A ZEALOT'S DESTINY

A Novel
by
Braxton DeGarmo

Christen Haus Publishing

Copyright

Dedication

While this story talks of kings, past and present,
there is only one King of kings.
I dedicate this story to my King—
my Lord and Savior, Jesus Christ.

Acknowledgments

The list of acknowledgments for this book is shorter than usual, largely because the story required more historical research than my previous books. That, in itself, was interesting, as I delved into books from the 19th Century, and even earlier literature.

First, I'd like to thank my friend, Mike Hodge, for getting me interested in the throne of David. He has produced his own book looking at the subject from a different, non-fictional perspective—*Where is the United States in Bible Prophecy?* I recommend it to anyone looking for more information on the topic.

I also wish to thank Dr. James Williams of the National Churchill Museum in Fulton, MO for information regarding the museum and campus on which it sits, Westminster College. When we first visited the campus, I suspected there might be tunnels for the utilities and, for the sake of my story, I really *wanted* there to be tunnels. He confirmed that, albeit reluctantly, without revealing their actual locations. I hope he doesn't get too upset with all the damage I inflicted on his beautiful church and museum . . . in the book, of course.

My thanks once again go to my editor, Patrick LoBrutto, whose suggestions always improve the final result, and to Lenda Selph for her valuable proofreading.

I'd like to thank the members of my "street team"—you know who you are. These folks always provide helpful feedback that improves my books, allowing them to become what you have today.

And last but never least, I want to acknowledge and thank my loving and talented wife, Paula, for her valuable assistance, whether it be proofreading skills, general help, feeding me when I'm wrapped up in writing, or all-around encouragement.

AUTHOR'S NOTE

A friend of mine piqued my interest when he asked, "Who sits on the Throne of David?" My answer was one of rote, Jesus Christ. After all, that's what most theologians today would say. And yet, my friend challenged me to investigate his question further. So, I did. And what I found led to this book.

For those of you scratching your heads, God had promised King David, of ancient Judea, that his earthly throne would be established forever—2 Samuel 7:13-16—and that someone would sit upon that throne throughout eternity. And yet, in 585 B.C., King Zedekiah, the last of David's royal descendants, was captured and taken to Babylon, where all of his sons were killed in front of him and he, then, later died. Other descendants of David carried his blood line forward. Indeed, Christ was born of that blood line, also as promised. But what of David's throne? Who sat upon it during the 400+ years between Zedekiah and Jesus' time of ministry? Even then, Jesus never sat upon the throne and won't sit upon an earthly throne again until He returns. None of David's descendants sat upon a throne of any kind after Zedekiah. Or did they?

More in my Afterword. . .

One

Prince Gregory raised his nose in the air and sniffed. He furrowed his brow at the odor and summoned his Chief of Staff from across the room.

"Is that gas I smell? The rest of the family will be arriving shortly."

Gregory turned 56 that day and the extended family now began to assemble to celebrate. Some of them had already arrived, and the last thing he needed was to evacuate his home because of some minor gas leak.

The aide sniffed the air as well and shook his head. "I don't believe so, sir. The exterminators were out this morning while you were in the city. They assured me there would be no residual odors but I'm afraid they were in error."

The prince looked at his watch and then back toward his assistant. "Are you quite sure? I've never smelled bug spray like this."

The man smiled and looked at his employer. "Sir, can you tell me when you've ever smelled bug spray?"

The prince cocked his head, looked askance, and then smiled. "Right, Geoffrey. Now that you say that, I'm not sure I have. Well, at least since boarding school."

Geoffrey was correct. The Royal Family never had to put up with certain occurrences of daily life. Services such as exterminators, plumbers, and the like worked whatever hours were necessary to avoid inconvenience to the family.

Besides, The Royal Lodge in Windsor Great Park, a 30-room mansion on the Grade II list of royal residences, was in tip-top shape. The prince had spent £7.5 million to fully restore the grand building, its grounds with eight additional staff buildings, and the private chapel. The buildings underwent inspection routinely, and maintenance was scheduled and proactive. The odds of a gas leak were nil.

He walked about the room, sniffing. The odor was indeed faint but seemed strongest near the front hallway.

"My older brother should be here momentarily. His youngest son is escorting the Queen and they're running late. Please inform security." He reflected on the still present odor. "And, please have someone check the gas lines."

The aide nodded. "Yes, sir. In fact, I will check the basement area myself, for expediency. It might take time to get one of the maintenance workers here, being supper time and all."

"Thank you, Geoffrey."

Geoffrey Hand had been Prince Gregory's Chief of Staff for over 15 years and adored the Royal Family. As a boy, he had daydreamed of being a rugged prince and finding a beautiful princess to take as his bride. Of course, that would never be, but the idea had led him to work hard at school, excel at sports, and join the military for a brief stint.

And yet, it was the one sport he failed to master that caught royal notice. Polo. He nearly fell off the horse with every swing of his mallet. After one disastrous practice match, where he did indeed fall from his mount, he rose from the ground to find the prince offering him a hand up, while calling him the worst polo player he'd ever seen. From there, the friendship grew and this position had been offered him. How could he refuse? Now, he and his wife of 30 years lived on the grounds and they hobnobbed with royalty . . . within limits. He would do anything for the family.

Geoffrey walked through the kitchen and found the staff scurrying about. They didn't cater to the Queen frequently, so he knew they were seeking perfection. Besides, the entire, immediate Royal Family would be attending. They sought to please more than just Her Majesty.

"Are any of the maintenance fellows still about?"

Simultaneously, half the heads in the room shook negatively.

"Do you smell gas?"

The head cook looked at him askance. "Seriously? We're in the kitchen. Look about. How many gas burners do you see working at the moment? Do we smell gas? When *don't* we smell gas in here?"

Geoffrey chuckled. "Sorry. The prince is smelling gas and I'm to investigate."

Another cook pointed with her thumb over her right shoulder. "That way to the basement."

He nodded. He knew how to get there. Walking down the hall, he came to the door leading to the basement and stopped. He looked around for other staff members to question about what he had found but saw no one. Of course, it was late and only the kitchen staff remained to prepare for the birthday party and to feed the drivers who would be missing their own meals while carting the family members from place to place.

Again, he turned toward the door and stared at it. Someone had sealed the door with clear tape, like that used for packages. Someone walking past would be unlikely to notice it in the dim evening light. In fact, he had not noted it until grabbing the doorknob and feeling resistance.

Curious, he thought. Was there some reason for this?

He began to peel away the tape, taking care not to damage the paint, if possible. Soon, he freed the door and opened it. Gas! Prince Gregory's nose had been correct. He had to warn them and clear the building.

He turned and found himself facing a member of the security team.

"You there. There's a gas leak. We must evacuate the building immediately. I'll go alert the prince."

The man's hand flew up toward Geoffrey and a piercing pain shot through his chest toward his back. He looked down to see a narrow blade thrust upward into his chest from just below his sternum. He knew it to be a fatal injury.

The man made two quick, additional movements and Geoffrey could feel the warmth of his life's blood filling his chest, his breathing becoming difficult. His death would be quick, but he feared for the Royal Family. Were they about to die in a fiery explosion?

His thoughts turned toward his wife and children. He longed to see them one more time, to hold his wife, to tell his kids how proud he was of them. To tell them all how much he loved them.

He could no longer talk, to ask "Why?" Yet, in a flash he understood why. He . . .

"*Allahu akbar*," whispered the man.

The man opened the door and Geoffrey felt strong hands grab him. The last thing he remembered as he toppled down the stairs was the smell of gas and the door closing behind him.

Prince Gregory paced in the foyer as his extended family gathered in the drawing room. His daughters had been excited to see their cousins. His younger brother and his family had arrived first, followed by his sister and her family. The latest to arrive was his older brother, Peter, the Prince of Wales and next in line to the throne, with his wife. Peter's youngest son, Prince Alexander, was escorting the Queen.

The smell hadn't changed and Geoffrey had not returned. Gregory had not forgotten the plot to assassinate his mother that had led to a drone strike killing two British citizens who had joined ISIS in the Middle East.

"Sir?"

He turned to find one of his security men extending his hand with a note.

"Have you seen Geoffrey?"

"No, sir. Do you wish for me to chase him down?"

"Yes, please."

The prince took the note. His mother had just left Windsor Castle and would be there in minutes. The note also mentioned that Prince Arthur, the Duke of Cambridge, Peter's eldest son and second in line to the throne, and his family would be delayed. No explanation was provided.

He walked into the drawing room and approached Peter.

"Mum is on her way. She should be here within minutes. I just received this note." He handed it to his brother.

After reading the message, his brother nodded. "Morning sickness. This third pregnancy has gotten to Helen more than the first two. Arthur must have anticipated something like this. He had us bring a small gift for you in our car." He looked about for someone on the staff. "Do you know if our drivers are still outside? I'll have James bring it in."

"I believe they've all gone to eat," said his wife.

"Very well. Then, I'll be just a minute. I'll retrieve it and greet Mum at the same time."

The two men walked together toward the front door.

"Tell me, Peter, do you smell anything? Gas, perhaps."

The Prince of Wales stopped and sniffed. "Can't say as I do, but the sniffer isn't what it used to be. Mum's the one to ask. Her nose still seems to pick up everything." The security man opened the door and the Prince of Wales walked out into the evening chill.

Gregory stood in the doorway and watched his brother. He could see headlights in the distance. A car, presumed to be their mother's, had come through the front gate.

At that moment, he felt a grumble in the floor that preceded a deafening roar behind him. He turned in time to see his home collapse around him and a fireball racing toward him. Unlike in the cinema, he had no time to escape.

Two

Karolus Karling sat on the balcony overlooking the courtyard of his *palazzo* on the outskirts of Rome. As Director of The Assembly, as well as the new Secretary General of the United Nations, he had the most advanced intelligence network in the world. Few things caught him by surprise, with the biggest in past months being the surge of the new American Party in the United States' 2016 election. Bradley Graham's resilience, as well as his uncanny knack at escaping their attempts to bring him down, caused Karolus concern. And if it caused him concern, he could only imagine the thinking of those in the Executive Council.

Francois, his aide, stepped onto the balcony.

"Sir, the latest from Britain." He handed Karolus a three-page report.

"Thank you."

Karolus breezed through the brief and frowned. Why couldn't these people get it right? Like the attempt on candidate Graham's life months earlier, the original operatives assigned to the task of eliminating the Queen had failed. This time, progress had been made, even if he had fallen short. Not every plan was foolproof and sometimes these tasks had to be done in stages to escape deeper scrutiny.

The command to eliminate the Royal Family had come from the highest authority, the one man that even the

Executive Council answered to. The master plan had been 50 years in the making. Their time of global control was on the horizon. When that man claimed his position of power, Karolus would be there, as his spokesman. And at that time, the man wished to claim the Throne of David, the Throne of Promise, to prove to the world that he was the man destined to fulfill that ancient prophecy of a Messiah who held the right to reign in judgment. Karolus, himself, held little stock in a bunch of 2,000-year-old letters called the Bible, but he understood the need to satisfy those who still believed in fables.

The Assembly had spent over a decade infiltrating the Metropolitan Police's Special Operations 14 group, also known as the Royal Protective Service. Abdul Aziz ben-Hadad, going by a well-crafted and deeply entrenched alias, had been a loyal guard for the Royal Family for almost a decade now. Karolus had called his sleeper cell into action the previous week.

Upon completing the report, Karolus walked into his study, turned on the television, and tuned into the BBC news. The famous door to 10 Downing Street appeared behind the reporter.

"We are awaiting comments by the Prime Minister's office. The country is aghast at the news floating through social media that an attack on the Royal Family has been successful. What we do know for sure is that the family was attending a family party for the Duke of York's 56th birthday at his residence, The Royal Lodge. We also . . ." The reporter stopped and turned.

Karolus watched the door behind the reporter as it opened and the Prime Minister himself stepped out and approached the podium holding a dozen or more microphones. It seemed that no one wanted to depend on a single, press-pool relay of the words about to be spoken.

"Ladies and gentlemen, I . . . I am saddened, and angered, to report that an explosion at The Royal Lodge in Windsor Great Park has claimed the lives of many members of the Royal Family, who had gathered to celebrate the birthday of the Duke of York. The Duke and his entire family . . . the Earl of Wessex and his entire family . . . the Princess Royal and her family . . . and the Duchess of Cornwall were killed in the blast. The Prince of Wales had stepped outside and the explosion threw him more than two dozen meters into a row of hedges surrounding the private entrance to the home. He is comatose and hospitalized in critical condition. His prognosis is unknown at this time."

The Prime Minister paused and wiped an eye. His distress appeared obvious.

"The Queen, accompanied by her husband and her grandson, was riding up to the residence and witnessed the explosion. Fortunately, she had been delayed at Windsor Castle. Her . . . her grandson, the Duke of Cambridge and possibly the heir apparent to the throne. . ." He paused and cleared his throat. ". . . along with his wife and children had been prevented from . . . from attending due to issues of the Duchess' third pregnancy."

Karolus sat there, intrigued by the man's emotions. He had never seen the Prime Minister so distraught. One would think the man's own family had been murdered.

"A full and extensive investigation into this tragedy has already started. Although there have been social media reports of the odor of gas, it is premature to believe this was caused by a gas leak. My administration will be fully transparent with the findings of our investigation." He appeared to be regaining his resolve.

"In the meantime, we ask, and the Royal Family asks, that you lift up a prayer for them tonight and keep them in your prayers in the coming weeks. The Queen has canceled all royal activities for the next two weeks, and the family has moved to secure quarters for added protection. We hope to have more information for you tomorrow. Thank you."

With that, he took no questions and turned to re-enter his residence. The reporter turned back to the camera and began her drivel.

Karolus muted the television but kept it tuned to the BBC. He smiled. He loved the word "transparent." So open, with such promise, and yet when used by most politicians, a most deceptive word.

A truly transparent report would have confirmed the fact that the Prince of Wales was one step from death, not in critical condition with no mention of prognosis. And that the Queen had to be sedated secondary to her emotional distress. Her doctors feared she might have a stroke otherwise.

He pressed a button on his desk and Francois appeared within a moment.

"Sir?"

"Please see to it that our man is rewarded and reassigned to the Duke of Cambridge's security detail."

Three

Citizens of the western hemisphere headed to lunch that Saturday hearing the tragic news out of Britain. Talking heads everywhere gave their own take on what had happened and their own unsubstantiated reports as to the cause. Yet, they couldn't alter the fact that the Prince of Wales remained in critical condition. The Queen's press office remained uncharacteristically silent. The press in Canada said it felt much like its friends in the U.S. had felt on 9-11.

Amy Gibbs sat at home fighting a carousel of emotions. Yes, she felt horrified and saddened at the reports about the Royal Family, but something closer to home roiled within.

Richard Nichols, her fiancé and Chief Social Media Strategist for the Bradley Graham campaign, as well as the American Party, was supposed to have flown back to St. Louis the previous afternoon. He was to have the weekend off . . . to spend with her. This would have been his first weekend off in over three months and she had big plans for them, plans she had now spent the previous afternoon annulling, giving away tickets to that evening's Arlo Guthrie concert at the Touhill Performing Arts Center and canceling reservations at various places.

Her cell rang. Richard. She debated about not answering but gave in. She accepted the call but said nothing.

"Amy? Are you there?"

"Yes. I'm here."

"Sweetheart, what can I say to convince you how sorry I am? This wasn't my idea. And now, with the situation in England, I . . . I don't know when I can get back."

She knew the cancellation of his trip home had not been his decision. That didn't make it any easier.

"Richard, I . . . I know it's not your fault. But you've been in Washington for almost a year now. I thought the Party's offices were here, in St. Louis. You've only been able to come home a few days each month. We haven't been able to plan anything for the wedding. Heck, we haven't even set a date yet. This long-distance relationship is not what I had in mind when you said you took a job in St. Louis to be near me."

She felt that she was whining now. She hated whiners. She'd had enough of them in the Emergency Room, where such behavior seemed guaranteed to lower the staff's empathy for you.

"Sweetheart, I know. This isn't what I thought I was signing up for either, but . . ."

She waited for him to continue, but he didn't. She could hear it in his voice. The unsaid truth. The meaning between the lines. He was where the action was. The adrenaline junkie in him loved the rush of being there.

"Look, the election isn't far off and then—"

"The election is nine months away, Richard! And then what? If Graham wins, he's going to want you in the White House. That would be four more years, maybe eight. You know I don't want to live there."

"But if he doesn't win—"

"If you think that, why are you working so hard?" She regretted the tone in her voice as soon as she said that.

He was silent on the other end.

"Richard, I need to go. Let me know when you actually board a plane to come home." That came across much too curtly, but she wasn't happy. This was supposed to be *their* time together, planning for the big day. Instead, she felt snubbed, coming in second to the man's job. It hit her that this was the exact reason why Lynch had stopped calling her just when their relationship looked to be getting serious. He hadn't wanted her to take second place to his career. And then he almost died, lost his memory, and disappeared for months. Richard filled the void and more.

Now, it was Richard who seemed to be putting Amy second after his career. And an interesting thought hit her, a different perspective. Lynch had enough concern that he broke things off rather than take her down a path where she'd play second fiddle. He hadn't wanted to hurt her, although the course he took did just that. Richard, on the other hand, didn't seem concerned that he had put his career first.

"Hey, look, I'll try to get back as soon as possible. Again, this England thing has our schedules all up in the air. I promise. I'll try. I love you, Amy. I want to make this right."

She sighed. "I-I love you, too, Richard. Bye."

What had her pastor once said? Love wasn't an emotion; it was an action. It wasn't Hollywood's portrayal of heated passion. It wasn't lust. Not even that warm, tingling feeling when you're with someone. You choose to love. You make it a commitment. You act, and the emotion follows. You make it work through all the ups and downs.

The problem was . . . there hadn't been any ups recently.

The news from London had Lynch Cully working overtime. Who would have thought that, as the Chief of Security for the Bradley Graham campaign, such news would almost double his workload overnight?

They had received official notification of the accident well before the Prime Minister made his televised announcement. They had released a statement of condolence about the same time as that presser outside 10 Downing Street.

However, inside information provided to them stated that this might not have been an accident. The Brits had promised them confidential information as the investigation progressed, working under the assumption that the explosion had been an inside job. Based on this information, and Graham's previous run-ins with The Assembly, specifically its director, Karolus Karling, Lynch now worked to double the protection detail around Graham. That required vetting, re-vetting, and re-re-vetting new applicants for the security team.

As he reviewed the credentials for another man, an ex-Navy SEAL with exemplary recommendations, his secure, encrypted phone rang. Only three people had that number—the boss, his campaign manager . . . and Amy. He doubted she'd be calling and was surprised to find himself wrong as he glanced at the Caller ID.

"Hey."

"Hi, Lynch. Sorry to bother you. I'm sure you're swamped as usual."

"Not too bad," he lied. "What's up?"

He listened to her litany of complaints and tried not to smile. He had been stupid enough to let her go a few years earlier and a major life setback, just as they were working things out, resulted in his losing her again. This second time posed a more serious problem, though. She had become engaged to a guy that he, Lynch, really liked. He had been nonchalant about their announcement, had tried to convince himself that he was over her, and had failed at that latter task. Still, he couldn't bring himself to compete with Richard. If she was happy, that's what counted. Or so he told himself . . . over and over and over again.

The smile crept onto his face anyway. Richard had once again found himself stuck in Washington, while Lynch was in St. Louis. He would be more than happy to offer his ear for listening or his shoulder for crying. He had made a vow, of sorts, not to actively compete. That didn't mean he wouldn't be there if things fell apart between Amy and her beau.

"Sounds like you need to go out for lunch. Up for Sugarfire?" The bar-be-que place was close to her home and one of his favorites. When she didn't jump on that suggestion, he added, "Or La Bonne Bouchée?" He knew that to be one of *her* favorites.

"Okay."

She didn't continue.

"So, okay for which one?"

"La Bonne Bouchée."

"Sounds good. My treat. Umm, can I ask you to meet me there? I'm more swamped than I let on and that would help me out time-wise."

"What time?"

Lynch looked at the clock on his desk and then at the stack of files next to it. Well, he needed to eat. Now was as good a time to take a break as any.

"I can leave right now."

"Me, too. See you there."

Lynch beat Amy to the restaurant and stood just inside the door, waiting for her while being tempted by the incredible bakery display he kept to his back. His stomach grumbled. Maybe he could spring for a treat, "for the office."

He warmed up enough to slip off his coat and continued to peer out the window. He stepped aside to allow a petite woman past him and returned to his vantage point. No sign of Amy's car, but then, his office was a good ten minutes closer than her home. And if Amy said she could leave immediately, that meant 15 minutes later, at a minimum. He had tried to compensate and stall at his office, but he might as well have finished reviewing the file he'd been perusing when Amy called.

As his resolve to avoid the bakery began to weaken, he saw her car pull into view in the parking lot. He took a deep breath and stepped closer to the door. A minute later, he opened the outer door for her.

"Hi." She smiled as he moved to open the inner door. "I hope you haven't been waiting too long. I got another phone call just as I walked into the garage."

"Not long, but I almost gave in to those cinnamon rolls over there. They seemed to be calling to me."

She laughed. "I'm surprised you didn't head straight to the counter when you got here."

Now inside, he offered to help her with her coat. She refused.

"I need to warm up a bit. It's brutal outside."

Lynch nodded. For being the third week in February,

the weather had been unusually cold with more snow than expected. Now, only remnants of the latest storm remained in dirty piles along the borders of area parking lots.

He felt good, being there with her, like old times. Yet, he reminded himself that she was engaged to another and this was *not* like old times.

At the table, she allowed him to assist her with her coat and pull out her chair for her. As he did so, she gave him a curious look. He couldn't quite make out what lay behind that look, but she seemed surprised. He thought for a moment. Hadn't he always helped her with her coat and chairs and such, those things expected of a gentleman? Maybe not. There were still many areas of his memory that he had not recovered.

He wondered whether or not to mention Richard, or to let her bring him up. They made small talk about family and the weather, passing the time until placing their order. She went with the "Choose Two" selection with French Onion soup and Adriatic Chicken Salad, while he ordered the slow-roasted top round of beef sandwich. He knew he'd been to the restaurant before but couldn't recall having a favorite menu item.

As the waitress left to put their order into the kitchen, Amy placed her hand on his and said, "Thanks."

Lynch cocked his head, questioning. "For what?"

"For being a friend and, well, for lunch. You did say your treat, right?" She seemed uncomfortable for a brief moment.

"I did. Happy I could be here to lift your spirits."

She nodded and sighed. "So, how's work?"

"Busy. That incident in England—"

"Isn't that awful?" Her eyes widened and she leaned

toward him. "Has that somehow affected *your* job here?"

He knew he couldn't tell her anything privileged, but he could at least acknowledge that it had. He nodded. "I'm increasing the security for Graham."

She sat back, but as her next words formed on her lips, his secure phone rang. Caller ID revealed it to be the boss, Bradley Graham, himself.

Lynch chuckled. "It's him. He must have heard me mention his name. Excuse me while I take this call."

He answered the call and whispered, "Yes, sir. Give me a minute," and then pulled away from the table and proceeded to walk outside, into the cold.

"Yes, sir. I can talk now. I'm at a restaurant getting lunch and had to walk outside."

"Lynch, I know you're in over your head screening new members of the security team, but I have another task for you."

Lynch took a deep breath and hoped this new task would still allow him a minimum of four hours of sleep.

"Yes, sir?"

"You might not know that I'm on the Board of Trustees for Westminster College in Fulton."

Lynch was aware of that and had, in fact, already organized a plan to protect his boss while at the college for their quarterly board meetings.

Graham continued, "I think you're aware of the National Winston Churchill Museum that sits on the campus property. Well, the seventieth anniversary of Churchill's famous 'Iron Curtain' speech is in two weeks there. The Prince of Wales was planning to attend and give a speech there to honor that anniversary. We thought for sure that they'd cancel, with his being in the hospital. But, evidently, the Queen has insisted that after the family memorials to take place this week, she wants his son, Prince Arthur, to keep that commitment here."

"So, what's that have to do with us?"

"Well, I've been invited to attend. Plus, I'd like you to liaise with his security team, give their plans a review. I don't want to see anything happen to the young prince, and I sure don't want anything to happen on a campus where I'm on the Board."

Lynch pondered that for a moment. "Sir, he'll have personal security from members of his own Royal Protection squad, as well as the Secret Service, or State Department, or both. If State's involved, they might even use Delta Force guys, and those guys don't mess around. They'll shoot first, disappear into the mist, and let someone else ask the questions later."

"I know, Lynch. I'm sure they'll have every angle figured and every inch of ground covered, but I *know* you and I value your opinions, your foresight, and your gut instincts. I can't say that about any member of the prince's protective detail. And we know how lax the Secret Service has become. If they miss people climbing the White House fence and entering the building, can I trust them protecting a foreign royal?"

"Well, thank you for the vote of confidence. Do we know the advance team's ETA?"

"Three days from now for the U.S. side of the team, including someone from the highway patrol, and one week for the Royal Protection advance team. I'll forward details to you in a moment."

"Yes, sir. I'll be on it."

When Amy saw Lynch standing at the door waiting for her, a sense of déjà vu also greeted her. However, when he offered to assist with her coat and pulled out her chair, she realized that he *had* changed. Following his "return from the dead," where he'd lost his memory and almost lost his life, he had commented that he'd changed. Others had told her the same thing. She hadn't believed him or them, until now. His gentlemanly offers hadn't seemed affected, just natural.

When she thanked him for being a friend, she felt surprise in thinking she now somehow cheated on Richard by having lunch with Lynch, while Richard remained stuck with work in Washington.

What would her fiancé think?

Yet, what troubled her more was the fact that she had called Lynch while upset with Richard. Why? As some subconscious payback? To make Richard jealous? Or did it have more to do with Lynch? All three possibilities flitted through her mind as Lynch left the table to answer his phone call.

She fidgeted in her chair as she waited for him to return to the table, in that moment becoming uncomfortable at being there.

"Ma'am?" Their waitress looked at her with concern. "Are you okay?"

Amy realized she had been staring off into some other dimension.

"Yes . . . um, no. Would it be too much trouble for you to put our food into to-go containers? I, uh, think I need to go home."

"Yes, ma'am. No trouble at all. I hope you're okay."

Amy nodded. "Thanks. I will be."

A few minutes later, as the waitress set the foam food containers on the table, Lynch arrived and stood over the table, his mouth open in apparent disbelief.

"Wh—"

Amy stood up and grabbed her coat. "Lynch, I-I'm really sorry. All of a sudden I'm not comfortable with this. I should never have put you in this position. I-I . . . thank you for lunch, but I think I need to leave."

With that she donned her coat, grabbed her food, turned, and left.

Four

Sir David Spencer-Hough, Commissioner of Police of the Metropolitan, commonly called the Met, paced the debris-strewn grounds of The Royal Lodge as he watched crime technicians combing through the remains of the royal residence. No resources were spared and days off had been canceled for members of SCD 4, the Forensics Services. The Met had mobilized its Specialist Crimes Unit, Evidence Recovery Unit, and Counter-Terrorism Team within minutes of the call to work the scene 24/7 until they answered certain questions.

The rising sun had topped the trees an hour earlier but had made no headway in taking the chill away or in dispersing the mist that had settled across the region overnight. He thought it fortuitous that the sun was visible at all, given that February saw a daily average of two hours of sunlight, which meant that on most days the sun remained hidden behind the clouds. They had been functioning with the aid of intense floodlights for the past 38 hours and the rare blessing of sunlight might help them see things differently, more clearly.

As he turned back toward what had been the front of the home, he saw the head of their Homicide and Serious Crime Command walking his way. The man's full unit had also been called into action, as it contained the Coroner's Office, the Disaster Victim Identification Unit, and Homicide Task Force among its several divisions.

Sir David nodded at the man's silent greeting.

"Robert, you look exhausted."

"Yes sir, because I am. I've been on scene since the word went out."

Sir David understood. He, too, had been working since that terrible news—at the scene, in London, and at Windsor Castle where the Royal Protective Branch had cloistered the remaining members of the Royal Family.

"We've located three more bodies and identified them as members of the kitchen staff and the Prince of Wales' driver." He handed Sir David a clipboard containing several sheets of paper. "That brings the death count to 23. The 17 members of the family and six staff. We still have half a dozen unaccounted for, including Geoffrey Hand, Prince Gregory's Chief of Staff and two members of S.O.14."

The commander glanced back at two members of the coroner's team lifting a body bag onto a gurney.

"The worst part was finding the children. That was hard for all of us." He frowned. "The med techs say it looks like what they'd expect from an explosion, but the pathologists will make the final call on cause of death. I understand we have full permission for the autopsies."

Sir David nodded and exhaled deeply. "Her Majesty was insistent on it. She quite plainly stated that she wanted to know that the explosion wasn't to cover up something else."

The commander took a step back and said, "Well, sir, back to work."

Sir David placed his hand on the man's arm to stop him. "Not quite yet. Here comes Quint. He might have information you'll need."

Quinton Lindley was the director of the Forensics

Services. Sir David knew that he also had been here for the past 36 hours.

Quint nodded in greeting. "Sir David, Robert. Quite the mess, isn't it? On so many levels."

Both men acknowledged his statement.

"Well, sir, we do know for sure that gas was involved. We've had a slow go of it, but we've finally turned off all the supply lines and are speeding up our work through the rubble to clear the basement level where those lines entered the building so we can examine them. If they were tampered with, we should know within an hour or so. We did find one curious thing. Fragments of a door with tape along the edges. Not quite sure what to make of that, but it appears to have come from the staff area of the home. Also curious is that the explosion seemed to occur from at least four, maybe more, points. At each of those points we can identify debris patterns consistent with that spot being its own ground zero, so to speak. Since the basement had multiple rooms, it may be that certain rooms contained the gas better than others and became focal points of their own explosions amid the overall cataclysm. We'll need to perform—"

A young female technician, her face smudged with dirt and wearing protective overalls to match, stood facing them. She seemed out of breath from running. "Sirs, sorry to interrupt, but I think you need to see this. We've found Geoffrey Hand's body, sir. At the bottom of a set of stairs to the basement."

The men followed her and arrived at that part of the home as the coroner's team hoisted a body bag up and over the debris. They laid it on the ground and unzipped the bag.

The senior man on the team pointed to the dead man's

chest. "The autopsy will need to confirm my suspicion, mind you. But to me, it appears this man was stabbed and pushed down the stairs." He opened the man's shirt to reveal a small linear wound just below the breastbone, a wound that had bled profusely at one point if the amount of blood on his shirt was an indicator. "And these bruises . . ." He lifted up the man's right arm and pulled back the torn sleeve to reveal the skin. ". . . were ante-mortem and are shaped in a way consistent with the body hitting the edge of a step." He lowered the arm back into the bag. "One last thing, the burns on his face indicate he was below the main explosion. Natural gas is lighter than air and would have collected along the ceiling of the basement first. As the explosion released the gas it would rise and only a small fraction would flash back into the basement. His burns are much less severe than those we've found on the other bodies. So, it would appear he was on the basement floor when the explosion occurred, not thrown down there by the explosion. The lack of debris under him would confirm that as well."

Sir David and the others stepped away to let the coroner's team complete their gruesome task.

"Well, Robert, it would appear you definitely have one homicide to investigate." He turned toward his forensics director. "Quint . . ."

The man had turned away from the group to confer with another technician. He appeared grimmer than before, as he turned back toward the commissioner.

"No, sir. He has 20 definite homicides to investigate. We've found evidence of Semtex in at least two locations. I think it's safe to say that the gas was used to increase the power of the explosion, but that it was the plastic explosive that set it off."

"Semtex?"

Sir David didn't like the sound of that. The Israelis and Czechs were known for using Semtex, but in the UK, it was the Irish Republican Army that made Semtex a name that everyone recognized. Being difficult for dogs to detect, Semtex was the IRA's explosive of choice during its reign of terror against England. Despite a resurgence in violent activity in the past few years by what was now called the Real IRA, their attacks seemed limited to Northern Ireland. Would they have gone so far as to attack the Crown in such a direct fashion as this? No doubt they understood that if the evidence pointed to their involvement, every last one of them, and their families and accessories, would be hunted down and arrested or killed if they resisted.

No, Sir David couldn't see them going this far to make a statement. He would need more evidence to believe that. What was clear was that this was no accident. Someone had murdered half of the first two dozen successors to the throne . . . and would have killed the Queen had circumstances not delayed her.

Five

Prince Arthur, the Duke of Cambridge, and his younger brother, Alexander, sat by their father's bedside. The Prince of Wales lay still, a breathing tube emerging from his mouth and numerous intravenous lines inserted into veins in his arms. He couldn't move if he wished to. He was still in a medically-induced coma for the serious head injury he'd suffered. The paramedics called to the scene had deduced that the explosion had thrown him headfirst into his car and then over the vehicle into the shrubs. The neurosurgeons had confirmed the seriousness of his cerebral contusion—as they termed it—and had drained a large collection of blood—they called it a subdural hematoma—from his head.

As teenagers at the time of their mother's death, they knew too well the anguish of losing a parent. They also lived through the torment of the many speculations surrounding her death, that such-and-such group staged it, or this group, or that one. Or worse, that their own family had done so to avoid a Muslim influence gaining access to them as future heirs to the throne. They had discussed it many times, as siblings do, and neither one wanted to know the truth. The whole thing had simply been a horrible accident. End of story.

The pregnant Duchess, Helen, entered the room with tea for both men.

"Thank you, dear." Arthur took the porcelain cup and

held it, not even looking at the contents.

"Take a sip. It's your favorite."

The young man looked annoyed. "Of course it's my favorite. Everywhere we go they make sure my favorite is on hand. Maybe, just once, I'd like something different."

"Like a pint of Guinness," quipped his brother.

Arthur shook his head and turned toward his wife. He held the cup in one hand and took her hand with the other. "I'm sorry. I shouldn't snap at you. I . . . I . . ." He sighed.

She used her other hand to touch and massage his shoulder. She then stepped around behind him and massaged his neck and both shoulders.

"You know, they have a room next door where you can try to get some sleep. Perhaps you should try."

The prince shook his head and reached up to touch her right hand as she rubbed his shoulder. "We'll need to leave shortly, as much as I don't want to. Grandmum is insistent that I take over father's schedule in his absence and go on this blasted trip to the U.S. The family memorial will be over, but I don't wish to leave with father like this."

"I'll be here. And you can be home within hours if something changes."

He turned and looked at his wife. "Actually . . . I've decided that you and the children will come with me."

Her eyes widened. "What? Without talking with me? I . . ." She looked away, uncertainty in her eyes.

Alexander rolled his eyes and gave him a look. "I, uh, think I'll step out. Maybe I can roust us up those pints," he whispered. Arthur gave him a stern look in return and turned back to his wife.

"I do not wish to be separated. You were with me when we got word that this was a deliberate attack on the family.

I want you to be with me."

"But, dear, my morning sickness. And toting two toddlers along. I just—"

"We will have their nanny to help with the children, and I'm arranging for a nurse to accompany us to help you. In fact, their nanny is already packing for them. We need to go home and select clothes for the trip and then the staff will pack them for us. Our protection detail continues to insist we stay at Windsor, so the trip home will be quick."

The Duchess looked troubled. "Oh, dear, I just don't know—"

The bedside alarm cut short her words. They both turned their heads toward Arthur's father to see his monitors flashing. The heart monitor showed an erratic pattern.

Within seconds, a doctor and three nurses ran into the room, followed by the youngest prince. Another nurse entered the room with a crash cart, while a fifth nurse came up to them, urging them to move out of the room.

"V-fib!" announced the doctor. "Paddles."

"Charging," said a nurse, as he handed the defibrillator paddles to the doctor. "Charged."

The doctor looked about. "All clear?" The medical staff eased away, so as to not be touching the bed.

"Clear," another nurse stated.

The Prince of Wales' body jerked as the electrical charge ran through his body.

From the edge of the room, Arthur could see that nothing changed on the monitor. The medical team repeated the process and the doctor ordered various drugs to be given through the IV lines. The scene became a blur to Arthur. This wasn't how his father's death was supposed to occur. He was supposed to live to a ripe old age and die in his own bed, peacefully and surrounded by family.

The team worked frantically. The monitor's tone changed and Arthur saw that his father's heart tracing had changed to a flat line. Helen began to cry. Alexander's head dropped as tears began to flow from his eyes as well. This couldn't be happening.

The team didn't stop, but time seemed to. And then, suddenly, everything stopped. The female nurses started to cry. The doctor said something like, "We did all we could," but even those words were a blur. His father was gone.

Six

Lynch had walked into the breakroom and was filling his mug with his second cup of coffee for the morning when one of his security team members found him. The news from England had gone from awful to horrible. A one-car accident outside London had killed three more members of the Royal Family—the Queen's nephew and the nephew's son and granddaughter. Possibly part of the same plot? Lynch wondered.

And on top of that, the Prince of Wales had died from injuries incurred during the explosion. Prince Arthur, the Duke of Cambridge, now rose to title of the Prince of Wales. How did those Brits keep up with all of these titles?

"Lynch, the new guys are here. We're all assembled in the conference room, except Jack and Roscoe. They're watching the Graham residence."

Lynch took a sip of coffee and nodded. He put his hand on the man's shoulder. "Then let's get this show on the road, Tony."

Lynch saw his new hires sitting outside the conference area, erect and face forward, as if they'd been called to the commander's office. Lynch tried to recall just how long ago these two had been released from each respective service. Whatever. They'd have to fit in . . . or else.

Mack Gilman waved his hand toward the door to allow Zach Darst to go first. "After you, swabby." He grinned. "By the way, there's your first assignment." He pointed to the janitor's mop and bucket down the hall.

Darst shook his head. "No, after you, green face. We've always covered your six."

Lynch took a deep breath. *This could get old fast*, he thought.

"Inter-service rivalries? C'mon, guys, we're one big, happy family here." With his free hand he ushered them through the door together. He caught Tony rolling his eyes and laughing. "Careful, or I'll put them both on your detail." The man gave him a look as if daring him to do that.

After the men sat down, Lynch approached the head of the table. "Good morning. Everyone rested? We're going to have a busy next couple of weeks. But, before delving into those details, let me introduce the two newest members of the team." He pointed to Mack. "This is Mack Gilman. He's ex-Green Beret, Master Sergeant, with 15 years of service. He got a bum deal from the current administration after 'interfering,' shall I say, with an Afghani police commander who gets his kicks out of abusing little boys. Since we stand up for morality around here, we weren't about to let him go unrewarded. He's got skills we need, the moral fiber we like, and more patriotism than the entire West Wing staff combined."

Mack raised his hand to acknowledge Lynch's introduction.

"Hey, we read about that," said Jim, who along with Tony and Alex had been among the first men hired for Bradley Graham's security. "Good for you. Glad to have you aboard."

Other team members murmured their agreement.

"Next up is Zach Darst, ex-Navy SEAL, Senior Chief Petty Officer, retired at 20 years. And like Mack, he's got skills we need and patriotism overflowing." The others again voiced their welcomes. "By the way, between the two of them, they speak and read six languages fluently, so we're pretty sure we'll know when the boss is being insulted by some foreign indignitary."

"Good one, Lynch," replied Alex. Nicknamed 'Bubba' for being the good ol' boy that he was, his shooting skill had downed the drone that had previously attempted to take Bradley Graham's life—a fact subsequently proven by forensics.

Lynch handed out a two-page briefing list. "As usual, these sheets don't leave this room, so pay attention." He continued into their upcoming electoral rallies and two town halls and gave the men their assignments for each. He then brought up the visit to Fulton, Missouri. "We've been informed that Prince Arthur, the new Prince of Wales and heir to the British throne, will be keeping his father's scheduled appearance at the National Churchill Museum, followed by visits to Washington and New York. Since the boss is a Trustee at the college, he's been invited to, and will attend, the prince's speech." He went on to detail certain specifics of the trip, as they now stood.

"Our friends at MI5 in Britain have been gracious enough to provide us with information they've gathered in the past few days. The explosion that took the lives of so many members of the Royal Family was clearly an attack on the monarchy. They've identified six separate locations within the building where plastic explosives were detonated, and the building's natural gas lines were deliberately opened in an attempt to make it seem an accident, to increase the explosion, or both. They've also uncovered some chatter among terror groups about plans for attacks here in the U.S., with the upcoming elections as a target. We can assume the Prince of Wales will continue to be a target, possibly while here."

"Why is he still coming? Makes no sense to me."

Lynch shrugged. "Not our call. All we can do is be prepared to protect our boss."

Mack, keeping his elbow planted on the table, raised his hand level with his eyes.

"That brings up a good point," said Tony. "Will we be allowed to do our jobs? I mean, Secret Service, State Department, Royal Protection detail, and anyone else involved might not like our being added to the mix."

As Tony spoke, Mack lowered his hand. Several around the table nodded, as did Lynch.

"The boss is working to smooth that out for us. I'm slated to join the advance team in two days. It's going to be interesting to say the least."

Mack raised his hand again.

"Taking anyone with you?" asked Alex.

Mack lowered his hand.

"Yes, the new guys are coming with me. The rest of you know the boss and his routine, so I'm entrusting him to you, while I'm tied up."

Mack raised his hand again. This time Lynch acknowledged it.

"Inside job."

Lynch looked at the man, expecting more. "What do you mean?" he asked.

"England. It had to be an inside job. I worked with SAS for a while and saw how the Met—that's the Metropolitan Police—and MI5 work. Royal Protection is a branch of the Met. Terrorists wouldn't have made it within 200 meters of

The Royal Lodge, much less inside with time to set charges and tamper with gas lines."

Zach chimed in. "I agree. Whoever got in had to be able to get the explosives into the compound and past several sets of dogs. Most likely one guy. Odds are against more than that, but we can't rule out the possibility. And the guy would have needed, say, 15 minutes to place and arm the charges. More for dealing with the pipes, especially if they're as stubborn as gas lines tend to be. You got to be careful with those. One spark and . . ." He raised and spread his hands to show an explosion. "Yep, inside job."

Lynch had planned to take the new guys with him for the sole reason of getting to know them and seeing how they worked. With their special forces training, he also figured he might learn something from them. Now he realized that taking them had other advantages. Mack and Zach. That name combination hadn't struck him before and he almost cringed thinking about how the others might capitalize on it for a little friendly hazing. But then, he had no doubt at all that these two could take care of themselves.

Mack continued, "I got a friend in MI5. I'll touch base with her . . ."

Lynch saw smirks cross several faces at the mention of "her."

". . . and see if they're holding anything back from us. Actually, make that *what* they're holding back, not *if*. I'll let you know what I find."

Several others at the table nodded as he mentioned things being withheld.

Mack spoke up again. "Oh, one more thing. My kid brother went to Westminster College. I know a few things about that campus you're gonna want to know."

Seven

Karolus entered his penthouse condo in the CitySpire building in New York City with bittersweet feelings. Over a year earlier he had left, convinced that the city and the nation it symbolized were about to tumble into economic collapse. But the Chinese had refused to play ball, to use a distinctly American metaphor. They hadn't believed it within the power of The Assembly to hurt them. They were learning that lesson.

The Chinese economy had stalled and seemed in retreat. The Chinese national bank had found it "difficult" to function in isolation and had to slow down. After a time, it had to stop new loans to Chinese companies. Those companies also found it "more difficult" to obtain other financing. The international media played up those "difficulties" to the aggravation of the Chinese government.

The end result had been a major correction in the international stock markets, and then the U.S. Federal Reserve used the Chinese economy as a reason for delaying until December the interest rate increase that the market had expected of them. That the Fed had reservations about the world economy reverberated through the markets leading to additional losses.

Karolus entered the living room and stepped to the windows overlooking Central Park. He still relished the view. At the sound of someone entering the room, he turned.

"Sir?"

"Yes, Francois. Please tell the staff they did a marvelous job reopening the condo. The place is immaculate."

"Thank you, sir. They'll have your bags unpacked shortly, and I will pass your praise on to them. They will appreciate it. However, that is not why I interrupted."

A well-dressed man in his late seventies stepped out from around the corner and behind Francois. He appeared slim and fit, muscular actually, for a man of his age.

"Good afternoon, Karolus."

Karolus nodded toward his aide. "Thank you, Francois. Please see that we are not interrupted." His assistant nodded and left. "Good afternoon, Martin. To what do I owe this surprise?"

The man joined Karolus by the windows. "A marvelous view. I see why you like this place so much." He then turned, walked back to one of the two leather couches positioned perpendicular to the windows, and sat down.

Karolus felt an edge of uncertainty and he didn't like that. Martin Mabry was a man much like himself, one used to getting things done . . . his way. And his way had been profitable. With assets into the double-digit billions, he controlled an empire of far left-wing, liberal organizations. He had broken the economy and government of at least one Eastern European nation and had almost destroyed the Bank of England. And while The Assembly had never questioned his loyalty, Karolus felt uneasy in his presence. Mabry was the only man who could challenge Karolus for the Directorship and perhaps succeed.

Karolus debated sitting across from the man but decided he liked the "power" position of standing over him.

"Oh please, Karolus, have a seat. You're not going to

intimidate me by standing." He gave a dismissive wave toward the facing couch.

"I've been sitting for the past eight hours on the plane. I prefer to stand for a while."

"Very well. I suspect this was a bittersweet return for you, but I understand your needing to lay low in Rome for the past year. After that unpleasant business with Bradley Graham and his exposing you as he did. I'm surprised the American government allowed you back into the country."

Karolus was about to reply, but Mabry continued.

"Of course, they had few options. You are the U.N. Secretary General after all."

Karolus sensed a sneer in the man's voice, although his face held no tells.

"So, again, Martin, to what do I owe this surprise visit?"

"I'm here as a friend, Karolus. I realize you see me as a competitor for the Director's chair, but I want you to know that I have no aspirations for that position. I believe you've done a good job and I would take the chair *only* if drafted by unanimous vote of the Executive Committee. It's a job for a younger man than me. Someone like you."

Karolus hadn't expected his praise, but his suspicions remained on alert. He also noted the man's choice of the word 'good' in describing his performance. Others had told him he had outperformed all previous directors. Others used words like great, superb, and distinctive in his presence. Yet, Mabry chose the word 'good.' Still, Karolus had never heard Mabry use higher superlatives. Maybe, this would be the highest level of compliment he would ever get from the man.

"So, as a friend, I'm here to give you warning. Several members of the committee have approached me to feel out my interest in your job. They will remain unnamed and would not be pleased to know I've come here to rat on them, so to speak."

Karolus began to answer, but Mabry held up a hand to stop him.

"Please let me finish. The debacle with Fawaz and Bradley Graham upset a lot of people, as you know. There was talk at the time of removing you then, but you had been selected and installed as the Secretary General by that point and they didn't want to upset what had taken years to achieve. Now, however, the dissatisfaction has resurfaced. The Queen still lives, as do her two grandsons and the elder grandson's family, all heirs to *the* throne. In addition, and you might not be aware of this, having been in transit here, but the attempt on the lives of Viscount Linley and his issue did not succeed. They, too, remain as heirs to *the* throne. Security has now doubled on these individuals."

Mabry was correct. Karolus had not had time to update his information between landing at JFK and arriving at the condo. Francois, however, was likely correcting that deficiency as they spoke. He steepled his fingers in front of his mouth and looked out the windows as he contemplated this news.

"Yes, I see that you haven't heard this."

Karolus turned back to his guest. "What did you hear about this attempt?"

"A supposed mugging in a park near their home was interrupted."

Karolus smiled. "Hmmm. That must have been a real mugging. We had nothing to do with it. Unfortunately, in light of the other incidents, this now complicates *our* plan which is to take place next week."

"And the others?"

"Well, we had hoped to remove them all at The Royal Lodge, but no plan is foolproof, as you know. Our man had time constraints to work under. We anticipated all of the family to have been there by a certain time and he disrupted the gas lines to give us a maximum amount of gas by that time. Then the Queen was delayed, which we couldn't anticipate. If our man had delayed, the family would begin to detect the gas and the building might have been evacuated before the blast."

Mabry nodded. "Unfortunate but understandable."

"The back-up plans have gone into effect."

"And you're aware that MI5 and the Met have found the remains of the explosives and timers?"

"Yes. Also unfortunate, but anticipated. Their Forensics Service is excellent and we lost the one person who could have thwarted their discovery to a heart attack two weeks ago."

Mabry stood and joined Karolus at the windows. "You are under scrutiny, Karolus. Your plans had best succeed, or, well, you know The Assembly's *involuntary* retirement plan better than anyone."

Karolus stared out the window. Indeed he did.

Sir David walked into the conference room at Scotland Yard and went straight to the head of the table. The murmuring around the table stopped and those present focused on the Commissioner. He wasn't happy and he didn't care whether or not he showed it. But for these men and the lone woman sitting there, he wouldn't let his frustration and anger control the meeting. They weren't to blame.

"Good morning. If you want tea or coffee, please get it now. I don't want any interruptions once we start."

Quint and Robert both lifted their mugs to show they were ready. Leslie Snow, the interim head of Royal Protection, stood and claimed a cup, tea bag, spoon, and small pot of hot water before returning to her seat. The rest appeared content with whatever they had.

"Very well. Let's get started. It's been a week since the destruction at The Royal Lodge. Quint, please bring us up-to-date on what forensics has found."

"Yes, sir." He stood and walked to an easel of paper where he flipped to the second sheet. He presented an outline of the building along with blast patterns and locations of key findings—areas where Semtex had been detected, locations where pieces of the detonation devices were found, more fragments of a door with tape along the edges, and more.

"The door," he continued, "has been identified as a door to the basement. We surmise that it was taped to prevent gas leakage and detection by the staff and family. The detonation devices were simple digital timers with no phone connections. The good news is that they are of a completely different construction than those used previously by the IRA. The bad news is that somebody had to be present to arm them—"

"And that points to an inside job," Sir David interjected. "This is why Ms. Snow is with us today."

Quinton completed his detailed presentation with a single sentence. "We've seen this detonator before, connected to Muslim terror attacks."

The group remained quiet. The impact of that simple

statement did not appear lost on them.

"Ms. Snow," said the Commissioner.

"Yes, sir." She stood and moved toward the front of the table. "I have to agree with Sir David that this appears to be an inside job. The difficulty we're having is from where. There are close to 20 staff members, eight full-time and the remainder part-time, who had access to the residence. In addition to the staff, our Royal Protection detail varies, with at least 30 individuals who had access to the grounds and buildings during the three days preceding the explosion."

She eased back toward her chair, took a sip of tea, and resumed. "We've identified these individuals, re-checked their backgrounds, their travel histories, bank accounts, the usual. We have come up blank. They all appear to check out, so we're looking again and digging deeper."

"Which leaves us in a difficult spot." Sir David cleared his throat before continuing. "We have to assume that each person is suspect. The household staff will remain under close scrutiny until we solve this. The security personnel are being re-assigned to non-critical positions and being kept—"

A knock on the door interrupted the Commissioner. He waved the young woman into the room and she rushed up to Ms. Snow and handed her an envelope. As the woman hurried from the room, Ms. Snow opened the packet and perused its contents. A frown crossed her face.

"Ms. Snow? Leslie? What is it?"

"We appear to have a bigger problem than we thought. Internal Affairs started interviewing the security personnel in person last evening. They finished just 30 minutes ago. It would appear that five members of the detail, whose IDs were swiped to allow them access to the grounds, were nowhere near The Royal Lodge at that time. They were all off-duty, with two men at local pubs with friends, one at a meeting with his football team, one out-of-country, and the last in Scotland on assignment. All of their alibis check out with numerous people attesting to each one's story. Not a one of them reported a lost ID badge and each had his on his person at the time of the interview. Whoever orchestrated this has the ability to produce flawless credentials as well as blend in. This wasn't the act of a sole terrorist. This involves a team of five and they appear to be members of my department, able to use a colleague's credentials and go about without raising concern among the others there."

"But who?" asked Sir David.

No one had that answer.

Eight

Amy's week had been hectic with continuing education classes for herself as well as those she taught to the MedAir crews. She flew fewer missions than in the past, a fact she didn't relish, but she didn't push it with Craig Sheehan, her boss. Although she knew he was jesting when he made comments like "We've only lost two aircraft, and you were on both of them," she recognized he was correct. Twice she had gone down and nearly died.

Having experienced that, she prayed regularly for the safety of their crews. Still, she realized that her faith wavered in that arena. She prayed . . . but did she trust Him to honor that prayer? She joked about not wanting to put God to a foolish test, but her heart raced every time she boarded an aircraft, even the Cessna 172 Skyhawk she co-owned with her father.

She thanked God that two years had passed since the last incident, her leg had healed without complication, and she remained healthy. However, every time she thought about that she reminded herself that it had also been almost two years since Richard had asked her for her hand in marriage. Her father had given his blessing. Recently, he'd stopped asking when they would decide on a wedding date.

She pulled into the Ferguson Community Center's parking lot, parked, and found herself sitting and staring out the windshield. Her friend, Brittany, had started teaching Zumba classes there and had asked Amy to help her with the larger Saturday morning class. This was her first time there and she wondered if maybe she'd taken on more than her schedule could comfortably fit.

A knock on her car window disrupted her daydreaming. She looked up to see Brittany, who nodded her head toward the entrance.

"C'mon. The class is this way."

Ninety minutes later, as the last participant dragged herself from the room, Amy walked up to Brittany while toweling off.

"Boy, that was some workout. I didn't know you were part drill sergeant. I had a hard time keeping up with you at the end. Are you sure you want me as an assistant?"

Brittany laughed. "Hey, you'll get used to it. This *was* your first time and I thought you kept up just fine."

"Amy? Amy Gibbs?"

Amy turned toward the voice at the doorway. Mary Southworth. Just hearing the woman's voice lifted Amy's spirit. It had been far too long since they'd shared time over a cup of coffee, a fact that Amy accepted as being her fault, even if unavoidable.

"What are you doing in my neck of the woods?" Mary's face took on a broad smile as she stepped into the room.

"Hi, Mary. My friend Brittany here is teaching this class and asked me to help." She introduced the two women. "Wow, it's good to see you."

She had come to know Mary and her husband, Mike, through Lynch. After Amy's helicopter accident, Mary had become a frequent visitor and a source of great encouragement. Amy, whose own mom had died of cancer just as Amy entered her teens, had begun to see her as a surrogate mother, full of the wisdom that only age and experience can offer . . . and as a woman of faith, a faith she wished to emulate. Work and circumstances in Amy's life had led to their relationship drifting apart over the past six months.

"For me, too. You know, there's no such thing as coincidence. You've been on my mind for the past few days. C'mon, let me walk out with you."

Amy donned her coat, grabbed her bag, and joined the older woman.

Upon exiting the building, with no one around them, Mary asked, "So, how've you been?"

"Way too busy. I'm sorry I haven't called recently. Life has, well, sort of gotten in the way."

"And how's Richard?"

Amy looked away. "He's, uh . . . he's fine."

Mary placed her hand on Amy's arm and stopped her. Looking right at her, she said, "I've seen that look and heard that tone before. Sounds like we need to talk. Why don't you come over to the house for coffee?"

Amy didn't want to burden the woman. "I don't know. I'm still sweaty and . . ."

"Nonsense. Like I've never been sweaty? And Mike sure won't care. He's been working in his shop. Probably covered in sawdust by now."

Five minutes later, Amy pulled into the drive behind Mary and together they walked into the kitchen of the two-and-a-half-story, 100-plus-year-old historic home. Mike had spent two decades restoring the place and Amy always felt at home here. The loving care that went into every detail of the restoration wasn't lost on her, but it was the home's sense of comfort and acceptance that Amy loved most.

Mary went to work preparing coffee and Amy wandered into the dining room. Despite the massive, mirrored mantle over an old fireplace and the glistening brass chandelier hanging from its ornate ceiling medallion, Amy's attention went straight to the large dining table covered in books, a couple of open Bibles, and charts. Curious, she began to inspect the charts first. She found Biblical time lines, the genealogies of the Old Testament from Adam and Eve to Jesus, and one—that she found too complex to absorb with a glance—that was titled "The Heritage of the Anglo-Saxon race." Next to that lay printouts from a book titled "History of the Anglo-Saxons," printed in 1805. Another, from 1902, was titled "Judah's Sceptre and Joseph's Birthright."

Mary carried two mugs of coffee into the room. "Mike's latest rabbit trail."

"What is it?"

"Better to let him explain it. I get it mixed up too easily. Come. Let's sit and chat in the parlor."

Nigel Barrington had been re-assigned to the young prince's security detachment without question or hesitation. Well, no more than anyone else considered for the position. He had heard of the intense manhunt underway for those responsible for The Royal Lodge explosion, while he had undergone a new level of scrutiny before being placed. Once assigned, he went through training designed to familiarize him with the family. As such, he had not been tasked within the investigation in England.

"Eh, Nigel. Ever been to the States before?"

The pilot announced that the government Lear jet was on final approach to the Spirit of Saint Louis Airport outside St. Louis. Nigel looked out across the rolling hills of the Ozarks just south of the city. They passed over several small rivers and the farmland quickly gave way to small towns and then suburban development.

"First time. You?"

"Been 'ere several times. They call this part the Midwest. We'll 'ave to make sure to try some bar-be-que. Distinctly American and I'm told it's quite good around here."

"Sounds good. Any idea where we are?"

Another man, a Secret Service agent named Mark, leaned forward from the seat behind him. "That's the Missouri River. We're coming into the airport from the west, so we follow that for a couple of minutes and then bank right and have a direct line into the airport." He started to sit back but stopped. "And Aaron is right. Outside of Texas, the Midwest has the best bar-be-que in the States. Memphis, Kansas City, and St. Louis—each has its own style, but none of 'em can beat Texas."

Another agent sitting across the aisle protested. "Not even close. You want the best Q, go to North Carolina, where we invented it."

Nigel sat back in his seat and let them debate their All-American food. He had other things on his mind. The Director had made it clear that The Assembly wanted the prince and his family killed while in the States. He understood their desire. Taking out their primary targets while on foreign soil would embarrass the host government and create a subtle wedge between two staunch allies. Nigel would not let them down.

However, at the moment, the "how" and "where" of accomplishing the mission remained uncertain. Of the four other S.O.14 members on board, two were members of his cell. Two more remained in England to accompany the prince and his family while traveling to the U.S. He felt hamstrung by the Director's requirement that the assassination take place on U.S. soil and make it look like gun-loving American criminals had killed the family. *That*, he did not understand. It was too dicey. His men could easily take out the family while in the air, or even take down the entire plane. They would gladly die for their cause. But his place was not to question the Director.

Also, complicating *his* mission was the fact that they were now accompanied by six Secret Service agents whose allegiances were unknown to him. A minimum of six more U.S. agents would join the party upon the prince's arrival on U.S. territory, plus state and local police officers. He had been told he would have support. He just didn't know *who* would provide that support.

And if he didn't know whom to trust, he couldn't trust anyone.

Amy and Mary talked for over an hour before Mike interrupted them. Mary had been correct. He appeared covered with sawdust. She gave her husband a stern look.

"Mike! Go back outside and dust yourself off. You're dragging all that stuff in here."

He gave his wife a sheepish look. "Oops. Just wanted to see about lunch. If you're not ready to eat, I was going to do a little more. Hi, Amy. How've you been?"

"Out!" said Mary. "And try not to leave any of it

behind."

Amy smiled. She'd never seen that side of the couple. Mike reminded her of her father. *Must be in the Y chromosome*, she thought.

A few minutes later, Mike returned, looking clean. At least, Mary didn't protest this time.

"So, what's up? You two look like you've been having some serious girl talk."

"We have, and it's none of your business," said Mary.

Mike grinned. "I learned a long time ago not to poke around in stuff like that, so I won't ask. Don't ask, don't tell works better here than in the Army. You two ready for lunch? I can fix us some sandwiches."

Mary stood from the couch. "Better yet, let *me* fix something edible and you can tell her all about your project."

Mike grinned. "Yep. Better yet." He stepped aside and with a wave of his arm, ushered Amy back toward the dining room with its cluttered table.

Amy looked at the table and back to Mike. "Sooo? Um, what's all this about?"

"Well, the deaths in England reminded me of something I'd heard years ago and I decided to research it myself to see if there might be any validity to it. What do you know about the history of the British people?"

Amy gave a subtle shrug of her shoulders. "Not much. I was bored enough with *American* history. I do know my Gibbs surname has the same roots as Gibson or Gipps and is common in northern England and Scotland. I was also told it goes back to the Norman conquest of England, but I can't say I really know who the Normans were. My dad's the guy you want to talk with about history."

"Well, most historians today would say this idea is rubbish, but in the seventeenth and eighteenth centuries, it was accepted as fact. The idea is that Western Europe, which would include the Germanic Anglo-Saxons and the French Normans, originated from the lost tribes of Israel. The tribe of Dan, for example. It's more commonly accepted that, as a seafaring tribe, they had settlements along the coast of Spain and Portugal. But it would seem they also settled Scandinavia and the British Isles. This history book of the Anglo-Saxons from 1805 says . . ."

Amy worked to keep her eyes from glazing over. Her father would love this. She wondered if Mary needed help in the kitchen.

"There is even an ancient Irish tradition that the prophet Jeremiah came to Ireland. When the Babylonians invaded Judah, he fled to Egypt, then to Greece . . . or was it Sicily? . . . and then Spain before ending up in Ireland."

Her interest perked up a bit. "Jeremiah went to Ireland?"

"Yep. That's the part I'm working on now. If true, and if what I'd heard long ago is true, then the attack on the English monarchy has its roots in prophecy and the spiritual realm. I'm pretty sure there's more going on here than meets the eye."

Nigel and the others sat in the conference room of the British Consulate offices in Chesterfield, Missouri, located just minutes from the small airport where they had landed. The Secret Service and Missouri Highway Patrol briefed them on transportation. The Prince of Wales and his entourage would land at the same airport the evening before his visit to the National Churchill Museum.

A captain with the Missouri Highway Patrol addressed them.

"Departure will be at 0900 by helicopter, weather permitting. The flight will be approximately 45 minutes to the Elton Hensley Memorial Airport outside Fulton, Missouri. The motorcade will be waiting and the route secured between there and the museum, a five-minute drive. We will have officers controlling the roads and bridges, with assistance from the Fulton police within the city limits. I'm told the prince will be at the museum for a tour, short speech, and some kind of presentation, plus a luncheon. The visit is expected to take three hours after which he will return to the Spirit of St. Louis Airport."

Aaron raised his hand. "And if the weather does not permit flying?"

"Should the weather forecast be unacceptable or even questionable, you folks are to make that determination by 0600. We will have the motorcade at his hotel ready for departure at 0800. The drive takes two hours, give or take, and we will control the roads with the assistance of local law enforcement along the way to and from."

One of the Secret Service agents piped up, "Let's hope for good weather, 'cause closing off that interstate is *not* going to be easy and will upset a lot of people."

Nigel contemplated that comment. Which would be easier? Taking down a helicopter, or taking out a limousine traveling at 130 kilometers an hour?

Nine

"So, Mack, I understand you did three tours in Iraq and two in Afghanistan. That right?"

Lynch sat in the front passenger seat as Mack drove one of the campaign's SUVs. They were to meet up with an Agent Michael LaPierre at the museum at eleven a.m. He wanted to be there early enough for them to get their own lay of the land before the meeting.

"That's right, but I can't give you any details on where or what we did. You know the gig. I could tell you, but then I'd have to kill you." He gave Lynch a goofy grin.

"Yeah, that's 'cause he doesn't want to be embarrassed. Probably spent his time on post," said Zach from the back seat where he sprawled across the entire seat. "Cleaning and re-cleaning his pellet gun while SEALs did the dirty work."

The rivalry had continued since their first meeting but never moved past the chiding banter and one-upmanship. If it had, both men would have had one warning to straighten out their game or find new employment. As it was, Lynch found it comical.

"Sure. Nothing like a SEAL in the desert, floundering around, confused, and looking for water. How many tours didja do, Flipper?"

Lynch knew the answer but wanted to see this play out.

"Two in Iraq and four in Afghanistan, and my call sign wasn't Flipper, Greenie Beanie."

"Okay, so what was it?"

Zach was silent and Lynch turned around to see his face. He could almost see the mental gears moving as the man debated answering.

"Don't know if I can do that."

Lynch found that curious. It was just a call sign. Richard Nichols had earned the 'Thor' moniker because of that hammer incident. Was there something Zach Darst had failed to include in his application?

"Hey, we're not over there. What's it going to matter?" asked Mack.

"When were you there?"

Mack listed his dates 'in country' while serving there.

"Yeah, well, we overlapped on more than one occasion. I don't know."

"Oh, c'mon, Aquaman. Be a good SEAL and I'll reward you with a fish."

Zach rolled his eyes and shook his head. "Okay, I was Zombie 10."

Lynch was about to ask if there was a story to be told, as with Richard, but the sudden change of countenance on Mack's face stopped him. There *was* a story to be told. And he suspected it was one he was likely to never hear.

Mack's voice wavered as he said his next words. "Zombie 10, this is Ghost Rider. We're clear."

Richard couldn't sit still. He'd spent most of the weekend at the office but had tried to reach Amy on multiple occasions. Since his temporary move to Washington, they had Skyped every day using their Android phones. For the past two months, the frequency had dropped to three times a week.

As of that morning, they had gone nine days without talking, much less sharing any video calls. Nine days.

He knew she was upset with him. She had every right to be, but he felt it unfair of her to blame him. The campaign could be blamed. He could even go so far as to blame their campaign manager, Stan McGonagle, who kept making requests for breaking new ground in social media. Richard was supposed to be their expert, but Stan's foresight had been on target every time. He saw potential venues that Richard hadn't thought of, requested features in their software that proved invaluable, and pushed the team into territory where they had become the best of the best. Their social media reach and the grassroots support it generated had caught the opponents scratching their heads wondering how they'd achieved such goals.

"Richard Nichols?" There followed a soft knock at his office door.

He turned to find a stunning redhead standing there. Clothed in a chic, skirted suit that flattered every curve, with heels that accentuated a pair of athletically toned calves, she almost took his breath away.

Except for one thing. She wasn't supposed to be in these inner offices.

Summer Stanton, probably a stage name, was a so-called journalist for one of the big news networks, one not in tune with the politics of the Graham Campaign. How had she slipped past security to gain access to his office?

It had only taken one monthly report to the Federal Elections Commission, in which they had reported fundraising numbers that blew away the competition, to induce members of the media to begin probing for the answer as to how they'd achieved such results. Richard and his team knew to look at each member of the media with caution. Just that morning, he had again forwarded requests for interviews and information to Stan. Stan was the clearinghouse for all such requests.

And now, Summer Stanton stood in his doorway, uninvited and out of bounds.

"Ms. Stanton, you're not supposed to be here. I'll need to call security."

He picked up his phone and pressed four numbers. She rushed forward and disconnected the call before he could talk.

"Please. Not until you hear me out."

Richard shook his head. "Not on your life." He refrained from saying anything more but dialed a set of four different numbers. This number would summons security as an emergency whether he talked with them or not. They would converge on his office within a minute.

"Look, I'm not here to ask questions. I have information for *you*. Information I don't think you'd want to go public. About what you did in Afghanistan."

He shook his head again. He wasn't about to take that bait. He heard two sets of hallway fire doors open and close.

Summer stepped back and glanced both ways in the hallway. She turned back to him. In a hurry, she stated, "I can take this to your boss, or just blow it wide open to the pub—"

Two burly security agents stood on either side of her. They never touched her, but their presence alone was intimidating.

"Ma'am, you're not authorized to be here. You need to come with us."

She grabbed the door posts with her hands—as if that could stop them if they decided to get physical.

"Nichols, did you hear—"

"Now, ma'am. We know who you are. You will lose all further access to the campaign if you don't come now. That will include press conferences, press releases, and interviews . . . all of it."

Richard knew she couldn't afford to become *persona non grata* with the campaign. Her career depended upon access to all of the campaigns.

He was correct. She dropped her hands and shrugged her shoulders. She looked at the two men next to her. "I won't say anything else, but don't say I didn't warn you." She turned and headed down the hall for the exit, with the two men following.

Richard walked to his office door and watched until they passed through the nearest fire doors. As those doors closed behind them, he returned to his view of the Capitol Building. And what was she talking about in Afghanistan?

Karolus' morning had been uneventful. His presence in New York City seemed to have gone unnoticed. So far. His physical return to the U.N., however, had been met with applause. Even he had to admit that attempting to direct that august body from its European headquarters had not been as fruitful as he would have liked. Too many items on their agenda required direct hands-on management.

His luncheon meeting also required his direct attention, although it had little to do with world affairs. His guest arrived as his secretary set up their catered meals.

"Charity, it is good to see you again."

She extended her hand and he noted her firm grip. At first look, one would never expect that of her, but he knew it to be the result of her love of rock climbing. Charity Lovelace, who went by many names, had been and continued to be one of his best operatives. Others might describe her as mousy and unassuming, but that was her most endearing quality. She could blend into any environment and go unnoticed.

"Thank you, Director. I feel honored that you asked me to join you for lunch. I'm not quite sure what to say . . . or to make of it."

Her eyes looked keenly into his, and her face held no hint of a smile. He loved her direct nature.

"Make nothing more of it than being a token of my respect and gratitude for your service. Please have a seat. I hope you don't mind that I took the liberty of ordering for you."

She looked at the food on the table and a subtle glint of pleasure showed in her eyes. "My favorite. But then, I shouldn't be surprised at that."

He chuckled. "No. I did not expect you to be."

From her extensive dossier he knew more about her than she likely knew of herself. As they ate, he brought up mutual friends and her recent travels. They talked as if they were old friends, although her reserve made it clear that she would never think of their relationship that way. She still worked for him.

She dabbed her napkin to her mouth and then leaned over to open her bag as it sat next to her chair.

"You had me divert to St. Louis on my way here. I did what you asked, although the agenda wasn't clear. I might have done a better job had I understood."

She pulled out several 8x10 photos, plus a thumb drive and slid them across the table to him. "The image files are on the drive. The photos were the best I could get under the circumstances. There are a couple of phone conversations on the drive as well, but nothing in them that seemed useful for anything. At least, not to me. She uses her cell phone at home, no land line, so I couldn't tap that. Her office phone was also problematic. The security where she works was tighter than I anticipated and you didn't indicate that this was a high priority job so I saw no point in risking it."

Karolus perused the photos. Amy Gibbs and Lynch Cully at lunch together. A couple of them with her holding his hand, head forward as if in intimate conversation. Those held promise, but they would have been better had they shown Cully being more responsive to her.

The young nurse wasn't his target. He admired and respected nurses, unlike those five women on that insipid morning talk show. He could never recall the program's title, but *My Silly Opinion* is what he would call it. As if their opinions mattered to anyone.

Cully, however, was a different story. Cully had a prime role in exposing and embarrassing him. He had placed a target on Cully's forehead, but payback required more anguish than death would deliver. Besides, Cully's unexpected demise, or the deaths of his family or close friends, would point to him and The Assembly. Karolus searched for something more subtle.

"What about Cully's phone? Any luck with that?"

"Not a chance," she replied, shaking her head. "He uses his business cell for pretty much everything, except calls to his family. And it's not your run-of-the-mill Android or iPhone. They're using the highly encrypted Blackphone II.

128-bit encryption. All calls go through their private server and remain encrypted from end to end. That one's beyond my skill level."

Karolus nodded. He was familiar with the phone, but they had yet to penetrate its security. Its programmers had had a previous run-in with a sub-group within The Assembly. The result of that tumultuous encounter contributed to the phone's development, making it one of a few communication systems they lacked access to.

"I've put someone else on Cully's tail. Have you made any progress in Washington?"

"We're just getting started. I'll have someone for you inside Graham's campaign within a week, two at the latest."

Karolus wondered who she had targeted. He already knew that money wouldn't work. Or, perhaps they hadn't found the right target for bribes. He wanted to know what she had planned, out of curiosity, but he couldn't. His ignorance of her methods was safer for both of them.

Ten

To say that the remainder of their drive to Fulton was quiet would be like trying to hear a pin drop in an anechoic chamber. Lynch's gut told him something significant had happened to these two while in Afghanistan and that it was a shared incident somehow. In the silence of the ride, he started his usual 'what if' game only to realize he could spend the entire afternoon coming up with potential scenarios. At some point, he would simply have to ask them.

They found a parking spot on Westminster Avenue right across from the museum. All parking within two blocks of the site would become restricted 36 hours before the Prince's arrival and they would tow all cars still within that area 24 hours later. This would allow the Secret Service time to recheck the area for explosives. And, after the events in England, they would be taking every precaution possible.

The trio walked across the street and stood looking up at the Church of St. Mary the Virgin, Aldermanbury. The original twelfth-century church had burned to the ground in 1666 and the famous architect, Sir Christopher Wren, rebuilt it in central London. The Nazi bombing of the London Blitz during World War II left it gutted. To commemorate Winston Churchill's visit in 1946, the college raised funds to move the ruins and rebuild it on campus as the college chapel, an effort that began in 1964 and ended in 1969. The museum occupied the space beneath the church, extending underground toward the nearby auditorium building.

"First impression?" asked Lynch, as they walked around the perimeter of the building.

Both men shrugged.

"Could be worse," replied Zach. "The entrance of the museum offers quick egress to a car, but it's still a wide-open space."

"The doors to the church are a total bust," said Mack. "They all open onto that plaza which is wide open and fully exposed to a number of sites."

A man in dress slacks, shirt and tie, and a blue zip-up jacket, holding a German Shepherd on a tight leash, approached them. "I need to see some identification, please." The dog sniffed each man and offered no reaction.

"Lynch Cully and this is my team." He showed his ID, as did Mack and Zach. "We work for the Bradley Graham campaign and have an 11 a.m. meeting with Agent LaPierre."

The man nodded. "He'll meet you at the museum entrance. You can wait there."

"If you don't mind, we want to get a lay of the land for ourselves."

The agent shook his head. "Please wait at the museum entrance. Agent LaPierre will brief you on everything you'll need to know. We know what to do and have it all under control."

The disdain in the man's voice made it obvious that he saw the trio as a bunch of rent-a-cops, private security with no real experience. And the look on Mack's face clearly showed annoyance.

"Look, Agent whatever, we don't know who *you* are.

Why don't you show us *your* ID?" Mack stepped into the man's personal space, ignoring the dog's guttural objection to that move. He then said something in a foreign language that sounded Eastern European to Lynch, and the dog promptly sat, with ears perked up as if expecting a treat.

That caught the agent's attention. He showed his Secret Service badge and credentials.

"Thank you, Agent Davidson. Now that we've established that you're a 'friendly' and we're on the same team, why don't you give your dog the treat I promised him while we finish our reconnaissance?" He said something else to the animal, reached down and rubbed his ears, and the dog's tail began to wag.

As they began to step away, Mack turned back to the agent. "Oh, and if you want to know how I did that, I might find time to give you a lesson on handling your dog. He should never be so easy to subvert."

The man's cheeks flushed and a scowl crossed his face.

Lynch leaned toward Mack as they continued walking away from the church and said, "*I'd* like to know how you did that. Will that work with Bandogs and English Mastiffs?"

Mack gave him a curious look.

"Long story. I'll tell you about it sometime. In the meantime, we have to work with these people, so let's not get them too riled."

They walked along an extended perimeter around the church. The two men validated Lynch's own opinion as to what buildings would be emptied and secured, the "high ground" where Secret Service snipers would be stationed to control the area, and more. Together, they watched men with dogs working the bushes, trash receptacles, dumpsters, and other potential hiding places in search of explosives. One team even had a Geiger counter scanning for radioactive material. No stone would remain unturned.

Outside Marquess Hall, Lynch glanced at his watch and said, "It's almost time for the meeting. Let's head that way." Lynch turned back toward the museum entrance on the opposite side of the church.

Mack spoke up. "Hey, do you need me in that meeting? This is the dorm my brother stayed in. I want to check out something he told me about it."

Lynch had forgotten Mack's comment about that during their staff meeting.

"Yeah, what's up with that?" asked Zach.

"I'll tell ya if I find it." He looked at Lynch. "Yes? No?"

"Sure. We can fill you in on what LaPierre says. Just don't start any trouble . . . and don't seduce any more dogs."

Lynch waited for Zach to pounce on that line, but nothing happened. No snide comment. No grief at all. Just a thumb up. What *happened* in Afghanistan?

Lynch and Zach glanced at each other, with Zach rolling his eyes, as Agent LaPierre gave them a five-minute tour of the building. Lynch wanted to scream as the man pointed out the obvious. The only entry and egress of the building would be the main entrance, while the underground exhibit hall connecting to the auditorium would be their emergency exit. All of the church doors would remain secured.

"And if there is an emergency, what *is* the evacuation plan through Champ Auditorium?"

Agent LaPierre looked at him as if he was asking for nuclear missile launch codes.

"We're finalizing that today, but the plan will remain secure with us. Suffice it to say that you are to manage your people and protect your asset. The Royal Couple will be given top priority in any evacuation and you are not to get in the way."

Lynch almost spoke up to remind the man that his *asset*, as he put it, had already been targeted twice before and that the Royal Family might not be the only people with a bulls-eye on them. He stopped, though, when he realized that such a reminder might get Bradley Graham un-invited to the party. Although that would make Lynch's job easier, he knew the boss wouldn't like that turn of events. And Lynch would have to take ownership of being the reason for the change.

"May we at least walk through, to, and around the auditorium, so that we know what our options are?"

The agent hesitated in answering but relented after a moment's thought. Lynch and Zach reconnoitered the underground passage, the auditorium and backstage areas, as well as the hallways and then returned to the museum. They found Agent LaPierre talking with others in the advance party.

"Thank you, Agent LaPierre. We have what we need and I promise we won't get in your way on the fifth." Lynch extended his hand to the man, who returned the gesture with a hasty handshake and turned back to his team.

"Mr. Personality," said Zach as they walked out of earshot.

"Yeah, and so helpful, too. I think they all look at us as being third string."

"Harrumph. If they only knew," muttered Zach.

Lynch looked at him, wondering, and thinking, *Why*

Outside, they found two other agents retaining Mack. Mack looked filthy. The arms of his jacket appeared to be smeared with what Lynch guessed to be brick dust, with its characteristic red color. Sooty dirt smudged his cheeks, and the knees of his trousers looked stained with all of the above.

"What's up?" asked Lynch. "He's with us."

One of the two agents nodded at Mack to join Lynch, but both men kept a close eye on them all.

Mack grinned. "A guess I do look like someone who lives under a highway overpass, but I showed 'em my ID. They wouldn't let me inside."

Zach laughed. "Maybe they didn't want the janitorial service working overtime in there."

"Maybe."

Lynch had expected a better comeback.

"Didja find it?" asked Zach.

"Funny thing. Agent Davidson walked back through the area and his dog came right up to me, wagging his tail. But Davidson didn't say a thing. He wouldn't acknowledge that I was cleared to be here, even though his dog did."

Mack tried to brush more grime from his coat and pants. Or was he wiping off his hand? A second later, he lifted the hand for a high-five. Zach complied.

"Aw-right!"

"It's there. I found it in the basement of the dorm, just like little bro said. It took some doing to uncover it. Someone went to great lengths to close it up and hide it."

Lynch felt a little perturbed at being kept in the dark. Mack had confided in Zach. They seemed to have formed their own little mutual admiration society.

Lynch stopped in his tracks. "Okay. So, are you planning on filling *me* in, or was this just some scavenger hunt for your brother?"

Mack grinned again. "Lynch, you're gonna love what I found. Trust me. I'll fill you in when we're back on the road."

"Thank you. And while we're at it, what's with this sudden change between you two? You were trading barbs with each other like college football rivals until 90 minutes ago, and now you're like BFFs. All kissy-kissy, let's make up."

Mack and Zach looked at each other. Lynch could see the mental gears at work again.

After several seconds, Zach turned back to face Lynch.

"So, as a major presidential candidate's chief of security, what's *your* security clearance?"

Lynch furrowed his brow, as he recognized he had no "need to know."

"Top secret."

The two men looked at each other again, as if trying to communicate telepathically.

"Tell you what," said Mack. "Me and Zach need to discuss this first. Then, we'll tell you what we can." Zach nodded. "But it won't be today."

Eleven

Nigel watched with interest the trio that walked away from the museum. As a member of the Royal Protection advance team, he had full access to all plans devised by the Secret Service, as well as input into the approval of invited guests. He didn't have final say, but that made no difference.

He walked up to their team leader and asked, "Charles, who are those men walking away?"

Charles Abbott looked up from his notebook and scanned about the area. His gaze stopped as he looked in the direction toward which Nigel pointed. He returned his gaze to his notebook and replied, "They're the advance team for one of the American political candidates. The chap is on the board of trustees at this college." He resumed writing.

"Do you know which candidate?"

Abbott looked up again, seeming annoyed at the interruption. "Afraid not, off the top of my head. LaPierre will know."

Nigel decided to break from his current task and find the Secret Service agent. As he neared the museum's main entrance, one of the other agents with his dog approached.

"I saw you pointing at those three guys over there. Did they do something?"

Nigel shook his head. "No. I was just curious who they worked for."

"Bradley Graham, the conservative presidential

candidate. Buncha rent-a-cops if you ask me."

"Rent-a-cops?"

"Yeah, a nickname we have for guys who want to be policemen but can't cut it. They become security guards."

The dog became antsy around Nigel and the agent had to calm it down. Nigel didn't like working around dogs. They had a habit of getting in the way.

Nigel chuckled, but inside he rejoiced. The Director would pay handsomely if he were to eliminate both the royal heirs and this conservative candidate who had twice escaped the death he deserved. Still, he needed to play his role.

"I'd be careful who you say that to," he replied to the dog-handler. "I've known some pretty rough chaps who went into security because they thought police work was too tame. British SAS types. And as I recall, some of your military's best and brightest left their services to work for firms like Blackwater and Sabre International in the Middle East." He grinned. "But, don't worry. They won't hear what you said from me. Hahahaha . . . rent-a-Bobbies. I rather like that one."

He turned back toward the auditorium's outside entrance on the building's south side and hurried to the glass double doors. Once inside, he ran up the nearest stairs and found the small control room where he and his comrades were to meet. The other two were already there.

"*As-salaam 'alaykum,*" he said as he entered the room.

"*Ahlan wa sahlan,*" replied one of the others. "You are late. We don't have much time."

"Sorry, old man," said Nigel, slipping back into character. "It couldn't be avoided. I have some good news for the Director. We will be twice rewarded in Paradise when we complete this mission." His team knew that this mission would likely lead to their deaths, but they were pleased to be of use to Allah and The Assembly.

He told them of his discovery that Bradley Graham would be attending the reception, and then explained just who the man was and why his attendance—and subsequent death there—would please The Assembly. Of course, he still required a green light from the Director, but he had no worry that the additional targets would be turned down.

"What have we found out about the final plans?"

"Nothing more than what you had already surmised. We are to protect the Royal Family while in route and within the buildings. The Secret Service will direct everything on the outside and supplement the security within the building. They have provided us with the details of their plan and the locations of their men. Abbott has approved the plan."

Nigel nodded. "As we expected him to do. And their emergency plan?"

"Also as we expected. They had no real choice." The other man pulled a folded letter-size sheet of paper from his jacket pocket, a map of the campus buildings. He began to point to various locations. "Their snipers will have oversight from these buildings. Should the main entrance become hot, they plan to evacuate through the auditorium building. Here." He pointed again to the map. "They will exit through the service area in the back. However, that area remains a blind spot for their snipers."

"And thus, for us, too, since we will have removed their snipers and replaced them with our own. That means we will have to be prepared to finish our job in the exhibition chamber connecting the museum to the auditorium. To take out our targets and give glory to Allah before they can escape."

Nigel glanced at his watch. They had two minutes before they had to rejoin the protection team for a final briefing. He rushed through the presentation of his plan and refined it with their input. Satisfied that they would succeed, they checked the hallway outside the room, and finding it empty, left as a group.

Karolus found his day at the office extending into the evening. He had no issue with that, as the day had been brutally cold with intermittent snow that threatened to become what the locals called a nor'easter. As he understood the term, the storm would be a severe one, dumping enough snow on the city to paralyze it by morning. He didn't want to chance that. He had items on the agenda that required his direct attention.

And so, he continued working at his office—to the dismay of his staff.

He buzzed his secretary in her front office. "Annette, do you have the report I was promised by the Russian Ambassador?"

"It's on your desk, sir. Front right corner."

He rummaged through the pile of papers there until he found it. *My fault*, he thought. He had stacked half a dozen reports on top of it.

"I found it. I'll also need the white paper on current efforts on gun control in the U.S."

"In the same pile, sir. Three or four packets below the one you just found." She paused for one second and continued, "Sir, may I release the rest of the staff to go home? The weather is worsening and public transit has slowed to a crawl. They're afraid they won't get home at all if they don't leave now."

Karolus stood and walked to his window overlooking the city. Snow swirled about and the street lamps seemed distant. Traffic seemed to be at a standstill. His typical two-mile commute took about 20 minutes. Tonight, he might be fortunate if it took under an hour. He wondered if he, too, should head home. He could read in the car.

The clock revealed the time to be a few minutes after seven. Yes. It was time to call it a day.

"Yes, Annette, please do. I just looked outside. I did not realize the weather had deteriorated. Please call for my car and have a safe trip home."

"Thank you, sir, and be careful. Have a good evening."

He searched the pile on his desk for the other briefing and placed it, along with other papers he might need, into his briefcase. By the time he had finished, the announcement that his car was available came across his intercom.

A few minutes later, settled into the back seat of the limousine, he opened his briefcase and retrieved the brief on gun control. The vehicle inched along as he read. He didn't like what he saw. All of the rhetoric from the current administration had had little effect. The conservative arguments for greater gun freedom seemed to strike a chord with the American people. The conservatives were correct, of course. He knew their logic and their statistics were solid, but that didn't fit the need of The Assembly. Should a forced take-over of the United States be required, they couldn't have millions of armed citizens resisting their effort.

He made a mental note to contact the President's Chief of Staff about upping their game. School shootings no longer made people blink. Gun registration by executive fiat would produce the alternate result. They needed to find some other means to make people abhor guns. In the meantime, two members of The Assembly had begun using their wealth to buy arms and ammunition manufacturers. Their control of these industries had already resulted in making it difficult for the average citizen to buy weapons or the ammunition needed to use the ones they had.

He glanced about the outside of his vehicle. The traffic had returned to a standstill and they had traveled less than half a mile in the past 20 minutes. He sighed but was glad to have left when he did.

He started to review the Russian brief and his secure phone chimed.

"Director, Barrington here."

Karolus frowned. The man had instructions not to contact him directly. Such direct communications with an operative named Fawaz over a year earlier had led to Karolus being implicated in an attempt to bring down the U.S. New safeguards had been put in place. New levels of containment.

"I hope there's a good reason for this call."

"Yes, sir. I took it up the new chain of command and at the end of the chain, I was instructed to contact you."

Karolus made note to have that claim validated and to discuss the result with whoever told the man to call him.

"Very well. I've been told that you are in St. Louis as part of the protection team for the new Prince of Wales during his trip there. I hope there are no serious problems with this mission."

Karolus could only suspect that something serious enough to warrant his direct attention would have led to Barrington's call. His stomach churned. And in St. Louis, of all places. His public embarrassment and temporary, forced exile from New York had begun with previous events in St. Louis. His mind wandered to that time and the circumstances surrounding that failed mission.

"No, sir. No problems. A bonus, in fact. One that I'm told should please you but that you alone could green light."

That caught Karolus' attention and made him perk up.

"Go on."

"One moment please, sir."

There was silence on the other end. Concern again raised its head in Karolus' mind.

"Sorry, sir. An extra set of ears passed by and I didn't wish to be overheard. We thought you would like to know that Bradley Graham will be attending the prince's luncheon and presentation, and that his chief of security will be there as well."

A smile crossed Karolus' face. Those two men had been the focus of his thoughts more than a few hundred times. Was the opportunity for payback now at hand?

"Would you like them to become collateral damage?"

Yes, his assistant had been correct to pass this along to him. This decision was his to make and no one else's.

"Most definitely. Yes."

Twelve

The cold front that had blasted through the Midwest had joined forces with another frontal system to pound the East Coast from Virginia north into New England. Amy watched the weather reports from their op center with interest, while being thankful that snowfall had spared the St. Louis area. She'd had enough of winter. Cabin fever now infected her as the first weekend of March was but days away.

The latest report informed her that all flights into and out of Boston, New York, Washington, D.C., and points in-between had been canceled. If the storm lasted more than a couple of days, she knew the chances of Richard coming home this next weekend lessened with each day the bad weather persisted.

Her long day had ended without incident and now she faced going home to . . . to what? Another microwaved meal alone? She didn't feel like preparing a meal just for herself, as much as she enjoyed cooking. A year ago, she had anticipated sharing that home with Richard and yet, after numerous discussions—long distance discussions at that--he still couldn't agree on a date for the wedding. Her house seemed emptier than when she had been single and without expectations.

She grabbed her bag and coat, said goodnight to those colleagues still at their desks, and emerged from the building into the frigid evening air. She climbed into her car and once more mentally debated her need for a remote car starter so she could enter an already warm car. Now, she would be lucky to have any heat at all by the time she reached home in 15 minutes.

As she pulled up to her house, she noticed through the windows that several lights were on. *Did I forget to turn off the kitchen and living room lights this morning?* she asked herself. Perhaps. Nothing seemed out of order as she opened the garage door and pulled inside.

As she emerged from her car, an incredibly wonderful aroma of food cooking met her. She couldn't place what it was, but it smelled delicious. But *who* was doing the cooking? She didn't see her father's car outside at the curb. Plus, he was supposed to be out of town for two more days.

She opened the door with caution.

"Surprise!"

She dropped her bag and ran into Richard's arms. He was here. In her house. And he was real, not a hallucination. He smothered her with a lingering kiss and held her tight to his body.

After a moment, he eased his grasp on her. "Wow. I've really missed that . . . you, that is."

She stepped back and slid off her coat, which he grabbed and tossed onto the back of a nearby chair.

"What? How? I mean . . . I wasn't expecting to see you anytime soon."

He nodded and grabbed two wine glasses already filled with red wine. Amy glanced at the nearby bottle to find it over half full.

"And no empty bottles in the recycling bin. Unlike somebody I know, I refrained from drinking while I cooked." He gave her a devilish grin and she blushed at recalling the first time she invited Richard to join her for a home-cooked meal. That had been a disaster.

"But, to answer your question, I talked the boss into letting me out of the office to join him for two weeks on the campaign trail. Since he's home right now and will be going to Westminster College this weekend, I decided to fly in this morning before the weather deteriorated back east. I was going to call and then I decided to surprise you. Hungry?"

"I am now. It smells wonderful."

"Chicken spedini with rice pilaf and green beans. I hope it's okay. I don't have much time off at work and when I do, since I couldn't come here, I actually started taking some cooking classes. I think I've mastered this recipe, but I'll let you be the judge."

"How long 'til it's ready?"

"I can dish it up now."

"Umm, okay. Give me a minute to clean up."

She rushed over to her bag on the floor, grabbed it and then her coat, and left the kitchen to put both away. In the bathroom, she looked into the mirror and felt dismayed. She looked a wreck. As much as she liked the surprise, maybe 15 or 20 minutes advance notice would have worked better. She quickly brushed her hair, passed her mascara wand over her lashes once, and added a touch of blush. Her uniform would have to do.

She sped to her bedroom door and yelled, "Ready yet?"

Richard answered, "Almost."

Okay, maybe she had time to put on something else. Two minutes later, she returned to the kitchen.

"Hey, you changed clothes. You didn't have to do that."

"Yeah. I did. I feel much more comfortable now. How can I help?"

"You can follow me." He offered his arm to her and led her to the dining room.

She stopped at the entrance and stared. Candles. Her best china and linens. Four bouquets of fresh flowers, including a dozen pink roses. Tears came to her eyes. How could she have doubted him these past few weeks?

"It's beautiful," she whispered.

He ushered her to her seat and pulled out the chair. As he then sat across from her, he offered a toast. "To the next three days together."

She smiled and they clinked glasses. "You do realize I still have to work, right? I don't really have vacation time to burn right now, if we want time for a honeymoon."

He nodded. "But we can still do lunch together, and dinner, and the evenings. I'm sorry I missed the concert you wanted to go to, but we don't have to do anything special. I just want to spend the time with you."

She took her first bite of the meal and savored it as it melted in her mouth. "This . . . is . . . delicious. You keep taking those lessons and you might end up doing the cooking. And all of this." She waved her hand across the table. "How in the world did you find my good stuff? It's been in storage so long, I'm not sure I knew where it was."

He went on to describe what he'd spent the afternoon doing. They talked of work and events. The conversation continued as they shared the task of cleaning up. That done, he opened a second bottle of wine and they moved to the living room. She snuggled into his arms and enjoyed the warmth of his body.

"Oh, wait." He slid away.

"Come back. I was just getting comfortable."

"I made dessert, too. Be right back."

Five minutes later, he returned and handed her a dish.

"Is this what I think it is? It looks as wonderful as dinner."

He smiled. "Well, if you're thinking chocolate mousse, then yes, it is."

"Did you—"

"Yes, I made it, too. Along with the chocolate leaves for decoration."

She dipped her spoon into the creamy, dark chocolate mousse and sighed as it filled her mouth with its rich flavor. She picked up the chocolate leaf and sampled it as well. Heaven.

Deep inside, she knew he was working extra hard to make amends, but at that moment, she didn't care. He was with her. The meal had been delightful . . . and the dessert was to die for. Sure, marriage won't be like this, her pragmatic self kept saying. But it would have its special moments as well.

If the wedding ever took place. She tried not to spoil the mood.

The drive home from Fulton wasn't as quiet as the last half of the trip there. Zach drove this time, so Mack could make good his word to brief Lynch on what he'd found while there.

"So, let me get this straight. You found an old utility tunnel." Lynch sat twisted around in the front passenger seat so he could see Mack in the back.

"That's right. My brother told me that in the early days of the college, they had their own power plant and generated steam there to heat the buildings. The steam pipes, as well as the electric service ran through tunnels from one building to another. They were brick lined and big enough for two men to walk through. The tunnels still exist, but they aren't used. The students used to access them for kicks, until the college closed them off with more than wooden doors."

"So, how does that help us?" asked Lynch.

"Not sure yet. I found one that heads from Marquess Hall toward the museum. I was able to get it open and, using my cell phone for light, walked through it to a point where it angled off to the left. At that point, the walls changed from concrete to brick and the passage is blocked by a brick wall. From the looks of it, the wall is just a blockade to keep someone from going farther. It looks like the tunnel continues on. I can't tell if it reaches the museum or not. I'm thinking they didn't destroy the tunnel when they built the museum in the '60s in case they ever needed it again for utilities."

Lynch absorbed this information and mulled it over but saw no benefit.

"So, again, how does that help? If we can't access it from the museum somehow, or if it's blocked by walls, it does us no good in an emergency."

Mack looked contemplative. "Well, that's what I was thinking. I mean, I thought it might be useful in an emergency. But you're right. I don't know about the access. I need better light and more time to inspect it."

Zach spoke up. "I think Mack is on to something here. Look, from what they told us, and from what we saw, there will be only two ways in and out. The main door is too easy to hit as a target. If the intel we received from Mack's friend in MI5 is correct about the attacks being an inside job, and there's one or more British officers on this suspected hit squad, then the emergency exit plan *has* to be their target zone. If I was them, I'd attack the main door somehow, force the emergency plan into action and make the hit there. That exhibit hall and the way it empties into the auditorium building is like funneling fish into a net."

Lynch didn't take long to think about that because he was in agreement.

"I think you're right. But how do we use it if we don't have access from inside the museum? We have to consider other methods of extraction, like the windows on the east side of the building. They open onto a small garden that's adjacent to the sidewalk and Westminster Avenue. We have less distance to cross to get to the cars from that garden than we do from the main entrance."

"But there's a fence to deal with. And the opening to the garden is next to the main entrance, so that's the same as using the main door."

"Zach has a point, Lynch. We could be prepared to blow an opening in the fence and use smoke for cover, but that will draw the attention of both the good *and* bad guys. Do we tell LaPierre of that contingency plan? And if we do, can we trust it to remain confidential? Not likely. He'd share it with his agents so they wouldn't be surprised and come shooting. And that makes it info the bad guys would have access to and could use."

"And what if the bad guys already have those windows covered? One shooter across the street is all that would take. If they gain the high ground we talked about earlier *and* have a shooter across the street, that puts the main door in a deadly crossfire situation and makes the garden a killing zone as well. I mean, think about it. Also, we're thinking about those windows as an emergency exit. What if they're planning to use them to get *into* the building?"

Lynch liked the way these guys thought. What if this. What if that. Playing the 'what if' game had always been one of his strong suits. Like a game of chess where a master player could think a dozen steps ahead, looking at all of the possibilities made it easier to find the trouble spots.

Yet, something ate at him about these scenarios. Were they missing something? Surely, the Secret Service would know about the old tunnels. Did they have an access point somewhere that remained their ace hidden up their sleeve?

Lynch glanced at his watch as they pulled into the campaign headquarters parking lot. The sun had set half an hour into their two-hour drive back from Fulton. The time was now 1930 hours and he was famished. He wondered what Amy was doing. He considered driving to one of her favorite take-out restaurants, Zorba's, and surprising her with Greek food. Two things stopped him.

He halfway recalled the last time he'd eaten Greek food from Zorba's with her. That evening had not gone so well, although his recollection of it was spotty, thanks to the anoxic brain injury and resultant amnesia forced upon him by that monster, the L.A. Rapist. More recently, however, was her abrupt departure from lunch just a few days earlier.

No. He would have to be patient. Surprising her with dinner would be too forward.

Thirteen

By the time Lynch arrived at their campaign headquarters, he had already imbibed three cups of coffee. His restless night had been bad enough. Now caffeine jitters added to the beginning of his busy day. And as the sun began to peak over the eastern horizon, he still couldn't shake the feeling he had missed something. And his gut warned him to remain vigilant.

Within ten minutes after his arrival, the entire security team assembled. He glanced at the stragglers. *They look as frazzled as I feel*, he thought. They had been on point, guarding the boss at a fund-raising dinner until late the evening before only to turn around and start the day early. Under normal conditions, they would have had the day off. Today was not a normal day.

Lynch whistled to get everyone's attention. The conference room quieted.

"Zach, Tony, and Alex. You're with me. We're driving the SUVs to Fulton. When we get there, Tony and Alex, you need to gas up the vehicles for the next leg of the boss' trip. Zach and I will meet up with the Secret Service for last minute instructions."

Tony raised his hand to show that he had the keys. "Why are we taking four? I thought we planned on just two vehicles for his trip to Kansas City."

"Just a precaution. Jim, Andre, Roscoe . . . you guys take one car and head to Kansas City to organize the security for that rally. The rest of you are on point with the boss. Pick him up at home no later than 0745 and move directly to the Spirit of St. Louis Airport. He will be introduced to the prince and his wife and, together with the governor, will fly to Fulton. They will have a total of four helicopters, two of which will be decoys. Once there, one car of the motorcade will be yours. The Secret Service expects you to protect our boss and him alone. You are not to interfere or even offer to assist them when it comes to the Royal Couple. Got it?"

The four men nodded.

"Questions?"

"Emergency plan?"

Yeah, about that, thought Lynch. He'd have to go with the official plan. "Secret Service will direct any emergency exit. The Royal Couple has top priority. After that, I'm sure the governor expects next priority, but that's debatable . . . in my opinion."

Several men chuckled. Bradley Graham had spared no criticism of the governor after his failure to protect Ferguson businesses during the rioting that occurred in 2014 and 2015. Lynch had to agree. To call up the National Guard and purposely withhold them when the riots began was shameful and cowardly. And when the lieutenant governor had outed the man for acting on orders from the White House, exposing the Administration's political motives for fomenting the protests, the Graham campaign applauded. The governor might smile in public around Brad Graham, but he'd need Super Glue to hold that smile in private.

"Actually, in thinking about it. You guys need to make sure you sit between the boss and the governor, in case the governor decides to act up." He grinned.

"Yeah, won't happen," cracked one of the men. "There'll be too many news cameras around."

"Maybe we should all wear body cams. We might come up with something truly newsworthy."

As the men laughed, Lynch thought that might, in fact, be a good idea. He made a note to look into them.

"Okay, guys, 15 minutes 'til game time. Do what you need to do and get ready to hit the field."

Lynch glanced at his watch. The caffeine had worn off by the time he had arrived in Fulton, but now the adrenaline surged.

"Motorcade should be leaving the airport. They'll be here in five," said Zach.

Lynch nodded. "Any word from Mack?"

The ex-SEAL nodded. "He's good."

"And what's that mean?"

"You know, he's, uh, good. Look, he said not to tell you anything. Plausible deniability and all that."

"So, he *is* somewhere around here then? I hope he knows to stay clear. I haven't added his name to the attendance roster. The Feds won't be expecting him anywhere in the controlled area."

Zach shrugged. "You sure you want to know?"

Lynch gave up. He suspected the man had come ahead on his own to inspect the tunnel system. Yet, Mack was treading on thin ice to do so with the level of security surrounding this royal visit. Wrong place at the wrong time would get him detained at the minimum, despite his credentials.

Lynch scanned the area. He and Zach stood at the

museum entrance, behind a phalanx of Secret Service and Royal Protection agents who would literally form a human shield for the Royal Couple's entrance and exit from the museum. The Secret Service had told him that snipers were in place to provide oversight and protection, but he couldn't see them even though he knew their most likely positions. The agents waiting in front of Lynch would disperse to positions in the auditorium, within the church, and at each door of the church once the Royal Couple was inside. Only a presidential visit might have garnered more manpower.

"One minute out!" yelled Agent LaPierre.

Lynch took a deep breath and put his mental gears in mesh. He heard the sirens of the highway patrol escort coming closer.

True to form, one minute later, the first vehicle pulled to a stop outside the entrance. As the door opened, a dozen men circled the Prince of Wales, with his wife, the Princess of Wales, at his side. They hustled the couple inside, looking much like a rugby scrum. Then they surprised Lynch by returning to the vehicle. Another woman and two young children emerged. The scrum re-formed and rushed into the building.

The children! Nothing had been said about the children accompanying their parents. They, too, were direct heirs to the throne, but. . .

"They brought their kids with 'em?" exclaimed Zach in a tone that revealed his own astonishment. "Why in the world would they expose their kids to the potential for danger here? Are they crazy?"

Lynch had no answer. He had no children so he could not imagine what the Royal Couple's thinking might have been. No matter. What counted was whether or not

LaPierre had been briefed about this before assigning his manpower to their tasks. Having the children there could quickly complicate matters should the worst-case scenario come into play.

He had little time to ponder the possibilities. The governor was now inside. A third car rolled up and Lynch was also surprised to see both of Missouri's U.S. Senators emerge. Agents escorted them inside. Both politicians had first announced they had scheduling conflicts that would prevent them from attending. Obviously, the photo ops here were too compelling to miss.

Finally, their car brought up the rear. Lynch knew the boss had no problem with that. The man didn't seek fame or have an ego to feed. He was a grassroots candidate whose main desire was to break the heavy yoke of liberal progressivism and its choke-hold on Washington, D.C. Plus, he was here because of his position on the board of trustees. No other reason.

In fact, five other members of that Board rode with him in the car. Together, they exited the car and walked into the museum. Lynch and his team surrounded them all, watching their perimeter for potential trouble.

Five minutes later, all were seated inside the church, awaiting the prince's speech and presentation. As the head of his team, Lynch stood at the back, while the others waited downstairs.

Introductions were made and the young Prince Arthur thanked his hosts for their hospitality and the red-carpet treatment, something he was still getting accustomed to. As he began his speech, promising to keep it brief, Lynch heard a voice in his earpiece.

"Lynch, can you come downstairs?"

He eased away from the back wall and eased toward the central spiral staircase, the only inside access between the church and the museum. He found Alex and Tony waiting for him.

"Something's happening outside. They've found a dog-handler and his dog dead in the garden along the east side. And one of the snipers isn't answering his comm."

Fourteen

Nigel swore under his breath. A member of his team had jumped the gun and the Secret Service had already discovered the body. He rushed to the top floor of Marquess Hall and from there gained access to the roof. Before the Secret Service sniper could recognize there was noise behind him and turn to see who it was, a bullet from Nigel's silenced 9mm Beretta sliced through the back of the man's head. Nigel clambered across the shingled roof to make sure the man's rifle didn't tumble off his perch.

With the rifle in hand, he pushed the body aside and took up a prone position. Using the telescopic sight, he eyed the second sniper nest. A short sequence of light flashes indicated his other team member was now in position and in command of the opposite side of the church.

Together, they began removing members of the protective details. First to go down were the agents at the church doors, followed by two who came running around the corner of the church. Nigel would keep his side of the church cleared, but he had to rely upon his comrade to deal with the main entrance. By plan, the others should have now converged on the auditorium doorway into the exhibition hall.

An explosion in the tower of the church told him that someone had tried to access that sniper nest and, in his haste, had triggered the booby trap his man had left behind when he dealt with the original occupant of that position.

That had been the only point high enough to threaten his current position. Now that it was inaccessible, he could focus on the area in front and around him.

He watched as the upper bell tower began a slow topple to one side, its descent accelerating as more of the tower's stone structure below gave way. Smoke started to curl up from the ruins. Within seconds, he witnessed the first flames of the incendiary device leap from the tower. If all went as planned, that would quickly engulf the lower tower and its spiral staircase from the museum to the church, the only interior route between the two. Cutting off that access point would force people within the church to evacuate through its outer doors, onto the plaza that he and his fellow sniper now controlled.

No one else appeared on the north side of the building, but the chaos inside the museum mounted, if the clamor in his earpiece was any indication. He checked his watch. Forty-five seconds until the next step in their schedule.

Lynch's mind raced. By best count, a dozen agents lay injured or dead on the ground. To check the bodies was suicide. But that was LaPierre's responsibility. Right now, he had to do *his* job, protect Bradley Graham.

He ran up the spiral staircase, assessing his options as he moved. As he entered the sanctuary, he saw the Royal Family huddled under the elevated pulpit with LaPierre standing in front of them. Next to him stood Charles Abbott, the head of the Royal Protection detail. Both men had guns drawn and appeared to be discussing their next move.

He ran to Bradley Graham.

"Sir, we need to get out or find a better defensive

position."

"We need to help the family out first. I want you guys to assist them, then worry about me."

"Sir, we were told in no uncertain terms not to interfere or offer assistance."

"Forget that. I don't think the Secret Service anticipated losing two-thirds of their squad before they could even respond. Don't worry about me. God has a plan for me and I'll get out of this just fine."

As he finished talking, the tall, arched, glass windows along the side of the sanctuary began to shatter. Glass rained down on the people inside. Two agents stationed in the balcony toppled over the railing to the floor below, crimson stains spreading across their upper chests, above their protective vests.

People began to scream and rush for the spiral stairway. Lynch noted the governor leading the pack and felt instant disgust at his cowardice. As the crowd surged to the top of the stairs, the glass window next to them shattered and a man next to the governor collapsed over the rail. The crowd turned and fled back into the main room.

In his mind, Lynch pictured the high points around the building. They needed to move people to the corners of the church, next to the doors and under the balcony. The shooters would be unable to penetrate the stone of the walls and wouldn't have a line of sight to those corners of the building.

"Back this way! Into the corners!" he yelled.

LaPierre must have understood his logic and joined him in moving people out of the line of fire. "C'mon, people. Listen to him. They can't get you there! Into the corners." As he said that, he stood his ground in front of the terrified Royal Family. A bullet shattered the upper edge of the elegant, carved wooden pulpit above them. LaPierre didn't flinch. Abbott held his ground as a human shield as well.

Lynch saw the danger they were in. Any attempt to move the family toward safety would expose them to the line of fire. Off to his left sat a grand piano, sitting upon the custom dolly used to move it. He ran to it and began to push it toward the center aisle. As he reached the aisle, a bullet hit the lid a foot away from him. Alex joined him and together they reached the altar area in seconds.

"Quick. Get under the piano!"

Abbott grabbed the oldest child, whose screaming pierced the sanctuary, and handed him to Lynch. He then shielded Princess Helen who clutched her toddler daughter tightly to her chest. As she found safety under the instrument, Lynch handed her son to her. Abbott stepped up to protect the prince as he moved to the piano. It was his last act of loyalty as a bullet ripped through his neck.

Lynch, LaPierre, and Alex ducked behind the piano and began to push it toward the safe end of the church. They weren't moving fast enough. The prince and princess couldn't crawl and keep up as they tried to manage the children as well as themselves. A thought came to Lynch, and he jumped up, opened the lid, and propped it open to act as a shield.

He leaned over to speak to the prince. "Put the kids on the struts of the dolly. Your wife, too, if she can. That way, only you need to keep up with us as we push."

He watched the man do as suggested, but then Prince Arthur rose and squatted next to him.

"I'll help push. Thank you."

Three more bullets hit the lid of the piano by the time they reached the area under the balcony.

Taking a breather, they rested next to the instrument as LaPierre radioed for a status update. He looked beaten as the news came through his earpiece.

Graham joined Lynch.

"Agent LaPierre, I've instructed my team to help in any way possible. We need to get the family out of here."

"I-I appreciate your help. I'm down to four men, plus four from S.O.14, the Royal Protection detail. They're converging on the emergency exit as we speak. I, uh, just got word that my team at the airport is gone. They were in route to assist when the car they were using exploded. The highway patrol is flying in a SWAT team from Jefferson City. They should be here in ten minutes and plan to land on the athletic fields."

Lynch shook his head. "Did all that info come through the radio?"

"Yes."

"Then this hit squad knows what you know."

He nodded. "We were told by MI5 that the assassinations appeared to be an inside job. But they assured us that no one on this detail was implicated. Obviously, they were wrong."

"But now, whoever it is, is forewarned and will be prepared."

He nodded again.

The sound of bullets hitting stone caught Lynch's attention. A second later, Zach was at his side.

"Lynch, we need to move out of here."

LaPierre shook his head. "No, we're out of the line of fire here. We can hold out until reinforcements show up and neutralize the threat."

Zach shook his head. "You don't have time. I just found and deactivated a C-4 charge near the main entrance. If there's one charge, there's bound to be more. Plus, I smell smoke. I don't see its origin yet, but my guess is the tower, the explosion. If that gets to the staircase before we move through, we're trapped."

LaPierre looked as if he'd been pummeled in the gut. The words whispered were more than salty. "Th-that means my team has traitors as well. Davidson and his dog were on explosive patrol. They were the first to die. No one from S.O.14 has been near the entrance since Davidson last cleared it. He had to have known about it, and he must have been eliminated to keep him from telling anyone about the charges."

Lynch shook his head. "Maybe not. They might have used the confusion of finding his body to place it. Don't judge him yet."

LaPierre looked as if he appreciated that thought. "Look, we have no chance up here if there really are more explosives. We can get out if we can get down the stairs."

Lynch wasn't so sure of that, but he did have an idea.

Zach smiled. "I came prepared." He held out a smoke canister. "They might think it's smoke from the fire. Either way, it'll give us cover in the stairwell."

Lynch smiled back and clapped him on the shoulder. "Perfect."

After instructing everyone who remained in the sanctuary, Zach prepared to ignite the canister. Lynch led the prince and his family to the edge of the doorway. Graham stood with them.

"Your people first, Agent LaPierre. I insist." Prince

Arthur pointed to the crowd of remaining guests, while the princess nodded in agreement.

"But, Your Royal Highnesses, we have to get you out. Our government would not—"

"Then do it now. These people first." Prince Arthur pointed to the last 20 guests.

LaPierre sighed. Lynch could only imagine the mental turmoil the man must be suffering. Finally, he nodded.

Zach lined everyone up at the opposite side of the doorway, pulled the pin on the canister, and tossed it to the bottom of the spiral staircase. Within seconds the alcove filled with dense white smoke.

"Now!" Zach yelled. "Remember, keep hold of and follow the railing to the bottom, then turn right into the museum. I'll be right there with you."

As the line of people snaked down the stairs, Zach disappeared into the smoke.

Lynch looked back as the last of the line disappeared. The smoke began to dissipate. "Now, Prince Arthur!"

The Royal Family stepped forward. Lynch took their son, while the prince took his daughter and urged the princess to take the stairs first. The prince was followed by Graham. Then Lynch and LaPierre. A bullet pinged the stone above him as Lynch raced past the window. The open window allowed the smoke to clear more quickly than it should have, but they made it.

They emerged into the museum and Lynch looked about.

"Where are the people who preceded us?"

Zach shook his head. "One of the agents told them to run for the auditorium. They all took off that way." He pointed through the exhibition hall with its new display of

Churchill artwork.

LaPierre seemed to be listening to a status report through his earpiece. "And we need to go that way, too," replied LaPierre. "C'mon. Quickly."

Lynch didn't like that idea, but the agent urged the family to move ahead. As they came to a final doorway leading into the empty exhibit hall just before entering the auditorium building, Lynch stopped.

"Your Royal Highness, please wait. Let us clear it first."

The prince nodded. LaPierre looked at him, appearing puzzled.

"It's clear. My people said it's safe. Look around the corner. Do you see a pile of bodies? The other people ran right through here and got out."

Lynch's gut said "no."

"I'll go ahead," continued LaPierre. He stepped into the open, took three steps, and stopped. As he slumped to the floor, Lynch could see the blood running from his forehead.

"He's dead. Your Royal Highness, we need to retreat. Find a better defensive position and hope those reinforcements show up as expected." The idea that had come to him earlier returned. "This way."

They ran back into the museum. The main hallway was deserted, except for a half dozen bodies scattered across the floor. Lynch knelt between two of the dead men—his men—and said a silent prayer. He felt a hand on his shoulder. His boss had joined him.

"They were good men. They'll be missed."

Lynch began to stand when he noticed both men wore no earpieces. Had they fallen out somewhere in the chaos, or had the enemy taken them to be able to listen into their conversations as well. Lynch thought about that for a moment and realized one thing. Had they considered Graham nothing more than collateral damage, they would have had no reason to take the communication devices. Why would they care where he was or what he was doing at any given time?

He looked around and did not see them, which reinforced his thought that they had been taken. And if they were taken on purpose, then Graham was also meant to be a target.

He looked at his boss. "Sir, whoever is behind this took their earpieces. They know everything we discuss through our comms. The only logical explanation for that, is that you, too, are a target."

Graham stood there in silence for a moment, before whispering, "The Assembly is behind all of this."

Lynch nodded. Who else had a stake in killing Bradley Graham? But what was behind their killings within the extended Royal Family?

"We need to find a safe spot," said Graham.

"This way, sir." He approached the prince and his wife. "Please follow me."

Lynch led them through a room that held Churchill's writing desk and several pieces of his artwork and into the room within the museum titled the "Wit and Wisdom" room. It held an interactive display of Winston Churchill's quotes and sayings on every aspect of life. At the far end was a full-wall china cabinet filled with Churchill memorabilia.

"Your Royal Highness, please keep your family near that back wall. There's one way in and out of this room, so we should be able to hold off anyone who comes hunting this way."

Actually, there were two ways. The first room, holding the desk and art, had one wide doorway into the museum. However, that room's eastern wall also contained the museum's only windows, the windows that viewed the garden which they had discussed as an emergency exit route. Anyone attempting to breach a window or come through the main doorway was in their direct line of fire from the "Wit and Wisdom" room. It was a dead-end room, but at least they didn't have to watch their backs.

"Zach, we can't use our comms. They're listening in. Check out the windows and see if you can get a cell signal. If so, contact Alex or Tony by phone. Warn them not to use their comms and to stay put with the vehicles. We may need them fast."

Lynch watched as the man inspected the windows. At least no bullets came flying through any of them as he checked. And at one spot, he appeared to get cell service. He gave Lynch a thumb up.

Now, all they had to do was sit and wait . . . and hope the cavalry showed up before the enemy came hunting for them. As he sat by the doorway, watching the entrance to the adjacent room, he heard a curious noise. It seemed to echo around him. Not loud but distinctly noticeable. Yet, he couldn't identify it.

Fifteen

Nigel checked his watch. Their time was running out. The SWAT team would be on the ground in a few minutes. He scanned the sky to the south—the direction toward Jefferson City—and saw nothing. But then, he didn't expect to. That helicopter would come in hot and fast, flying nap-of-the-earth above the treetops as soon as it came within view of the town.

They needed to finish the job.

He signaled his counterpart on the library roof and then descended from his perch on the dorm roof. Making sure he had not been seen, or worse, videoed by some college coed with a cell phone, he ran in a bee line to the Champ Auditorium building. Inside, he joined his fellow shooter and together they ran to the basement level to join the others at the entrance to the museum.

They arrived just as a dozen-plus civilians ran through the checkpoint. He scanned their faces as they ran past. No sign of Lynch Cully or Bradley Graham. That meant they still had to be within the church or the museum, possibly with the Royal Family.

Nigel smiled at that thought. *So convenient*, he mused.

Having led the last of the guests to the service area at the back of the building, two Secret Service agents returned. Nigel counted heads. Three Secret Service agents to his four-member team.

"We need to extract the Royal Family," said the lead

agent. He clicked on his lapel mic. "LaPierre, the emergency egress is secure. The remaining guests have come through and have been staged at the service area. I left one agent with them there. We're clear to bring the Royal Family through. Copy?" He listened and nodded. "They're moving this way."

Nigel nodded to one of his men. Five shots in rapid succession took down the three agents. Two of his men dragged the bodies out of view.

"Should we go meet them?" asked the man on his left.

"No, let's wait here. LaPierre's in a rush. They'll be here in a moment."

And true to that word, Agent LaPierre appeared in the doorway across the room. A spit from a silenced gun stopped the man's progress.

"Fool!" whispered Nigel in a rage. "You should have waited until *all* the targets were visible." He cursed in Arabic and, in anger, turned and shot the offender. He addressed the remaining two. "Now *they* have the advantage. They know the threat is still here and will retreat to a defensive position. Time is on their side and the SWAT team has no doubt landed."

He debated on his best course of action. "Move quickly. We must find them and finish this."

"Don't shoot. It's me." Zach ran back into the first room and then up to Lynch. "They're coming. Three of them. All with the Royals' team."

Lynch nodded. "Did they see you?"

Zach gave him an 'are-you-kidding' look. "I kept an eye out for other explosives while out there. Didn't see anything. Maybe the main entrance was their only target."

Lynch could see that possibility. The group of dignitaries would have gathered there while awaiting an escort to the cars outside. An explosive at the door would have inflicted maximum casualties.

Lynch felt a tap on his shoulder. He looked to see the prince kneeling beside him.

"Do you hear that?"

Lynch nodded. The noise he'd been hearing since entering the room seemed louder.

"It seems louder by the cabinets where we've been sitting."

Lynch looked at Zach. "Watch the doorway. Be right back."

He rushed to the back of the room with the prince following and listened. The noise was definitely louder here. He moved to the opposite end of the cabinets. Still there but not as loud.

He knelt in front of the lower cabinet and looked inside. A small computer and other electronics sat on the single shelf. These appeared to control the room's display of Churchill quotes. He noticed that the wiring disappeared through the back panel of the cabinet. To where?

The opening was large enough to allow passage of his hand. He reached through but jumped back and inspected his hand. Something had grabbed him.

A moment later, the back panel of the cabinet fell away and Mack's grimy, grinning face appeared.

" 'Ello, mates. 'Ave I missed the fun?" The man's gaze fell upon the Prince of Wales and his wife. He dropped the Cockney accent. "Oh. Sorry, sir. No insult intended. I-I didn't know you were there."

Within seconds the shelf with its electronics disappeared behind the cabinet, leaving a space large enough for a man to squeeze through but no more.

"Mack!" Lynch turned to the Prince. "Your Royal Highness, he's one of mine and his appearance here means we have a way out."

"It's really dirty back here."

Zach spoke up from across the room. "Whatever you're going to do, do it now."

This time Princess Helen spoke up. "A bit of dirt never hurt. Bullets, however . . ." With that she passed her daughter through the opening to Mack. Their son followed on his own accord. A minute later, the hole had engulfed the princess as well.

"Your turn, sir," said Lynch to the prince. As the man began to inch his way through, Lynch ran back to his boss and Zach. "Boss, you're next."

Graham shook his head. "Nope. Zach and I discussed this while you were over there. If we all leave, they'll wonder how and begin searching. If we stay, we can help delay a search and give you more time to get away."

"Sir, I really don't think—"

"You don't have to. I already have and you now have your orders. Make sure the Royal Family stays safe."

Lynch processed this for a second. "Zach, you go. I'll stay with the boss."

Zach shook his head. "What? And leave me out of the fun? Do you think you have a better chance at keeping the both of you alive?"

Lynch didn't think that. "Well, no. It's just that it's my job as head of security. I—"

Graham interrupted. "Go. You're wasting time."

Zach looked at him. "A couple of days ago, you asked about Mack and me. I still can't answer that, yet, but I can tell you this." He leaned forward and whispered into Lynch's ear.

Lynch made an immediate about-face and began to work his way through the opening in the cabinet. On the other side, he glanced back into the room in time to see Zach move into the first room and throw a smoke canister into the main part of the museum. Smoke began to filter back through the doorway. As Mack replaced the shelf and electronics, they heard one gunshot. As Mack replaced the back panel on the cabinet, Lynch could hear only the sounds of their own breathing.

Mack picked up a bright LED flashlight, moved to the lead position, and said, "This way."

Sixteen

Richard and Amy decided to get breakfast at a First Watch restaurant closest to the campaign's headquarters. These few days back in the Lou had been great and he and Amy seemed back on track. They still hadn't managed to find a suitable date for the nuptials, but that would happen in time.

He finished off the last of his side order of pancakes, downed his now tepid coffee, and took her hand across the table.

"Hey, look, I'm sorry this is so rushed, but if I don't make it to headquarters in time, I'll miss the last van to Kansas City."

Amy hurried to finish eating. "I know, I know. You'll get stuck riding the press bus." She ate the last of her fruit plate while he paid the tab and then joined him at the cashier.

She was his chauffeur for the morning. He had already parked his car at his place, double checked his home's doors and the utilities, and repacked by the time she picked him up for breakfast. Now, he relied on her to take him to the office as well.

"Hey, thanks for driving. I really appreciate it."

A short while later, they pulled into the parking lot to see the bus but no vans. He groaned inside at the thought of dealing with reporters for the three-plus-hours trip to Kansas City. He asked Amy to wait until he found out what was going on, and after doing so, returned to say goodbye.

"From the sour look on your face, I'm guessing you missed the van."

He nodded. "Yeah. Last minute change and they had to leave 15 minutes early. So, I'm going to stake out my place on the bus, in the far back, where I can avoid as many of the others as possible. That means I need to go now, before the crowd arrives."

He leaned into the car and kissed her. He wanted that kiss to linger and sensed that she did, too, but he hadn't the time to stick around. He'd made a deal with the boss to get the time off and now he faced two weeks on the road with the campaign.

"I . . . I gotta go. I wish I could stay. I'm going to miss you."

"I'll miss you more," she replied.

He smiled. How many times had she said that to him over the past year? Too many.

The ride to Kansas City proceeded without incident. He hadn't been harassed, probably because he didn't personally know any of the reporters on the bus and they didn't recognize him. But he noted a dramatic change in the tone of the trip about the time they hit the I-470 intersection near Independence, just east of Kansas City.

His phone rang three times in quick succession. Three times he answered to dead air. That was his first inkling of trouble.

Then, he saw animated excitement in several reporters as they talked near the front. The disturbance spread from one seat to the next. More than one reporter whipped out a cell phone or tablet. He saw them searching for something online. He overheard the words "mass shooting" from several of them. The crew two seats in front of him were trying to rent a car, from the screens he saw pop up on their tablet.

But when he overheard someone ask how far it was to Fulton and in which direction, his heart began to race. A mass shooting in Fulton?

He fumbled his cell phone trying to dial Stan. The call went straight to voice mail. He left a message. He tried to reach two members of his social media team with the same result. In desperation, he dialed Lynch Cully. No answer there either, but his voice mailbox was full. That was strange in itself because he knew Lynch made an effort to keep his box clear in case of an emergency. And it hit him. *Only* an emergency would fill his voice mailbox.

The last 15 minutes of the ride seemed like it took a day. As they pulled into the destination, the reporters stumbled across each other in their efforts to get their gear and rush off the bus. For the first time that morning, Richard regretted having sat in the last seat.

As he, too, moved ahead to leave the vehicle, the driver stopped him.

"You Richard Nichols?"

It took a second for Richard to register the question, but he looked at the driver. "Yeah, that's me."

The man held up a sealed manila envelope with Richard's name printed in block letters across the front. He handed it to Richard.

"I was asked to give this to you as you left the bus."

"Okay. Uh . . . sure. Thanks."

The man nodded as Richard tucked the package into the outer pocket of his overnight bag. Whatever it was would have to wait.

He rushed to the campaign's operations center inside the hotel. Normally, the conference room turned-ops-center would be filled with tables, each manned by volunteers handing out press packets, bumper stickers, yard signs and more. The atmosphere would be one of barely-controlled pandemonium. Today, the place seemed more like a morgue. Groups of people clustered around televisions that had been wheeled in on carts. Half a dozen men and women sat with their cell phones glued to their ears.

"What's—"

"Shhhhh!" came from every direction.

It didn't take long for him to find out what was happening. An attack at the National Churchill Museum that was being labeled an assassination attempt on the Prince of Wales and his young family. Witnesses and survivors were calling it a bloodbath. Intercepted police calls suggested a SWAT team was in route to the location. Missouri's governor and both senators were safe, but the status of the Royal Family was unknown, as was the fate of presidential candidate, Bradley Graham.

Amy drove about town running various errands, her mind blissfully lost in reminiscing about the previous three days. She already missed Richard and hoped their next time together wouldn't be far off. As she waited for a traffic signal to turn green, her phone rang in a distinctive melody with the words, "Your daddy's calling you. Wants to see what you're up to . . ."

She answered before the song could continue. "Hi,

Dad."

"Hey, sweetheart, um, you sound cheerful. Richard still in town?"

His tone seemed distressed.

"No. He had to leave a few hours ago. I'm out running errands. Umm, is something wrong? You sound upset."

"I guess you haven't been listening to the news."

"Uh, no. Haven't had the radio on. Wh-what's going on?"

Her first fear was that the campaign bus had been in an accident. Her mind raced to thinking that something had happened at the rally in Kansas City, but she realized it hadn't started yet. What could have her normally nonplussed, retired Army father so concerned?

"There's been a mass shooting in Fulton. An apparent attack on the Prince of Wales. The latest reports say the prince, his family, and . . ." He paused. ". . . and Bradley Graham are still inside the building."

The light turned green and Amy sat there, too stunned to drive. Horns behind her began to blare. Her mind in a fog, she moved ahead and looked for a place to pull off. She adored the Princess of Wales, her fashion sense . . . and her two young kids. They were as adorable as the Prince of Wales was handsome. How could anyone want to harm them? But then, why had the Royal Family been under attack in England? None of this made sense.

It took a moment, but her father's last words hit home. Bradley Graham was unaccounted for. That meant Lynch was. . .

She didn't want to think the worst. Yet, Lynch would not have abandoned Mr. Graham. He would go down fighting to protect the man. He would take a bullet for his boss. Tears began to flow as she recalled how he had taken a bullet for her. *Had* he taken a bullet for his boss?

"Sweetheart, you still there?"

She sniffed. "Yeah. I-I'm heading straight home."

Sir David paced in his office at New Scotland Yard. The Home Secretary, Helen Ward, had requested regular updates on the Prince of Wales' trip to the States, and the Commissioner was tardy in giving her the afternoon briefing. They were having communications problems with the commander of the S.O.14 detail protecting the prince, and now rumors had started that MI6 was reporting trouble in Missouri. Sir David wanted a direct report, not rumors from another agency.

He turned at a knock at his door. His Deputy Commissioner stood there, ghastly white, and looking like the world was about to explode. Sir David felt an acid tsunami in his gut.

"MI6? Bad news?" he asked.

The deputy shook his head and lowered his gaze. He looked up at the Commissioner and replied, "Disastrous news, I'm afraid. And in a direct report."

Sir David walked behind his desk, opened a drawer, and retrieved a bottle of antacids.

"Charles Abbott and 16 members of his detail are dead, as well as Prince Arthur's aide-de-camp, Major Alistair. The Secret Service reports over a dozen of their men dead, including the head of their squad. We have four wounded, three in critical condition. They have eight. Conditions unknown. Several members of other security details were also killed, sir."

Sir David felt his face blanch. His legs became unsteady and he braced himself with his desk.

"We . . . we have only four . . . *four* men left standing?"

"Five, sir. One casualty, Nigel Barrington, has just a flesh wound in the arm. He managed to kill the last three traitors, just as a SWAT team descended on the building. Of the others, two were on guard at the family's lodgings in St. Louis, and two protected the helicopters."

Sir David didn't want to ask the most pressing question. He didn't want to have to report to the Queen that her grandson and his family were dead. Yet, he had little choice.

"And Prince Arthur, his family?"

"To our knowledge, not dead, sir."

Sir David furrowed his brow. Not dead? What kind of answer was that?

"What do you mean, not dead?"

"Just that, Sir David. Their bodies were not among the dead." The deputy hesitated.

"And?"

"We don't know, sir. They are nowhere to be found. They've, uh . . . vanished."

Seventeen

Nigel sat alone in the empty exhibit hall, nursing his left upper arm, which still burned from the through-and-through gunshot wound he had received. Had he not dodged right as soon as he saw the smoke discharge, they would be counting him among the dead.

He knew the layout of the museum well. So, evidently, did his targets because they had chosen the best defensive position possible within the structure. He had quickly surmised that they had little chance to kill the family before the SWAT team entered the building, so he made a tough decision.

Two men, obviously federal agents, entered the room and pulled up chairs across from him.

"Officer Barrington, I'm Agent Croft and this is Agent Zimmerman. We're from the St. Louis office of the Secret Service. Agents from the FBI will be joining us as well."

Zimmerman pulled out a digital recorder. "First off, we need to record this. If you have any object—"

Nigel shook his head. "No objections. I fully understand."

Zimmerman recorded details of time and place and placed the recorder where it could register the interview.

Croft continued. "Can you please tell us what you observed? Please start with where you were assigned and proceed."

Nigel took a deep breath. He had already formulated

his story, but he wanted to appear as if this was coming off the top of his head. "I, and Officer Warren, we were assigned to monitor the vehicles, to prevent any nobbling." The men looked confused. "That's, um, tampering or sabotage for you Yanks. Anyway, the Royal Family, their nanny, and their personal detail had entered the museum about eleven-ten. We drove the vehicles to the service area of the auditorium building where they'd be available in case of an emergency. At eleven-eighteen, Officer Warren needed to take a jimmy. You know, use the loo. 'Bout the time he returned, we heard the situation starting via our comms. We wanted to assist, but someone had to stay with the cars in case they needed them straight away."

He continued on with his story, complete with details as to the time and what he heard through his earpiece.

"As things deteriorated, we felt like we were just diddling about with the cars, but we knew they might come running from the auditorium at any moment. When word came that Abbott was down, Warren insisted we go to their aid. One of us needed to stay with a car in case it was needed, so I told him to go."

He lifted his head to gaze at the ceiling and slowly shook his head. "Warren was talking on the com and halfway through a sentence he groaned and stopped. At that point, no one was talking on the comms except Agent LaPierre and a couple of others. I knew they needed help, so I ran into the auditorium and toward the museum. I arrived at the entrance, just over there . . ." He pointed with a nod of his head. ". . . in time to see Worthington shoot LaPierre." He looked to the other end of the room where the lead agent's body lay, still draped with a sheet.

"Worthington and Boswick took off into the museum. I

heard Boswick say something about finishing the job. I followed them, being careful not to let them see me. I was about to confront them, when smoke started billowing up from a smoke canister and a shot was fired. I caught it in my arm. I guess I made a noise because that's when the two traitors turned and saw me. They were about to shoot when I took them down. Moments later, the SWAT team stormed the main entrance."

The two agents looked at each other and seemed satisfied with his testimony.

"The Royal Family . . . are they okay? Were they injured?" asked Nigel. In truth, he knew nothing about their status and he needed to know where to find them.

Both men furrowed their brow in unison.

"We were hoping you could tell us. We haven't found them anywhere in the area."

As they prepared to emerge into sunlight, Lynch held the group back.

"Please, sit tight and let me go first. I need to make sure we're not spotted and I don't want Alex and Tony to know what we're up to. The fewer people who know the better. I'm going to send them to the main entrance."

He heard no argument to that and took off in a sprint toward the campaign's SUVs parked in the northern lot. He held his .40cal as if prepared to stop and shoot.

"Lynch, what's . . . you're filthy. Where's the boss?" asked Alex as he joined them next to the vehicles.

Lynch didn't have to pretend being out-of-breath. "Back in the . . . museum . . . with Zach. Don't . . . worry about the . . . vehicles. He's going to be here for a while. They . . .

attacked the Royal Family, and I think Graham was included in the target list. But, he's okay. I want you both to head to the main entrance. See if they'll let you in to help Zach. If not, it's okay to use your comms now and you can call me back. Right now, I need to contact Stan McGonagle, and I need to plug into one of the Traverses. My phone's dead."

"On it," replied Tony and both men took off running.

Lynch ran back to Gage Hall. In the light, the group didn't look too worse for wear. Thanks to Mack's flashlight and his own cell phone they had been able to navigate the narrow tunnel without much difficulty. Lynch had noted what took Mack so long to do that morning. Two piles of brick lay where someone in the past had built walls to prevent the curious from traveling too far into the tunnels. He had also managed to open the tunnel between Marquess and Gage Halls so they could move undetected as far as possible before being forced to surface.

Lynch looked at the prince. "Your Royal Highness, are you sure you want to do this? It appears that reinforcements have arrived. We can get you back into the hands of your own people, let them take you home."

Prince Arthur shook his head. "Not on your life, or mine, as the case may be. It was my *own people*, as you put it, who tried to kill us. I don't know if they've all been dealt with or not. I prefer to go to ground, to lay low, or however you Yanks put it, until I can get people I trust to get us home."

Lynch gave him a questioning look. He happened to agree with that assessment, but he didn't want to sway the prince one way or the other. The last thing he needed was to become a suspect in the kidnapping of the Royal Family.

"He's right, Lynch," replied Mack. "We don't know who

to trust."

Thanks for chiming in, thought Lynch.

"Well, we have one other complication here. If we all go together, we'll be a lot more conspicuous, so I think we need to split up."

"By all means," said the prince. "I have to think of the Monarchy here. If we're together, we're one easy target and three heirs to the throne could be gone as quickly as my cousins. We *must* split up. I need to go with one of you, and dear, . . ." He looked at his wife. ". . . you must take the children and go with the other."

She nodded without hesitation. That was too easy. Lynch did not want to take on protecting the whole family, at all, and yet, he couldn't abandon them either. Particularly if The Assembly was behind this. He and Graham hadn't succeeded in taking down Karolus Karling, who still reigned as the Director of The Assembly, as well as Secretary General of the U.N. While they had no expectations of eliminating The Assembly, removing Karling as its leader held a small chance that someone more reasonable and less cutthroat would take his place.

"Okay, but we still have a problem. If we split up and take two of the vehicles, it will become obvious. The investigators will see that they've disappeared and begin to question why. At that point, the authorities will be on the lookout for them. Or worse, they could activate the GPS tracking remotely."

The look on Prince Arthur's face showed that he had no solution to that dilemma.

And then Mack grinned as he held up two sets of keys. "I worried that our vehicles might be targeted, so I had some friends help me out. One pickup truck for you." He handed the key to Lynch. "And a late model sedan for me, complete with children's car seats. I added those in case the long odds came in that we'd have the Royal Family to tend to. Always plan for every contingency, they taught us. Oh, and don't let their appearance fool you. Totally reliable. They could take us to Afghanistan and back, but they're intended to blend in."

Lynch didn't know what to say, but he had no doubt that God had brought Zach and Mack to him and helped him decide to hire them.

Mack turned to the prince. "Your Royal Highness, now you all need to blend in, too." He handed the young man a Westminster Blue Jays sweatshirt, followed by a Westminster Women's Volleyball sweatshirt to his wife. "Sir, I suggest you ditch the coat and tie. Ma'am, I'm sorry the sweatshirt doesn't compliment your dress better, but it's all I have to work with." He gave them the most disarming smile Lynch had ever seen.

With the Royal Couple dressed as much incognito as possible, Lynch said, "You first, Princess, Mack."

Mack looked at Lynch. "First, try to follow me but not too close. I'm sure by now they have all the main roads blockaded. If we get separated, I left a map with two usable escape routes highlighted on it. Where should we meet up?"

Now Lynch was faced with the dilemma. Where could they go? Within an hour, the Royal Couple's faces would be plastered across television and social media, not that they weren't already well known. Everyone and his Facebook friends would be aware they were missing and would be on the lookout for them. Motels were obviously out. They could crash at his place in St. Louis, but once it became evident that he, too, was missing, his home would be watched 24/7 as well. They needed to regroup in short order and plan their next steps. Plus, the sooner they got off the roads, the better.

He knew where to go. He had keys and the security codes, and the boss wouldn't mind. Besides, the area was almost deserted in winter. He gave Mack the address for the Graham family's home at the Lake of the Ozarks.

Eighteen

For Sir David, the situation had gone from bad to worse. He had requested an urgent face-to-face with the Home Secretary, who had taken the news more calmly than he'd expected. Had it not been for the arteries in her temples, he might have thought she was unconcerned. The fact that they became bounding and that her pulse rate had accelerated belied her outwardly calm demeanor.

He watched as she made a hasty phone call. From the look on her face, he understood whom she was calling. After a brief, and private, conversation, she looked up.

"David, we have an appointment with Her Majesty in one hour. Can you get us there in time?"

He nodded and in short order, they were in her car with his driver acting as a police escort. They skirted along the Thames River on Grosvenor Road and joined up with traffic leaving the city on the M4. Fifty minutes later, they passed through security at Windsor Castle and parked near the Queen's private quarters. Shortly, they stood in a private drawing room awaiting her.

"Madam Secretary, Commissioner."

As their elderly monarch entered the room, they curtsied and bowed respectively. She sat in a cushioned chair and directed them to sit across from her. Nearing 90 years of age, Her Majesty had always seemed quite vigorous. Tonight, Sir David noted how frail she appeared. The recent family deaths had taken a significant toll on her, it seemed. He dreaded what was to come next.

"Is there news of my grandson? Please, do not spare me of any details."

The Home Secretary deferred to Sir David.

"Your Majesty, I am afraid we have no news of Prince Arthur or his family. They seem to have vanished." He went on to outline the details of the attack as he understood them, while holding back on the number of dead.

"And how many of our good men did we lose? How many families must we console in the morning?"

Sir David glanced away for just a second. He didn't want to answer, but to avoid her eye contact would be disrespectful. To ignore her question would be disobedient.

He cleared his throat. "Out of the contingent of 25 officers, we lost 17 and have three with critical injuries. Their prognosis is guarded. One has a flesh wound to an arm. The remaining four were on duty elsewhere. Prince Arthur's aide-de-camp was also killed."

Tears formed in the Queen's eyes. He had never, never witnessed his monarch crying. Sir David felt responsible.

"But Arthur was not among the dead."

"No, Your Majesty." He felt desperate, wanting more to tell her—but good news, not bad.

"Thank you. Please excuse me."

They stood as she did and prepared to show her the proper respect, but she hung her head and walked from the room with the assistance of an aide, a private nurse by the look of her uniform. She never looked back to them, but the nurse gave them a worried look.

An equerry for the Royal Household joined them in the drawing room. "I will escort you out. Please follow me."

As they neared the door, they heard a scream. A

moment later, the nurse came running toward the equerry.

"Call her doctor! Call the ambulance! Her Majesty is having a stroke!"

Prince Arthur scrutinized the man driving the truck. From the moment the man had put himself into the line of fire to push that piano to them as protection, he knew inside that he could trust this man. He already felt indebted to him for saving their lives. Yet, he feared the hard part was still to come.

As they followed the sedan holding his family, Arthur ignored the fact that they were driving on the wrong side of the road. In truth, he enjoyed sitting in the front seat, something he rarely had the opportunity to do, being chauffeured about as he was at home and in his travels.

As they meandered along small streets, he saw a glimpse of the States he was unlikely to ever see in the course of one of his usual trips. Small homes with dirt drives. Rusted vehicles and appliances in barren yards. Boarded up businesses. Whoever would have thought such poverty existed in what the world considered the richest nation on the planet? But then, the idea of poverty was relative. The poor of the third world nations would consider these small houses mansions.

As they crossed one major intersection, Arthur saw police lights in the distance on the intersecting road. A blockade, just as the other man, Mack, had mentioned. Someone had done his homework to determine the route they were taking.

He looked back at the man. "So, might I ask your full name? I heard you being addressed as Lynch, but we had no time for introductions."

Lynch smiled. "That is an understatement, Your Royal Highness. My real name is Carson Cully, the second, but as a young teen I somehow got pegged with the nickname Lynch. We always joked that that was what my father wanted to do to me on more than one occasion. Anyway, sir, the name stuck and now the only people who call me Carson are my parents."

Arthur smiled back. "I rather like the name Carson Cully. It has a certain ring to it. But after seeing you in action, Lynch is quite fitting as well. Might I call you Lynch?"

"By all means, Your Royal Highness. You may call me—"

Arthur interrupted. "Please. Please call me Arthur. In private, of course. People, my family and staff in particular, would insist on more formality in public."

Lynch's face became one of questioning. "I-I'm honored, sir, but I don't know if I can do that." He shook his head as if in disbelief. "Wow. I mean, you are the future king of England and I'm just, well, me. It might take me some time to wrap my head around the idea that I could ever call you by your given name."

"Nonsense. We're not that far apart in age. My school chums call me Arthur when we're together. And, after all, you saved my life and the lives of my family. Plus, I suspect we're going to be together in close quarters for a while. I believe the term 'foxhole friends' is fitting. You have joined me in fighting this battle."

"Sir, um, Arthur, protecting lives is what we bodyguards are *paid* to do. I'm sure any member of your protection detail would have done the same."

Arthur shook his head. "Except they didn't, and *some* of

them wanted to take our lives. The difference is that you carried no responsibility for our lives and yet, you did so willingly and bravely. I owe you much and would be honored to have you in my circle of friends."

Lynch had no trouble following Mack and hadn't needed the map. He did, however, require an explanation from Mack. Why had he arranged for these vehicles? And car seats? How in the world had he anticipated the need? Just who were these friends of his and what did they know? And then there was Mack's preplanned destination. A quick glance at Mack's map had shown Lynch that the Lake of the Ozarks was Mack's destination, too. How had he known to do that before Lynch had settled on their destination? Did they think that much alike?

Too many questions without answers. Mack was becoming the proverbial riddle wrapped in a mystery inside an enigma, as Churchill had once said about Russia.

He did have to give the man credit for one thing, though. His ability to map an escape route was unparalleled by anyone Lynch had ever met. About the only drivable surface they hadn't encountered was someone's private driveway and there were a few times Lynch thought they were about to include one of those in the circuitous route they'd been driving. Just once, when they crossed U.S. Route 54, had they come within half-a-mile of a police blockade. And when they passed the Hensley Airport, as emergency vehicles with lights flashing passed them heading *into* town, he prayed a silent prayer for invisibility.

But nothing in their escape came as close to blowing his mind as when his charge, the man who would be king, gave Lynch permission to address him by his given name. He sat there amazed that he was driving a pickup truck with the Prince of Wales as his passenger in the middle of Missouri. Who could ever have dreamt up such a scenario?

"...be honored to have you in my circle of friends," said the prince.

Had he heard that correctly? Prince Arthur wanted to include him as a friend? At first, he sat there not knowing how to answer. Of course, he couldn't say no. How could you turn down such an offer from royalty at any level?

"I, uh, don't know what to say, except thank you. I'll do my best not to disappoint you."

"So, Lynch, what can you tell me about the man protecting my family? Mack, as you called him."

Lynch proceeded to tell the prince what he knew of Desmond Macklemore Gilman. He hadn't thought of it in such terms until he said the man's full name, but they both carried nicknames as their common name. Yet, Mack proved to be much more of a mystery man than Lynch.

Nineteen

Richard's afternoon became more hectic than he could have imagined. He and his team monitored every social media venue for news of the shooting, as it related to the Graham campaign. Rumors, innuendos, lies, and more vilification filled the liberal blogosphere, taking on a tone that somehow George Bush was responsible and that Bradley Graham now carried on that legacy. They put out fire after fire, calling upon the campaign's legal team more than once as some reports took on libelous character.

On the opposite side of the ideological aisle, the conservatives blamed everyone from Irish separatists to Islamic jihad in its many forms. They focused on the ills of the British Monarchy, while also expressing sincere hope for the safety of the Royal Family. The one common thread through many of their posts was the danger posed by the thousands of Muslim immigrants that had invaded Europe. The United Kingdom had resisted the call for accepting these people and had successfully turned back thousands who had attempted to cross the English Channel either by boat or via the Chunnel beneath it.

Stan McGonagle, their campaign manager and immediate boss, had laid out specific goals for the team prior to his leaving for Fulton with extra security. Meeting those goals had proven to be a challenge, but Stan was due back in Kansas City within the hour, with Bradley Graham and his bodyguards. Curiously, no mention was made about

Lynch Cully.

Taking a break, Richard took the elevator to the first floor to pick up a box lunch from the ops center. The doors opened and he stood there face-to-face with Summer Stanton, looking marvelous in a form-fitting dress in a color block of cream and forest green that accentuated her silky red hair. She was the last person he'd hoped to run into.

"Mr. Nichols." Her greeting was curt.

"Ms. Stanton," he replied. He tried to step out and allow her to enter the elevator car, but she pushed in and quickly hit the button to close the door. He moved aside to step past her before they closed, but she blocked his way. Obviously, she wanted to say something to him. He watched as she held the button in an attempt to keep the doors closed. He stepped to the opposite side of the car.

"Look," she said. "First, no hard feelings about last week. I shouldn't have been there. And I didn't expect to run into you here. I thought you were still in Washington. But since I have run into you, what do you have to say?"

Her stare bore into him as if trying to search out some hidden answer. He had no idea what she was talking about.

"Ms. Stanton, I haven't the foggiest notion of what you mean."

She raised her brow in surprise. "You didn't get one?"

Now he didn't know whether to be concerned or not. She had expressed a quick but cryptic warning at their last encounter. Was he missing something? Or was she simply nuts?

"One what?"

Now she looked worried, even fearful.

"You didn't get a manila envelope?" The door alarm on the car began to chime and its safety override would open the door at any moment. She released the button and as the door began to open, she handed him a card. "Call me if you get one." She rushed from the car.

He stood there, unsure how to respond. He looked at her card and then back to her fleeing figure. As the door began to close again, he used his hand to stop it and stepped out. A petite, mousy-looking woman stood there staring at him. She shrugged and shook her head, and then walked away down the opposite hall.

Richard was about to write off Summer Stanton as crazy, until he remembered the bus driver handing him an envelope.

Charity Lovelace once again blended into the crowd outside the Bradley Graham campaign's operations center. She had been watching Summer Stanton and was as surprised as the reporter when the elevator door opened to reveal Richard Nichols. She stood there waiting to see what might happen and wished she could have heard the exchange inside the car.

Yet, no matter. Her plan would work. Graham was her target, and Nichols was nothing more than her means of getting to him. Stanton, in turn, was nothing more than collateral damage. Who better to use against Nichols than the gorgeous Ms. Stanton? Okay, so maybe there was a bit of jealousy over the woman's perfect hair and slim, yet voluptuous, body. Bodily injury was not in Charity's playbook. To ruin her character seemed fitting.

Charity watched as Nichols rushed to the food table, grabbed something to eat, and ran back to the elevator. His face showed apprehension. Perhaps the chance meeting with Summer had resulted in speeding up her timetable.

All the better if that was so. The Assembly, and Karolus Karling in particular, approved of timely results and they showed their appreciation well.

"Hey guys, everything under control?" Richard looked about the suite where they had set up their social media center. The three men and one woman looked up from their computers and nodded.

"It's not as crazy as it had been earlier," said the sole female on the local team.

His crew back in Washington had a female majority, but most of them had families and liked the fact that their single co-workers had signed up for the road duty. That made it easy for Richard as well.

"I'm going to my room to eat and turn on the evening news. See what the talking heads are saying. Call me if you need me."

"Will do," said one of the men.

Richard took off down the hall for his room. Once inside, he double locked the door and turned on the television. He wouldn't lie to his team. He was going to monitor what he could. The room's TV set allowed one picture-in-picture, so he planned on setting them to CBS and NBC. Yet, he didn't have to tell the team everything. Like, maybe, his attention might wander to a mysterious envelope he had received on the bus. He wasn't even sure that he *wanted* to look inside. There was something threatening about it. So ominous, he worried about delaying this task any longer.

He took a bite of his sandwich. The lead story would be

on in five minutes. As he chewed, he searched for and found the envelope from the bus. He grabbed another bite and sat on the bed. The envelope didn't look suspicious. No mysterious white powder or greasy stains. He took a whiff. Just the smell of paper. He had smelled enough C-4 and Semtex in Afghanistan that he felt confident in his ability to detect it here.

As he felt the package, it seemed to contain paper along with something rectangular and hard. Whatever that was must have been nestled within the papers because he couldn't ascertain discrete edges. In fact, it must have been taped or somehow fixed to something that kept it in the middle of the packet. He couldn't work it out near the edge for a better feel. Thinking of edges, he traced his fingers along the edges of the envelope, trying to determine if any wires were present. He found nothing suspicious.

The news was about to start, so he waited. He had no doubt that the events in Fulton would lead off the news. He wasn't disappointed. The news media had converged on the small Missouri town and its college of 950 students. Fuzzy scenes of the church taken from far distances, as well as aerial video, also from a distance, dominated both channels. The reports mentioned only those facts as released by the Secret Service, and they were sparse. Both broadcasters went to commercials within seconds of each other.

His sandwich now finished, Richard decided to focus on the envelope. He repeated his examination—working to recall instructions he had received in the Army on how to detect a letter bomb. Satisfied that he wasn't about to die in an explosion, he took the plastic knife from his box lunch and carefully slit open one end.

He eased out the contents. He had been correct about

the hard object being taped to something. The throw-away cell phone was taped to a piece of shirt cardboard. The papers looked to be photo paper, but the stack was upside down so all he saw at first were the white backs. He flipped the stack over and felt his heart flop, before beginning to race. Pictures of Summer Stanton in bed . . . with him.

Numb, he wanted to destroy what he saw but seemed mesmerized and drawn from one photo to the next. After nearly a dozen pictures, the scene suddenly changed. Afghanistan. What he saw produced an instant wave of nausea, and he ran to the bathroom to empty his stomach.

Twenty

Despite the cold, Nigel paced the plaza outside the church, his bandaged arm in a sling for comfort. He could still use his arm—although with a great deal of pain—and had refused the paramedics' offer to take him to the local Emergency Room. What were they going to do? Clean it? He had done that and knew how to care for it. There'd be no suturing. Closing a deep wound such as his would increase the risk of infection, and he didn't care about cosmetics. He'd been shot before. What was one more scar on a body destined for Paradise?

He felt he might benefit from antibiotics, and he had access to some in their emergency kits. And yes, he could use something for pain. Unfortunately, he would have to tough it out. He couldn't afford any mental impairment.

His new acting team leader, Harvey Chelmsford, exited the museum and walked up the steps, past the Churchill statue, to him.

"Nigel, 'ow's the arm?"

Nigel nodded. "Bearable, Harv, bearable. Have we any news?"

"None, but we've got hold of the nanny now. Secret Service had 'er sequestered away with the others what escaped from the church. Thought you might like to join me in talking with 'er."

"Definitely. Where is she?"

"Inside. C'mon." The man turned and headed back

down the concrete steps.

Nigel found it hard to keep up with his new supervisor. Chelmsford had six inches on him and his stride was long and brisk. Yet, it was the pain in his arm that slowed him. Trying to keep up meant jostling his arm and that meant more pain.

Chelmsford slowed his walk and looked at him. "You sure you're okay?"

Nigel nodded. "Just have to take it slow. Sorry."

"You know, you really should get that looked at."

Nigel shrugged with his good shoulder.

Inside, they found the Royal Family's nanny seated in a folding chair in the hallway outside the auditorium. Two empty chairs sat facing her. Nigel and Chelmsford introduced themselves and sat down.

"Aye, I know who you are, Constables. And the Secret Service has questioned me at length. Do I need to go through this all over again? I need to get to the children. They must be frightened beyond imagination."

"Yes, ma'am, I'm afraid we 'ave to ask questions as well. It's 'ow we do things," replied Chelmsford.

"Please tell us in your own words what you recall."

She started with waking the children at the hotel in St. Louis, to prepare them for traveling. Nigel wanted to cut her short, to have her start when they were in the church, but he had to keep his place and let Chelmsford lead. He listened as his leader peppered her with questions as she told her story. Was anyone acting unusual? Did she have any inkling that something might happen? Had the Royal Family mentioned anything, anything at all, about being fearful of an attack, about having their own emergency plan? He was picking at straws.

Nigel's attention perked up as her narration arrived at the church.

"Her Royal Highness took the children from me so they could join their father at the front of the church. As he was talking, the shooting started. Glass started flying everywhere. People scattered from their seats. It was pandemonium, total chaos. I saw the family take shelter under the elevated pulpit and Sergeant Abbott moved in to shield them. I wanted to come forward and claim the children, get them to safety, but I was instructed to stay put and get down. It was horrible. People getting shot and falling around us. We were then ushered to the back."

Tears began to well up in her eyes as she recalled the events. She took a handkerchief from a pocket and dabbed her eyes.

"Thank God for that one man. I don't know his name, but he put himself in harm's way to push that piano to them for cover. The Lord bless his soul. When the family made it to the back, I wanted to take the children, but His Royal Highness wouldn't have it. Her Royal Highness even insisted on carrying their diaper bag and took it from me. When one of the men triggered a smoke grenade, we were pushed down that spiral staircase and into the museum. From there, we were led out into the auditorium. I expected the family to follow us and then I could relieve them of the children, but I never saw them again. Please tell me they're safe. I fret so about needing to help them. I'd like to get the children, now, if I might."

Chelmsford said nothing in reply. Nigel knew that only those with a need to know were aware that the Royal Family was missing. Royal Protection Command had been informed. He felt sure that by now the commissioner had been alerted. From there, the Home Secretary and, ultimately, the Queen would be told. The six-hour time difference between Missouri and London would not matter. Her Majesty would be awakened in the middle of the night if necessary.

"Thank you, ma'am. This officer will escort you back to the others." Chelmsford nodded to one of the other officers standing nearby.

"But I need to help with the children. They're likely scared to death."

Nothing more was said as the officer escorted her away.

After she had left, Chelmsford looked at Nigel and said, "So, tell me again what you saw as you entered from the auditorium."

Nigel took care to keep his story straight and repeated for the sixth time what he saw and did.

"And there's no way they could 'ave gotten past you? Could they 'ave escaped through the main door? We are all totally flummoxed."

Nigel shook his head. Even with the smoke, they couldn't have gotten past him. If they had, they would have joined the others.

"I have no clue, Harv. Maybe they realized the shooting had stopped outside and took a chance to flee through the main door."

"Then, where are they?"

At that moment another officer ran up to them.

"I think we found something, Harvey. This way." The man led them to the Wit and Wisdom room. "This is quite the fluke. Angie there . . ." He pointed to a female Secret Service agent nearby, wearing a sharp, Navy blue, skirted suit. ". . . was just kind of eying the exhibit here, the one with all of the Churchill teacups and the like, when she noticed a cool draft on her legs. She called me in to check it. I couldn't feel anything through my trousers, but I put my hand down here . . ." He repeated what he had done. ". . . and, sure enough, there was a draft."

He knelt before the lower cabinet and looked up toward them. "All of the electronics for the room are controlled by a computer in here, and the wires exit through a hole in the back. At first, I thought the draft was just coming through the conduit for the wires, but I took a closer look and saw one corner of the back board seemed off, like it had been removed and not put back in its proper place. I started to push and blimey if I didn't pop the whole thing off. There's a bloomin' tunnel back there."

"Can you get into it? Is it big enough to move in?" asked Chelmsford.

The officer nodded. "That it is. I'm waiting for a torch to inspect it."

Two minutes later, flashlight in hand, the constable crawled into the cabinet and disappeared. A few minutes after that, the light appeared in the opening, followed by his head.

"Harvey, it's an old service tunnel. Heads west for about 50 feet then turns north, toward the dormitories. From the looks of it, someone made quite the effort to open this up. In two places it appears the tunnel was blocked with brick walls, but those blockades were taken down. Recently, from what I can tell. Whoever did it was smart enough to take his tools with him. I'm going to follow this to the end."

As Nigel turned to leave the room, the female agent

was already talking into her lapel mic. He cursed the injury that slowed him down. By the time he made it to the dormitory, there'd be a crowd.

He descended to the basement of Marquess Hall in time to see a filthy constable lead a contingent of S.O.14 officers and Secret Service agents down the length of the basement to the opening of a second tunnel. He had no doubt where that one led and retreated back up the stairs. He managed to beat the others—those who didn't wish to dirty themselves in the tunnel—to Gage Hall.

Those who had used the tunnel were already crowded around another opening. The tunnel system continued toward the dormitory sitting perpendicular to the one they stood in.

"They must 'ave stopped here. This tunnel doesn't appear to 'ave been opened," said one of the officers.

A murmur of concurrence rose within the group, which as a whole turned and clomped up the stairs. Nigel followed. The central hallway down the length of the dorm led to an outside door that opened to allow access to the north parking lot.

Nigel had no doubt they had found the escape path for the Royal Family, but where had they gone from there? And how?

He noticed the glares from his fellow officers as they stood apart from the U.S. Federal agents. He watched as Harvey conferred with the other officers who had survived the ordeal. He then approached Nigel.

"You were here for the advanced screening. Did the Secret Service know about these tunnels? Did they make any effort to secure them?"

Allah had just given Nigel an opportunity to create a

new wedge between these services. Inwardly, he thanked him.

"If they knew about them, they didn't alert us to their presence. They made no mention of them at all, so it appears they neglected to do their due diligence to find all possible avenues of a threat. No one was stationed near these dorms, except the sniper on the roof, and we know how easily he was taken out by the traitors."

Chelmsford appeared ready to dress down the senior agent, but one of the officers who had flown in from St. Louis interrupted him. The officer handed a cell phone to the team leader.

After 30 seconds, Chelmsford dropped to one knee and tears welled up and began to flow across his cheeks. Regaining his composure, he rose and faced his team. The senior agent began to say something, but Chelmsford cut him off.

"Please, we need a moment."

Nigel tried to read the man's face. Had the prince turned up? Was he dead? If not, why the tears?

"Chaps, if you're of the praying sort, please do so now. I just received word that Her Majesty, our Queen, suffered a major stroke just an hour ago upon receiving word of the incident here and the disappearance of her grandson. It is no longer our Prince of Wales and his family who are missing but our new king."

Lynch entered the six-digit code into the gate at the head of the driveway, watched the gate open, and led their two-car parade into the Graham's Lake of the Ozarks hideaway. He stopped a dozen yards in and watched to make sure the gate closed. Satisfied, he continued the drive to the home.

To call it a "lake cottage" was a hyperbole of understatement. The six-bedroom, eight-bath home nestled within a ten-acre compound, along with a two-bedroom apartment above a three-berth boathouse on the Gravois Arm of the reservoir. The four-car garage was in addition to one bay built exclusively for the 40-foot motor coach that Graham now called "Campaign Central," his home on the campaign trail.

Despite the lack of foliage, the home had its privacy, privacy that cost Graham significantly more since the attempt on his life over a year earlier. State-of-the-art technology covered the perimeter, the grounds, the shoreline, and the house. Routine manned patrols kept an eye on the property and Lynch needed to make a call to keep that patrol from barging in on their "party."

He jumped out of the truck and approached the man door to the garage complex. He entered another code that allowed him access to the building, where he opened the doors to two empty bays. He waved Mack into one of them and then pulled the truck into the other. Before closing both doors, he stepped outside and dialed the security company, provided them with an authorization code as well, and informed them that the Grahams were allowing guests to use the home.

He returned to the garage to find the Royal Family laughing.

"Lynch, my dear wife loves your man, Mack. She says he had her and the children laughing in stitches all the way here."

Helen smiled and touched Lynch's arm. He almost

flinched.

"Lynch, what an interesting name. May I call you that?"

Lynch nodded. He had once heard that she was called a "Princess of the people," as had her late mother-in-law. He found her very disarming and genuine.

"Yes, dear, by all means. Lynch and I have already had this chat. I've told him that he may call us by our given names. We are, after all, beholden to him . . . to both of them really."

"Thank you, Lynch. Arthur is right. You've saved our lives." She looked at her husband. "And I've already told Mack the same thing. I hope you don't mind."

"Not at all. Now, Lynch, please show us around. We need baths . . . although, I'm not sure what we're going to do about clean clothes."

Lynch unlocked the door to the home and showed them in, starting his tour in the kitchen. Mack soon joined them and approached Lynch.

"The perimeter appears secure and no one is home on either side of us. Those homes looked closed up for the winter."

"Thanks, Mack. I hear you entertained the family."

"Oh yes," said Helen. "He does wonderful impersonations, but I bet you've seen them all. I must say, he certainly made our children forget this awful day. Thank you again, Mack."

"You are most welcome, Helen. I'm glad I could help. Say, where are those little rug rats of yours? I found something to show Amelia."

Lynch wanted to choke. That Mack had warmed up to using their first names was, well, okay. But to call the little heirs to the throne "rug rats"?

Helen laughed. "And I believe you called Albert an ankle biter. Some of the names you Yanks come up with. My little nippers, my adorable children, are asleep on that couch over there, until we figure out sleeping arrangements."

Lynch stepped back into the conversation. "Yes, that. Follow me. You get the master bedroom. We can move an extra mattress into the room if you want it for the children. With it on the floor, they can't get hurt if they roll out of it."

Prince Arthur nodded. "Good thinking."

They wandered through the living room with its expansive windows overlooking the lake.

"This is beautiful. I would love to see this in the summer," said Helen.

They continued on to the bedroom wing. Lynch showed Mack where he could bunk and pointed out his quarters. He ended the tour in the master bedroom.

"The room is big enough to keep your family together. I don't like that it has the big windows, but we're both just feet, um, meters away if you need us. You might want to keep the drapes closed."

At the reminder of the danger they faced, Lynch could see the sadness overtake the princess's demeanor once again. He hated spoiling the mood that Mack had worked so hard to create.

"I'm sorry. I didn't want to bring up all the things that happened earlier today, but we can't let our guard down. We have to remember why we're here."

His cell phone buzzed. He looked to see that his voice mailbox was full. He made a mental note to clean it out ASAP. The notification, however, was a text message on a secure account known only by his boss and two others—

Stan McGonagle and Jim, his second-in-command for the security team.

"Give me a minute. I need to take this." He walked into the hallway and opened the text from Bradley Graham.

> They found the tunnel. Going door to door in Fulton. Don't know where you are or how you got away without one of our vehicles, but be very cautious. I don't think all of the attackers are dead. Just my gut feeling. Also, if you can, turn on the news. You are now protecting. . .

He finished reading the text and didn't know what to say. He hesitated walking back into the bedroom. To show Prince Arthur the news now could greatly complicate his task. The man would insist on going home. And yet, how could he deny him the news? Lynch understood the value of family. He decided to inform the prince and let the chips fall as they might.

He walked back into the master suite and walked straight to the television.

"Your Royal Highness, there's something you need to see."

He found the Headline News channel and turned up the volume. The top of the news was five minutes away and the current story covered yet another strong earthquake in Southeast Asia, stronger than the October earthquake in Afghanistan which had measured a 7.7 on the Richter Scale.

The Royal Couple looked at him with questioning stares. He didn't want to be the bearer of bad news. Besides he knew nothing other than what the text had told him.

The news cycle began again and the pain in Prince

Arthur's eyes told Lynch what he needed to know. Somehow, he and Mack needed to get the young king back to safety.

Nigel saw the news about the Queen as bittersweet. On the one hand, heartbreak had achieved what his bombs at The Royal Lodge had failed to do. The reigning monarch was now removed from her throne. Yet, the news instilled a new vigor in not just his peers under the Royal Protection Command but also the Secret Service, FBI, and regional and local police authorities. News of the Queen's incapacitating cerebral hemorrhage had already made it into international news channels, although the precipitating cause had not. He wondered how long that secret would remain intact. The United Kingdom would soon be clamoring for their new king to make an appearance. Coronation plans would soon be thrown into full gear.

The discovery of the tunnels had opened a new channel of investigation, a concrete lead, as the detective shows on the telly would call it. Still, it unleashed a dozen new questions. Why, who, and where were at the top of the list. Nigel wanted to know how. How had they managed to leave the city? Or had they? Perhaps even now, they were holed up in a residence or an abandoned business building, waiting for assurance that their safety was secure.

Unable to help with the active search of the city, Nigel volunteered to assist in reviewing the evidence. His motive, however, was less than admirable. He had built into their plan a fail-safe. The interruption of the tunnel's discovery had disrupted his chain of thought. It was as he walked back from the dorms to the museum that the nanny's words came back to him.

The fire department had extinguished the tower fire in record time, and the fire marshal had released the scene as being safe and secure. A small army of forensics agents had arrived from the state capital and had initiated their investigation on campus. Nigel joined in and systematically began to search the museum and then the church for the item he sought. In the church he saw an FBI forensics agent photographing, bagging, and cataloging personal items dispersed throughout the sanctuary.

"I have a question. Are all of the personal belongings and the like still in place, or have you begun to collect and store them some place?" he asked.

The agent looked up. "Most things are still here, where people dropped them in the church, but I think my counterparts working the museum have started to move things to a secure spot awaiting transport to our labs."

"Thank you. You haven't by chance run across a diaper bag, have you? High quality, navy blue with pastel yellow panels."

She shook her head. "Not that I've discovered up here. I haven't made it to the choir loft yet, but no one was up there except the two agents who were killed there, and it received a lot of fire damage. I really doubt we'd find it there."

"Might I take a fast look? I won't disturb anything."

"Sure, but please put on fresh booties, um, foot covers. I don't know what you guys call 'em. They're over there, by the north side stairs. And take care near the back walls. That's where most of the fire damage is."

He complied and used the north stairs to the choir loft. Other than blood stains and a bloody suit jacket, he saw nothing of note. As he left the loft, he changed shoe covers again. Evidently, this agent wanted to make sure no trace evidence got tracked from one location to another. When another agent confronted him at the bottom of the spiral staircase to change once again, he realized the entire forensics team had been briefed to take all precautions.

"There, new covers. You chaps are taking this to an extreme, aren't you?"

The agent shook his head. "Not when you consider what happened here. The slightest bit of trace, like a hair with DNA on it, might tell us who was where. We might find something that helps us nail down a time sequence, or proves someone was someplace he wasn't supposed to be."

Nigel felt a twinge of apprehension. Might they find something to place him in that sniper's nest? He now had his incentive to work quickly, before that might happen.

"Say, have you chaps seen a diaper bag?" He repeated its description.

"Not that I've seen or heard about." He pointed toward the museum's gift shop. "My partner is over there. If he hasn't seen one, we have one other agent who's manning the evidence locker now. She worked the scene, too, until we needed to start moving things out. She would have everything in the locker cataloged."

He thanked the agent, checked with his partner, and found his way to the small room off the auditorium's backstage that they now used as a temporary evidence locker. That agent had not cataloged a diaper bag, which meant one thing. There was a better than excellent chance the princess still carried it . . . and that he could find them using the tracker he had sown into its lining.

Twenty-one

"C'mon, Lynch. Answer your phone," muttered Richard. He hadn't much time before his crew might send a search team for him. Yet, he knew he had to tackle this new dilemma head-on and Lynch was the one he trusted most to help him.

Why wasn't he answering his phone? They had received word that the boss was on his way from Fulton to Kansas City. Lynch rarely drove one of the vehicles, so he should be available to answer his phone. Right? A new thought hit him. Had Lynch been injured, maybe killed? No. He didn't want to entertain that thought. Plus, they would have been informed, as they had been about the others.

He knew that Lynch disliked texting, ever worried about the security of that practice. He tried one more time. No answer, but one thing was different. He was able to leave a voice mail. That meant the man was making an effort to clear his mail box. So, if he was using his phone to clear his mail box, why wouldn't he answer it?

Richard shook his head. He had no choice but to leave a message.

"Lynch, this is Richard. Man, I need to talk with you, like, right now. Something has come up that could cause trouble and you're the only one I trust to help. Please *call* me, or find me when you get here."

He clicked off his phone and tossed it onto the bed. All he could do was wait for Lynch to respond.

He returned to the table and leafed through the items on top, taking care to touch no more than the edges of the photos. The photos of him with the reporter looked very real—and compromising. He was a healthy, all-American male and she was a gorgeous woman, with no inhibitions according to the photos. In the court of public opinion, they would be tried and found guilty within minutes if these were released on social media.

Had she received copies of these as well? That would explain her anxiety.

The embarrassment to the Graham campaign would be immediate as well. The boss campaigned on a platform that included Christian morality and conservative family values. Yet, here was his engaged head of social media cavorting with another woman. In fact, the woman was someone who had a certain dislike for the Graham campaign. The question would be raised as to whether he had sold out to the liberal side.

Yes, the photos could be damaging, despite being expertly Photoshopped. He'd never so much as had coffee with the woman and anyone with even minimal investigative chops would be able to discover that. Or would they? Whoever was behind this might have the ability to manipulate credit card charge records. Forge motel receipts. Create new photos.

What did this person, or group, want?

He dialed Lynch again. Same result.

Whatever they wanted, they were serious. That became obvious as Richard once again looked at the first of several images that appeared to be him in Afghanistan . . . killing, no, executing a young woman and her child and then butchering their bodies. He had seen death while there—

even a few things most would call atrocities, but he had not participated in such things. He wished he could unsee the images before him.

Then he took the thin cardboard sheet to which was taped a disposable cell phone. Printed above the phone: "Call the pre-programmed number within 24 hours, or these photos will be released to the media and police."

He assumed the 24-hour period began upon receiving the packet. That meant he had 20 hours left. First, he wanted to find Lynch and ask him what to do.

He dialed again. "Lynch, it's Richard. I really mean it. I, uh, we have trouble and I need your help. I have 20 hours before bad stuff hits the fan. *Call* me."

Amy sat in her front room, her eyes glued to the television. As Yogi Berra had said, "It was déjà vu all over again." Not too many years past, she had found herself in the same position watching for any sign that Lynch Cully was still alive.

The doorbell interrupted her thoughts. She found her father waiting on the stoop.

"Hi. I figured you might want company."

She nodded. "Thanks." She stepped back and allowed him to enter the front room. As he removed his coat, she asked, "Can I get you something to drink? Or a snack?"

He shook his head. "Thanks, but I'm good. Any word from Richard? Did he make it to Kansas City?"

Amy sat back into her chair and took a sip of her tea. "He made it there fine. I got a text from him that things were crazy when he arrived, so I doubt I'll hear from him again until late."

Her father looked at the television. "What's the latest?"

Amy sat there, silent, staring at the screen.

"Amy?"

She looked at her father. "Huh? Oh, sorry. I think they said something like two dozen killed or wounded. They still haven't reported on the status of the Royal Family, which has most of the commentators worried. With the Queen's stroke, protection for Prince Alexander has been tripled, which has the talking heads speculating that Prince Arthur and his family have been killed, too. What a mess."

Her father nodded and stared at her. "But that's not what's really bothering you, is it?"

Her father knew her too well. Despite her belief that she'd been able to fool him since age 12, he had proven time and again that she hadn't. She lowered her gaze to the floor and fought the tears that tried to well up.

"No. They're saying that Bradley Graham is okay and now in route to Kansas City. But they've also reported that several on his security team were killed. I've been watching for a report on the names of those men. I have no idea what's happened to Lynch."

"Ah," he replied, saying nothing more as he settled back into the cushions of the couch and watched the screen. "So, how was your time with Richard?"

"Um, great. We had a good time. I hated to see him leave."

Her father nodded. "But?"

Once again he proved his knack to read her moods, maybe even her thoughts.

"But I'm afraid that this long-distance relationship is going to go sour. I don't like it."

"Is that all?"

Now she was beginning to feel pestered. Why couldn't he leave it at that? She didn't feel like having her emotions, her thoughts, probed.

"You know, maybe it's time you think about moving closer to him. Find a job in northern Virginia. I realize you don't want to move away. Your brothers and their families are here, and I'm still here because of them. But, if you're serious about this relationship, maybe it's time to uproot and go where he is."

Her eyes widened and she gazed at him with her mouth slightly agape.

"I didn't say move *in* with him. Just move closer. I realize this goes against political correctness and all things feminist, but once upon a time, a woman expected to follow her man. What's your real reason for staying here? With your experience, you should be able to find work anywhere in this country."

Amy felt a wave of relief. She had sworn to remain chaste until marriage and, at times, still wore the purity ring her father had given her to honor her pledge of abstinence. She felt embarrassed that she just now had thought her father no longer expected that of her.

And yet, he had once again asked a question that made her dig deep into herself. Just why was she resistant to leaving?

"Tell me if I'm wrong, and I know you will, but are you having second thoughts?"

She didn't answer right away because she wasn't sure herself. Second thoughts. Cold feet. Weak knees. Perhaps a yellow streak down her back. She tried to tell herself she had no doubts, but. . .

The doorbell rang. She felt saved by the bell, literally.

She found the postman waiting.

"Need your signature on this one. Thanks."

She signed the slip and took the manila envelope, along with the rest of her mail, from the carrier. "Thank you."

She looked at the envelope with curiosity. She expected no special deliveries, and the Washington, D.C., address was not familiar to her. She laid the other mail on the coffee table and opened the packet. She hadn't finished pulling the contents from the envelope when she gasped. Was that Richard in the photo? With another woman?

Nigel took a head count of the killed and wounded, and compared that to the roster of agents, officers, and others who had been granted access to the museum and church. He also reconciled the list with those who had been debriefed and allowed to leave. One person stood out. Bradley Graham's team had left town less than an hour earlier for a campaign rally somewhere west of Fulton, minus one man.

Lynch Cully, the man who had become something of a thorn in the Director's side—and now his. Putting two and two together, he could think of just one conclusion. Cully had snatched away the Royal Family from their destiny and now hid them. But where?

And again, how? Yes, through the tunnels to the northern parking lot, but they had accounted for all vehicles. To have escaped the city meant having a clandestine vehicle. The logical conclusion when one's thoughts traveled down that road was that the man had been clever enough to arrange for an emergency egress path that he had not informed the Secret Service about. He probably had not, however, expected that his escape would be with the Prince of Wales and family.

For the first time that afternoon, Nigel held hope that he would complete his mission. On the assumption—and he recognized that for what it was—that the Prince now knew of his grandmother's incapacitation, he would become increasingly insistent on getting home. And in that hurry, the clever Lynch Cully would be bound to make a mistake.

Nigel found an isolated hallway on the second floor of the auditorium building and, deep in thought, paced.

"You okay, Nigel?" The question startled Nigel. He looked up to find Alistair Squyres, one of his peers.

"I am, Al." He thought quickly for a reason to be there. "I keep thinking I missed something prior to the family's disappearance. Thought maybe getting away from everyone might help me clear my mind."

"Oy. Chelmsford is asking for ya. I'll tell 'im you'll be along in short order."

Nigel nodded. "Thanks, mate."

As Squyres left the area, Nigel pulled out his cell phone and called up his tracker's app. He tried it one more time, but the result was the same as the previous four attempts. Nothing. He could activate the tracker within 25 miles. His failure to do so meant one of two things. The tracker had been broken, a not unlikely occurrence considering the circumstances. Or, they had moved beyond its range, also a possibility. They could be a hundred miles away by now.

Nigel had a decision to make. He could make the absence of Lynch Cully known to the Yanks and bring the full force of their Federal police agencies to bear against the man. He could even make the accusation that the man had kidnapped the Royal Family. He doubted he could make that stick, but the charge might be enough to further motivate the Secret Service and FBI. The extra manpower would no doubt shorten the hunt and then he'd be in position to finish the job he'd been sent to do and perhaps find himself basking in Paradise with his harem of virgins.

On the other hand, if he could find them first, he might be able to take out Cully, then the family, and make it look as if Cully had done the dirty work. He could tarnish Cully's name, eliminate him to please the Director, put that political campaign on the defensive, and remain among the living to further the work of Allah and The Assembly.

He chose the latter. He would be first to admit that he had fallen short of honoring the *salaat*, the Islamic ritual of prayer and second among the Five Pillars of his religion. While he felt a degree of assurance that Allah would forgive him under *taqiyya*, the doctrine of deception that arose from the Quran 4:29 and made it obligatory for Muslims to lie in order to advance the will of Allah, he felt it best to live. Upon completion of this task, he would seek a penitent's life and travel to Mecca for the first time since going underground to work for the Metropolitan Police and working his way into S.O.14.

In choosing the latter option, however, he was at a disadvantage. He had no transportation, did not know the geography of the area, and did not have total freedom to move about. He was restricted, not the least of which was having to report regularly to Chelmsford. The Assembly had promised assistance, but by not identifying themselves early, Nigel feared that assistance had died in the attack. He needed two things, no, three. He needed access to the internet, an excuse to leave the team for at least a day, and a car.

Twenty-two

"Here, dear," said Helen as she handed Arthur a cup of hot tea. She stroked his head with her free hand.

Arthur glanced up, took the white porcelain mug from her hand, and watched the steam rise from it. In a way, it mesmerized him like watching the flames of a fire.

"I once heard it said that life is like this vapor that rises from a cup, just a wisp in the flow of time. Everything in life seems so immediate and important at the time, but when you lose someone, someone special in your life, you have the choice of putting off the circumstances surrounding you and honoring them, or not."

He returned his gaze to the lake across the lawn from the house where he now sat. A baker's dozen of pintail ducks paddled a meandering path along the shoreline. He took a sip of the tea and shook his head.

"What is this?"

"Well, they have two dozen flavors of tea in this home, but you got your wish. Not one of them is in your list of top five favorites. I thought you might like this one. It's called Snickerdoodle tea. The name caught my fancy but I had to ask Lynch about it. They have a cookie by that name. Like the cookie, the tea has a blend of vanilla, cinnamon, and cream flavors."

Arthur took another sip. Yes, the vanilla and cinnamon were definitely there. Different, but he began to enjoy it.

"You know, Helen, I never envisioned this for our lives.

I mean today. And now . . . poor Grandmum. I must get back to her before it's too late. To let her know that we are alive, that her plan for succession will be carried out."

The Queen had informed him over a year earlier of her plan to skip his father and name him, Arthur, as her successor to the throne. Despite her nearing 90 years of age, her vigor had been that of a much younger woman and he had no hint that her plan would be set into action so soon. He wondered now, as he had many times over the past few years, whether he was ready. Would he be a good king for his people?

Many things weighed heavy in his mind.

"But how do we get home? Whom do we trust?"

He looked up at his wife. "I have an idea. Even on short notice, I've come to trust Lynch and Mack. I don't know how game they might be to my idea, though." He stood up and kissed Helen on the forehead. "First, I must get hold of Alex. Thank you for the tea. It did perk up my spirit."

They walked into the kitchen to find Lynch cooking. It smelled delicious.

"I hope you enjoy Italian. It's all I could come up with using ingredients at hand."

All three turned at the noise of Mack snorting and whinnying as he came into the kitchen on his hands and knees, two-and-a-half-year-old Prince Albert laughing and clinging to his back. The boy saw his parents and raised his arms to them. Arthur picked him up and hugged him, as Mack stood up.

"I'm a little rusty at this child care thing, but I managed to change Amelia. She's sleeping in the next room." At that moment his demeanor changed, becoming more serious. "It was purely a fluke, but as I was looking for, what do you call

diapers? Nappies? Anyway, the light of the setting sun coming through the windows hit the diaper bag and I noticed a shadow. There was something in the liner of the bag. This." He held up a small electronic device.

Lynch stepped around the kitchen island and looked at it. "A tracker."

Mack nodded. "We used similar devices to track suspect cars. They come in a variety of ranges, but I can't tell from looking at this one what its range is."

Arthur didn't like the implications of this new information. He would never believe their nanny was in on the rebellion, but someone with close contact to the family had been. That meant someone, or someones, on their personal protection detail, not just the Royal Protection team assigned to this trip.

"Please disable it," said Arthur.

"Sir, we could use this to lure them in, find out who they are," replied Mack.

"We might already have," said Lynch. "I agree with Arthur. Break it."

"Yes, please," repeated Arthur. "Lynch, I have an idea how we can narrow down the field of suspects. I need to call my brother."

Lynch looked at him, questioning. Arthur had already thought this through. He wanted Alex to know they were alive and well. Plus, Alex could get him the information he needed with one call.

"Are you sure, sir?"

"Quite. I saw your phone earlier. It's a Blackphone II, correct?"

Lynch nodded.

"Then, we shall have no problem. May I?"

Lynch handed him the phone.

Sir David stirred at the sound of his phone ringing. His irritation grew as he noted the time. Two in the morning. Sleep had been a rare commodity for him for the past 16 days and this night had been the first where he'd forced himself to go to bed at his usual time. *This had better be important*, he thought, or he'd give the bloke more than a what-for in the morning.

"Hello," he said.

"Sir David, this is Alexander. Sorry to have awakened you."

Sir David wanted to fall back to sleep. His mind wasn't clear.

Alexander? "Alexander who? And do you know what time it is?"

"Alexander Henry Charles David Windsor, Sir David. And yes, I know that it is precisely two oh eight in the morning."

This caller seemed absolutely amused. Alexander Henry Char . . . Sir David came to full awareness that instant.

"Please forgive me, Your Royal Highness. I am quite awake now. Yes, quite awake. How, how may I serve you?"

The prince chuckled and Sir David sighed internally. In all of his years as Commissioner, he had never received a direct call from a member of the Royal Family. One of their aides on occasion might call. And he received regular calls from the Madam Home Secretary. But this was a first and highly irregular.

"First, let me be the one to inform you that my brother and his family are quite well. I received a call from him just an hour ago. He assures me that they are secure and in the very capable hands of a Yank with an unusual name: Lynch. I will spare you the details at this time of day. However, they fear they are still the targets of whoever is behind all this madness and they do not know whom to trust."

Sir David felt a wave of relief flood his mind, and yet, he also did not know who to trust. He had men he did trust working on deep background checks on everyone on that protection detail. So far, no anomalies had been uncovered.

"I'm calling you in person because we fear the Home Office might be compromised as well. You should take this as the vote of trust we have *in you*, Sir David. We do not expect you to let us down."

Sir David felt honored indeed. He would work tirelessly on their behalf, as he always had.

"Thank you, Your Royal Highness."

"My brother has some information that he wishes to keep guarded until they can put together a few more pieces. To do that, he has asked that I provide him with a list of the Royal Protection officers who were killed. Please send me that list via this number, the one I'm calling you from."

"Right away, Your Royal Highness. Anything else?"

"Yes. We need to get Arthur and his family back home. This is what we need to do."

Sir David listened intently as the young prince outlined their plan.

Twenty-three

Lynch and Mack decided to split the night as watchmen over the house and the Royal Family, with Lynch taking the first shift since Mack had spent the day doing the physical labor of clearing the tunnel and needed to sleep. He assured Lynch that he'd be at 100% after four hours of rest.

Lynch used the time to work on the voice mail backlog. He figured he'd made a dent in the calls, most of which expressed the caller's concern and hope that Lynch was okay after the shooting, when he heard movement in the bedroom wing of the house. He grabbed his .40cal and eased toward the hallway, only to be met by Prince Arthur.

"Everything okay, sir?"

"Quite. It took a while for Helen to nod off, but she's sound asleep now."

"You should be, too. We have a busy day ahead of us."

Arthur nodded. "About that. Do you think we can stay ahead of whoever is behind this? You made no comment on my idea."

Lynch thought about that. If indeed The Assembly was behind the attacks, they would not stop until they completed the task . . . or were exposed openly and definitively as the source of the attacks. Even then they might not have the incentive to stop. Their mistress, the mainstream media, would turn a blind eye to any evidence presented to the public. Only through the power of social media and the internet could they exert pressure on the elitists to stop.

But that brought another question to mind. Since the monarchies of Europe were among the elite of the elite, why had the British Crown come under attack?

"Sir, may I ask you a question?"

"Certainly."

"Is your grandmother, your family in general, a member of The Assembly? Are you?"

The question appeared to catch the prince off-guard. He turned away and glanced toward the lake, wringing his hands. He then turned back to Lynch and scrutinized him.

"I am aware that Karolus Karling was embarrassed by some event here in St. Louis, something that forced him to flee the U.S. until recently. I paid little attention to those reports at the time. Maybe I should have been more attentive."

The prince's statement was one of admitting that he knew of The Assembly.

"Were you involved in that incident?"

Lynch nodded. "Yes."

"Then I am doubly glad that you are looking after my and my family's welfare."

Lynch found that statement odd. If the Royal Family was involved in The Assembly, would they not agree that Lynch was an obstacle to avoid, if not eliminate altogether?

"To answer your question, yes . . . and no. Of course, the monarchies of Europe have been intimately involved in ruling world events over the course of a millennium. My family has been no different. However, two decades ago, The Assembly became dominated by Big Business and Big Banking. They pushed and bankrolled the formation of the European Union. My family urged our government to resist.

That resistance came but only in token form. Members of The Assembly within the government succeeded in getting what they wanted and our family's role became more marginalized. We became little more than patrons of charities and a memorial to the monarchy's grand past."

The prince followed Lynch to the kitchen and both men sat down at the table.

"As time progressed, two things have happened. Their success in forming the EU emboldened them to push for total globalization and a one-world system. They've had to focus on diminishing the role of the U.S. to make that happen. The second thing is more recent. Someone in the Middle East has gained control over The Assembly. The result is an increasing trend of Islamizing the group. Some are calling him Islam's Mahdi."

Lynch and his Christian friends knew the Mahdi's role in future events by a different name. Some even suspected that the man already walked among us. Could this "someone" be that man?

"What I still don't understand, though, is that if The Assembly is behind these attacks on my family, why? We have continued to play our role and it's something important to my people, even if we don't have a direct say over the governing of the United Kingdom."

Lynch pondered what Britain's soon-to-be king had said. Did he personally believe The Assembly was behind the murders? His gut said yes. Still, he had no further insight as to why.

"Your Royal Highness, I, for one, believe The Assembly is responsible. Why? I don't know, but I have a friend who might be able to shed some light on that question. As for your question about being able to stay a step ahead, I think we can until that point when you leave us. From there, The Assembly will have roughly eight hours to plan ahead for your return home. *That* will be your most vulnerable point unless. . ."

Lynch paused. He had only an inkling of a plan forming in his mind. He needed time to work it through, like playing chess ten moves ahead.

"Unless what?"

"Unless we can expose them openly enough to make it impossible for them to act."

To say that Nigel awoke that morning feeling better would have been an outright lie. His arm ached more than it had the day before, making him wish he had taken advantage of the offer for pain medication despite his need to remain alert. He wished to let the warmth of a hot shower in his room at the local motel where they'd set up their operations center pound relief into his arm, but he'd been instructed not to get the wounds wet for at least 24 hours.

He prepared for the day, still trying to come up with a plausible excuse for remaining absent from the search for their sovereign. Considering the fact that they now searched for their new king, only death would have been an acceptable reason.

He grabbed a cup of hot water and the American excuse for tea, along with several Danish, and walked to the conference room that had been commandeered by the Secret Service and FBI for their use.

" 'Ow's the arm, Nigel?" asked Chelmsford upon seeing him.

"Not too poxy. Nothing some brekky and a paracetamol

won't help tame." He held up his breakfast.

Chelmsford shook his head. "You know they've got the makings of a real English breakfast in there, don't you?"

Nigel smiled to disarm the man's health rant. "Well, when in Rome . . ."

"Well, eat up. I was to have you working here with the comms, but your assistance has been requested. One of the Yanks wanted one of our boys to join him and he asked for you by name."

Nigel raised his brow. Had the Director come through? Was this his backup? The timing could not have been better.

"Go on, eat up. He'll be back straight away."

Nigel sat down and pulled the tea bag from his cup. He added a bit of milk and downed the first Danish in short order. He had two bites left of his second when an agent he did not know walked up to him.

"You Barrington?"

Nigel swallowed before answering. "I am, and you?"

"Special Agent Muntz, with the FBI. I flew in with the reinforcements this morning. Someone in our Washington headquarters got a tip on the possible whereabouts of Prince Arthur and they want me to check it out. For some reason, they want me to include you. Any idea as to why?"

Nigel shook his head, although he suspected he knew the exact reason. What he didn't know was whether or not this agent was sent by the Director and could be trusted. He would have to play it safe.

Lynch and Arthur talked further into the night, to the point where he finally came around to Arthur's insistence on calling him by his given name. Almost. Of course, Arthur made it quite clear that when he became king, that any jokes about a round table would lead to immediate imprisonment in the Tower of London, where visitors on guided tours could throw rotten fruit at him in the stocks.

Due to their talking, Mack had been rewarded with an extra hour of sleep, which he appreciated immensely. In turn, Lynch received an extra hour as well. The final result, however, was not to their satisfaction. By the time everyone convened in the kitchen, it was mid-morning. Lynch had hoped for an earlier start, as he followed his nose to the brewing coffee.

Mack had been busy, of sorts. Two grocery bags sat on the counter next to mugs and plates.

"Coffee ready?" asked Lynch. "Smells great."

"Almost, and thank Helen for that." Mack turned toward her and smiled. "You know, if this gig as Queen doesn't pan out, you could fit in as a barista at any Starbucks."

Helen laughed. "I most certainly will keep that in mind." She pointed to the grocery bags. "And just what is the master chef going to prepare for royalty today?"

Lynch looked at Mack and raised one brow. Mack got the message.

"Sorry, Lynch. The family was already up because of the little nippers; we had nothing for breakfast; and they said it was okay for me to leave to get something. It did take longer than I expected. Not much around here except waterside bars and cafes. Sorry."

Lynch nodded. "Just think you should have woken me first."

Helen stepped up closer. "Lynch, please blame me. I insisted on letting you sleep a bit longer."

Lynch relented. "Thank you." He turned back to Mack. "So, master chef, get with it. We have to get moving."

Mack grinned as he placed his arm in the first bag. He pulled out a characteristic, green polka-dotted box.

"Krispy Kremes!" Helen softly applauded. "We love Krispy Kremes."

"Huh?" Mack looked disappointed. "I thought I'd treat you to something distinctly American."

Arthur walked in with both children in his arms. Young Prince Albert reached for the donuts. "Kispy Kemes. Ummmmm."

"We have these throughout the United Kingdom. Helen is correct in saying that these are a favorite indulgence of ours."

Lynch poured a cup of coffee, grabbed a donut, and moved into the living room. He had a concern with the way Mack seemed to be handling their current situation. His way of making light of things did make the family more comfortable, but he worried that it made him less alert. He made a mental note to talk with him about it.

In the meantime, he wanted to finish clearing his voice mailbox. He had no idea how much longer that would take and they also needed to get on the road. After a dozen messages, he came to one from Richard. He sat up. Trouble? What kind of trouble would Richard contact him about— and him alone?

When he heard Richard's second message that included a time reference, he checked the time stamp on the message and compared that with his watch. He had *two* hours remaining. Even if he left for Kansas City now, he couldn't get there in two hours.

And what would he do with the Royal Family? He

couldn't risk taking them to Kansas City with him. Too many opportunities for being spotted. Plus, the plan they had put into motion required them to be in Saint Louis. They couldn't change the venue to Kansas City without alerting the bad guys.

Lynch walked into his boss' study and closed the door before dialing Richard.

"Oh Lynch. Thank God you're okay. The rumor mill here is rotating at light speed."

"Yeah, I'm okay. I'm on special assignment, you might say, and I won't make it to Kansas City before you all move on to Wichita. I hope to catch up with you in Garden City. What's up?"

Richard proceeded to inform Lynch about the packet of photos and the requirement that he call the number with the enclosed phone by noon. At Lynch's request, Richard described the phone. Lynch shook his head. The outdated phone offered no way to record the conversation.

"Lynch, I need your help. All of this is fabricated. Not a shred of truth here, but the media will have a heyday with this and I'll be crucified in public opinion. The campaign will be put on the defensive. It will be a disaster."

Lynch could hear the panic in his friend's voice, as well as the sincerity that none of the allegations made by those photos was true. "Richard, I'm stuck. I can't get there to help. I suggest you take it directly to the boss. He'll know what to do. In the meantime, I'm going to get someone to help. He won't be able to get there right away either, so stall. Maybe pretend the phone was damaged on the bus, call from a different phone, and record the conversation if you can. Sound cooperative."

"I-I don't know. I trust your judgment, though. I'll get

hold of Graham. Who do you think is doing this? And why me?"

After his discussion with Prince Arthur, he had a pretty good idea who was responsible. Their choice of Richard also made sense. He had contact with the news media on occasion. He had been away from his fiancée for an extended time. He served in Afghanistan. All of those circumstances gave them openings for their lies. His main question wasn't why Richard but why Summer Stanton? Why a reporter known for her liberal reporting and dislike of almost everything Bradley Graham stood for?

Staying in one place posed a risk. Staying at the Graham's lake house would stand out to anyone who connected the dots between Lynch being missing along with the Royal Family. The place had been convenient for one night, but they couldn't stay. They needed to get back to Saint Louis, to a safe place that no one could openly associate with Lynch or Graham. He needed to make one more call and they needed to move on.

"Mike, it's Lynch. I need your help again."

Mike Jurgesmeyer, a tall, athletic, tech genius with a ponytail to between his shoulder blades had been the county's computer forensics expert until the new county crime lab went over budget and they downsized his department of eight to just him. He had lasted six months before throwing up his hands in frustration over the case load and lack of help. He quit to do independent consulting and never looked back. His workload was his to manage and he was never without work. The fact that his clients never blinked at his consulting fees wasn't as much a source of pleasure as was the fact that he now had the state-of-the-art toys that most geeks only dreamed of.

More importantly, Mike's work had been the key to breaking open The Assembly's plot to destroy the U.S. economy and exposing Karolus Karling once before. Like Lynch, his one regret was not destroying the entire operation and seeing Karling remain in power.

Lynch briefed Mike on what Richard now faced.

"Let me read between the lines here, Lynch. Are you thinking we get to have a do-over? I can be in KC in four hours."

Twenty-four

About 15 minutes into the trip, heading south by Nigel's reckoning, Agent Muntz glanced at him.

"So, you're the guy that got shot in the arm, eh?"

Nigel was in the mood to make a sarcastic response but thought better of it. He needed this man's cooperation and assistance, not enmity. Besides, he still had no clue as to the agent's loyalties.

"That I am, and I have to say, it's not feeling great this morning. So, if you can avoid the potholes and rough spots, I would appreciate it."

Muntz nodded. "I've been there. I know just where you're coming from. Although, in my case, they gave me the week off. Don't know what I would have done if I had been on assignment overseas like you are. I'll do my best with the driving."

Nigel watched the scenery go by. He didn't feel like talking. He had a job to finish and he didn't know whether he was being led away on a snipe hunt or not.

"So, since you were in the middle of things when the shooting went down, what was it like?"

Nigel *really* didn't want to talk about the previous day. He decided to change the subject.

"So, where we headed? You mentioned having a new lead."

The agent glanced his way.

"The Lake of the Ozarks. It's a huge reservoir behind a

hydroelectric dam, with hundreds of lake homes and resorts. Specifically, we're heading toward one branch of the lake called the Gravois Arm, formed along the Gravois Creek that joins the lake from the west."

"And the lead?"

"Well, one of the Secret Service guys was comparing the list of dead to the list of people in attendance. Other than the Royal Family, one other person is unaccounted for."

Nigel was not surprised that he had not been the only one to notice that. He did wonder, however, whether the agency had more information about that than he had. They must, otherwise he wouldn't be riding in a rental car south, having just passed the state capital.

"The Director thought it interesting that Bradley Graham and one bodyguard were discovered in the same room as the tunnels that were found later, and that it's his chief of security who is the other missing person."

The Director? thought Nigel. Perhaps they were on the same team after all.

"He thought that a bit too convenient. We did some digging and learned that Graham has a lake house on the Gravois Arm of the Lake of the Ozarks. If Graham's security guy snatched the family for safekeeping, that house sure would make a cozy place to hide out. So, we're gonna check it out."

"Why am I along?"

Muntz nodded. "The Director wanted you there in case the family is in hiding there. I figured he wanted a member of the Royal Protection detail along to be a firsthand witness if we find them. I wasn't told why it had to be you specifically, but that choice was above my pay grade."

Nigel relaxed a little. If the Director was behind this

escapade, he had no room to complain.

"Do you think this security chief kidnapped the family?" Nigel knew better but couldn't resist planting that seed. His hope of yielding a crop withered within seconds.

"Not at all. We've checked his credentials and background. He's as clean and honest as they come. More likely he took on the role of guardian when it became clear that the attack was an inside job. If we're right, and we find them, I'll deal with the bodyguard while you take care of the family."

Nigel smiled at that comment.

Lynch glanced at his watch. Ten-twenty. With Richard's situation, he had no time to dilly-dally and they were already running well behind his initial schedule. He had figured it wouldn't take long for folks to figure out he was missing as well as the family. And with Brad Graham as his boss, he suspected the lake house would quickly emerge in their minds as a place of possible refuge. As a detective, *he* would not hesitate to investigate such a lead. He reasoned that since he didn't see himself as being exceptional or better than the FBI and Secret Service agents now on the case, they would, too. Plus, if they learned which home security company covered the property, all they would need is one quick phone call to that company to find out that the proper entry codes had been entered and someone had been there all night.

"Mack, just pack the remaining food in the car with you and get the children loaded into their seats. We need to get out of here."

Lynch imagined several helicopters loaded with armed

agents descending on the property at any moment. He rushed through the bedrooms, dealing with linens and the like and piling them all up in the laundry room. He could notify the family's housekeeping service later.

He returned to the kitchen to find Helen tidying up the area. It struck him as odd, but then, why wouldn't a future queen know how to do that?

Arthur entered the kitchen. "The children are strapped in and ready."

Helen held up the paper towel in her hand. "Where?"

Lynch took it from her and escorted them to the garage. He locked the door to the house and opened both garage doors.

"Where's Mack?"

Before anyone could answer, he peeked around the corner of the garage. "Right here. Did a quick recon of the drive and exit. We're good to go."

The two men pulled their vehicles from the building and Lynch jumped out to arm the security panel before closing the doors. He noticed something taped to the door post and smiled. Mack had done more than reconnoiter the area.

As they pulled out of the gate and onto the main road, Lynch glanced at his watch again. Ten thirty-six. So far, so good.

Nigel sat in the car, fuming. He wanted to throttle whoever had rented a car for them that had no GPS. His own smartphone's map app didn't have U.S. addresses, only those in the U.K. Muntz's system had them driving in circles. In frustration equal to his own, the agent gave in and pulled into a petrol station to ask for directions to the address of the Graham lake house. He glanced at his watch. Ten twenty-eight local time. They had been driving around, lost, for nearly 20 minutes.

Muntz came running back to the car. He waved a piece of paper as he climbed in.

"Got it. We must've passed the place four times. It's just minutes from here."

The agent pulled out and sped down the county road heading back toward the lake. Ten minutes later, he pulled into a driveway and up to a closed gate. He pressed the intercom button awaiting an answer from the house. Nothing. He tried a second time with the same result.

Nigel opened his car door. "C'mon then. Let's hoof it."

The agent shook his head. "Can't do that. Close the door."

Nigel closed it, thinking the man had another plan. Instead, he pulled into a turn-off big enough for a delivery truck to turn around if unable to pass the gate, parked the car, and turned it off. Nigel opened the door again and began to climb out.

"Where you going?"

"To the house."

"We can't yet," replied Muntz.

"What do you mean, we can't. C'mon, chap, we have our jobs to do."

"That's exactly what I'm doing. We can't enter the property without permission or a warrant. I'm waiting on my office to text me the warrant."

Nigel couldn't believe what he heard. What in blazes did they need a warrant for?

"I thought you said the Director wanted us to take care

of things."

"I did. We just have to do so legally. The guy who owns this place is running for president. Can you imagine the fallout if we entered his property illegally and he wins the election eight months from now? Director Winchell would have my head if I did that."

"Director Winchell?"

"Yeah, the director . . . of the FBI."

In that instant, Nigel no longer had any confusion as to which side the agent played for. He climbed out of the car, pretended to stretch, and removed his backup handgun from his leg holster. He continued to pretend to stretch as he walked around the back of the car. Coming up to the driver's window, he raised the gun and fired once, shattering the window and hitting the agent in the left temple.

His thoughts moved into high gear. Now that he was on his own, he needed to make it look good. He pulled out his pocket knife and cut the back of his left hand. He let his blood drip across the passenger seat and out onto the driveway to form a small pool. He disturbed the brush along the drive to make it look as if something, or someone, had been dragged through it, adding some of his blood to a large log along the way. Satisfied with the scene, he walked toward the lake, allowing blood to drip along the way. He proceeded to the nearest dock, where he re-opened his wound and created another small pool of blood on the deck. With a little luck, he'd finish his task before the divers finished looking for his body in the lake.

He again placed pressure on the wound and worked his way toward the house, taking precaution to avoid being seen from any window. He saw no lights or other sign of activity inside, so he worked his way up to a window. The kitchen. No sign of anyone. Slowly, he moved from window to window. Those through which he could see inside all revealed the same thing. Nothing. An empty house. Bedrooms were vacant and the beds had no linens. He decided against breaking in, which would have triggered an alarm.

Having circled the house, he came to the garage. Refuse cans outside contained only a wadded paper towel. No household trash. No fast food garbage. He neared the man door and glanced inside. A jet ski and other lake toys. No cars. He was about to walk away in search of a car to steal when he noticed something pinned to the door post. His anger rose as he recognized his tracker, broken and taped to a piece of paper along with a small wood screw and a large letter 'U.'

Twenty-five

Amy never made it to bed the night before. Sleep could not overcome the anguish she felt after seeing the photos of Richard and another woman. Worse yet, her father had seen them as well. He hadn't intruded. She had been so shocked, she dropped them to the floor and he moved to help pick them up before she could react.

Yet, after that, he had refused to go home. She wanted to be alone. He wouldn't allow it. She was too numb to talk about it. He held a one-sided conversation, most of which she never heard. She wanted to sleep as a way of escape but couldn't close her eyes. He wanted to stay awake, in case she needed him for support but fell asleep in the overstuffed chair in the living room. Even now, as the sun rose high enough to top the home across the street, his snoring had the Space Station crew complaining.

Amy walked into the kitchen and prepared her coffeemaker for a pot of medium roast. Between the two of them, they would need the whole carafe. Maybe more.

"Did you sleep at all?"

She turned to see her father standing at the doorway to the kitchen. While she didn't feel like laughing, she couldn't help but smile. It was just like her father to wake up at the first waft of brewing coffee.

"No. I'm glad you got a couple of hours sleep, though."

"Sorry. This old body can endure a lot still, but pulling all-nighters isn't in my repertoire anymore."

He walked to her cabinets and pulled out two mugs, placing them on the counter next to the coffeemaker.

"Have you thought about what you want to do?"

She sighed. "That's all I've done all night. Think about it, that is."

"I should rephrase that. Have you *decided* what to do?"

She looked away and took a deep breath. Deciding. That was the hard part, wasn't it?

"I don't think you heard a thing I said last night, so I'm going to repeat two points. At a minimum, you need to call Richard and confront this. You need to hear his side of the story. You just can't let those pictures rule your life. Maybe ruin it. And my second point is that you can't trust them, the photos."

He was right on both counts, but something in the way he stated point number two caught her attention.

"Can't trust them?"

He nodded. "That's right. You can't trust them. In this day of digital photography and photo manipulation software, anyone could create photos like that. So, your next question is, why? Why would someone send you photos like that? If someone wanted to split up the two of you, why send such explicit photos? Wouldn't photos of Richard and this other woman holding hands at a restaurant, or kissing on the sidewalk work to accomplish that? Another question is who. Who would benefit from sending you these photos? The other woman? She seems to have more to lose from these photos than Richard. This is the type of stuff I'd expect from that Darko Komarčić character, reaching out from jail with his depraved mind trying to ruin both of your lives."

Amy stared at her father. Maybe she should have paid

closer attention to him last night. It might have spared her hours of torment. She, too, could see Darko doing just this sort of thing as payback for Richard's helping to take down his human trafficking and prostitution ring.

She poured coffee into both mugs and added an ice cube to hers to cool it down before taking a sip.

"Dad, you're right. I need to call Richard, and sooner, not later."

He took a long drink of his coffee and she wondered how he did that with it as hot as it was. The man had a mouth and esophagus made of iron.

"Good. It's much better to put this fire out quickly than to let it smolder."

Amy took her coffee with her to the front room and grabbed her phone. Her father followed but stopped at the doorway.

"Do you want to do this alone, or should I stay to offer moral support?"

"By all means, please stay. I'm even going to put it on speakerphone. I'd like your take on what he says when we're done."

"I'm here to help." He walked back to "his" chair and sat down with his coffee. Amy speed-dialed Richard.

"Hello."

As soon as she heard his voice, Amy wanted to back down. She faltered in her reply, as her father gave her a "thumbs up."

"Hi, Richard."

"Amy! It's, uh . . . yeah, I'm glad you called. I miss you and it's been a day from Hades here. How are you this morning? Oh, hey, good news. I heard from Lynch and he's okay. I know the media has gotten wind of his being missing and you might hear something about that. Don't pay attention to what they might say."

That aroused Amy's curiosity, but she wouldn't let that sidetrack her. She also noted a nervousness in his voice, as if she was the last person he wanted to talk with at the moment.

"Richard . . . that's, um, not why I called."

"What's up, sweetheart?"

She felt her heart start to race. Not being fond of confrontation, she became uncomfortable. No, *more* uncomfortable.

"Umm. Richard, I received a packet of photographs yesterday in the mail. Pictures of you and a redheaded woman."

Silence from the other end of the line. Then she thought she heard a whisper, "Dear Lord, please help."

"Richard?"

"Amy, I am so sorry you had to see those. I-I just got them yesterday, too. And I think the woman allegedly in the photos got them, too. Please, please, please, please, please . . . do not believe what you see there. They're a total fabrication. I only know the woman peripherally from the campaign, but we've never so much as even had coffee together."

"Who is she, Richard?"

Amy rolled her eyes, chastising herself for that question. What difference did it make who she was? Why didn't she ask why someone would do this?

"Her name is Summer Stanton. She's a reporter with MSNBC and not exactly a friend of our campaign. Which makes it even stranger that she would be used in those photos."

"Why, Richard? What's going on?"

She heard him take a deep breath. "That's the question of the day. I have a meeting with Brad in ten minutes to show him the photos and decide how we want to handle this. Lynch thinks they're a ploy to embarrass or discredit the campaign."

So Lynch already knows about these? she thought.

"I don't know where Lynch is. All he told me is that he's on a special assignment, but he's sending someone here to help. I think it's the computer guy that helped him uncover that stuff about Karolus Karling awhile back. I don't know the man's name, but he's supposed to be on his way here, to KC."

Amy didn't know his name either. Lynch had always been protective of that friendship, and she understood why. But, if Lynch was sending him to Kansas City to help, he also had to be convinced that Richard was being set up.

"Amy, one other thing you need to know. There was an ultimatum in the packet I got. I have just over an hour to respond to this blackmailer or the photos go public."

Richard left his room having mixed feelings about the conversation he'd had with Amy. He was dismayed that she had been exposed to those raunchy photos. Yet, he felt confident that she understood the situation and would not be surprised by anything that might pop up on the news.

He knocked on the door to Bradley Graham's suite, and the door opened in an instant. Stan McGonagle, the campaign manager, ushered him inside. Brad sat on the couch and opposite to him, in a chair, sat a surprise guest. Summer Stanton.

Richard's assumption that she had also received the photos had been correct. Brad had them in his hands.

"Richard, come on in and grab a seat." He pointed to the envelope in Richard's hands. "I take it those are the photos you received."

Richard had briefly explained the nature of the photos when he called Stan earlier to set up the meeting. However, the stack of paper in Brad's hands was smaller than his.

He nodded in greeting toward Summer Stanton. "Ms. Stanton. I didn't expect to see you here."

The sour look on her face showed that she wasn't pleased to be there. She held her arms across and tight to her chest.

"After you mentioned that she was implicated in the photos, I thought it only appropriate that she be here and take part in whatever decision is made. I told her that despite our differences, I was not one to throw her under the bus for our benefit. Whatever approach we take, she will be in on it."

"And I appreciate that, Mr. Graham. I tried to warn Mr. Nichols about these photos in Washington. However, I still don't know how *I* am somehow implicated in these photos." She pointed to the papers in Brad's hands.

Richard gave her a questioning look. "You said something about Afghanistan." Had she seen only that set of photos? Richard handed his boss the envelope he had received. "May I see what you have, sir?"

Brad nodded and handed him the photos he had been perusing. Richard glanced through them. They were the same Afghanistan images that had branded themselves into his mind, but *only* those of the alleged atrocity.

"Are there more?" Richard asked Summer. He

wondered if she had received them all but withheld the sex images out of embarrassment.

Summer replied, "No. Just those."

"I'm sorry, Ms. Stanton, but you've been dragged into this in a very explicit sense." Brad now held the other photos out to her.

The woman's eyes widened and her breathing accelerated. Her hands began to tremble as she leafed through the new set of images. "I . . . I . . ." Tears formed in her eyes.

Richard imagined the thoughts racing through her head at that moment. They were probably the same thoughts he had experienced.

"I . . . we . . . we've never been . . . together," she managed to say. "Wh-who would do this to me?"

Richard took a deep breath and exhaled. "I've been asking the same question. However, on our side of the political aisle, we have a pretty good idea. Whoever is behind this must want to guarantee my cooperation. In your case, maybe you didn't act quickly enough on those photos to satisfy this person, or group. For the record, I can state without equivocation that I never did such a thing while overseas. Just as we've never, ever, been together."

Brad gave a groan of disgust as he looked again at the first two Afghanistan pics. He set them on the table, face down, without looking at the rest. Richard couldn't blame him. He wished *he* could unsee those images.

Brad pulled the cell phone from the envelope.

"And this is the phone you're expected to use? What kind of time limit do we still have?"

Summer looked shocked, as if bitten a second time by the venomous snake they now dealt with. "What's this about?"

Richard looked at Brad. "We still have 45 minutes." He switched his gaze to Summer. "I am to contact this person using that phone at a number pre-programmed into the phone. I assume I'll get this person's demands then. If I don't call, this person will release the photos to the public."

The woman's perfect ivory complexion looked bleached. Again, he guessed her thoughts weren't that different from his own. The public ridicule. The condemnations. The nightmare of defending oneself in the court of public opinion. Or, in his case, a military tribunal, too. Being a civilian now would not spare him should the military wish to investigate the atrocity alleged by those pictures.

"Richard, you mentioned talking with Lynch about this."

"Lynch?" asked Summer.

"Our chief of security and a man you want on your side if anything might go wrong," replied Stan.

Richard nodded. "That's right. He's on some sort of special assignment..." He couldn't help but notice a glint of recognition in Brad's eyes. He went on to detail his conversation with Lynch.

Summer appeared unsure. Brad and Stan took a few minutes to reflect on Lynch's suggestion. For the first time, Brad seemed unsure how to proceed with Summer in the room. He hesitated with his reply.

"This guy he's sending our way, is he the guy I think he is?"

"I'm assuming he is. You know he's never given any of us his name."

Summer held up both hands. "Hold on, guys. I'm feeling

like a useless cog in this machine. First, Lynch and now some nameless, mystery man. What guy?"

Richard didn't want to be the one to answer her. Stan pursed his lips and didn't seem eager to answer either. They both turned toward Brad.

"Ms. Stanton, it's probably best that you not learn anything more. Your *health*, if you catch my drift, could depend on your ability to deny knowing anything."

She crossed her arms and frowned. Richard wondered if they had now waved a red flag in front of a journalistic bull.

"Trust me. *He* poses no danger to you. It's the people he's exposed, who would do anything to find him, you would have to worry about. Very *powerful* people."

Twenty-six

Lynch and Mack had debated the best route back to St. Louis but had agreed that the city should be their final destination. The royal jet, the family's means to return home, sat on the tarmac at the Spirit of St. Louis Airport. So, getting the family within close proximity to their transportation seemed easier than moving that transportation to them. Any attempt to fly the jet elsewhere would give their enemy more time to plan and another opportunity to strike. Of course, that would also be the case when they left for England, but they had no control over that leg of the trip.

The biggest issues they faced once getting the family there would be securing the aircraft from sabotage and vetting the flight crew and protection team. Lynch could do little but pray that the royal sibling, Prince Alexander, had that part of the plan under control.

Lynch's mind moved from one threat assessment to the next, to curiosity about Richard's new situation, to what if this, what if that. He drove on auto-pilot.

"Graham Stewart and Nigel Barrington."

Lynch glanced at Arthur. "What? I'm sorry, sir. Did I miss something?"

"You do seem a bit pre-occupied."

"That's an understatement, for sure."

Lynch tried to focus on the road that now dipped, curved, and rose again as they moved through rural

Missouri. Having passed through the small town of Vienna, they headed east toward St. Louis using small state highways and avoiding the interstate system.

"I said, Graham Stewart and Nigel Barrington. I've been looking at the list of men assigned to our protection detail and these two are among the living. Both were assigned to my family *after* the explosion at The Royal Lodge. In fact, I believe both were assigned to my uncle's home at the time of the incident. They would be at the top of my list of suspects."

Lynch slowed down for yet another small community that took the speed limit from 60 miles-per-hour down to 30 without warning. He knew they had no police force to enforce the limit, but he didn't want to take any chances that a county sheriff's deputy lurked around a corner. The last thing they could afford was being stopped, for any reason.

"Sounds like they both had opportunity and access. We just can't ignore the possibility that others are involved. Remember, you said your brother had been told that authorities back home estimated at least five men were involved."

Prince Arthur shifted in his seat and turned to face Lynch. "Quite. And we know nothing about what they've discovered at the museum. Perhaps they've identified all five and they are all dead." He seemed ebullient at the thought. "Perhaps we are safe to board our plane and fly home."

"Sir, I think the key words were *at least* five. We can't trust that all of the assassins are dead. I would still wait for your brother to work out his end of our plan."

The prince looked down for a moment and then sat

facing forward again. "Yes, that would be the safest route. I must admit, though, it was nice to think we are safe, even if for a moment."

Lynch's cell phone rang. He had thought they were still out of range of any towers. Obviously not. Caller ID told him it was Mack, who was supposed to be about a mile behind them with the princess and the children.

"Lynch, you might want to turn on the radio."

"Okay. You guys good?"

"Sure. Still behind you. I almost caught up with you, but I backed off as soon as I saw you up ahead. But, turn on the radio. We might have to change plans. You *do* have a Plan B, right?"

"I'll call you back."

Lynch clicked off the phone and turned on the radio. He dialed right to KMOX, "The Voice of St. Louis" that could be heard in 44 states.

". . . as we've been reporting for the past 15 minutes, federal and state authorities in Fulton have now informed the media that the Prince of Wales and his family are missing and they are still believed to be in great danger after what the authorities are calling an assassination attempt yesterday. A major manhunt is now under way for them and we've just been informed that travelers can expect significant delays as road blocks and checkpoints are being established on all interstates and major state highways. Local police are also screening all suspect vehicles, and all airports except Lambert International and Kansas City International are on lock-down. Even Amtrak rail service has been curtailed. Folks, if you think a presidential visit is a traffic nightmare, you haven't seen anything like this before."

The station cut to a commercial and Lynch turned down the volume.

"I thought your brother informed your people back home that you're safe. Why haven't they communicated that to the people here?"

The prince shuffled around in his seat. "Yes, well, I would not go so far as to say he told *my people* at home. He told family members who need to know and he told Sir David Spencer-Hough, the Commissioner of our Metro Police. Our protective details, the Special Ops 14 group, or Royal Protection command, are under his office. I directed Alex not to tell our Home Secretary, MI5, or MI6 because we don't know where the traitors are. Sir David, however, I trust explicitly and he's in the position to assist my brother."

The radio personality came back on the air and began to comment about the manhunt again. Lynch turned the volume back up.

". . . more about the manhunt that is now underway. Although police will not confirm this, our sources say that one other man has been listed as missing. We do not have his name, but our source says he is with the Bradley Graham campaign. The authorities are considering him a person of interest."

Great! thought Lynch. *Now they're looking for me, too.* That was going to make it hard to call in favors, but he knew one guy he could always count on. No, make that two guys.

He glanced at the prince to find the man smiling.

"You know, Lynch, over the past 24 hours I have found you quite interesting as well."

Lynch didn't know what to make of that comment. "Sir, person of interest means—"

"Yes, yes. I know what it means. I have watched American television more than a few times. I've always found the term to be a peculiar euphemism."

Lynch now realized the comment was meant to be a humorous compliment.

"The problem, sir, is that now it's going to be a lot harder to get you to St. Louis. Not impossible, just more difficult. And I can't call in favors from some old friends without jeopardizing their careers."

"But, as Mack said, you do have a Plan B, correct?"

Lynch nodded, as he worked feverishly in his head to formulate one.

Nigel now regretted his burst of anger that led to killing Agent Muntz. The man had been his ticket to searching for the family, and Nigel had not just burned that bridge but bombed its piers as well. He needed transportation and having found none at the five homes nearest to the Graham home, he had one choice. He would have to take the agent's rental car—bloody seats, broken window and all—and use it to help him find another car.

He jogged back toward the car but stopped as he neared the property. Men talking. At least two. And in the distance, he heard sirens. The car and its contents had been discovered.

He circled along the property line toward the lake. A new plan, a better plan, formed in his mind. He scanned the property around him and watched the house for activity. He saw no one. It appeared the men were waiting for police at the rental car. He wondered how long it might take for them to realize someone else had been in that car. He realized his original plan to leave a blood trail to the lake might have now become his salvation.

One thing he had to do first. He approached the shoreline and tossed his spare gun and its holster as far into the water as possible. He couldn't risk having the ballistics test of the bullet in Muntz's brain traced back to his weapon. Besides, he wasn't authorized to have a backup weapon on U.S. soil. If he were to be found with one, or worse, with an empty holster, his freedom would disappear.

Then, using every stealth method he'd ever learned, he crept back to the dock where he'd left the small blood pool. Now, he simply had to wait.

Intent on the land activity, he almost missed the boat speeding his way in the distance. He couldn't be seen on land if he wanted the plan to work. Witnesses stating they saw him sitting next to the dock would destroy his story.

He took a deep breath and slid into the water, keeping as low a profile as possible and hoping the boaters hadn't seen him. The frigid water took more than his breath away. The cold numbed his limbs to the point he could barely move and he began to worry he might actually drown. He knew the stats. In water that cold, he had five to ten minutes to be discovered and pulled from the water before hypothermia took the last of his strength. At that point, he would not be able to move on his own.

He felt his mind beginning to go dull. How long had it been? He tried to count off the seconds but couldn't focus on one to ten, much less ten to 60. Was that someone yelling?

He thought something just snagged his coat. Maybe he imagined it. Then, two sets of hands grabbed him by the arms and yanked him up. He sputtered water from his mouth. The boat. He was on a boat. Wasn't he?

"This guy's still alive. Get an ambulance. Grab those blankets."

Nigel tried to open his eyes, but the muscles didn't obey his brain. He began to shiver. That was a good sign. The shivering would create heat.

He felt someone probing his pockets. They would find his credentials and identification. Yes. He felt someone pulling those items from his pockets. He then felt warm blankets engulfing him and within a short time, he opened his eyes.

His mind became clearer. He was indeed on a boat. He saw a sign identifying the boat as a state Water Patrol craft. He overheard the officers talking on their radios.

"382, Jefferson City, we're on scene with the J4 on Blue Valley Circle. Be advised we need EMS for a man found in the water. Alive but appears to be hypothermic. Please notify the FBI that the man in the water is a British Royal Protection officer by the name of Nigel Barrington. I will have the ID of the J4 for you shortly."

Nigel's mind continued to clear as he warmed up. He had made the correct move. After an obligatory night in the hospital, he would be able to resume his hunt.

Twenty-seven

The decision had been made and agreed to by all parties. The Graham campaign, along with Summer Stanton, would play along. Richard would make the call, try to stall, and allow them time to formulate a better strategy, while learning what it was the blackmailer wanted. In his room, alone, he had half an hour to prepare.

Richard started first by making some calls. Assuming his room might be bugged and taking extra precaution, he went into the bathroom, turned on the shower for background noise, and placed his first call.

"Clive, old buddy, it's Thor."

"Hey, how's life on the campaign trail? Sounds like you're standing in a waterfall."

"Brutal. I don't have time to chat. Here's why I'm calling." He proceeded to inform his friend and fellow Army squad member about the attempted blackmail and their decision to play along with the monster in the closet.

"So, if something goes wrong and those pics get into the media, you want me to support you in denying the claims about Afghanistan? You got it. You were a Boy Scout the entire tour. What else can I do to help? Want me to call the others on the squad?"

"Thanks, that's exactly what I'm asking. They might never go public but if they do, I don't want you guys blindsided. But I'll call the others. I think I need to make those calls myself. That's why I don't have time to talk. I've got half an hour."

They said their goodbyes and Richard repeated the process with the other living members of his squad: Hassle, Capt. A, Walts, and Sasquatch. They offered their support without hesitation, knowing that Richard was innocent of such cruelty. Snarky was the one team member he couldn't reach . . . besides the three friends they had lost while there. Calls to the squad never failed to bring back the bad memories of the firefight in which they had died.

He shoved those thoughts aside. He had to focus on the now. He rehearsed what he wanted to do . . . and hoped it would be convincing.

The time had come.

He retrieved the cell phone from the envelope, turned it on, and pulled up the sole number listed under contacts. As a group, they all agreed that this number was likely to be a burner phone but hoped it would become the first lead in tracking down the person behind this.

He took a deep breath and pressed the call button. Two rings.

"Your time was almost up." The voice was deep and mechanical, distorted but not so much to make it unintelligible.

Richard launched into his spiel. "Hello? . . . Hello? This, um, is Richard Nichols. I-I don't know if you're there, but I'm calling as instructed."

"Quiet! And listen," replied the voice.

Richard realized he would be distracted and could not be convincing if he could hear the person, so he flipped the phone upside down. He could talk into the mic but not hear anything. He talked over the person on the other end, as if he really could not hear.

"I can't hear anything on this phone. It looks like it got stepped on, damaged in the stampede off the bus yesterday. The glass is cracked and it looks like the case is, too, near the earphone. I tested it last night and the earphone doesn't work." He paused for a second. "I hope you can hear me. I'm calling as instructed. Even though I know those photos are faked, I can't prove it and I don't want to embarrass the campaign or put it on the defensive. I . . . I don't know what else to do. I can't hear anything on this phone. It was damaged. I have to join my team in an hour or they'll wonder why I'm not there. I have to leave it up to you to contact me somehow."

He paused. He could hear the person on the other end saying something, but he ignored it and started into an abbreviated version of his speech one more time. He finished by adding, "I hope you can hear me. There's nothing else I can do with this phone, so I'm hanging up now. Please contact me somehow."

He disconnected the call, placed the phone on the floor and stomped on the end near the earphone. He did it again and cracked the glass this time. He used the phone to call his personal cell. He could make the outgoing call, but he also could still hear through the earphone. He stepped on it again and tested it. He smiled. Now the phone worked as he had told the blackmailer, in case the person somehow requested to see and inspect the phone.

Using his personal cell, he texted Stan. "Call made. Gave them one hour. Waiting." He then texted Lynch. "Did as advised. Boss and Stan in the loop. Made call and pretended phone was broken. Waiting to hear back from blackmailer. Wish you were here."

Charity rarely felt flummoxed, but she faced a problem she had never foreseen. And she prided herself in being able to see all possible outcomes to her endeavors. Yet, she had been on that bus. The tension that had built up during the final 30 minutes of the trip, after folks started learning of the shooting, did lead to a stampede to get off the bus, just as Nichols had said. She hadn't lingered to watch him get the envelope, a move she now regretted.

She replayed the conversation in her mind. He sounded sincere in not wanting to cause trouble for the campaign. He also truly seemed to not hear her. Few could ignore someone else and keep talking without some minor hesitation. She sensed no hesitation, no indication that he had heard even a portion of what she had said.

She walked over to the room's small closet and pulled her suitcase from inside. Within it were a couple of extra burner phones. She had not used her personal cell phone and in this case, she had to avoid using it at all costs. The number she had programmed into the damaged cell phone led to a relay that called another burner phone in her possession. While traveling as they were, from campaign stop to campaign stop, that was the best she could do. One layer of protection that she could pick up and move in a hurry if necessary. In a more static environment, she might have had multiple relays.

She picked up a new phone and programmed it as she had the previous one. Now she had to figure out the best way to make a switch. Despite his apparent sincerity on the phone, she would not leave it at that. She would inspect the phone he'd been unable to use.

She grabbed her bag, placed the phone inside, and

went downstairs through the lobby to the business center. As expected, a flurry of activity hovered around the room as various journalists awaited their turns to use a computer or printer. She knew she had to be patient.

Twenty minutes later, she moved to one of the workstations and typed up a simple set of instructions. While waiting on the printer, which had multiple jobs in its queue, she leaned over and pretended to search through her bag on the floor. Instead, she grabbed the phone, peeled off the protective layer from the two-sided tape she had affixed to it previously, and as she sat up, she thrust it up and stuck it to the underside of the table.

The business center was a perfect drop, busy enough that anyone watching would never be able to label her or her actions as suspicious. She was but one of dozens of journalists covering the campaign and most, if not all of them, used the business center at least once a day.

She retrieved her printout before someone else could snatch it from the printer, folded it in thirds, and placed it in a motel envelope. Outside the room, she found a drinking fountain and used some water to dab the adhesive. No way would she lick the flap of the envelope to seal it and offer up her DNA to someone trying to find her.

She walked up to the front desk. Using one of their pens, she put Nichols' room number on it using simple block letters and numbers. She was about to place it on the desk for a clerk to discover but noticed the video camera to her right. No, she did not want to be seen leaving the envelope there on a video replay.

Instead, she retrieved a $20 bill from her purse and found a young bellhop.

"Do you think you could deliver something for me and

totally forget that I gave it to you? My colleagues and I want to play a prank on a competing network journalist."

She held up the envelope with the image of Andrew Jackson showing prominently on top of it.

"Yes, ma'am. I never saw you." He pocketed the bill, took the envelope, and headed toward the bank of elevators.

Charity smiled. She had other work to do now. After all, she still had to earn her paycheck from Al Jazeera.

Twenty-eight

Lynch knew that a major intersection of two state roads was ahead, so he pulled off into the lot of an abandoned gas station to plot his next move. Could he risk driving on and run smack into a checkpoint? No. He needed to find an alternative route.

Yet, he also needed to come up with a final route to get him back to the hotel where the Royal Family were guests, not just a way around one checkpoint. Once returned to and safe within their suite, he and Mack would remain with them until Prince Arthur's brother contacted them. Hopefully with good news, such as the flight crew and remaining Royal Protection officers had been fully and deeply vetted and found to be trustworthy. He doubted that would be the case.

He knew he could count on one close friend who would be in the loop regarding police activities and the search for the Royal Family. He waited for Mack to pull into the lot beside them.

Mack almost drove past them but turned at the last minute and pulled up next to them, driver's side to driver's side. Lynch rolled down his window.

"Sit tight. We need some intelligence on the police checkpoints and I know just the guy to call." Mack gave him a "thumbs up."

Lynch speed-dialed Seamus O'Connor.

"Lynch, you're a wanted man. Every police unit in four

states is on the lookout for you and the Royal Family. What are you up to?"

Lynch chuckled. "Well, hello to you, too."

"No, I'm serious, Lynch. There are even rumors that you've kidnapped the family."

Lynch shook his head. "I hope you're vouching for my good name." He put his thumb over the phone's mic and looked at Arthur. "Would you mind saying hello to police Sergeant Seamus O'Connor and reassuring him that I've not kidnapped you?"

Arthur smiled. "Most certainly."

Lynch clicked the phone to speaker mode.

"Sergeant O'Connor, it is indeed a pleasure to meet you. This is Arthur Windsor and I assure you that Lynch Cully has not kidnapped me or my family. Quite the opposite. He saved our lives and I have put my complete trust in him."

Silence. Just as Lynch had expected. He grinned as he wondered how long he should let O'Connor dangle. After 30 seconds, he continued.

"Shay, the Royal Protection team is still dirty. Well, we suspect one, maybe two, of those who lived through the shooting are. We have two names and we've come to the conclusion that The Assembly is behind all of the killing. No proof, as usual, but this has the fingerprints of Karolus Karling all over it. We've been discussing it while driving."

"Where. Are. You?"

"Someplace west of the city, and that's why I'm calling. I need some intel on the location of the checkpoints that are being set up. I'm trying to get the family back to their hotel. The prince's brother is working to secure the family's travel back home. Until then, I'm personally keeping watch over the family, along with one of my guys."

Silence again greeted him.

"Shay, I'm trusting your discretion. I need to keep them safe and I don't trust delivering them into the hands of the feds. If The Assembly is really behind this, then there may be FBI or Secret Service agents in on the plot, too."

Lynch heard a deep sigh on the other end. "You're killing me here, buddy. You're asking me to set aside my responsibilities as a police officer."

"Yeah, to do the *right* thing."

"Okay, okay. There are checkpoints at all major state highway intersections, and I mean all, between Fulton and St. Louis, Kansas City, and I-44 to the south. They've called on local jurisdictions to assist with checkpoints to the north and south, but those efforts are spotty right now. When you say you're west of the city, I don't know exactly what that means, but right now your best route to remain undetected is to get south of I-44 and approach the city from the south. Once you get inside the I-270 outer beltway, you're pretty much clear. They're trying to avoid major traffic issues in the cities."

"What about the Chesterfield area?"

"I was gonna bring that up. They have the area around the hotel and airport locked down. This hasn't made the news yet, but they discovered a makeshift bomb on the family's jet. All of the crew members are being interviewed and scrutinized, as well as the flight services folks at the airport."

Arthur's upbeat attitude of the morning dissolved at the reminder of the danger they still faced.

"Please, do not tell Helen of this."

Lynch nodded.

"Shay, I'm going to have to go to Plan B. Thanks for your help."

"Anytime. I think. Just don't tell me where you are or where you're going. It's better that I not know."

"Not a word, not a word, old friend. You know how to reach me if needed."

Lynch disconnected the call and pulled up the map app on his phone. He waved Mack over to join him and together they worked up a route using county roads to move south of the I-44 corridor, then east, and finally north into the city. The drive that would normally take two hours evolved into a five to six-hour journey. Lynch hoped they wouldn't have to stop for gas.

Their route decided, Lynch pulled out to take the lead again.

"Can we trust your friend?" asked Arthur.

"Beyond a doubt." He told Arthur about Seamus O'Connor, so that he could understand the type of man he was being asked to trust. He talked of his role in taking down a white supremacy group that had almost succeeded in its plan for global genocide. Arthur learned of the man's role in exposing Karolus Karling and The Assembly, and much, much more.

"So, this is how he became known as Famous Seamus, as you called him?"

"Yeah, but if you call him that, he'll know it came from me and I'll never hear the end of it."

Arthur smiled. "So, tell me, Lynch. Why are you doing this?"

"What?"

"This. Protecting my family and me. You could have taken us right to the Secret Service once the shooting was done. You would have been correct in doing so and you would have been able to get back to your own duties. I overheard part of a phone conversation you had. I know you have a friend in some kind of trouble. You could be there helping him. Instead, you're helping us."

Lynch thought about that. Why was he taking this task so seriously? Arthur was correct in that he could have turned them over to their protection detail and would have been done with it.

"Arthur, I don't know how you feel about religion, but—"

"As king, I will soon become the head of the Church of England. I have been raised in all the tenets of Christianity."

"Yes, sir, but do you know Christ as your personal Lord and Savior? There is a difference. I came to learn that not too long ago and since then, I believe I have felt the Lord urging me to do certain things. I know it sounds strange to say I can feel His presence or to say that He speaks to me, but He does that. He wants a personal relationship with each of us. Anyway, I feel that He is directing my steps and wants me to protect you to the best of my abilities."

Lynch glanced at Arthur. He felt *he* was still learning what it meant to be a Christian. As a result, he often balked at talking with others about it, but that timidity was fading. Here he was, after all, talking with the future head of the Church of England about Christ, and that leader now looked contemplative, not offended.

"I don't know why, but I feel that it is important that you remain alive and that I'm just one of God's instruments to make that happen."

Arthur said nothing and Lynch could not tell if his words had made an impact or not. Lynch drove on and nothing more was said for close to an hour. During that time, Lynch formulated his Plan B. Its success would depend on another set of good friends. It was time to give them a call.

"Hello."

"Hey, it's Lynch."

"Oh, thank God. Lynch, we've been worried about you. News of the shooting has been the only thing the media's been covering since yesterday. And now, with the Royal Family missing—"

"Yeah, about that. Do you have room for six?"

Again, the expected silence came.

"I hate to put you out, but I need a safe place for six and you two, with that big empty house, came to mind."

"You're kidding, right?"

Lynch could hear the bemusement in Mike Southworth's tone. The man thought Lynch was pranking him. Lynch said nothing.

"You're *not* kidding. Am I reading between the lines correctly here? Um, are we going to get into trouble?"

"Not at all. You'll love 'em. They're really a great family. I'll explain when we get there. If it's okay, that is. If you can hide us."

"Just don't tell me you're 15 minutes away. Mary will have a heart attack. We'll need at least an hour to clean the place up. She might have a heart attack anyway. I can't believe this is happening, but this is definitely God at work. Man, I've got something to tell *you* when you get here."

"We're roughly two hours away."

"Oh gosh, that puts it at supper time. Yep, she is going to go spastic, but don't worry, we'll have something thrown together for a meal."

Lynch laughed. He'd been there before to witness Mary getting frantic about a last-minute meal. And yet, she always pulled it off with grace and great food.

"I'll call to give you a 30 minute heads-up."

"Thanks. You know what I'll be doing for the next two hours."

They hung up and Lynch wished he had a video feed into the Southworth home to see what was happening right now.

"It's all set. I've got the perfect safe house for us."

"So, where are we going?" asked Arthur.

"Ferguson."

Arthur looked aghast. "Ferguson? *That* Ferguson?"

Twenty-nine

Richard wondered if his nerves would get the better of him. He had not been able to keep his focus on work during the afternoon. Stan understood and had stopped in several times to call him into an impromptu meeting that was nothing more than an excuse to give Richard some breathing room from his subordinates.

The boss' late afternoon speech had concluded, and their role in monitoring the social media response had begun to taper off. Thankfully, Richard now had the time to go to the hotel's business center.

"Here you go. It's all yours."

"Thanks, but I need that specific workstation there." He turned around to the person behind him. "Go ahead. I saved something on that specific computer and need to wait for it." He pointed to the table where he was to find the phone.

He began to get restless as he watched the woman still sitting at the computer he needed. He had seen her before but couldn't recall a specific place or time. Maybe she'd been on the bus with the other journalists. Maybe he'd simply seen her around the hotel. Right now, he just wanted her to move along. *What's she writing, a novel?*

Fifteen more minutes elapsed. He passed up two other workstations. Ten minutes later, the woman gathered up her bag from the floor and left, smiling at him as she walked by.

Finally! He sat down and logged onto the system. He

placed a flash drive into a USB port and pretended to download a file, while his right hand fished around under the table. *There it is.* He tugged at the device, but it remained stuck in place. Using his finger, he pried it part way from the table's underside and was then able to pull it free and let it drop into his hand. He slid it into his pants pocket. Glancing around, he saw that no one seemed to notice.

He pulled the flash drive free and logged off the computer. He smiled at the next person in line. "All yours."

He wanted to run to the elevators but forced himself to walk and remain inconspicuous. He felt as if someone was watching him. He had no doubts that the blackmailer was a guest at the hotel. No one else could have sent him the instructions he had received earlier in the day so expediently. Plus, the person had used a hotel envelope. While that in itself wasn't proof, it sure pointed toward a guest as the culprit.

As he walked through the lobby toward the elevator bank, he saw Summer Stanton heading his way. Even though she had agreed on their plan, he felt awkward around her and wanted no one to have an opportunity to photograph them together or even in close proximity to each other. He veered to the right. He saw her swerve to the left and wondered if she'd had the same thought.

Waiting at the elevator, he looked about and scrutinized those around him. They all seemed intent on their own business. Was one of them his tormentor?

The elevator chimed and the door opened. He started to enter and realized he still needed to perform act two of his instructions. Flustered, he turned and walked into the hotel's atrium. Sitting on a designated bench near some semi-tropical plantings, he eased the damaged phone from his left pants pocket. He glanced around, as well as up to scan the balconies around the atrium. No one watched him, so he moved his hand behind the plant in the pot next to him and hid the broken phone there.

Now, he was to enter the elevator and go straight to his room. Act three would take place there when he called the pre-programmed number on the new phone.

The elevator waited for him this time. Several people had boarded the car by the time he walked in. He noticed the petite woman from the business center, the novelist, as he had called her in his mind. She was unassuming. Quite average actually. And she showed no interest in him, or even a hint of recognition. He looked at the others. Maybe the perpetrator was one of them.

Charity stood less than three feet from Richard Nichols as they rode together in the elevator. She ignored him.

Yet, inside she gloated. She had relished tying up the workstation in the business center and watching him begin to sweat. She had observed him scoping out everyone around him, no doubt wondering if one of them was behind his trouble. She thought that to be a good assumption. Human nature was, well, human. Under the circumstances, anyone would question those surrounding him.

He hadn't even noticed her. She had watched his every move in the atrium and he had looked right past her. Even on the elevator, he had paid her but a cursory glance.

She loved her anonymity. That—and her innate intelligence—were what made her so good at her "job."

She rode the elevator one floor beyond Nichols, exited the car, and caught the next descending car. She walked about the atrium, observing the flora, taking pictures of the Bird-of-Paradise in bloom with her cell phone. When she came to the planting where Nichols had ditched the damaged phone, she circled around it, looking at the mandevilla vine in bloom through the eye of her camera. She picked off two dead leaves and checked her camera again. This time, while removing a little more dead foliage, she grabbed the phone and stuffed it down the front of her blouse while still bending over the plant. Then she snapped her photo and worked her way to the next flowers.

She stopped at the bar and ordered a glass of red wine. With glass in hand, she retreated to her room. Once inside, she placed the glass on the table and removed the phone from her blouse. It appeared as Nichols had stated. Using another phone, she tested it. It functioned as he had stated. Satisfied that she had him on the hook, she sat on the couch with her wine, and awaited his call.

Richard felt a sense of relief once he slipped into his room. He had retrieved the phone and ditched the broken one without stumbling. True, he still had the call to make, but now he had moral reinforcements.

"Got it," he said, holding up the phone.

Mike Jurgesmeyer looked up from his work. One corner of Richard's front room looked as if the NSA had taken over. Two desktop computers and a laptop, along with four monitors, a scanner, and equipment that Richard could never begin to identify had been set up in his absence.

Mike smiled and stood up. Richard, at six-foot-two, still had to look up at the man and marveled at the guy's ability to grow a ponytail to the middle of his back. Lynch had once told him of his friend's appearance, as well as his genius. The first part was as advertised. He hoped the second area was as well.

Mike held out his hand for the phone. "How much time we got?"

Richard handed him the phone. "I'm to call at seven pm, according to the time on the phone itself."

Mike powered on the device and inspected it. "We've got plenty of time then. Let me show you what I've been up to so far." He walked back to his makeshift computer lab. "I took a close look at the photos you received. Whoever did this is an expert with Photoshop. And he took his time doing it. That's what it takes to get a cut-and-paste job to look real. He adjusted the margins pixel by pixel but even the best can miss things. This guy did, too. I found several areas along your hair where he missed some pixels. Makes it obvious that it's a cut and paste job."

"So, we're good then. We can prove it was doctored, a lie."

"In a court of law where I might be credentialed as an expert witness, I could make that case. But, in the court of public opinion, I think we need more. Here's what I'm doing. I took two each of the bedroom and Afghanistan photos and scanned them into my system. I then selected portions of each photo as objects for a search, kinda like doing facial recognition. My software then took each area, turned it into the mathematical model that would be stored on a computer, and has started searching websites on both the worldwide web and deep web. With a little, no, make that a lot of luck, we might find the original images that were used."

That sounded good to Richard.

"Okay, so if we luck out, then we can at least short circuit this blackmailer's plan. But, how do we catch him?"

Mike's look turned more somber. "That's the hard part. I've been thinking about that as I worked, trying to get my head into this person's. At the minimum, he would have to have been in St. Louis and in close proximity to you, in order to know that you were on that bus and to give the driver the envelope for you. To have orchestrated this phone switch, the odds are good this person is here, with the campaign, and not calling the shots from afar. Too many things could go wrong trying to get a hireling to make such a switch without calling attention to himself. Better to do it himself."

"That makes sense. I've been thinking the same thing and watching people to see if they're watching me."

Mike shrugged. "He, or they, won't be so obvious. He might actually *be* watching you, but you'll never see him. This is a pro." Mike plugged a USB cable into the phone and connected it to one of his computers. "So, my next question is, how would a pro handle this phone call? The voice distortion you mentioned would seem to be a given. Yet, what about the phone call itself? Too easy to trace a call these days, so there are going to be layers of separation. But how many? Will the call go through one relay or more than one? I'm betting on just one or two if this person is here and following the campaign. They'd have to be portable."

Richard saw some logic to that but wasn't convinced. "Why couldn't he have relays set up elsewhere? He could have them anywhere in the country."

"He could, but what if he had to make a last-minute programming change? Like when you faked the broken phone. What if a relay system went out? Or the relay phone's battery died? Or the local power went out? No, I suspect he wants the system close by and portable, for easy maintenance."

That made sense to Richard. "So, back to my original question, how do we catch him?"

"Eating the elephant one bite at a time."

Richard furrowed his brow in confusion. "Huh?"

"We need to track each step in the relay. But, in the end, I don't think we want to *catch* him. Not just yet."

That wasn't what Richard had in mind. He wanted this person exposed, prosecuted, and gone from his life.

"We want to track the person down and then move to whoever hired him. We want the big fish. If The Assembly is behind this, we want proof. And here's how we're going to do that." He went on to explain.

Thirty

Lynch and Mack had closed ranks as they drove north into the city. That had been a fortuitous move, as they witnessed a new roadblock go into effect and begin stopping cars just moments after they passed that point on the highway. Had Mack been lagging behind, as he had been earlier, they would have been stopped.

Twenty-two minutes after that near miss, Lynch pulled into the parking lot of their old campaign headquarters.

"This doesn't look much like the Ferguson on the news," said Arthur.

Lynch glanced at the building under reconstruction. "It's not, but a few months ago, it might have looked the part. This used to be our campaign headquarters until The Assembly planted a bomb here."

Lynch pulled a key ring from his jacket pocket. He crossed his fingers that he'd grabbed the correct set from the glove compartment of his SUV back in Fulton.

"We still keep some of the campaign vehicles on the lot here and I guessed right that the feds didn't think to watch this place. Anyway, I thought it best to change cars. We can all finish the trip in one car."

As he opened the door, the prince started to do the same.

"Sir, not just yet, please. I need to make sure I have the right keys and then I'll move the car closer. The less exposure you have the smaller chance we have of someone recognizing you."

Arthur nodded and closed his door. Lynch stepped up to Mack's window, and he responded by lowering it.

"What's up?"

"I'm gonna get one of the spare campaign vehicles and we'll put the family together for the trip to the safe house. I want you to ditch these cars, get 'em back to wherever they came from." Mack looked upset. "Something wrong?"

"Uh, guess not. Just figured you'd need my help."

"I can manage from this point. Call me when you've finished and I'll let you know what you can do to help next."

Mack gave a mock salute with two fingers.

Lynch walked to the nearest Traverse and tried the keys. No good. He had the same results with the second. Three more vehicles to go. The keys had to work on one of them or they'd be stuck with the current cars, cars that had been useful and reliable, but cars he didn't know anything about. Had they not been procured by Mack, he never would have used them.

Fourth car. Success. And with a full gas tank, too.

Within minutes, the Royal Family was together in the vehicle, with car seats secured, and Lynch headed toward Ferguson.

Nigel recalled little of his trip from the lake to the hospital, other than the helicopter ride had been a bit rough. Throughout the trip, the paramedic's emphasis had been on warming him and, after his dip in the lake, he relished that warmth. The fact that his "swim" might have been fatal was not lost on him. Indeed, it was that very risk that would make his story convincing.

"Mr. Barrington, your X-rays look fine and your labs are normal. We're going to move you to a room shortly." The Emergency Room physician smiled as he thumbed through the chart in his hands. "You're very fortunate they found you when they did. Do you have any questions?"

"When can I leave?"

"Well, we'd like to watch you overnight. Your body temperature is still a little low. Your superiors have also asked that we watch you for that time. So, if all goes well, you'll get to leave in the morning."

His superiors. Did that mean Chelmsford was there, waiting? Probably. Along with who-knows-who else. He needed to finalize his story in his head.

A short while later, before he even had the chance to order some hot tea in his new room, he heard a knock at his door. He figured he was as ready as he'd ever be.

"Come in," he said.

Chelmsford and two other men entered the room. A nurse followed, holding a chair, and the three men sat around his bed, Chelmsford closest to his head.

"How ya feelin', Nigel?"

"Been worse. Ready to leave, if you'll take me." He didn't want to seem overeager.

"Tomorrow morning. Besides your body temperature, the doctors want to make sure that shoulder wound hasn't been infected."

"Officer Barrington, I'm Assistant Director David Lloyd, with the FBI, and this is Special Agent-in-Charge Chad Warren, from Jefferson City, the state capital. We'd like to know what happened."

Nigel had decided on the strategy that least would be best. He shook his head.

"I would like to know that as well. It took Agent Muntz some time to find the address we were looking for. When we did, the gate was locked and no one answered the intercom. We were waiting for a warrant to access the property and my shoulder was feeling stiff and sore. I thought maybe getting out of the car and walking a little might help. Next thing I know I was hit on the head. I vaguely remember hearing a gunshot and being dragged someplace. The next thing I recall is incredible cold and then being on a boat. How is Agent Muntz?"

The three men exchanged glances. Chelmsford answered. "He's dead. Shot in the head through the car window."

Nigel appeared saddened and proceeded to claim ignorance of the answers to their additional questions. But he had a question of his own.

"Harvey, where do things stand? Have you found the family?"

Chelmsford shook his head. He appeared emotionally drained. "No. No sign of 'em in Fulton. We haven't a clue where they might be. No one has come forward with anything about them, no ransom demand, nothing. The State Highway Patrol and local police departments statewide have established checkpoints to examine vehicles. Airports are locked down. We're moving our team back to St. Louis in the morning. You'll be coming along with us."

Nigel tried to match Chelmsford's mood externally, while inside he rejoiced that he'd have yet another opportunity to complete his task.

Waiting at a stop light at the end of the interstate exit ramp, he texted the Southworths about their pending arrival. The plan, to Mary Southworth's great dismay, was to have him park in the garage and enter through their laundry room, into the kitchen, allowing the family to enter their home unseen by neighbors' eyes. Mike had relayed that she was aghast at having the future king and his family come to her home that way. She was frantic enough at just the thought of the visit.

However, the trip had taken longer than anticipated and the sun would be setting soon enough. Perhaps Lynch would be able to spare Mary.

"I saw on a sign that historic Ferguson is one mile ahead. Are they claiming a spot in history because of what happened there?"

Arthur seemed appalled at the concept. Lynch agreed. That would not be right.

"No. I think most residents hope that event never makes it to the history books. Ferguson is over 120 years old and was one of the first suburbs of St. Louis. Residents would take a train into the city to go to work. The train station, one of the elementary schools, and several other buildings are on the U.S. Register of Historic Places. It's a beautiful small town that was descended upon by a media eager to create news, not just report it. Tell you what. There's still some light. Let me give you a quick tour."

Princess Helen shook her head. "No, no. That's not necessary."

"Helen, if you're worried about your safety, I can assure you, we'll be fine."

He continued down the main road, past the police station, and then east toward the area that had been damaged. A few buildings remained in disrepair, but the vast majority of the damaged buildings had been removed, leaving empty lots. Lynch pointed out the locations of some of the "highlights" of the turmoil.

Arthur looked from side to side as Lynch drove. "This is all? The international news made it seem as if the whole city was on fire. Why, this covers what, maybe half a kilometer?"

"That's right. Ninety-five percent of the agitators were bused in from across the country, and they were egged on by the media to give their cameras something exciting to cover. Now, let me show you the side of Ferguson the media refused to reveal."

Lynch drove them through calm, tree-lined streets of small homes and then into the historic district with beautiful century-old homes on large lots, churches, and small businesses in equally old storefronts. He pulled in front of one large, two-and-a-half-story home, set back from the street, and said, "And this is where you'll be staying."

"These homes are lovely, Lynch."

The last light of dusk now faded and Lynch saw no one outside. He pulled into the driveway and parked. "I think it's safe to use the front door. Follow me." He assisted them with young Princess Amelia and led them along a brick walk toward the front.

Helen looked at Arthur. "Dear, look at these gardens. They even have the plants labeled. I think this would be a delightful place to visit in the summer."

"Perhaps," he replied.

They walked up a short flight of concrete steps to a broad, covered front porch. Lynch looked at Helen. "The garden is incredible at full bloom and sitting here on this porch, sipping a drink while enjoying the color is a relaxing and wonderful experience."

He rang the bell and the door flew open. Lynch stopped Mary in the doorway and led them all back inside. The last thing he needed was a neighbor seeing Mary curtsying to her visitors.

"Welcome. Please come in. Welcome." Mary curtsied again. Mike joined them and bowed.

Lynch spoke up. "Your Royal Highnesses, this is Michael and Mary Southworth, your hosts until we get things settled. Mike, Mary, this is Arthur, Prince of Wales and his wife, Helen, the Princess of Wales. And these little nippers are Prince Albert and Princess Amelia."

Mary began to curtsy again, but Arthur stopped her. "Please, don't hurt yourself. Under the circumstance that is not necessary."

"I-I'm sorry, Your Royal Highness. I haven't a clue how to act around royalty. I—"

Arthur stopped her by raising his hand. "And please, call me Arthur and my wife, Helen. We cannot begin to thank you for opening up your home to us."

Helen nodded. "Oh yes. Not only have you opened your home to us but at some danger, too. We very much appreciate your assistance."

Mike placed his arm around Mary's shoulders and chuckled. "Seems that danger has become a given, ever since we met this man." He pointed to Lynch. "Perhaps later, I can show you the bullet holes near the front door from the last time Lynch brought us guests."

Arthur's and Helen's eyes widened.

"That's true," said Mary. "Each time Lynch calls and

says he's bringing us guests, we wonder if we should invest in Kevlar body armor."

Lynch protested. "Hey! Remember that *I* was first brought here as a guest, too."

Mike laughed and Arthur joined him. "It would seem that you might have some stories to entertain us while we're here. I look forward to that."

Mary took control. "Please, let me show you around. Dinner will be ready shortly."

"You are most generous," replied Helen.

As Mary led them into the library, Lynch's cell phone rang. Expecting it to be Mack, he was surprised to see the caller ID reveal that it was Zach. He retreated to the front porch to take the call.

"What's up, Zach? Is there a problem?"

"Yeah. Like, isn't there always some problem?"

"The boss?"

"No, no. Graham's just fine. Grapevine tells me something is going on with Richard Nichols, but I've not been privy to any of that."

"I'm aware of the problem. I sent someone there to help."

"Yeah, I believe that someone is here. Is Mack there with you?"

Lynch wondered where this was going. It wasn't like Zach to take the indirect approach.

"No, he's dealing with the vehicles we used to get away. Why?"

"Don't trust him. I don't think he's the real Desmond Macklemore Gilman."

Alarms blared inside Lynch's head. How could he have missed something like that? But then, how would he have caught the lie? The man's credentials had checked out.

"What?"

"Yeah, I don't think that's the real guy. Look, remember how you wanted to know why we got so buddy-buddy during the Fulton trip. You entrusted me with Graham's safety after I told you I was not just a SEAL but a member of DEVGRU."

DEVGRU, Seal Team 6. It had, indeed, been that revelation that gave Lynch the assurance that he was leaving his boss in capable hands.

"I had to get permission to tell you anything more. What I'm about to tell you stays with us. Got that?" He didn't wait for Lynch to respond. "Desmond 'Mack' Gilman wasn't just Special Forces, either. He was Delta Force. His squad was on a mission in the mountains of northeast Afghanistan when they got pinned down and surrounded. My team was sent in to help. It became like a game of leap frog with each squad helping the other until we were all clear. My call sign was Zombie 10, like I said. And Gilman's was Ghost Rider. His last call to me was 'Zombie 10, this is Ghost Rider. We're clear.' The wild thing was, none of us ever met in person. We only knew each other by our call signs, so when he reacted as he did when I mentioned my call sign a few days ago and quoted that last message from our joint mission, I thought for sure I'd met the ghost who helped keep my team and me alive, while we did the same for them."

At first, Lynch marveled at the thought that he'd hired two of the military's foremost warriors to work for him. But as Zach's story continued, he realized that maybe he hadn't.

"And now?" Lynch asked.

"As I said, I had to get permission to tell you what I just told you. When I was doing that, they informed me that

Mack Gilman was presumed dead. His car went off an icy road in Minnesota two years ago and into a river. They retrieved the car, but no body was ever found. I had my contact send me a personnel photo of Gilman. It's a bit dated obviously, and there is some resemblance, but I don't think our 'Mack' is the real Mack Gilman."

Thirty-one

Amy stood on her back patio, warming her hands near the fire that blazed in her grill. It had taken a few attempts to get a fire started in the cold, but now those photos burned as if they had been doused with gasoline.

She thought that eliminating them would help, but the images seemed seared into her brain. Yes, against her father's advice she had looked at them all. She had told herself that she was looking for something, anything, that could convince her that the man in the images wasn't Richard.

But who was she fooling? She had remained chaste and would remain so until their wedding night. Other than seeing him in swimming trunks only twice the previous summer and occasionally in shorts, she had no intimate knowledge of his body that she could use to compare to the man in the photos. The height, build, and general physique were close enough for a match.

She stirred the papers to ensure they all burned. The flames surged briefly again.

And who was she kidding? How many women had she seen over the years in the Emergency Room who had believed their boyfriends or husbands, only to discover the truth? She *wanted* to believe Richard. Yet, did she? She felt as if she was in a cartoon, with a little angel in white on one shoulder telling her one thing, while the little devil in red sat on the other shoulder giving her a conflicting story.

The only way she'd know the truth was to see it in Richard's eyes.

Richard sat on the bed in his room and took a deep breath. There would be no pretending, no ruse involved this time. He looked across the room at Mike Jurgesmeyer, who nodded and gave him a thumb up.

He took one more deep breath and glanced at the clock on the phone's display. Show time.

He pressed the speed dial key for the sole number that the blackmailer had pre-programmed into the phone. It rang three times before someone picked up.

"Good. I like that you are punctual."

Again, the creepy mechanical voice made it impossible to tell if a man or woman had answered.

"I've done as you asked so far. We both know that isn't me in any of those pictures. I doubt that's Summer Stanton, too. So, why us, and what do you want?"

"The why is unimportant. And how far will your protests of innocence go in the court of public opinion? You can avoid all of that by providing me with information."

Mike gave Richard the hand signal to keep the person talking.

"W-what kind of information?"

"I want the names and demographics of *all* of your donors and I want advance notice of major policy speeches and your planned campaign stops."

Richard was incredulous. This person wanted him to be a mole inside the campaign. Even worse, he wasn't in a position to have that information. Now anger swelled within him.

"That's all? Check our FEC filings and try the calendar on our website. Besides, I don't work in either of those areas. I don't have access to donor names."

"Then get access. I want *all* names, not just those required to be reported by law. And I want event plans *before* they're posted on the website."

"You don't understand. I don't have *access* to donor information or anything financial. I work in Washington. That office is in St. Louis. It's not like I can just ask for that data and have it given to me. It's like the need-to-know basis in government security clearances. I have no need to know that information."

Mike gave him a thumb up. He had located the phone.

"You have 48 hours to figure that out. Call me again in two days, same time, to arrange the drop. I want it on a flash drive."

The person hung up.

After entertaining guests for the early evening, Karolus sat down for dinner in the kitchen, rather than his customary place in the dining room. The cook had a sick child and had been discharged earlier in the day but not before preparing his evening meal and placing it in the oven to stay warm.

With a glass of wine paired to the chicken cordon-bleu, he reminisced over pleasant times eating in the kitchen with his favorite tutor while growing up. Those times had been rare, but he found the casual atmosphere a delightful change to the formal meals he had with his parents . . . when they were at home and not overseas on some political or business foray. Even in their usual absence he had been expected to maintain the formality of separation from the servants. He was, after all, being groomed for a dominant global position, a position he now held.

Francois entered the kitchen. "Sir, a phone call for you. As requested, I've been screening your calls and this one is important."

"Thank you, Francois." He didn't know what he would do without his aide. The man was as diligent in his duties as he was a stickler for details.

"It's Mr. Avery, sir."

Indeed, any call from Wallace Avery was important. The man was his biggest supporter on the Executive Council and his confidential ear for news within The Assembly.

"Good evening, Wallace. It is a pleasure to hear your voice."

"And yours, my old friend. I hope you are doing well."

"Personally, never better. There have been a few setbacks in our mutual business, however. They are under control."

"I'm happy to hear that because I'm hearing some voices of dissatisfaction among our colleagues. We lost some good men."

"We did, and I am still waiting to learn how that happened. Our two remaining men on the ground are to deal with the family first. Then, they shall be debriefed as to what went wrong."

"You might wish to get that information sooner, my friend. Questions are being asked."

Karolus thought about that. If Wallace Avery considered that important enough to call on a Sunday evening, he should take that as a special advisement.

"These must be more than whispers you're hearing, Wallace, if you felt compelled to call. I will take heed to your advice. Thank you. Perhaps we shall get together soon for a fine meal and your favorite brandy, and discuss old times."

After a few more pleasantries, Karolus ended the call. Francois was there to take the phone.

"Francois, see if you can track down Nigel Barrington."

"Sir, he's in a hospital in Central Missouri at the moment. I've been keeping tabs on him, as well as Ms. Charity." He proceeded to inform Karolus of the death of the FBI agent and near drowning of Barrington.

"And the family remains missing, I assume, or I would have heard about their fate, one way or the other."

"Yes, sir. From the fact that this latest incident occurred at the lake home of Bradley Graham, I believe they suspected that Graham's missing security chief might have been hiding the family there."

Karolus nodded. His aide's deduction was sound. And yet, the mention of Graham and that security chief, Lynch Cully, brought a flush of anger from deep within. Usually able to compartmentalize his emotions, he found it difficult with these two. They alone were responsible for his great embarrassment and had made him look weak. He blamed them for his failure to economically bring down the United States.

"When Barrington is available, I need to talk with him firsthand. And our other remaining asset there?"

"Still in play, sir, as the failsafe."

Karolus had learned one thing from the fracas with Abdul Aleem Malik Fawaz that had led to his defeat by Graham and Cully. He had relied on one man that time. Never again.

"Excellent. Please get hold of Charity Lovelace."

"Yes, sir. It might be half an hour, though. I believe she is in the middle of business."

"That will do. We don't wish to interrupt her. I'll be here, in the kitchen, awhile longer. Then I will retire to my study."

"Very good, sir."

His meal had cooled during the delay, so he placed the dish in the microwave and stood there. He realized he had never been called on to use the machine and he had no idea what to do. As he studied the various options on the control panel, he felt a presence at his side.

"Allow me, sir." Francois had re-entered the kitchen and now prepared to warm his meal. "Thirty-seconds should suffice. This button . . ." He pressed one labeled **Add 30**. ". . . will do it."

"Thank you, Francois." Again, he wondered what he would do without Francois as his aide. "I think I can take it from here."

Francois offered a subtle bow and left the room. Forty minutes later, Francois appeared at the door of his study, where Karolus sat sipping his second glass of wine while reviewing a brief from the U.N.'s Human Rights Commission. The man pointed to the phone.

"Ms. Charity, sir."

Charity hung up the phone and took another bite of her room service dinner. She gazed off in the direction of Nichol's room and wished she had placed a remote video feed from it. She imagined him squirming. Nothing like being asked to do the near impossible while having a

Sword of Damocles dangling over your head.

She had made a request that was nearly impossible in order to best fit her plans. If he actually came through with the information, that would indicate to her that at least one more person in the campaign was capable of being swayed. She could then focus on that indiscretion to further penetrate the organization and begin to wield some influence on them. If he failed, well, the embarrassment and distraction to the campaign in general would prove overwhelming as the media picked them apart.

As she finished her salad, her cell phone rang. A glance at the Caller ID motivated her to pick up without hesitation.

"Good evening, Director. I wasn't expecting a call."

"Yes, well, remind me, should I ever call when you *are* expecting it."

Charity nodded. The man did have a penchant for calling unannounced. Yet, to call him unannounced, or worse, to fail to call him when he expected your call, look out.

"So, please tell me you have good news for me."

"Am I correct in reading behind that statement that you have received bad news?" She rarely questioned the Director, but if he had bad news that might affect her plan, she needed to know.

"Astute as always, Charity. And yes, the day has been full of bad news. The Prince of Wales and his family still live. Bradley Graham and Lynch Cully still live as well. Six of my eight operatives in Fulton were killed. So, again, please tell me something good."

"Sir, I thought you wanted plausible deniability about my plan to penetrate the campaign."

"I changed my mind."

She proceeded to inform him about her blackmailing of Richard Nichols and of her progress so far. She had promised the Director someone on the inside of the campaign. She would deliver on that promise.

"This had better not backfire, Charity."

"Have I ever let you down before, Director?"

"No, you haven't. I do have one question, why these two people?"

She reflected on his question. Nichols had asked the same thing, why him, why Summer Stanton?

"You asked me to get you someone on the inside. To me, that implied keeping Graham alive. So, I was a little surprised to hear your lament about the man still being alive. If you wish me to change the goal, I can do that."

"When we last talked, seeing Graham in someone's cross-hairs wasn't in the equation. An opportunity came up. But you're not answering my question. To me, Nichols is as good as anyone in the campaign. Stanton, however, is one of ours. She follows our drumbeat."

"Nichols was the easy choice inside the campaign. He's part of the inner circle. Served in Afghanistan. Has a long-distance relationship with his fiancée. His position is such that he's going to have to solicit help to get the information and that gets at least one other person on our hook. Or, he gets thrown to the wolves."

She wasn't quite sure how to answer about Summer Stanton. She couldn't yet admit to herself that she was jealous of the woman's great body, flawless hair, faultless skin, perfect teeth, and position with a wonderful news organization.

"As for Stanton, I needed someone who covers the campaign, travels with it, and was a likely candidate for

Nichol's advances. Would a stud like that go for a Dowd or Crowley?"

The Director actually laughed. She didn't think he knew how. At least she bypassed that sticky question well.

"No, I could not. Too old for him. Very well. Keep me posted."

He disconnected before she could say, "Yes, sir."

She took her glass of wine to the sofa and sat down to enjoy it. She felt pleased that she remained in favor with the Director. And yet, his unexpected call had been a distraction. She remembered that she needed to move her relay phone.

Thirty-two

"C'mon, we need to hurry. If this person is smart, he is going to want to move the relay ASAP. I need to access the phone before that happens." Mike grabbed a laptop and a couple of cables and urged Richard toward the door.

Richard still sat on the bed, stunned at the magnitude of what this person wanted.

"You heard what he wanted, didn't you? I can't believe it. This is, well, like the IRS releasing the names of members of conservative groups to its favored liberal groups. They could use this information to derail the campaign, intimidate donors to the point they'll never donate to a conservative again."

"Yeah, I heard. I have an idea to deal with that. Later though. We need to find this relay."

Mike stood at the door, tapping a foot on the carpet. Richard stood and, after checking to make sure he had his key, joined him.

"Like I thought, the relay's in the hotel. I took the opportunity earlier to place some relays of my own around the building. Kinda like mini cell towers. They helped me triangulate the phone's signal."

Together they rode the elevator to the second floor, where the conference rooms and a ballroom were located. Outside the ballroom, Mike opened his laptop and checked his screen.

"Not the ballroom. Someplace off to our left."

Richard saw a guide to the floor plan on the wall to his left.

"This guide says there are two small meeting rooms over here. Oh, and a coat room. Nothing's scheduled for either room today."

They hurried toward a sitting area just outside the rooms. Mike referenced the software on his computer again. "We're closer, but it's somewhere to our right now."

Richard saw only the coat room to his right. "Must be in there."

Mike nodded. "Let's check it out, but we need to be fast and thorough. The guy could show up at any moment, and he'll recognize you right off the bat."

The coat room was roughly a ten-by-twenty-foot space with little in it other than metal racks and hangers. They each took a row and inspected the racks. There was no place to hide anything within the frames themselves, but Richard noticed a coat hanging up at the end of the rack that Mike was inspecting.

"That must be it." He pointed. "In that coat."

Mike nodded, but after scrutinizing the garment, said, "Nope. Not in there."

At the far end of the room, they saw half a dozen metal folding chairs and headed toward them. Richard felt more confident that they'd find them there. He was wrong, again.

"Nothing there either."

Mike used his software one more time. "We should be right on it. I can't get us any closer than this."

They double-checked the room on their way to the door and had the same results. Outside in the hall, Mike re-checked the floor plan to see if they were missing a space. Richard walked along the hall looking for additional doors.

Perhaps there was a service hallway behind the meeting rooms. If so, he saw no access to such. On his way back toward Mike, he noted a cabinet marked "Fire." On a quick glance, he saw the fire extinguisher but he felt drawn to look closer.

"Mike, over here." He started to open the door, but Mike stopped him.

"Wait a second. Check it for any tells."

"Tells?"

Mike pointed toward the cabinet door. "Like this one." He pulled a single strand of hair off the face of the cabinet. "One of the oldest in the book. You take a hair, moisten it, and lay it across the gap between the door and the frame, so it sticks to both sides of the gap. If it's still there when you come back, no one has bothered your cache. If it's gone, someone has opened the door. Here, hold this." He handed Richard the hair, opened the door, and retrieved a cell phone. An iPhone 6 and it was active.

"Don't you need the PIN to access it?"

"Not for my special app." He grinned.

He connected the appropriate cord to the phone's charge port and then to his laptop's USB port. With a couple of keystrokes, he watched the screen for a few seconds and then disconnected the phone. He returned it to the cabinet, closed the door, and replaced the hair where he'd found it.

"Okay, let's skedaddle. Take those stairs over there."

"The stairs? My room's ten flights up."

"Yeah, I can use the cardio."

Just then, they both heard the ping of the elevator stopping on the floor and ran for the stairwell door.

*   *   *

Amy paced across the floor of her kitchen. After checking her schedule, she decided she would have to take the time off. She had plenty of accrued vacation days, but she was saving them for a honeymoon. Of course, if she didn't take this time off to see Richard and clear up her concerns, there would be no wedding. Plus, her mind would be in a state of constant distraction at work. Yes, she needed to take the time off and go to Kansas City. She could think of no reason why her boss would refuse her request.

She speed-dialed his cell phone.

"Amy? Are you okay? You weren't scheduled for any flights today, were you? Or, do I need to bail you out?"

She frowned. Ever since her accident in Illinois and her time in county lock-up for "housing" a fugitive, he never passed on an opportunity to give her grief about it. But then, even the pilots ribbed her about being on both helicopters that had gone down in MedAir's corporate history, and that maybe she wanted to fly with someone else. She knew it to be friendly jesting, and yet . . .

"Okay, Craig, that was almost two years ago now. The joke's getting stale."

"You're right, but you *are* calling me on a Sunday evening. So, if there's no emergency, what's up?"

He had a point.

"I'd like to take two days of vacation, tomorrow and Tuesday. I need your approval, and I didn't want to leave town tonight, only to have you turn me down in the morning had I waited 'til then to call."

"What's your schedule like? We do have a corporate staff meeting on Wednesday. So, you would need to be back for that."

"No problem. Richard surprised me by coming into

town, but he had to leave to meet up with the campaign in Kansas City. They'll be there three more days, and I want to surprise him. I know he's going to be busy, so I'll take my paperwork with me and work in the hotel when I can't be with him. And if something comes up where you really need me, I can be back here in a few hours, less if I commandeer one of our aircraft."

He laughed, as she had expected he would. Not even the CEO could "commandeer" an aircraft and remove it from its service area without leaping over tall mountains and promising gold to the air crew.

"Sure, consider it approved. And tell ol' Thor I said hi."

They talked business for a few more minutes and then Amy rushed to her bedroom, packed her overnight bag, and headed for the garage. She would be in Kansas City before midnight.

Thirty-three

Lynch paced a circle through the library, dining room and front hall of the Southworth home. This path had seen his pacing several times before. The movement felt familiar and the mindless loop allowed him to think.

A presence blocked his way in the doorway between the library and dining room.

"Arthur. I-I expected you to be resting with your family."

"The children are asleep, and Helen wishes to stay with them. I, on the other hand, need a drink."

Lynch pointed toward the kitchen. "Coffee and tea are in the butler's pantry. Iced tea, water, and soft drinks are in the kitchen. What can I get for you?"

"No, no." He pointed to a chest in the corner of the room. "I believe that is the bar, is it not? Would our hosts mind?"

Lynch laughed. "You know, I think I could use an adult drink, too. And no, they would never mind. In fact, they'd be offering it to you themselves if they hadn't gone out for groceries."

Arthur walked to the old chest and lifted the lid. He picked up a couple of bottles and inspected the labels. "We must apologize to them for the inconvenience."

"Trust me. We'll be hearing about your visit here for years to come. It is no inconvenience for them."

Arthur picked up another bottle and closed the lid.

"Yes, this will do just fine." He showed Lynch the label. Lamphroaig Single Malt Scotch Whiskey. "He has good taste in scotch."

"Neat or on the rocks? I'll get two glasses."

"Neat for me."

Lynch returned a minute later with one empty short glass and one with two ice cubes. "If you're pouring, two fingers for me, please."

Arthur poured and the two men sat down on the chairs adjacent to the fireplace. At Arthur's urging, Lynch told him about meeting the Southworths and told of their role in helping to bring down a human trafficking ring.

"That is a cause I am quite passionate about, as is Helen. I must say, I now feel honored to be staying here. These people are an amazing couple, from what you're telling me."

"They are. Generous. Caring. Godly, above everything else. I have been blessed to call them friends. Mike is also quite the trove of interesting information about the Bible, too. Sometimes, Mary has to calm him down and bring him back to earth."

The look on Arthur's face became serious.

"Tell me, Lynch, you were pacing when I interrupted you. Is there a problem?"

"I'm not sure yet." He informed the prince about his phone call from Zach.

"Zach is the one you left to protect Mr. Graham in the museum, correct?"

Lynch nodded.

"How well do you know *him*?"

"That's just it. I don't know him any better than I do Mack. They are both recently hired and both passed our security checks."

"Yes, and we've seen how well such scrutiny works. Or look at how a normally peaceful man can one day suddenly turn into a homegrown terrorist."

Lynch knew the prince referred to his own protection detail. And how many mass shooters, such as Syed Rizwan Farook in San Bernardino, had normal lives until something, or someone, turned them?

"True, but if Mack is working for The Assembly as a hit man, why are we all still alive? He had multiple opportunities to kill us all. He had the element of surprise on his side. He could have killed your family anywhere along the line and taken out both of us at any one of our stops. Something doesn't add up."

"Perhaps it is Zach you should be wary of."

Lynch savored his sip of scotch before replying. "I've considered that. If he's on their payroll, then why is my boss still alive? *We* are the ones who outed Karolus Karling as the Director of The Assembly and foiled his plans. It's taken the mainstream media two years to make people forget that and rebuild his image. He would love to see us gone and Zach could have killed Graham, or all of us for that matter, at the museum and blamed it on the gunmen. A perfect cover. No, something isn't adding up."

Lynch became alert to noises emanating from the kitchen. He set down his glass and moved quickly to make sure it was the Southworths. Mike appeared first, carrying two armfuls of groceries. He saw Lynch and smiled.

"Mary has set her mind on preparing meals fit for royalty. In this case, literally. We all should eat well for the next few days."

Lynch had no doubt of that. He had been the recipient

of more than one of Mary's meals.

"Are you the only one up?"

Lynch shook his head. "No, Arthur and I were talking in the library."

Mike looked excited and became animated. "Oh. Good. Stay put. Let me carry one more load in and I'll join you. I think I know what precipitated the killings."

Lynch raised his brow and was about to say something when Mike disappeared in the direction of the garage. He rejoined Arthur in the library.

"Might want to get another drink. Mike's home and I think we're about to get a Bible lesson."

They heard more noise from the kitchen and then Mike yelled, "Do you need drinks?"

Lynch replied, "We beat you to it."

Mike appeared with glass and ice in hand, tossing his coat onto the back of a dining room chair. He grabbed his Bible and laid it on the couch opposite the other two before pouring himself a drink. He looked across at the others and smiled. "I see you found the good stuff."

Sitting down, he asked a question, "What's the first lie in history?"

Lynch wasn't quite sure where this was going, but Arthur replied, "When the serpent told Eve she would not die if she ate the fruit of the tree in the center of the garden."

Mike looked impressed. "That's right. And by that, what was Lucifer, or Satan, saying?"

Lynch saw that answer right away. "He was saying that God had lied to Adam and Eve about the fruit."

"That's right, too. And that's a lie that Satan has been perpetuating throughout history. He continues to try to prove that God is a liar, and of course, God is proven correct at every turn. That's what's happening now. Satan is once again trying to prove God's a liar."

"Huh?" Lynch didn't see how killing a royal family would prove God to be a liar. He looked at Arthur and could see the same question in his countenance.

"Your Highness, sorry . . . Arthur . . . what have you been taught about your heritage?"

Arthur shrugged. "Probably little more than any student in English history. My brother and I were instructed on family lineage, how certain of our ancestors made rulings at the time based upon events of those times. Mostly, we've received instruction on how to act and function as members of the Royal Family. With the monarchy being more symbolic in modern times, we don't have the same power as before. We appoint people into certain positions. We bestow honors. But we no longer have total sovereignty."

"What do you know about the Stone of Destiny?"

Lynch was totally lost on that question. "The stone of what?"

"The Stone of Scone? I don't see how that fits in," replied Arthur. At Mike's prodding gestures, he continued. "The Stone is the traditional coronation stone coming from the earliest kings of Scotland and then to England. Although it is housed at Edinburgh Castle in Scotland, it has a place under the seat in King Edward's Chair, which has been used for the coronations of kings and queens since Edward the First."

"What about before that? Before Scotland."

"Oh. There are legends, of course, but geologists have identified the sandstone as coming from the region around Scone."

Mike nodded. "Yet, other geologists have pointed to the area around historical Bethel, in the West Bank of Israel, as matching the stone as well. And then there are all sorts of theories that the stone on display is a replica, with the real stone having been hidden years ago. That would fall in line with the sandstone matching that in the region."

Arthur looked contemplative. Lynch felt left out. He wanted to know more.

"Okay, I have no idea about any of this. I've never even heard of this stone. Tell me more."

"The legends Arthur refers to identify the stone as being the Lia Fail, or coronation stone of Ireland in its earliest days. But there is no such sandstone in Ireland, so how did the stone get there? Before I get to that, let me ask another question, what happened to the throne of David? In 2 Samuel, Chapter 7, God promised David that his throne would be established forever and that someone would sit on that throne throughout eternity. Most theologians today say that Christ now occupies that throne, but the reference in Samuel is to an earthly throne, not a heavenly one. We see David's line moving forward in history until Jeremiah describes the destruction of Jerusalem by the Babylonians. Zedekiah, the last of David's line in the Bible, and his sons were taken to Babylon, where his sons were put to death before his eyes and then his own eyes were put out and he lived there until his death. That was in 586 B.C., hundreds of years before Jesus walked among us. And even then, Jesus never sat on an earthly throne. So, where did the throne of David go? Or, is God a liar?"

Lynch saw where this was going; he just had no inkling as to how. Arthur looked incredulous.

"Are you saying that *I* am now about to sit on the

239

throne of David?"

"Are you saying that *I* am now about to sit on the Throne of David?"

"I am indeed. Bear with me here. A few early historians traced Jeremiah's life after Jerusalem. He's forced to go to Egypt with the Jewish remnant, where they holed up in a Greek Milesian fortress. Among them were the *daughters* of Zedekiah, who might also have been Jeremiah's granddaughters. God had warned him not to go to Egypt, so he and the princesses fled at the first chance, following the Milesians, who followed the path of the tribe of Dan to the coasts of Spain and, ultimately, they shipwrecked in Ireland. He took with him Jacob's Pillar, the stone Jacob used as a pillow when he had the dream of a ladder into heaven with angels going up and down. Jacob took the stone with him, believing the stone to be blessed. The House of Judah later used it for the coronation of their kings."

Lynch looked at Arthur. "If anyone can find rabbit trails in the Bible, it's Mike. Maybe you have some idea where this is headed, but, I sure don't."

"Listen and learn, grasshopper. Listen and learn." Mike poked Lynch in the arm. "Anyway . . . in Ireland, Zedekiah's daughter, Tamar Tephi, married Heremon, the King of Ireland. They lived at Tara, the royal residence, with the Lia Fail, Jacob's Pillar. Through Tamar Tephi, the line of David continued in Ireland, and then to Scotland through Fergus, and ultimately to England where the House of Windsor now fulfills that destiny. There's actually a lot more to it, but with the House of Windsor another distinction takes place. In Ezekiel 37, God says He will take the stick of Joseph, or the so-called lost tribes of Israel, and join it with the stick of Judah to become one in His hand. Not since David has the throne been united. The ten tribes of the House of Israel were lost to history after their Assyrian captivity, but many believe they merged with or even became the Anglo-Saxons and Scandinavians. The House of Judah, however, returned to the Promised Land after their Babylonian captivity and became the Jewish nation we now know. But not until the House of Windsor did the two come back together. Arthur, your great-grandfather, George VI, and his brother were the first people since David capable of sitting on his throne with the two ancestral Houses of Jacob being united. But not just united under the throne, but upon the throne, embodied in the monarch. I can show you the genealogy charts, if you wish."

Recognition lit Arthur's face. "So, getting back to your first question, The Assembly is trying to prove God a liar by eradicating my family, by making his promise to David null and void."

"Of course, they won't succeed. The sticky point is neither you alone, nor your children, are guaranteed to be the ones who fulfill that destiny. Your brother is eligible, as is a small group of second cousins. We can't begin to guess who God will use. So, you and your family are not out of danger yet."

Lynch saw the truth in that and watched it sink in with Arthur.

But then, Mike bolted up and he paced the floor for a few moments, lost in thought. He turned to face the others. "Another reason comes to mind. Actually, this makes more sense. They're not out so much to prove God a liar. The Antichrist, or Mahdi, or whatever name you give him, wants to claim the Throne of David. He wants that throne to legitimize himself."

Thirty-four

For Richard, sleep gave way to an all-nighter and now, he needed coffee and maybe Super Glue to keep his eyelids open. Mike had been with him until shortly after midnight but had left to get some sleep. Richard's personal anxieties about Mike's plan, however, had kept sleep far from his own turf.

Richard sipped the first of what he knew would be too many cups of coffee that day and watched the sunrise from his window. He knew it was not going to be his best day when the inane thought that "He didn't have to bet his bottom dollar about the sun coming up" floated through his foggy consciousness. *Where in the world did that thought come from?* he wondered.

He turned at a ping from one of Mike's desktop units. The computers had been running throughout the evening and night, working on Mike's search algorithms. Richard expected a call from management about overwhelming their wireless system, but Mike had assured him they could handle it . . . and that they had no way to track the data usage to his room.

He nudged the mouse of the closest computer. The monitor screen woke up but revealed nothing new. He did the same for the second system, but this time the screen presented a window saying a possible match to one of the search parameters had been located. He resisted the urge to click on the "OK" button. The last thing he wanted to do was lose whatever the search had found because he did something wrong. Besides, Mike was due to join him shortly.

As if on cue, there was a knock at his door. As he opened it, he said, "Mike, I think we got . . ."

Amy stood there.

Richard panicked for a second. He hadn't shaved. Or combed his hair. Yes, he had pants on.

"Amy, wh-what are you doing here?" That hadn't come out correctly. "I mean, c'mon in. I wasn't expecting you. I-I would have cleaned up."

He stepped back and allowed her to enter the room. She had no luggage, not that he expected her to stay with him. If she had driven in from Saint Louis, she had to have left at three in the morning.

Amy stepped into the room and he saw her gaze shoot straight to the array of computers across the room. A look of curiosity took command of her face.

"Richard?"

He set down his mug, stepped up to her, and reached out for an embrace. She took a step away.

"Amy, sorry. I haven't slept all night. I didn't expect you, but I'm glad to see you." He stepped closer again for a hug. She allowed him to do so but didn't give much effort in return.

"What's with all the computers?"

"Long story, but it has to do with those photos and blackmail attempt. Lynch sent his friend Mike to help and that's his equipment. The computer on the right just found something, but I'm not touching it and messing something up. Mike should be here soon. In fact, I thought you were him when you knocked."

She turned toward him and looked intently into his eyes.

"Richard, about those photos. I, uh … they're still really bothering me. That's why I came here."

He could see her concern in her body language. "Sweetheart, I swear—"

Another knock at the door. He turned toward the door.

"That must be Mike. Look, I swear that's not me in any of those photos. Stick around. Maybe I can prove it to you."

He opened the door to find Mike there, two more laptops in hand. "Morning."

"You look awful. Didn't you get any sleep?" At that, Mike appeared to notice someone else in the room. "Hey. You're Amy, right? I recognize you from the pictures Lynch showed me. I'm Mike."

Richard closed the door and turned back to the growing number of people in his room. Amy had taken a spot on the couch, while Mike headed directly to his equipment. Richard grabbed a shirt from a hangar and put it on. Shaving might have to wait.

"The computer on the right pinged about five minutes ago. Did it find what we're looking for?"

Mike moved to that system and called up his software. With a subtle flourish of the mouse and the click of a button, he called up a screen in a browser Richard did not recognize. From there, he popped up one window after another.

"Yes! We've hit pay dirt, lady and gentleman." He hit a couple of more keys and placed a thumb drive into a port. "Those raunchy sex scenes are from this site on the deep web. Here are four of the images which were used to create those you received. The others shouldn't be far away. I still have my software searching for the military images. Having found these others, though, I think we'll get lucky."

Amy stood and walked over to the nearby monitor. Within seconds, her body language relaxed as if a weight had been lifted from her shoulders.

"Richard, I'm sorry. I didn't want to doubt you. I . . ."

He put his arm around her. "Hey, no problem. I think I would have had my doubts and concerns, too, if I were in your shoes. We're good now, right? Your reason for coming here has been taken care of, right?"

She nodded and Richard felt a major release. He hadn't recognized that he still worried about Amy's reaction to those images.

"So, now that you have these source images, you're going to stop this blackmailer, put an end to this before it might go public?"

Mike answered her question first. "No, we're not. And I had to convince Richard to follow my lead on this, so don't blame him. Actually, this is Lynch's idea, but I concur. We want to use this person to get to whoever is behind it. We don't think this person is acting solo."

"The Assembly," whispered Amy.

"That's what we're thinking. Along with the current administration and leaders of the Democrat and Republican Parties. They'd all like nothing more than to squash the grassroots movement that identifies with Bradley Graham."

Amy shook her head. "That's playing with fire. It's one thing to put out a blaze here and there, and something else to take on the entire flaming forest."

"That's what I said," responded Richard. "But I've been outvoted. Graham and Stan agree with Lynch and Mike. Even Summer Stanton, the woman in the photos and a real liberal, seems intent on dealing out justice on the people behind this. *That* surprised me."

Mike grinned. "Yeah. We might make a conservative out of her yet."

Amy frowned. "But, *you're* the one whose reputation is on the line, whose name could get dragged through the mud. You should have the final say. You—"

Mike raised his hand to stop her. "We've promised him, we won't let it go that far. We'll go on the offensive if we need to. Promise."

Amy walked over to the window and gazed into the distance. Richard wanted to assure her, but Mike's presence intervened. He decided to move the topic along, to let her hear what they had planned. He wanted to hear that, as well, since he hadn't heard the entire game plan himself.

"So, what's our next move, Mike?"

He gave Richard a look that seemed to say he knew what Richard was trying to do, but he was also uncomfortable.

"Before I say anything more, I need assurances from you both that nothing I say leaves this room. Some of what I'm about to do isn't exactly legal, even if we are using it to bring down bad guys."

Amy turned back toward them and looked at Mike. Richard tried to read her mind. She had already experienced the results of breaking the law once, even though for the right intent. Richard, on the other hand, had already had this conversation with Mike.

"Seriously," added Mike.

"Do I need to sign some non-disclosure agreement?"

"No. Your word is good for me."

"Okay, you have my word."

"Me, too," added Richard, for her sake.

"Thank you. So, we have two things going right now. When we found the phone relay, I planted a small virus into the phone that will allow me to find it, even if the phone's location services are turned off. It uses the phone's unique identifier, its IMEI number, which it also transmits back to me along with its IP address on the system. With that, I can track it anywhere and see what numbers it calls. With a number in hand, I can call that phone and send it a similar virus from my laptop."

"Why not just let the first infected phone pass along the virus?"

"Because it wouldn't discriminate. I'm just out to get the bad guys, not cause trouble. If it were passed on automatically, then it would spread to friends and family, his favorite carry-out place, the bank, every phone that person calls. Then from those phones to every phone they call. It would spread like wildfire and that would do two things. It would overload my system and make it hard to isolate the calls we *want* to know about, and two, it would soon come to the attention of the anti-virus security companies which would develop a 'cure' for the virus and put it out of business eventually."

Amy returned to the conversation and sat down in her previous place on the couch.

"So, you get these numbers and can track the phone. Then what?"

"If we can locate the phone, we can find who is using it. It's our first step in identifying the blackmailer. More importantly, with the IMEI number, I can do the NSA thing and actually monitor the call, record it. That's what we did to expose Karolus Karling the first time."

Richard was impressed.

"You said there are two things going. What's the second?" asked Amy.

"With the campaign's blessing, I've obtained a copy of the donor records."

"What? You can't give that to him." That the campaign, implying Bradley Graham's consent, would give up such information shocked Richard.

"They're right here." Mike held up a thumb drive. "We need to stall for time and this is how we'll do it. The blackmailer will get this file with real names and demographic data, all of which will be scrambled so that none of it matches up. It's all randomized and can't actually be corrected, but if they test the data and discover the discrepancies, you'll tell them the data was scrambled using an algorithm that you will provide only to the person who hired the blackmailer, for, say, $100,000. That should guarantee a call to the person we really want."

Amy's eyes widened. "But, won't that guarantee they release the photos?"

"Not when we have the IP addresses on the dark web of their source photos. Richard can give them those addresses and make some additional threats if they won't pay the money, maybe even up the price to be more convincing. That'll change the rules of the game and I'm sure there will be a lot of communication."

"But they know I don't have access to the information. You were there. You heard him. He'll question how I got hold of the information."

"Likely. So, we give up a fictitious name and tell him that's part of the reason you need the money. You see, asking for money is a language he'll understand. They believe everyone has a price. If they question why you're working with them when you have the web addresses and can prove the photos false, the answer is money. It works every time."

That makes sense, thought Richard. Turn the tables. Blackmail the blackmailer in a sense. If you can't beat 'em, join 'em.

Amy sat on the couch in Richard's room, her emotions teetering from one extreme to the other. Relief. Richard had been truthful about the photos. She saw the source images with her own eyes, as much as she wished she didn't have to. Anxiety. They were dealing with some really bad players. People who did not hesitate to kill if that best served their purposes. She hadn't raised that concern with Mike and Richard.

In truth, she saw that the plan had a good chance of working. Mike was correct in stating that people such as these saw money as everyone's goal. They would understand if Richard asked for payment. A low six-figure request would be seen as plausible. High enough to make it worthwhile, while not being so high as to make Richard seem greedy. They might possibly laugh at that low number, knowing that they could afford much, much more.

She looked at Mike. "So, when do you take this next step?"

"That's up to Richard. He was given a deadline, but he could take control by calling now." He turned toward Richard. "You can say you were up all night, which is true. Maybe say you were able to get the data quickly because you found someone in finance who needed cash right away and you were able to pay them off. Again, use the money angle."

Richard shrugged. Amy watched his body language. He wasn't ready for this. The night without sleep wasn't playing in his favor.

She spoke up. "I have a better idea. Let me take Richard downstairs for some breakfast and then give him some time for a shower. He needs to be more alert if he's going to pull this off."

Richard smiled for the first time since she'd arrived.

"I think Amy's right. I'm not thinking as clearly as I need to be."

"Okay. Just realize that I can't do much more with their phones until this next call is made."

"Oh," said Richard. He seemed to be vacillating.

"Sure you can," replied Amy. "Just call the number yourself, ask for Harold or somebody, and then apologize for the wrong number."

Mike looked at her askance. "Well . . . um, yeah, I guess I could do that."

Amy rolled her eyes. Men. Why did they always want to do things the hard way?

Charity sat in the breakfast area enjoying the "free" hot meal and a cup of English Breakfast Tea. She felt good about her plan and confident that she would get the results she wanted. She wondered how Nichols might get the donor information, but that was his problem.

She reviewed her work notes from the evening before and prepped for her first report of the day for Al Jazeera. In her mind, she tried placing a different spin on the information provided by the campaign, one more suitable to her employer.

As she rehearsed and took another sip of tea, she caught a glimpse of Nichols in the hallway. He looked like he hadn't slept at all, which didn't surprise her. What did surprise her was the presence of the man's fiancée with him. She felt certain that receiving the photos would have upset their relationship and yet, here she was with him. Maybe she hadn't received the photos yet. She should have, but the postal service was, well, the postal service. Was she pulling a Hillary? Support her man at any cost.

She pretended to ignore them, while watching them all the while. Her phone startled her.

She glanced at the Caller ID. Her relay phone? But Nichols stood there, a mere 20 feet away, and had no phone. What was this call?

She wanted to ignore the call, but her curiosity got the best of her. She activated the voice distortion app.

"Hello?"

"Is Tayvon there?"

"Who?"

"Tayvon.

"There is no Tayvon here."

"Whoa, is this here the Death Star or sumpin? Sound like I got holt of Darth Vader."

He pronounced Vader as if it was radar, and the accent said redneck, or did it? Something inside told her to be careful.

"Sorry there, Darth. Must've dialed wrong. Just wanted to see when ma truck'll be ready."

The connection ended.

She put her phone away and tried to return her

attention to Nichols and his fiancée. But the call nagged at her. Was that really a wrong number? To a throwaway phone? That was possible, she figured. Two numbers switched. Hit one number incorrectly. Maybe that's all it was, a wrong number.

And yet, it took place while Nichols stood in the room with her. Another coincidence? It had to be. He didn't know who she was, after all. Or that she'd be there at that time for breakfast. Still, the timing of the call jiggled every suspicious bone in her body.

She turned her attention to the fiancée. Maybe she would need some insurance.

Thirty-five

Sir David sat with Prince Alexander in the lounge at RAF Northolt awaiting several aircraft. One was a hastily chartered transport plane from British Airways. The others were coming courtesy of the RAF. The United Kingdom remained the only G20 nation that did not have a long-range aircraft for top government officials and had to rely upon charters. Parliament had worked the previous November to correct that deficiency, and save some money, by authorizing the refitting of an RAF A330 from being a refueling plane to carrying dignitaries. That work had not been completed yet.

Alexander worked the phone, coordinating the deployment of members of the Royal Horse Guards and 1st Dragoons, or as they were officially called, the Blues and Royals regiment. Both Alexander and Arthur had joined the regiment as Cornets at the beginning of their military careers.

Sir David approached the young prince as he placed his phone back into his jacket pocket.

"Your Royal Highness, are we sure about these men?"

He had asked the question before. Yet, after the treasonous acts of members of the Royal Protection Command, he remained in doubt. They had continued scrutinizing the members of the team assigned to The Royal Lodge and, more importantly, those assigned to Prince Arthur and his family. After the death of that FBI agent in

Missouri, they focused again on one individual. Nothing had been found to incriminate him, other than circumstances. Yet, they kept digging.

"Sir David, Arthur and I have trained with these men, trusted these men with our lives in the past. We went through Sandhurst with all of them. I served with many of them in Afghanistan. They have sworn their loyalty to the Crown and will die for the Crown if needed. I am as sure as any man can be, that these men will do what is necessary to bring my brother home, safely."

Sir David still had his reservations, which is why he planned to travel with them personally. He took direct responsibility for protecting Prince Arthur and his family. Indeed, the entire Royal Family. As such, he had decided that upon returning to England with Prince Arthur, he would tender his resignation. He had failed the family. His only hope was to make up for that failure by bringing their new king home.

"Might I ask, Your Royal Highness, who will command this deployment of the troops?"

Prince Alexander looked surprised. "Why, I will, Sir David. I have been recalled to duty for this specific mission. With my grandmother out of commission and my aunt dead, I am now the acting Colonel of the Regiment."

Sir David was aghast. "But, Your Royal Highness . . . that would break protocol. You must stay here, should anything happen. I realize your mother was the first ever to break such protocol, taking you and your brother on outings with your father, but under the circumstances, is it wise to place you with your brother and his family all in one place?"

"Wise? Of course, it's not wise, Sir David. But they are what's left of my immediate family and that now takes precedence. You, sir, will command your men and I, my men. Together, we will make sure there is no problem."

Sir David shook his head. "I am not sure this is—"

"It's settled, Sir David. Air Chief Marshall Ramsey is coordinating our flight and taking care of other details. Upon reaching Canadian waters off Newfoundland we will have RCAF F-18s escort us to the U.S. border. USAF F-35s will then escort us to St. Louis. Both services will escort us in leaving as well. We will board and lift off once the Bentley is loaded and secured on the transport plane."

Sir David looked off into the distance past the tarmac. To take the armored Bentley limousine was a good decision. Still, he did not like this scenario.

Lynch watched the news off and on throughout the day. At times, he had to laugh at the floating heads of the news stations. The speculation as to what had happened to the Royal Family ran the gamut of their being tucked away in a government safe house to having been abducted by aliens. Their having been kidnapped by radical Muslims seemed favored by the more conservative "experts," while the liberals called it a far right-wing conspiracy.

One thing was certain, however. Their disappearance dominated the news. Even another mass shooting on a "gun-free" campus in "gun-free" Chicago had failed to topple the royal story from its current king-of-the-news-mountain perch.

Princess Helen joined Lynch in the Southworth's parlor.

"I would like to thank you again for assisting us. We hope to be out of your hair shortly."

Lynch smiled. "Helen, it has been my honor. And I know the Southworths, Mary in particular, are simply beside themselves at the chance to serve a royal family. I hope you have found the rooms and food acceptable."

"Our short stay has been lovely, and I'll compare Mary's food favorably to any chef who has ever served us. I think the most important thing is that you all have taken us away from the world that threatens us. Please understand. We recognize the danger. We don't take it lightly. But you have managed to give us a time of peace in the middle of incredible turmoil. Again, thank you."

Lynch nodded. He thought it strange to be sitting there with the next queen of England and being thanked by her. Of course, growing up in the U.S., he had no real concept of having a monarch. The idea was somewhat abstract. No doubt his English counterparts would gasp at the mention of his talking with their king and queen as if they were friends.

He started to ask about Arthur's whereabouts when his phone rang. The Caller ID failed to identify the caller, which made him guess about who it might be.

"Hello."

"Mr. Lynch Cully I presume. This is Alexander Windsor and I wish to speak with my brother."

Lynch's guess had been right on target.

"Yes, Prince Alexander, this is Lynch and I will track down your brother."

Helen put her hand on his shoulder and whispered, "I'll get him." She left the room.

"Your sister-in-law is fetching him. Is the cavalry coming?"

He heard Alexander laugh. "It is indeed. But we have

been delayed by the outfitting of the aircraft we've procured from British Airways."

Arthur raced into the room.

"Your brother is here, sir. One second."

Lynch turned to Arthur and handed him the phone. "They've been delayed."

Arthur took the phone and Lynch exited the room to give him privacy. He found a freshly brewed carafe of iced tea in the kitchen. A tall glass of that appealed more than hot coffee at that moment. Mary entered the kitchen from the back stairway.

"I thought I heard someone in here. I came to see if I can get anything for anyone."

Lynch had already procured a tall glass and filled it with tea. He lifted it toward her. "I just made myself at home."

She grinned. "And I'm happy that you do, Lynch. You are always welcome."

"I know. Thank you. I always seem to put you out though, don't I?" He loved this couple like a second set of parents. He hated to think he might overstay his welcome at some point. "By the way, Helen was quite complimentary of your cooking, so don't worry that you aren't living up to their ideal."

She looked relieved. "Ohhh, thank you, Lynch. That is a weight off my shoulders. In church, we're continually talking about serving others as if serving Jesus, *our* King, and here I am really serving a king. In all my life, I never would have imagined that happening. This has truly been an amazing past 18 hours. What a lovely family . . . and their kids are adorable."

"Lynch!" Arthur rushed into the kitchen. "Ah, there you

are. We must talk."

Lynch held up his glass and asked, "Iced tea? Coffee?"

Arthur slowed down. "Coffee would be great, thank you."

Mary nudged Lynch. "Go on. I'll make it and bring it into the library, or parlor. I'll find you."

Lynch led Arthur to the library, where they sat in adjacent cushioned chairs.

"As my brother told you, they have been delayed. They wish to bring our armored limousine, and the transport plane initially provided by the airline was not equipped to handle it and passengers together. It will take a few hours for the refitting of the aircraft. They anticipate taking off at 0530 hours, Greenwich Mean Time, which means they should touch down here around 0700 hours, local time. Alex has asked if we have a way to arrange traffic control on the ground."

Lynch's first thought was of the traffic nightmare that would result from closing off highways between Ferguson and the airfield in Chesterfield, until he remembered that the larger aircraft would need to use Lambert International Airport. The longest runway at Spirit of Saint Louis Airport remained at least 2,000 feet shorter than required for the long-range aircraft required to fly direct from London. Traffic control between the Southworth home and Lambert would be a cinch.

"Are they flying into Lambert International?"

"Yes, that's what he said. The airport we first flew into isn't big enough."

"No, it isn't, for the size plane I suspect they'll be using. In that case, we're just minutes from Lambert. I think I can arrange for a police escort without making a big to-do over it and snarling early workday traffic. Let me make a call."

"To that Irish friend of yours? The one who helped us with the roadblocks?"

"That's the guy. Seamus O'Connor. We'll get it worked out."

"He also requests vehicles for a motorcade. Enough to carry a score of men." He grinned.

Lynch thought about the vehicles tucked away at the old campaign headquarters. He could handle four men in each of the vehicles he had there. More if the vans were there, but he wasn't sure they were available.

Arthur nodded. "My brother said you asked about the cavalry. He thinks you must be clairvoyant."

"What?"

"He wondered how you could possibly have known that he had recruited the Household Cavalry to come here to extract and safeguard my family."

"The Household Cavalry? I was referring to old American westerns where the settlers would get into trouble and the U.S. Cavalry would come to their rescue. What's the Household Cavalry?"

"The Household Cavalry consists of Britain's two oldest military regiments and are the Monarchy's ceremonial bodyguards. Alex and I were commissioned into the Blues and Royals, the ceremonial mounted unit at Hyde Park Barracks. Quite literally, the cavalry." He laughed. "I think you are going to have quite a show, as they say."

Lynch thought about that statement. Arthur had mentioned the limo. Were they bringing their horses, too?

Thirty-six

Richard rolled over in bed, noticed the time on the bedside clock, and started awake. It was mid-afternoon. He had slept the day away. Why hadn't someone on his team awakened him? And then, he remembered Amy and Mike.

He checked his appearance in the mirror and walked from the bedroom into the front half of the suite. Amy sat on the couch reading, while Mike worked on his gear in the corner.

"About time." Amy stood and walked to him, gave him a hug, and moved toward the coffee pot.

"Sorry. I'm surprised someone from my team didn't come pounding on the door. I've missed most of the day for work, too."

She held up the carafe and he nodded. While she poured him a cup, she said, "I got hold of Stan. You're good. He's told the team you're dealing with a special assignment and might be tied up with it for a couple of days. They've got things covered."

Richard felt relieved. He had a good team and knew they could handle things in his absence.

Mike looked up. "So, you ready to go to work on that special assignment?"

Richard shrugged. "Yeah, I guess. Give me a few minutes and some coffee. I need a moment to wrap my head around what I'm supposed to say and do."

"No problemo. I'm going to need some time to get into

position anyway. I made that wrong number call, like Amy suggested, and was able to retrieve the phone number of the blackmailer's phone. Before I infect it with my virus, I want to confirm that it's the correct phone. And I figure this might be a good time to see if we can spot the guy. That would give us a huge advantage."

"How do you propose we do that?"

"Well, it's not 'we,' it's me. The guy knows you, Richard, plus you've got to make the call and that shouldn't be done in a public spot. And I suspect he knows who Amy is, too, since he sent you the photos. He doesn't know me, however. So, I'm going to take this tablet and stroll through the hotel. The tablet has an app that lets me see what cell phones are active within a hundred feet or so. I might get lucky and find him on it. If not, the same electronic grid I used to find the relay phone will help locate that phone and I can narrow down the search. I'm hoping he's in a public space so I can blend in better."

Mike placed an earwig into his right ear and checked to make sure it communicated with his tablet. "This lets me know what my app finds without my having to look at it all the time. That might look suspicious." He grabbed his coat and draped it over his arm. "I'm off. Amy's going to be my relay person. I'll call her phone and we'll keep an open line while I search. I'll let her know when to have you call."

Richard watched Mike leave the room and felt butterflies in his gut. It would be showtime shortly. He began to mentally rehearse.

Ten minutes later, Amy's phone vibrated and she answered. She looked at Richard. "He hasn't located the phone, so he wants you to call now."

"Okay." He walked into the bedroom, picked up the

phone and speed-dialed the lone number in its contact list. It rang four times.

"Hello."

"I have what you want."

"You were instructed to call tomorrow. Now is not a good time."

Richard needed an excuse.

"They're talking about sending me back to Washington in the morning."

"Call me back in ten minutes."

The call disconnected.

Amy peeked through the door.

"He disconnected."

"I know. Mike said he saw the phone go active and almost had the person pinpointed."

"Tell him I'm to call back in ten minutes. I suspect that means the person is going someplace more private. Maybe his room."

Amy spoke into her phone and then listened. "He says he'll be ready but to try to draw out the conversation."

The next ten minutes seemed like hours. Richard took that time to think through what he had rehearsed, several times, and then he called again.

Charity had just finished working with the on-air reporter for their late day report. While her job as a researcher and writer for Al Jazeera was useful as a cover, she sometimes resented the fact that she did all the work and the "pretty face" got all the credit.

As she talked with the cameraman, the only co-worker who seemed to appreciate her work, her phone rang. She saw the number and excused herself. Another wrong number? One unexpected call was upsetting enough.

With her app activated, she answered. "Hello."

"I have . . ." It was Nichols and he was early. She hadn't anticipated he would be so quick. Maybe he called only to try to stall. She couldn't allow that to happen.

She kept the conversation short and told him to call back. She needed more privacy, but she hadn't time to go to her room. She recalled the empty meeting rooms near her relay phone.

She walked briskly to the escalator that took her to the second floor and on to the meeting rooms. She glanced about and saw no one. The sign revealed no planned usage of the rooms that day. She walked on, entered the furthest room, and sat down in the dark in its far corner. Now, she had five minutes to await his call, while remaining suspicious of its nature.

Her phone rang. *Punctual again*, she thought as she answered.

"That's better."

"Like I said, I have what you asked for."

"So soon? You said you had no access to the information."

She noted that he hesitated. Why?

"I-I found someone who did. And he happened to be in need of cash for a family member's medical bills. I-It cost me ten grand. I have the information on a flash drive."

"Well done. In the breakfast room, the fourth table on the left from the back of the room. It's the only table with a green glass flower vase. Taped to the underside of the table you will find an empty envelope. Place the drive inside and leave the envelope in the same place. You have two hours to do so."

Two hours. Richard sat back on the bed and took a deep breath. Amy appeared at the doorway.

"Mike says to stay put. He'll be here in a minute."

"I've got two hours to make the drop. In the breakfast room."

Amy nodded. "Sounds like a good place. Few people use it after the breakfast hours are over. The staff has cleaned and readied it for the next day, so they aren't around. It should be empty. A good place for a drop this time of day."

There was a knock at the door. "Must be Mike."

As expected, the tech guru was there, grinning from ear to ear. "Got him. Or rather, *her*."

That surprised Richard. He hadn't expected a group like The Assembly to use a woman. He had no reason for that belief, and on reflection he recognized that throughout history some of the most effective and unsuspecting operatives had been women.

"I got lucky. The phone registered on the same monitors as the relay phone so I ran up to the second floor. Sure enough, the phone was in use in one of those meeting rooms, so I popped one of these babies onto the wall outside the rooms and then ducked into the closest men's room." He held up a small surveillance camera, like those used in baby cams or to spy on activities in a room.

"So, who is she?"

"Well, *that* I don't know yet. I mean, I don't have a name. But here she is."

He held up his tablet for Richard and Amy. The screen

showed a high-def image of a woman emerging from the meeting room. She was of average size and build, not homely but not pretty. Her hair needed the work of a good beautician. She could blend into any crowd, the stereotypical wallflower. In fact, as Richard thought about it, the perfect look for an operative. And yet, Richard thought she looked familiar.

"I've seen her before. Here, in the hotel." He wracked his brain to recall *where* he had seen her. "I can't remember, but it'll come to me."

Thirty-seven

Nigel arrived at the hotel outside St. Louis following several delays, first in his discharge from the hospital and then with transportation to join his group. He had learned through Chelmsford that they had exhausted all leads as to the possible whereabouts of the Royal Family in central Missouri. The regional authorities, likewise, had failed to find the family and its checkpoints had come up empty-handed.

After a shower and change of clothing, he joined the others for a late afternoon meeting.

"Hey Nigel, how you feelin'?"

"Too bad 'bout that FBI fellow."

"Good to see you up and about."

As the others peppered him with questions, he watched Harvey Chelmsford walk in and up to the front of the room.

"Okay, you blokes. Front and center. This won't take long."

The others moved into seats, as did Nigel, and gave their attention to their acting chief.

"I see you've welcomed Nigel back into the fold. For those of you who 'aven't talked with him yet, some hoodlum gave him a knock on the head and tossed him into the lake to drown. FBI Agent Muntz didn't fare as well. Nigel doesn't remember much, so don't be asking a lot of questions. We're just glad to 'ave him back."

Murmurs of agreement arose within the ranks.

"As for any leads on who did it, we 'ave none. The same goes with our missing family. Other than their likely escape through that old tunnel system, we 'ave no idea where they're off to. No cars or other vehicles have gone missing and been unaccounted for. No aircraft were in the area and haven't been since the lock-down. Yet, we also 'ave not received any ransom requests, claims of kidnapping, or any other indication of foul play. We can only pray for their safe return and allow the FBI to do its job, helping where we can, of course."

He paused and scanned the room. Nigel glared straight ahead, not wanting to meet the man's gaze when it came to him.

"I have other news. Sir David himself, with reinforcements, will be arriving tomorrow morning. So, be prepared, chaps. Look smart and be ready to work. Dismissed."

Nigel sat still for a moment as the others began to mill about and discuss plans for supper. He digested that last tidbit of news. Why would Sir David come here? Perhaps the man felt the need to personally oversee their work and assist the FBI in its hunt for the family. That *would* make sense, but was there some other reason? Did they have information they now withheld from the current team? That, too, made sense.

He made plans to join some others for the evening meal, at their insistence but returned to his room to rest and to ponder this latest turn of events. He didn't like to admit it, but his swim in the lake and the resultant hypothermia had taken more out of him than he had expected.

Within his room, he turned on CNN and watched the news. The missing Royal Family remained at the top of the news cycle. He gleaned nothing worthy of his attention from those reports. But then, he rarely did. North American news reporting, like that in Britain, was highly scripted by The Assembly, through their friends within the mainstream media.

He glanced at the clock and rose to leave, when his phone rang. Caller ID told him the Director wished to talk with him. The timing was good. As he thought about that, he recognized that the Director rarely called at an inconvenient time. It was like the man knew what he was doing at any given time of the day.

"Yes, sir."

"Nigel, I heard about your mishap. I hope I can still count on you."

"Oh yes, sir. That mishap, as you call it, was a calculated gamble on my part. I thought Agent Muntz was on our side. When I realized he wasn't and was likely to get in my way, I dealt with him. Unfortunately, the family wasn't at the residence we were investigating and I might have been premature in killing the agent."

"Perhaps. However, nearly dying of hypothermia should throw any investigator off your track. I'm calling to inform you that you might have only one more chance at the family. We're hearing murmurs that Prince Arthur has been in contact with his brother and that a team of men has been put together to retrieve Arthur and his family."

Now Sir David's arrival in St. Louis made sense.

"We were informed just half an hour ago that Sir David Spencer-Hough will arrive here in the morning. That would fit with what you are hearing. I will make sure I am there to *assist* them." He paused as the reality of the situation hit him. He was prepared. "This is likely to be our last conversation, sir. Thank you for the opportunity to serve The Assembly and Allah. *Allahu akbar.*"

Barrington is correct, thought Karolus. The combination of the information that had been reported to him, along with confirmation that Sir David Spencer-Hough would travel to St. Louis could only mean one thing. The Windsor family was alive and looking to go home, as he had heard and suspected.

Yet, it also meant something else. They didn't trust the protection detail assigned to them. They likely didn't know the exact identity of the traitor. Had they a name, they could have revealed themselves to local authorities and pointed out the culprit. No, they now avoided the entire team because they didn't know specifics. That meant Barrington still had a chance at completing his task.

"Francois." Karolus spoke into the intercom on the desk in his study. He knew his aide was in his private quarters eating his evening meal. He hated to interrupt. The man served him well and deserved his personal time.

"Yes, sir."

"I am sorry to interrupt your supper. I just spoke with Nigel Barrington and have a concern that he might not complete his task. I want reassurance that our backup operative is still in play?"

"Yes, sir. Very much so."

"And our man in England?"

"On point and on time, sir."

"Thank you, Francois. I don't believe I'll need you any

further this evening, but please keep me up-to-date on anything we might hear coming from England."

"Of course, sir. Have a good evening, sir."

He continued working on the joint resolution condemning the closure of mosques and mass arrests of Muslims throughout France, as well as the failure of the German authorities in stamping out the nationalistic tide sweeping through that country. Perhaps they had been premature in naming their Chancellor as *Time*'s 'Person of the Year' a few short months earlier, now that German citizens, in rebellion to their government, continued to burn mosques and kill Muslims. France seemed civilized in comparison. Even tame Sweden now saw an uprising of nationalism, after dozens of its citizens had been assaulted and nearly two dozen women raped by refugees.

Even as he put the finishing touches on the resolution, he feared that new outbreaks in adjacent countries would require yet additional revisions before the issue could be presented to the Security Council. Perhaps the U.S. would also have to be included as additional lone terrorist acts continued to stoke the fire of anti-Islam sentiment.

His desk phone rang. Very few people had that number and these days it rarely rang with good news. He did not recognize the number on the Caller ID.

"Hello."

"Karolus, it's Wallace. I hope I am not calling at a bad time."

"Not at all, old friend, although I'm reading concern in your voice."

"Indeed. Word from England is that the young Prince of Wales is very much alive and that an extraction team has been formed to take him home. They are to take off from

Heathrow at 0300 hours, Greenwich Mean Time. That is just a few hours away."

"So I have heard. There's a new team from S.O.14 going to the U.S., along with the Commissioner. That has been confirmed."

"Members of the Executive Council are not pleased. The chatter behind your back has grown since we last talked."

"Mabry?"

"To be honest, I don't think so, but I can't be sure. If he's agitating any of this, he is doing so very discreetly."

Karolus thought back to his surprise visit from Martin Mabry. Perhaps he had been truthful in stating that he came as a friend.

"Well, don't worry, Wallace. I heard about the rescue plan several hours ago and plans have been made. When the others on the council hear the next news out of Britain, please reassure them that I have things under control."

Thirty-eight

With less than 30 minutes to meet his deadline, Richard pocketed the flash drive, left his room, and descended to the first floor. Making his way to the breakfast room, he discovered a lone occupant of the room, a journalist working on her report it appeared. No doubt, she, too, recognized the privacy afforded by the breakfast room after hours.

Richard found a seat at the designated table. He pretended to work on his tablet. Well, actually it was Mike's tablet, now programmed to recognize the woman's phone should it become active. At the moment, it showed nothing.

He glanced at this watch. Ten minutes remaining and the reporter remained at work across the room. He didn't want to make the drop under any condition but total isolation from others. Even one set of innocent eyes could glance his way at just the right time and see what he was doing. He needed to get her out of the room.

He acted as if his phone had just vibrated, retrieved it from his pocket, and acted as if answering it. "What?" he whispered, as if trying to be respectful of the other's quiet space.

"Tell me that again." He spoke a bit louder and with a touch of irritation in his voice. And then he erupted as if angered. "You mean to tell me you broke it? A $25,000 camera and you broke it? What kind of idiot does something like that? Listen to me . . ." Out of the corner of his eye he saw the woman give him a look of disapproval. He continued his tirade. ". . . you better find someone who can get that equipment back up and running by . . ." She now gathered her belongings and stood up. ". . . morning or someone's head is going to roll. Losing your . . ." She now rushed from the room. ". . . job will seem tame to what . . ." She was gone, but he kept up the act for another minute to make sure.

With the room to himself, he quickly exchanged his phone for the flash drive in his pocket. He brushed his hand along the underside of the table and found it, the envelope. It was taped securely to the table and he didn't want to risk it coming loose should he remove it and try to re-attach it. So, he slid the drive inside and tucked the flap in behind it.

All he could do now was hope it stayed put, that she would retrieve it shortly, and that she plugged it into her computer to check it. That would allow the virus that Mike had written to infect her computer, which in turn would allow Mike to find her room. From there, he could place a monitor outside the room and track every phone used within the room. If, as expected, she had another phone that she used, Mike would call that number and infect that phone. If she used more than one other phone, they would have to think of a ruse to infect them all.

As he left the breakfast room, he noticed the reporter sitting in the lobby sipping a cup of the hotel's complimentary coffee. As he passed by her, he spoke.

"Hey, sorry about that. A bad day just got worse. You can have the room to yourself again."

She nodded but said nothing. He hoped she didn't know who he was. As he rose to his floor in the glass-enclosed elevator, he looked out across the open atrium of the hotel. A handful of people milled about on the open walkways overlooking the atrium. As he passed the fourth floor, he did a double-take. It was her!

His blackmailer walked toward the elevator bank as he watched. He forced himself not to react.

And that's when he recalled seeing her. On the elevator with him right after he retrieved the second phone from the business center. The same woman who had tied up the computer workstation while he sweated the time limit she had given him. She had passed by him without so much as a blink of recognition. This lady was one cool operator. Now it was time to turn up the heat.

He rushed toward his room and opened the door. Mike was there with Stan and Brad. He didn't see Amy.

"Hey, I was just giving them an update on where things stand," said Mike.

"Well, let me take over 'cause I think I can save us a bunch of time. This woman is staying on the fourth floor. I just saw her from the elevator, walking toward the elevators. She might be heading to the breakfast room as we speak."

Mike picked up some equipment and rushed from the room.

"I don't know what he told you already."

"He told us what you've accomplished so far and was about to show us her picture," replied Brad.

"I can do that." Richard used the tablet he had in his hand and called up the woman's image.

Brad's face took on a more serious look. "She works for Al Jazeera, as a writer if I recall correctly. I had to do a brief interview with their on-air reporter and this woman took notes and fed questions to the reporter through her earwig.

She's been with the campaign almost from the beginning."

Stan looked disgusted. "Hmmph. Gotta be The Assembly. And it would be just like them to put people into our campaign."

"I think that's what they're trying to do with Richard, get him on the hook to become an inside man." Brad put a hand on Richard's shoulder. "I'm not saying you come across as someone who'd do that. I know you aren't. I think they saw an opportunity and a vulnerability with your long-distance relationship with Amy."

Richard nodded. He certainly wasn't one who would turn on his friends for money and he sure didn't share the Progressives' goals or misguided worldview. Brad's reasoning seemed sound.

"Speaking of Amy, she was here when I left to make the flash drive drop."

"She said she was tired and headed back to her room. She said she has to leave first thing in the morning to get back for a staff meeting at work and that she'll call you."

Richard hated that he hadn't been able to say good-bye in person and took out his phone. "Excuse me a moment." He stepped away and dialed Amy's number, but the call went straight to voicemail. He left a message to meet him for breakfast at seven a.m. and rejoined his bosses.

Stan looked up from the couch where he now sat. "Mike said this phase of the plan might take a while. We're scheduled to leave for Tulsa in two days and Denver via Garden City two days after that. If we don't have what we need before we leave for Tulsa, he's going to stay in the background and follow us until he has it. Will you be able to rejoin your group?"

"Yeah, I think so. The exchanges have been made. With

some luck, she'll check out the data sooner rather than later, discover the problem, and contact me. Mike's the one who's going to be busy."

As if on cue, there was a knock on the door and it was Mike.

"If I believed in coincidence, I'd say we got really lucky. You were right. Room 460 and she had the flash drive in her hand as I passed her on the walkway. She's probably plugging it into her computer right now. Anyway, after I passed her, I waited a bit and then walked back past her room. Placed my monitor above a light right outside her room." He walked over to his computers and woke up one of the desktop units. "Now, I sit, wait, and watch. And if she discovers our data is jumbled, you'll be getting a call. I'm sure of it."

Charity had watched Nichols rising to his floor in the elevator. He had taken his time limit to the maximum. She wondered why.

Still, when she got to the breakfast room, she found it empty but the envelope full, as anticipated. Within a minute, she had retrieved the flash drive, while deciding to leave the envelope in place. It might be useful again before the campaign left for Oklahoma.

If anyone had been watching her, which she doubted— no one ever watched her—she didn't want her trip to the ground floor looking suspicious. She walked through the atrium again, admiring the tropical flora as she had before. She walked to the atrium bar of the adjacent restaurant.

"A glass of Chianti, please."

She charged it to her room and then returned to the

garden and sat there, enjoying her beverage. She took her time. No one seemed interested in her. She glanced up toward the walkways at each floor level. Again, no one appeared to be watching her.

After her last sip, she placed her glass on a nearby table and headed back to her room. Although anxious to see what was on the flash drive, she forced herself to act normally. To rush back to her room was to risk gaining attention.

She nodded to the couple she passed shortly after exiting the elevator. She hadn't seen them before, but they raised no concerns. Her spidey sense remained calm. Likewise with the hippy wannabe she passed not far from her room. Real men didn't grow ponytails to their mid backs. Someone needed to call the make-over squad for a fashion rescue for him.

Once inside her room, however, Charity rushed to her laptop, woke it up, and inserted the flash drive. It seemed to take a little longer to register with the computer than other drives she had used, but the directory opened without a problem. There, she discovered over 20 CSV text files. She clicked on the first one, which brought up the data in an Excel spreadsheet.

She quickly scrolled down to see how many listings it had. And kept scrolling . . . and kept scrolling. As she hit the 10,000[th] row, she knew scrolling would take too long. Using command keys, she navigated to the last row—row 1,048,576. The Excel sheet had been maxed out.

She sat back in the couch, dumbfounded. If all of the files hit the spreadsheet maximum, she had data on close to 30 million donors. That number astounded her. She had no concept of how many donors the Democrats and Republicans had, but this was a new party, its first election cycle. She did a quick search on contributions to the main parties and saw that the Republican Party had collected just over $250 million for the 2016 cycle as of that day. The Democrats weren't far behind. If the American Party's donor population gave just ten dollars each, they would far exceed the numbers of the Republican Party. No wonder both parties were concerned and The Assembly was willing to go to extreme measures to get this data.

But then a thought struck her. *Is this their mailing list, or donor list?* She had specifically asked for the latter. Unless their average donation was five dollars, their numbers didn't conform to those she now saw online from the Federal Election Commission.

She took a close look at several individual rows. *Is there a Wichita in Utah? I don't think so,* she thought. The east coast ZIP Code caught her attention. She checked another line. Cincinnati, Washington, with a Texas ZIP Code? What the. . .? Who did this Nichols guy think he was dealing with?

She prepared to dial his number and stopped. She had programmed her relay with only her number, not the reverse. She hadn't anticipated a need to call him directly. She faced a dilemma. Did she want him having this phone's number? There was an additional possible obstacle. He might not have the phone turned on.

She needed the relay phone. That would take care of the first problem. There was nothing she could do, short of leaving a message with the front desk, about the second.

She grabbed her key card and hurried from the room. Once she had the phone, it would take less than a minute to program a reverse call, from her phone to his.

The elevator stopped on the second floor. She had moved the relay phone, but since her prior hiding place had been convenient and worked well, she had simply moved it to a fire extinguisher cabinet on the opposite side of the ballroom. She surveyed the area. She saw no one, so she opened the door to the fire extinguisher and looked into the cabinet. The phone was gone. Instead was a note: If you lost your phone, check lost & found.

Thirty-nine

Sir David yawned as he sat in the terminal. For the past almost three weeks since the explosion, he had spent too many nights awake at 0300 hours. He longed for his bed and at that moment, retirement didn't seem so bad. If only he could have retired on a high note.

"Sir David, the plane is ready for take-off."

He nodded. "Thank you, Hadley."

At Prince Alexander's request, he was to fly with the prince and the Blues and Royals on the cargo jet. The passenger manifest of the plane about to lift off revealed the plane to be a government charter with nearly 30 of his best officers on board. He had publicly wished the flight Godspeed.

The runway was too far away to visualize, particularly in the dark of early morning. However, Sir David and the prince were provided a monitor in the lounge to watch it take off. He felt as nervous as if he were on the plane.

The great circle route to St. Louis would have them flying over Wales, across the St. George Channel and then south of Dublin and across the breadth of Ireland. Old RAF F-16s would fly alongside until it passed into international airspace west of Ireland.

The lift-off was uneventful. They heard the squadron leader of the escort flight report that all was well and they had smooth flying. Twenty-eight minutes into the flight, Air

Chief Marshall William Ramsey entered the lounge. They had met before at a social function in London, so no introductions were needed.

"Your Royal Highness, all is going quite well with the flight. I suspect some of our fears were unfounded."

Prince Alexander shook his head. "The flight is still early, Air Chief Marshall. I will relax a bit once the plane is over international waters."

"Yes, Your Royal Highness. Understood. Your plane is nearly ready and we are scheduled for the planned 0530 hour lift-off."

"Thank you, Air Chief Marshall."

The three men discussed other flight issues. At roughly 40 minutes into the flight, the squadron leader reported, "Crossing the St. George. All still appears smooth." Seconds later, they heard, "Oh, dear God. The plane . . ."

Lynch sat in the parlor at the Southworth's home and felt a little antsy. The Royal Couple had gushed over Mary's dinner and Lynch had to admit it was the best meal he'd ever had as their guest. And he had partaken of many meals with them. She had truly outdone herself.

He sensed a bit of sorrow on the part of Mike and Mary. In that brief time, they had come to know, admire, and perhaps even love the family they now sheltered. He had seen it before, the ease with which they became attached to those whom God had brought under their roof.

Mary found him in the room. "They've retired upstairs. Arthur expects a long day tomorrow and wants to be well rested."

"He's probably correct. Which reminds me, I still need

to get hold of Zach. We need vehicles for tomorrow."

"Can I get you anything? If not, I'm going to join Mike upstairs and see if I can finish this book I'm reading."

"I'm fine, Mary, and I know where things are if I need something."

"True. Well, goodnight."

Lynch checked the clock on the piano. The local evening news would be starting soon and he wanted to watch. But, first things first. He pressed in Zach's number.

"Hey, boss. I was beginning to wonder what happened to you. Everyone okay?"

"Yeah, we're good."

"And Mack?"

"I left him at the office and brought the family to my safe house solo." He paused, still wondering how his scrutiny had failed in that employee selection. "Look, I need you to roust up Tony and Jim and come back to St. Louis tonight. I'll clear it with Graham. I need five of the SUVs with drivers for tomorrow morning. They're parked outside the old headquarters, but the keys are in our office at the new headquarters."

"You said five. There're three of us. I figure you're counting yourself as number four. Who's got the fifth?"

"That's right. I've got one of the vehicles with me. You'll need to get keys for four. For the fifth driver, call Mack."

"Boss, are you sure you want to do that?"

"No, but I might need his driving skills and I'm willing to give him a chance. We can watch him closely. Plus, with what's coming, he'd have to be a ghost that can pass through walls to cause any trouble."

"What's coming?"

"You'll see in the morning. Be ready at 0700 hours. I'll

call to let you know where to go."

Zach didn't reply immediately. "You're the boss. We'll be ready."

Lynch disconnected that call and tapped in Mike Jurgesmeyer's number.

"Lynch, ol' buddy. What's up?"

"How're things going? I wanted to keep in touch, but my special assignment hasn't really allowed that. Looks like I might be joining you tomorrow afternoon, though."

"Good to hear. We've got things under control. Actually, better than that." He went on to explain what had transpired so far. "We've now identified her as Charity Lovelace but working for Al Jazeera under the name of Nadera Rashidi. We've been expecting her to call because I'm sure she's discovered the corrupted data by now. We did something else to throw her off balance. I took her relay phone. Left her a note to check lost & found, where it's forever lost, of course."

"That was fast. The ID, that is."

"Yeah, ran facial recognition through Interpol. Only took three hours to get a hit."

"That's amazing in itself. So, you gonna do the phone infection thing when she calls?"

"That, and since we know her room, I'm monitoring it for other cell phones in use. I'll deal with those, too. And with that, we wait for her to call her handler and keep our fingers crossed that it's the top guy again. He micromanaged the first encounter we had with him. I doubt the zebra has changed its stripes."

Lynch said a short prayer to the same effect. "Okay, see you tomorrow."

Lynch turned on the television in time to see the

opening of the early local news on the Fox affiliate. Again, they issued a brief appeal to the public that if anyone had any leads on the whereabouts of the Royal Family, to please call the authorities. He chuckled. As with the weather, if you don't like the news in St. Louis, just wait a day. Tomorrow their plates would be full again.

The news of another north St. Louis shooting, followed by more stories of local color, led into the weather. At least, the cavalry would have a calm day to fly into Lambert. Halfway through the sports segment, the anchors broke in.

"We have breaking news from England. A charter plane, reported to be carrying officers of the Royal Protection Command, has exploded over St. George Channel, the stretch of water between Wales and Ireland. It is being reported that the officers were coming to St. Louis to assist in the search for the Prince of Wales and his family. We will have more details in our ten o'clock news segment."

Forty

Charity felt out of control and that was both unfamiliar and discomforting. She should have found a different hiding place for the phone. Yet, the inspection ticket showed that the extinguisher had had its monthly check within the past week, so the inspectors likely didn't discover it. Perhaps someone on housekeeping had noticed it.

Nevertheless, this put a real kink in her plan. How best to get hold of Nichols?

She paced in her room as she debated her options. Soon, even that became tedious as she maneuvered around the bed. Why couldn't she have a suite, like the on-air diva who did nothing but speak the words that she, Charity, wrote?

She had but one extra cell phone now, which would have to become her new relay phone. She hadn't planned on deploying it so quickly. The thought to go out and buy a few additional phones came to her, but that thought was followed by her recall of a news story about a hundred cell phones purchased in the state only a few months before. The Middle Eastern name she used as a cover might cause suspicion.

In reality, she had two choices. Well, three, but that third option was definitely out. She would *not* use her business phone. So, that left putting the new phone into service or calling from her usual phone. If she used the latter, she might have to dispose of it, and yet, that phone contained her personal contact list. That made her choice easier. She would use the new phone.

She plugged it into her laptop and prepared it to relay all calls. Calls received from any number but hers would forward to her phone. Plus, a call from her number would now route to Nichols' phone via the relay.

She grabbed her keycard and left the room. Outside of the bar and business center, there were few people milling about. Several news crews had left that afternoon to precede the campaign in Tulsa, which resulted in fewer people in the hotel. She wandered about the atrium but found no suitable place to stash the phone, even for the one day before they moved on. The exercise room was empty, so she checked it for hiding places. The television sat elevated on a metal platform attached to the ceiling. The remote sat on a small stand underneath.

She found a plastic and metal chair and dragged it along the floor until it sat beneath the television as well. She climbed onto the chair and found a hidden spot on the platform behind the TV. With the raised edge of the platform to prevent it from falling out, the spot was perfect.

She returned the chair to its original location and hurried from the room. As she rounded the corner, she ran into another woman. At first, she saw only the woman's workout attire, but as she glanced up, she realized it was the fiancée, Amy Gibbs. She hoped she showed no hint of recognition. The fiancée, however, looked shocked.

"I-I'm sorry," she said. "I should have been looking where I was going. Please excuse me."

The Gibbs woman shrugged, once her look of surprise wore off. "No problem. Have a good evening."

Charity rushed back to her room. She needed to call

Nichols, put him in his place.

Amy couldn't get to sleep. *Why is life so hard?* she wondered, as she reflected on the past few years of her own existence. She hadn't expected to live a fairy tale where her Prince Charming would ride up on a white stallion, sweep her off her feet, and take her to his castle. But this? The only two guys she had ever fallen for were more like super magnets for trouble. Lynch had been dealt a near lethal blow and disappeared for months with amnesia, only to return to face The Assembly with its assassins and deadly drones. And yet, he had taken a bullet for her. Richard seemed so much safer, until now. Maybe she needed to call off this wedding and find a quiet accountant somewhere.

She decided to work off some of her frustration. So, she dressed in her exercise clothes and headed for the hotel's fitness room. As she walked around the corner in the hallway leading to her destination, she ran into another woman. Well, it was the other way around. The woman ran into her.

And the woman turned out to be *that* woman. The person behind this trouble for Richard, and thus, her.

She had been shocked to come face-to-face with her. And outside the fitness center at that. The images and video she had seen on Mike's laptop showed a woman she hardly expected to be someone who was into working out. Her mouth fell open at her realization of who the woman was, but she hoped her surprise appeared to originate from their physical collision. She recovered from the contact in time to respond, after which she wanted to dash away and leave this woman behind.

She ran to the fitness center and glanced about at the equipment offered, still focused on exercising. Then, she peeked back into the hallway. No sign of the woman.

She started to walk back toward the lobby, to follow the woman, but stopped. Why had she been in this area? The only thing she could access back here was the fitness center and she obviously hadn't been exercising. That made Amy curious.

She walked back into the room and began to nose around. She found nothing curious around the equipment. She walked over to the laundry bin and rifled through the dirty towels. Nothing. She ran her hands through the pile of clean towels. Same negative result. She stood upright and gazed around the room. There appeared to be a cabinet built into the mirrors on the side of the room, but she was wrong. The exposed brackets looked like hinges but only restrained the mirror. She stared about once more. This time the television platform stood out. She walked over and raised her hand to feel around the base of the TV on the steel shelf—one of the advantages to being five-foot-eleven.

There was something loose behind the TV in the back, least accessible corner. She grabbed it and brought it down to inspect. Another cell phone and identical to the one Mike had collected. As she watched, the screen lit up. A call was coming in. No vibration. No ring. The device was on mute and yet the screen had come alive and showed the incoming call . . . and it looked like the number Mike had been referring to in Richard's room.

She got a bit frantic. What should she do? If she ran back to Richard's room with it, the call might be completed. She couldn't leave it here. She did the one thing that seemed easiest. She hit the button to disconnect the call . . . and then ran for Richard's room.

Mike looked at Richard and then his watch, followed by Richard again.

"I think I'm going to take a cue from your girlfriend and head to my room. I don't think this woman is going to call. Maybe taking the relay phone wasn't such a good idea after all."

Richard looked at the man. The guy was a tech genius. Of that he had no doubt. But snatching the phone was an impulsive act that might have doubled back to bite them.

"Hard to say. I can't see it being a problem, unless she went to look for it."

"Which I suspect she did. When I examined the device, it could only forward calls one way, to her. She couldn't use it to call you. That was shortsighted on her part, particularly since she provided the phone for you to use. She had the number." He paused. "By the way, she did a great job of hiding her number in that phone. Totally encrypted. If we hadn't tracked her using my bag of tricks, I don't know that I would've been able to decrypt the number."

Richard plopped down onto the chair across from the couch. "So, you're thinking she didn't want to call me from some other phone and give away her number, and that would lead her to retrieve the relay phone to set it up to call me."

Mike nodded. "Exactly."

Both men flinched when the cell phone provided to Richard rang. Mike looked at the relay phone. He'd left it on, running on the extended battery case that held it. The call wasn't coming through that phone.

As Richard picked up the phone to answer it, the ringing stopped. Both men looked at each other as if saying, "What was that about?"

Mike examined the phone's call log. "Looks like she has a new relay phone set up. That's not the number I've seen on my monitor, the one from her room." He checked his laptop that was tied into his monitor outside her room. "Yep, she called out on her usual phone. That was her. Wonder what happened."

There was a soft knock at the door. Richard stood and approached the door. Looking through the security peep hole he saw Amy and she looked out of breath.

"Amy? What's up?"

She took a deep gulp of air and entered the room. "I . . . just . . . ran up . . . the stairs . . . to get here." She took another deep breath and extended her hand. She held a cell phone that looked exactly the same as the phone Mike had just examined. She appeared to be starting to catch her breath. "I think God is giving us favor." Another deep breath. "Guess who bumped into me coming out of the fitness center?" She didn't give either man time to answer. "That's right. Our blackmailer, but she wasn't out of breath or sweaty. I found this phone hidden on the TV shelf, behind the TV. It started to ring a short while later and I think it was her trying to call you. I admit, I got a bit flustered, so I hung up."

Mike started to laugh. "So, that's what happened."

Richard, however, saw it differently. He grabbed the phone from Mike, the one provided to him, and hit the call back button. "Shhh. She probably thinks I hung up on her and that's not good."

The phone in Amy's hand came to life. Richard's call was being relayed to the blackmailer.

The distorted voice answered. "You hung up on me. Do that again and you will pay dearly."

"I-I didn't hang up. The call just disconnected. But I figured it was you, so I called back."

The voice did not respond right away.

"What kind of game are you playing? Did you think you could fool me with a flash drive full of garbage? You will regret this."

The call disconnected.

Mike held out his hand. "Amy, quick, hand me the phone." He connected it to his laptop and went to work. A minute later, he handed it back to her. "I hate to do this to you, but this needs to go back where it came from."

Richard held back the grin that started to show on his face as he watched Amy's face. She had just run up a dozen flights of steps and Mike now asked her to run back down. She couldn't afford to run into Charity Lovelace again, so she really was restricted to the stairs. Amy gave Mike "the look."

Mike gave her a blank stare. "Hey, don't look at me like that. You're dressed for it, and you were going to the fitness room to work out anyway. Here's your workout."

She grabbed the phone from him, turned, and rushed out the door. Before it closed, she stopped and turned back. "Don't expect me to come back here. I'm going back to my room to collapse when I'm done." The door closed.

Richard realized too late that once again he had lost his chance to say good-bye and she hadn't mentioned meeting him for breakfast. He wondered if she had received his message. He wanted to run after her, but knew he had to deal with Charity Lovelace first.

Mike looked at Richard. "Call her back."

Richard hit the re-dial button and, together, they listened as the phone rang and rang. The blackmailer wasn't answering.

Charity didn't like being played and she didn't believe Nichols when he said they'd been cut off. He had hung up on her and that was the last act of rebellion she would tolerate from him. If Nichols thought he could dupe her, he was in for a rude awakening.

But then she started thinking. *Why* would he want to do that? Why would he think he could get away with it? Did he think she wouldn't release the photos? Did he think he was calling some bluff? Maybe she needed to show him that she meant business. Still, she couldn't release the photos. They were the only thing that she had to string him along.

Another thought struck her. Maybe he didn't *care* about the photos. Maybe they posed no threat to him. If not, why not? That idea bothered her more.

At the moment, the only advantages she had were the photos and the damage they could do to him and the campaign. But not for long.

That tall fiancée of his was in the fitness room. But she would be returning to her room in time. Charity would teach Nichols not to mess with her. Besides, the woman was attractive—like Summer Stanton—and Charity always felt inadequate around women like them. She didn't like that feeling of depression, of low self-esteem. She'd fought it far too often throughout life. If Nichols wanted to play games, she was happy to raise the stakes.

Charity returned to the elevator. She made her way to the woman's room and, using her key card spoofed as a master key, unlocked the door and let herself in.

Amy replaced the phone in its spot behind the TV in the fitness center and sat down in the chair along the opposite wall. Her legs felt like rubber. Her breathing came in spasms. Looking at the treadmill, she wished she had used it according to her original plan. That would have been a stroll down a Hawaiian beach in comparison.

Another woman entered the room and took a look at her. "Wow, I hope you didn't wear out the machines. Treadmill?"

Amy went along with her and shook her head. "Stepper," she whispered in between breaths. Amy wobbled as she stood. "All yours . . . have fun."

She walked slowly from the room and made her way along the hall. By the time she reached the elevators, her breath had returned and her legs followed simple commands again. Left foot, then right foot. She never wanted to use steps again.

She hoped the exhaustion would help her sleep. She needed to get up and check out early, if she was to make it home in time for the noon staff meeting. She also hoped that Craig would forgive her the extra few hours off in the morning.

She made it to her room and opened the door. The room was dark, but a faint glow came from the bathroom. She paused. *I'm sure I left lights on*, she thought. She flipped on the lights as she entered the room. Two steps into the room, just as the door clicked shut, she saw her. The woman. And the woman raised her hand. Amy saw the Taser as the darts hit her torso.

Forty-one

Lynch felt awkward trying to get Prince Arthur's attention from the base of the stairs to the third floor's bedrooms. He was certainly in no position to climb the stairs and possibly intrude on their privacy. Nor did he want to awaken the children. A switch at the bottom of the stairwell controlled the light at the top and he tried flashing the light a few times. The door at the top of the stairway was closed, so he could not tell if the bedroom doors were also closed. If they were, they would not detect the flashing light.

"Arthur!" he said in a voice just above normal volume. "Arthur!"

He tried a few more times but saw and heard no response. The late news was about to start and he didn't wish to miss the lead, so he headed back downstairs to the parlor. Mike Southworth was sitting there waiting for him.

"What's up? I heard you trying to get the prince's attention."

"A charter plane exploded over the channel between Wales and Ireland. It's reported that the Royal Protection team coming to get Arthur was on board. Details were sketchy with the first report and they promised more with the late news."

Mike looked saddened.

"The only thing is, I don't think they were on that plane. When Prince Alexander called earlier, he said they were at RAF Northolt. I looked it up. It's an RAF base about six miles north of Heathrow. The news said the plane took off from Heathrow."

"Well, maybe just the protection team was on it. You mentioned they were waiting to load the armored limo. Maybe that plane was at the airbase."

Lynch gave a half-hearted nod. "Maybe." He saw the news starting and took the TV off mute. The male news anchor started with the developing story.

"As reported earlier, a charter plane which took off from London's Heathrow airport just an hour ago exploded as it flew over St. George Channel, the strait of water between Wales and Ireland. Initial reports said that it carried a new Royal Protection team headed for St. Louis to aid in the search for the missing Royal Family. However, onlookers report the plane was being escorted by two RAF fighter jets, which has raised speculation that another member of the Royal Family was on board, perhaps Prince Alexander. We have since learned that the force of the explosion was so large that fragments of the plane also damaged the two escort planes. Those pilots were able to eject and parachute to safety. An RAF Sea King rescue helicopter was dispatched and both pilots have been retrieved from the water. We are awaiting a press release from 10 Downing Street for more information."

Lynch looked at Mike, who said, "That doesn't sound good."

The news anchor continued. "We have video of the explosion taken from a weather cam along the Welsh coast." The TV screen filled with a night scene showing lights along the coast and a few lights from boats bobbing in the water. The weather looked calm. Suddenly a bright flash of light fills the sky and trails of fire can be seen falling into the channel. Two parachutes are seen as well briefly before the fires extinguish in the water. "Chilling video from the UK. More details to come."

The broadcast moved to the next story and Lynch placed the TV on mute again. He didn't know what to do.

"Maybe I should go wake the prince. He'll want to know about this."

"I agree. He needs to know. How can I help?"

"Don't know."

Lynch stood and climbed the stairs to the second floor. As he reached the base of the next set of steps, his phone rang. He checked his watch. *Must be Alexander*, he thought.

"Hello?"

"Lynch Cully, this is Alexander Windsor. Might I speak with my brother?"

"Prince Alexander, I'm glad to hear your voice. The news here is reporting on the plane explosion and the loss of all those men. They were speculating you might have been on the plane, too."

"Good. Now, might I speak with Arthur?"

Good? wondered Lynch.

"Arthur and the family are asleep. He went to bed earlier than usual in anticipation of a long day tomorrow."

There was silence at the other end for a moment.

Sir David clicked off the phone call he had made and turned to Prince Alexander.

"Done, Your Royal Highness."

Alexander smiled back and pressed a number into his own phone. There was nary a delay as the call went through to the U.S. He remembered his father's continued amazement at the speed of current communications. Once upon a time such an international call had required two live operators and a series of relays that meant as many as 15 minutes before your connection went through. His father would have been equally amazed at what they had done that morning.

"Hello?"

Alexander heard the voice that was becoming quite familiar to him now. They spoke for a moment. The man now told him that news of the explosion had already been reported in St. Louis. He wondered if that might be the same for New York, Washington, or Los Angeles, or whether the Missouri news stations had picked up on it for obvious reasons, his brother and family "missing" in their state.

Alexander debated the need to wake his brother, but he needed to know what he and Sir David had initiated at home. This man Cully seemed quite capable of and trustworthy in briefing his brother. After a bit of research into the man, he knew they now battled a common enemy.

"Ah. Well, hmmmm. I see. Please don't wake him then but relay this information to him. I'm sure the news cycle will continue regarding the plane, but please assure him that no one was injured and the cost to the government was one expendable plane. Well, three, actually."

"No one was injured? That is a relief, but I'm not sure I understand."

"The RAF has an experimental program going on regarding remote flying. We had taken an old refueling tanker, a Boeing 777 like those we charter, and had fitted it with the electronics to allow a set of pilots in a simulator to fly the plane. They've been successful in test runs, with a live crew on board to take over in case there was a problem.

We had gotten wind of a plot to take down our plane, so we planted information with three suspect groups that this was the plane being used by our team and filed the flight manifest as such. To make it more convincing, we used Heathrow, arranged the escort with two out-of-service fighters, and then crossed our fingers. The remote team had never taken off from a commercial airport before and never as the sole pilots. They did their job perfectly, and fortunately for us, too. The scuttlebutt we'd heard was right on the money. A bomb had indeed been planted aboard that plane. However, we hadn't expected to lose the two F-16s and the Air Chief Marshall isn't happy about that. They were on loan from an air museum, so we wouldn't risk losing one of our F-35 Lightnings or Tornadoes."

"We suspect The Assembly is behind all of this."

"So Arthur had told me, and I understand we have you to thank for exposing Karolus Karling as their leader."

"Well, sir, that opportunity just kind of fell into my lap. Unfortunately, he's still at the helm and still working hard to implement the Progressive ideal. He's trying to gain control of my employers now, but..."

Alexander wondered why Cully stopped.

"Well, Lynch Cully, if it makes you feel any better, we're working on our end to deal with him as well. We've been complacent too long. The British people are tired of lack of leadership in our government, as are the American people with theirs. Now, they've attacked the Monarchy and our people want justice. Please tell Arthur that we have three suspect groups and our police commissioner, Sir David Spencer-Hough, has had three different stories about the crash planted within those groups. One will say that it has been confirmed that I was on board. The second will say the charter carried only freight and the crew, not the new protection team. And the third will say that the charter is now confirmed to have been secretly carrying Syrian refugees at the request of your current administration. We'll see which one hits the mainstream media and then go after them."

Alexander knew what that implied better than most. The attack on the Monarchy had now become a military matter and the group responsible would not find themselves in a cozy jail. For him, it was a personal matter and he resolved not to ease up on the pressure to remove The Assembly's tentacles from within Britain.

Forty-two

Charity had never resorted to violence before. Blackmail and emotional intimidation, not physical, had always been her forte. She sat in her room stewing about her action. Why had she gone to that extreme? She knew better than to act in anger, to *react* to a problem rather respond. Surely she could handle Nichols without harming his fiancée.

Now she had *two* problems facing her. Amy Gibbs sat bound and gagged in the bathtub of her room. She would have preferred dragging the woman back to her own room, but Gibbs was too big for Charity to manage without assistance, or perhaps a wheelchair. She would have to check on the woman in the morning and again throughout the day. At least the "Do Not Disturb" sign on the door would stop housekeeping from entering.

Her immediate problem was Nichols. She needed to get him in line without mentioning his fiancée or he would rush to her room and discover her. She reminded herself that she could think quickly on her feet and decided to call him again and play things by ear. She could always fall back on disconnecting after another threat, as she had earlier.

She keyed in the number to her relay phone. A sleepy voice answered.

"I do not like playing games," she said through her voice distortion app. "I have added an insurance policy to our relationship. You will give me the real data or else."

There was no hesitation in the answer and the man now sounded alert.

"I have a few new conditions. I scrambled the data with an algorithm, which I will provide if you meet my conditions. I told you I had to pay—"

"You are in no position to demand anything. You will give me the data I requested or else."

"Be quiet and hear me out."

The man's assertiveness startled her. He didn't sound like he would yield.

". . . As I started to say, I told you I had to pay for the data. That got me thinking. I want $150,000 for the algorithm. You asked for the data. I got you the data. You didn't say anything about needing it in usable order, so the algorithm is extra. $150,000. I am opening a bank account in the Cayman Islands and will provide you with that account number tomorrow. Good night."

"If you hang up, I will release those photos immediately."

"Go ahead. Do the following IP addresses sound familiar?"

Charity's jaw dropped as he told her the deep web addresses for the source images she had used to create the photos. She had underestimated the man's resources, *greatly* underestimated. Suddenly, she worried that he might also find out who she is.

She was the one to hang up.

Richard had been bone tired, having not slept at all a few nights earlier and poorly every night since. The fatigue wore him down. He knew that lying down on the bed would result in his falling into a deep sleep that no phone could disturb, so he propped himself up in the least comfortable chair in the front of the suite.

When the phone rang, he picked it up and answered, not realizing which phone he spoke into. When that registered in his brain, he became alert. He ran to the corner of the room where Mike's equipment sat and pressed the spacebar on one keyboard, as instructed by Mike. That did two things. That single key-press would have the computer send an alert to Mike's phone, as well as an alert to his monitors throughout the building to make sure they were "awake" and gathering signals from their immediate vicinities.

By the time she started making her demands, he had had enough and had no trouble getting into "character" to make his own demand. And when he threw in those IP addresses and shut her up, he knew he had won that round. As he recognized that she had disconnected, he pumped his fist in the air with a resounding "Yes!"

By that time also, Mike began knocking on his door. He opened it to find an ebullient geek in ratty bathrobe and black socks waving his tablet. "I heard it all. You were perfect. And the way she just ended the call, I think you really got to her."

Mike tossed his tablet on the couch and moved to the chair in front of his gear.

"Okay, Ms. Blackmailer, let's see what you do now."

He typed something into the desktop system that tracked his monitors. The screen on that system's monitor woke up to show a handful of phone numbers, the most recent of which was hers. "These are the phones that have been active within 50 feet of the monitor outside her room.

Here's her number . . . aannnd, wait for it. Yes! The virus I programmed into the relay phone has uploaded to her phone. Now . . . in a second or two . . . there. I have her phone's unique ID."

Richard watched him interact with his gear some more, but he had no idea what Mike was doing. The man thought in binary code.

"The phone is online with the hotel's Wi-Fi network, so . . ." He pressed another couple of keys. "Three, two, one . . . we have her phone. I planted my software on it via Wi-Fi. People have no idea how vulnerable they can be when they log into a public Wi-Fi network."

Richard looked at his personal phone, saw that it was connected to the hotel's network, and turned off the Wi-Fi feature. He wondered if he'd ever use it again after seeing what Mike had done in less than a minute.

He looked up to see Mike watching him. The man laughed. "Yeah. That's most people's reaction to learning that. Don't worry. I put my own special firewall on your phone yesterday. You are secure. I did Amy's phone, too. And all of the campaign's phones. You guys are almost as secure as Lynch's Blackphone II." He stared into the distance for a moment. "You know, maybe I should set up a secure server like the Blackphone guys, just for the campaign and friends. Hmmm, I'll think on that a bit."

He watched the screen again. "Hey, her phone's on again."

Richard waited but the phone on his end remained silent.

"She's calling a number in New York. Could we be getting lucky? Oh man, I would love to get my software on the Director's phone. Maybe I need to rethink allowing one phone to pass it on only once."

He hit another key on the keyboard. Richard recognized this one. The man was turning up the volume.

"Let's listen in, shall we? Oh, and I added a nice modification to this new-and-improved version of my app. I can turn on the camera on a smartphone and record video of who is actually making the call, as well as the audio. Seems like a good time for a field test."

For Richard, this foray into eavesdropping bordered on spooky. He thought maybe this was why spies were called spooks. Probably not.

The revelation that Nichols had somehow found her image cache had unnerved Charity. That he now made demands of *her* proved even more unsettling. Did he have more information than he let on to having?

She hung up and forced herself to calm down. Slow easy breaths. She would not give in to her old anxieties and allow hyperventilation to cripple her as it once did.

As she worked through what had just transpired, though, she realized Nichols might have just given her a Golden Ticket. The Director's first request had been to find someone they could put on their payroll. Her initial screening of key players had revealed no one likely to do that. Perhaps she had been wrong. Maybe circumstances had changed. If she could get Nichols to accept money, they would have a greater hold on him. Cayman Island account or not—they weren't as discreet as the media portrayed— they would have the money trail to hold against him.

She decided to call Karling. Yes, it was an hour later on the east coast, but he was a night owl. Plus, he would be pleased to learn they would soon have a man inside the American Party.

" 'allo, this is Francois."

Charity had met the Director through his aide. They had been close friends for years and yet, once she began working for the Director they rarely talked. The Director always preferred talking with her directly.

"Ah, Francois, this is Charity. I need to talk with him, if he's available."

"Sweet Charity, it is nice to hear your voice. I hope very much to see you on your next trip to New York. It has been far too long. As for him, he has asked not to be disturbed."

Charity wondered whether she should call back.

"Francois, please tell him I have someone willing to take money for the information he requested. Asking for it, in fact. You know how he loves to hold a money trail over people who receive payment for information."

"This is true. I will inform him at the first opportunity. He will, no doubt, call you. Please call me when you arrive in town. *Bon soir*."

Charity sat back in her chair. Yes, it had been far too long since she had enjoyed Francois' company. She made a mental note to visit New York and call him once this job was complete. As for Karling, she had no doubt he would call back. *When* was the question. Should she stay up awhile or was it safe to go to sleep?

Richard watched Mike jump from his chair, surprised that with his height he didn't hit the ceiling.

"Woot! Woot! Woot!"

The man turned to Richard and beamed.

"Got it all on the hard drive. You know something, I'm gonna do it."

Richard had no idea what that meant.

"Do what?"

"Send my bug to the Director's phone, now that we know she's using the infected phone to contact him, I can instruct my code through the Wi-Fi to send itself to whoever calls her. It's risky, though. If they're as sophisticated as I suspect they are, they might discover it or even be able to block it."

"What if she called a land line? Or, he calls back on one."

"Nothing will happen. The phone won't be able to accept the code and they both might hear a second or two of static, but that's all."

Richard wasn't sure he liked the idea. They already played with fire. Did they really want to pour gasoline on it?

"Can they trace it back to you?"

"To her phone, yes. To the hotel's Wi-Fi network, maybe. To me and my gear, no. The biggest risk I face is their detection of the code and adding it to whatever anti-viral protection they use. Then, I won't have a chance to penetrate them again."

"So, why risk that?"

"Because what better opportunity will I have? If they don't detect it, I will have direct access to every order he gives, every colleague he talks with. We might be able to unmask the top tier of The Assembly, the upper echelon. If I don't try now, I might not have another chance."

That was reasoning for which Richard had no argument.

"Then, let's go with it. Shoot for the moon."

Forty-three

Sir David sat in the web seat of the cargo plane, fingers crossed on both hands and a silent prayer on his lips. He looked about at the men seated beside and across from him and saw that they, too, had concern on their faces. They now neared the St. George Channel and the same altitude at which the decoy plane had exploded.

He knew that few organizations in the world excelled in intelligence as well as The Assembly. What if they had learned of the cargo plane as well? He didn't want to calculate the odds of falling into the sea as had the flight before them.

He saw Prince Alexander sitting among his military companions, eyes closed. He couldn't tell if the young man was in prayer, or half asleep. Yet, as they had boarded, he had been among friends with the 25, hand-picked members of the Blues and Royals. The men were clothed in fatigues right now, but that would change upon landing in St. Louis.

His own men, ten in number, sat together as well, with him. The segregation hadn't been intentional, just the result of friendships and corporate association.

He looked out the window and saw that they were now above water. From the military regiment, a sole voice began low but clear.

"Amazing grace, how sweet the sound . . . that saved a wretch like me!"

A few more voices joined him. "I once was lost, but now I am found. Was blind, but now I see."

Sir David joined them as they began the second verse of that favored hymn. By the end of the verse, most of the men were singing and somehow, they all knew the words.

"The Lord has promised good to me, His word my hope secures; He will my shield and portion be, as long as life endures. . ."

They finished the final verses as they passed over Ireland and a sense of relief seemed to wash across the men. Perhaps it was God's peace and the belief that their mission would succeed. Perhaps it was in knowing that they'd made it beyond the first plane's final point and remained in the air. Twenty minutes later, they cleared the western coast of Ireland.

Movement near the flight deck caught his eye and he looked that way. The military cargo chief made his way to Prince Alexander, who raised his head and listened to the man and then pointed toward Sir David. The chief worked his way along to stand in front of him.

"Sir David, I was directed to give this communiqué to you."

"Thank you."

He opened the paper and read it.

Early morning BBC news, followed by CNN, is reporting that the airliner that exploded off the coast of Wales secretly carried Syrian refugees slated by the United States government to come to the U.S. The plane carried 200 men and five women between the ages of 18 and 30. No children or families were aboard.

"We'll get you, you bugger," he said as he finished. *Let the purge begin*, he thought as he reflected upon The Assembly and its likely role in murdering the Royal Family. Within the hour, his men would take into custody for questioning the Homeland Secretary and her staff. She alone had been told of their plan to retrieve Prince Arthur, but they could not ignore the possibility that she had passed that information to someone on her staff. All would be suspect and none would be above prosecution.

Charity found herself fully clothed and sprawled across the top of her bed. She had given up on an immediate call back from the Director but hadn't found the energy to undress and simply crawl between the sheets. Now, though, she was cold and woke up to address that problem.

As she prepared for bed—for real this time—and emerged from the bathroom, her phone chirped. The screen told her it was one a.m., two a.m. Eastern Standard Time, and yet the Director now called.

"Good morning, sir. Thank you for calling back."

"It has been a long day, Charity, but I'm told you have good news."

"Yes, sir, Director Karling—"

"Please, do not use my name on the phone."

Charity became alert at her *faux pas*. She knew their security protocols. She heard a brief flicker of static, but the line remained open.

"I-I'm sorry, sir. I do know better. I was still half asleep,

I think. I'm surprised you are still up and working."

"As I said, it's been a long day. Please, back to where we were."

"Yes, sir. I believe it's good news. I have someone in the inner circle of the American Party who has asked for money in return for data. He's asking for $150,000 to be deposited into an account in the Caymans."

There was a long pause on the other end.

"The money is not a problem. However, I find it suspicious. You first said there was no one in that tier who could be swayed. Now, one of them is *asking* for money?"

"Yes. I created new circumstances that made one of them think, well, differently." She went on to explain the blackmail con using expertly doctored photos. She decided against mentioning that the con itself was blown by the discovery of the deep web images or that he had already delivered the data but had scrambled it. She didn't want the Director to think she was not in full control of the situation.

"Well, that is a change for the better. I will arrange for the money after you get the account number and routing information. Once we have that to hang over his head, with the money trail to prove it, we'll convince him to continue working for us. I am even willing to pay him for that effort. But I wouldn't mention that until the time comes."

"Yes, sir."

"Good work, Charity. Once again you have come through for me. Good night."

"Good night, sir."

Richard wanted nothing more than to sleep. He could not understand where Mike Jurgesmeyer got his energy. It was as if the guy made his coffee with Monster Energy® drink and "sugared" it with NoDoz®.

Richard stirred on the couch and Mike turned toward him.

"Go back to bed. You can't do anything to help right now."

Richard yawned as he stretched his shoulders. The couch was much too short for him to get comfortable.

"You sure? What're you doing?"

"I've been rewriting my code. I want to send Karling an extra-special present. No more relying on conversations he has with just the people we've run into. I want to catch everyone he talks with."

"You're right that I can't help you there. Are you close to finished? There could be another call at any time."

"I think I'm finished, but I wish I could test it somehow. I don't have a spare phone to use. I can get one in the morning."

Just then one of his computers bleeped an alarm. Mike looked back at the screen.

"Wow. Guess you were right. I didn't expect any calls until morning, the usual business hours, but there's a number calling into her phone right now." He un-muted the sound. "It's him." The man looked surprised and started typing frantically. "Field test coming up." He sat back and raised both arms like a victorious Rocky Balboa. "Sent."

Richard listened to the conversation and grinned as the woman called the Director by name. They had them both now. She then went on to detail what she had done, minus two important factors. Those omissions were obvious to both men, as they glanced at each other and gave a fist bump.

"I think I need to call Stan, maybe even Graham himself."

Mike nodded. "Start with Stan."

Richard grabbed his phone and keyed in his immediate boss' number. A groggy campaign manager answered.

"Stan, it's Richard. Sorry to wake you, but we have them. Karling and Lovelace, both mentioned by name and discussing their blackmail attempt. I think it's time for a press conference in the morning to blow this wide open."

He smiled at the man's agreement.

Forty-four

Lynch had slept well for the first time in 48 hours, and that said a lot considering he tried to squeeze his six-foot-two-inch frame onto one of the Southworth's couches in their parlor. After a quick shower in the downstairs bath, he felt human again. His "babysitting" ordeal was almost over.

He heard someone stirring upstairs and suspected it was Mary preparing to come down to the kitchen to cook breakfast. He produced a cup of coffee using their Keurig one-cup coffee maker and returned to the parlor where he turned on the television to CNN's Headline News. As the analog clock in the room moved its hands to announce seven a.m., the top of the news cycle repeated.

He watched as they reported the planted story about the airliner being full of refugees and tried to remember whose head would roll in England if that story came out. An image of the Tower of London entered his head and he wondered if that place still held rooms to imprison traitors, rooms the public tours never went near, rooms where tortured screams never emerged from their walls. He had received the impression that there were those in England prepared to use such rooms for those behind the attack on their Monarchy.

As he sipped his coffee, his phone rang.

"Lynch Cully, we've landed."

Lynch recognized Alexander's voice.

"Your Royal Highness, I hope the flight was uneventful.

By the way, please just call me Lynch."

"It was and I will. Thank you, Lynch. Is my brother available?"

"I've not yet seen the whites of his eyes, but I will go get him."

"No need, well, not to speak with me, that is. As soon as I get transportation, I will be arriving to bring him, and his family, suitable attire to be seen in public."

"I can come get you. I can be there in ten minutes. We're that close."

"Not necessary. I'll bring the limo. We will, however, need transportation for the others. My brother is our new king and he will be treated as such in a way you Yanks have never seen." The prince laughed. "Yes, indeed. It will be an escort befitting our king."

"One call and you'll have it within 15 minutes. Might take me 30 minutes to secure the route back, however."

"Then, let's get started. My country wants to see its new king."

Having informed Arthur of his brother's landing in St. Louis and expected arrival at the house, along with fresh clothes, he set about his own duties.

"Zach, it's time. Are you with the vehicles?"

"We are. They're cleaned up, gassed up, and polished up. So, who do we pick up?"

"There's a cargo plane sitting on the tarmac of the cargo area at Lambert. Meet me at the easternmost gate by the Air Cargo building in 20 minutes."

"See you there."

Lynch disconnected his call to Zach and keyed in

Seamus O'Connor's number.

"Lynch, I've got things lined up for you. St. Louis County PD will close off the back roads from the Ferguson city limit to the cargo area at Lambert with the help of Berkeley Police. Ferguson will have you covered within the city limits. The Airport Police are already on the job. County will also put its chopper in the air for support and oversight. Do you want EMS on alert? What about the media? You know they're going to get wind of something happening at Lambert."

Lynch thought about it for a minute. He didn't want to acknowledge the need for EMS, but he knew there was still at least one loose thread in this morning's tapestry of protection for Arthur. He prayed their shielding net would be sufficient.

"Yes, to EMS. Have them on standby at the cargo terminal. Let the media figure it out on their own. I'm sure they'll have no problem getting in the way."

"Got it. I need ten minutes heads up."

"I'll give you 15." He almost hung up but stopped. "Oh, you might want to take this in yourself. I've been promised a show like St. Louis has never seen."

Lynch heard the doorbell ring, followed by a shriek. He ran to the front door to find Mary with her mouth covered and amazement in her eyes, pointing to the door. Mike rushed up to her side and looked outside. His eyes widened.

At the door stood Prince Alexander in his full ceremonial uniform, as seen by millions of people at his brother's wedding four years earlier. At his flank stood six members of the Blues and Royals. Each soldier was dressed in the ceremonial blue tunic of the Royal Horse Guards covered with a highly polished, metal cuirass. They wore matching silver, spiked helmets topped with a red plume. Their legs were covered in black leather chaps and boots with spurs, boasting a spit shine a U.S. Marine would be envious of. Their white-gloved hands held a scabbard pointing to the floor in the left, while a full sword was held upright in salute in the right.

"Well, Mary, open the door and let them in," said Lynch. He laughed. He wanted to make a comment about toy soldiers but held his tongue.

Mike leaned toward Lynch and whispered, "They didn't bring their horses, did they?"

Prince Alexander stepped inside as Mary opened the door and then stepped back to give him room. She began to curtsy as she had when Arthur first arrived. Lynch stopped her after the third one.

Mike gave one curt bow and said, "Welcome, Your Royal Highness. I am Michael Southworth and this is my wife, Mary. Welcome to our home."

Alexander doffed his hat, tucked it under his left arm, and extended his right hand. "Thank you. I'm Alexander Windsor, as I'm sure you know. I am pleased to meet you." He leaned toward Mary. "I'm sorry I can't stay long enough to eat. I've heard you're a wonderful chef."

Mary blushed in neon.

Alexander faced Lynch. "And you then must be Lynch Cully. I am honored to meet you, sir. My family and our country owe you a debt of gratitude."

"The honor has been mine, Your Royal Highness." The men shook hands.

"Please tell me that brother of mine has not been insisting on titles while here. In private, please call me Alex."

"Alex!"

Lynch looked toward the main stairs and saw Arthur bounding down them. The two brothers embraced and began to talk. Lynch stepped away, not wishing to intrude on their reunion. He did see Alexander motion toward the door. Lynch looked to see one soldier sheathe his sword in one fluid movement and with his free hand, pick up a suitcase. With a sharp turn toward the house and four quick steps, he entered the foyer and placed the suitcase on the floor. With another easy move, he reclaimed the sword from its scabbard, saluted the two princes, and smartly returned to his position.

Alexander grabbed the luggage and extended it toward his brother. "Fresh clothes for you, Helen, and the children. How long will you need to get ready?"

"We need only to change clothes. With the children, half an hour, give or take a little, should suffice."

The three men discussed the logistics of transportation and Lynch left for the airport. His team had arrived before him and the drivers stood outside their vehicles, two additional SUVs and two passenger vans. Tony and Tim approached him as he pulled alongside. Zach and Mack remained in place, eyeing each other.

As Lynch powered down his window, Tony spoke. "They won't let us in, Lynch."

Lynch wasn't surprised. He wondered, though, what would be required to give them access.

"Well, follow me and let's see what we can do."

Lynch led the short caravan to the guarded gate. The guard was accompanied by an airport police captain and a very distinguished older gentleman. The captain approached his window.

"We're here to pick up the soldiers and Sir David."

"And you are?"

Lynch identified himself and provided a photo ID. The situation gave him a flashback to his days as a police officer and how many times those credentials had opened doors.

"Very good, Detective Cully."

Lynched looked at the man. "I'm not a detective anymore."

"I know, but you were one of the best this county ever had. Honored to meet you. These your guys?"

"That's right. The three SUVs and two vans."

"Good, I was instructed to let no one in except you and your men. I believe the older *chap* over there has been waiting for you, too. He's got one of those hyphenated names."

"Sir David Spencer-Hough."

"That's it." The officer waved to Sir David, who rushed over and climbed into the passenger seat.

"Mr. Cully, I'm David Spencer-Hough. I wanted to thank you personally . . ."

As Lynch drove through the gate and rounded the corner of the building to the tarmac, the man continued his effusive thanks. However, upon seeing the plane, Lynch could only give off a low whistle. There before them stood the remainder of the Blues and Royals Regiment, in full regalia, including two men he presumed to be officers atop horses, at attention surrounding the plane.

Forty-five

Richard watched as three staffers set up the podium and attached microphones for the press. Others raced about preparing press packets, which included DVDs that contained audio and video clips from the calls Mike had been able to record. Richard yawned. At least he'd managed to get three hours sleep. He keyed Amy's number into his phone and listened as his call went to voice mail yet again. He left no message, as there were two others that he'd recorded within the previous half hour.

Journalists with various news agencies began to filter in and take seats. He felt sorry for those who had already moved on to Tulsa. It never failed that Bradley Graham's impromptu press conferences provided the best material. Those reporters still present had learned that.

At seven-thirty on the nose, Brad walked in and went to the podium. He had no notes. None were needed.

Richard approached him.

"I hear you have a second item on the agenda this morning. So, that's what Lynch has been up to."

Brad smiled. "Yes. That's his special assignment."

"Mr. Graham!"

Richard turned to see Summer Stanton enter the room and walk toward them. She extended her hand to Brad.

"Mr. Graham, I want to thank you. Stan McGonigal briefed me on what you're about to say. You guys could have thrown me under the bus, but you didn't. You watched out for my interests even though I've not exactly been complimentary of you or your campaign."

That's putting it mildly, thought Richard. "Not exactly fair in your reports, either, in my opinion," said Richard.

Brad put his hand on Richard's shoulder to stay any further comments. "Ms. Stanton, I recognize our differences, but what was the truth? I will stand up for the truth no matter what or who is involved. If that had been truly you in those photos, with just Richard's head Photoshopped into the image . . . if that had been the truth, we might have left it there for you to deal with. But it wasn't. You were a victim here, too."

She appeared to think on that. "Fair enough, but again, I thank you. I will admit, this has left me thinking differently about you and your campaign."

Brad flashed a broad grin. "Good. Maybe we'll make you a supporter yet."

She smiled sheepishly. "I wouldn't go that far, yet."

"I'll focus on the *yet*. And, you're welcome, Ms. Stanton. Now, if you'll excuse me."

Richard took a seat in a row of chairs set to the side of the podium and was surprised when Summer Stanton sat beside him. Stan joined them.

Brad tapped the mics to make sure they were on.

"Ladies and gentlemen, please have a seat. I have two news items I wish to address this morning and I thank you for coming at such an early hour at the last minute."

As he waited for people to take their seats, Richard watched the crowd. It would be a bittersweet moment for some, particularly those who would soon wish they were on the other side of the state at Lambert International Airport.

"I have two things I'd like to bring up. First, the Royal Family, as I speak, is coming out from hiding and is prepared to return home. A special extraction flight has landed at Lambert airport in St. Louis. I have approval now to inform you that, as some of you speculated, my security team was responsible for hiding and protecting them. The shooting at Westminster College, as well as the bombing at The Royal Lodge in England, appears to have been perpetrated by some members of the Royal Protection team itself. The extent of that treasonous infiltration has yet to be determined, so I must leave further information to the Brits. Suffice it to say, Prince Arthur and his family are alive and well and about to return home."

He stopped and watched the reaction within the group. Richard followed his gaze, but he stopped when he spied one person in the back of the room, Charity Lovelace. He wanted to see her face as Brad spoke on this next topic.

"That now brings me to the next item for this morning. Two and a half weeks ago, Karolus Karling, the Secretary General of the U.N., was granted permission by the current administration to return to U.S. soil despite his now well-documented attempt to destroy the U.S. economy. At that time, he also had his henchman murder leaders of our American Party and attempt to assassinate me. It would appear that he, and The Assembly, of which he is the Director, still has it in for us. Just a few days ago, with our arrival here in Kansas City . . ." He went on to document the blackmail attempt against Richard and Summer Stanton and what had transpired to thwart that effort. He made no mention of Mike Jurgesmeyer or the method by which they had obtained the information now being made available to the press on the DVDs within the press packets.

"The FBI has been contacted and given the name of the woman who, at the direction of Karolus Karling, made this attempt to blackmail a member of my team in order to gain access to private campaign information. . ."

At the mention of this person being a woman, Richard saw Charity Lovelace's face go pale. She quickly gathered her things and rushed from the room. He arose to follow her. She was not going to simply disappear without receiving her due justice.

As he walked into the hallway and looked for her, his cell phone beeped.

"Hello."

"Richard, this is Craig Sheehan, Amy's boss."

Richard needed no introduction from the man. He recognized his voice after spending a day together looking for the downed helicopter that Amy had been on over a year earlier. Yet, two things stood out to Richard. First, why was Craig calling *him*? Second, the concern in the man's voice was unmistakable.

"Hi, Craig. What's up?"

"Amy was supposed to be at work this morning but hasn't shown up."

Richard's level of concern ratcheted up logarithmically.

"She was up late, for reasons I'm sure you'll hear about in the news today. But she was supposed to meet me for an early breakfast and then head out. I haven't been able to get hold of her, so I figured maybe she was already on her way." He paused as a comment from Charity Lovelace came to mind. "Uh-oh. Craig, I gotta run."

The woman had mentioned "insurance." Now, he understood what she meant.

Forty-six

Amy was exhausted and sore. Her shoulders ached as if someone had stretched her body on a medieval rack. She could tell that morning had come as light from the windows in her room filtered under the door to the bathroom. At least, she thought it was the bathroom in *her* hotel room. She wondered what time it was.

Never again would she lack sympathy for someone who had been Tasered, even if they deserved it. She might as well have licked an electric fence.

The resulting disability had eventually worn off. Unfortunately, the zip-tie restraints hadn't fallen off at the same time. Her wrists and ankles were bound. Her hands were behind her back.

As she became alert again, she realized she had two things in her favor, her long limbs and the ability to use the bathtub in which she sat to gain some leverage. She pushed her legs against the wall of the tub in order to raise her body up. With her butt off the bottom, she scooted her hands underneath her and began the task of working them under her butt, then her thighs, and finally, with her knees squeezed tightly to her chest, past her feet until they were in front of her. She found the effort more arduous and time consuming than she had expected and at one point wondered if her shoulders were going to dislocate as she stretched to her limit to get her hands past her feet. It looked so easy on TV.

She took time to rest and roll her shoulders around. During that time, she debated her next move. Zip-ties could not be easily broken like duct tape. With the latter, she could have raised her hands above her head, swung them down forcefully to her sides, and broken free. She had seen it demonstrated online and had tried it herself with success.

She needed something to cut through the zip-tie, but she had nothing in her purse or bag. She could think of no edges in the main part of the room that might help. The only thing that came to mind was the faucet of the tub, and she was already in position to use that. Her wrists were raw from the first chore. Now, as she rubbed the plastic tie back and forth along the edge of the metal faucet her pain became increasingly unbearable.

Charity could not believe what she had heard coming from the mouth of Bradley Graham. As soon as he'd said a woman was responsible for the blackmail attempt, a sense of foreboding rose within. With the mention of her real name, that foreboding became fear . . . not of Graham or the FBI but of The Assembly. She had seen colleagues "retired" before their time. There was no gold watch nor carefree beach strolls or traveling on a generous pension.

As she ran from the press conference, her first inclination was to bolt to her room, pack up, and leave as quickly as possible. But the man had said the FBI had been called. Were they waiting outside, maybe even inside, her room?

Anger at her predicament grew as she rose in the elevator. She had only one course for revenge, one action to make them forever regret having discovered and outed her.

She stopped short of her floor and made her way to the Gibbs woman's room. Her blood would be on their hands.

Amy worked and worked at freeing her hands. She felt sure her wrists now bled from her effort. She stopped to give her wrists a break and turned to freeing her feet. If she could walk, she could run. She would head straight to the front desk and ask them to call the police.

She lay back in the tub and raised her feet to the faucet. The undertaking proved to be more laborious than she'd thought it might be. She had to keep her legs elevated and had nothing to rest them on while sawing at the restraint. That was like doing leg raises for an endurance trial. Her thighs and abdomen began to tighten and spasm. Equally as bad, she didn't have the fine control of her legs as she did this. Twice the tie slipped off the metal edge and the faucet would have badly cut her legs had she not been wearing athletic pants for her previous night's workout.

To her advantage, however, was the strength in her legs. Yet, she felt the faucet loosening with each forceful thrust of her legs. She prayed to break free before the spout gave way.

After another four pushes, she felt the faucet break free and the metallic clang of it hitting the tub seemed almost deafening in the small, dark room. Crying at the thought of losing her means of breaking free, she reached down to her ankles with both hands and felt the tie.

She was close! The plastic was almost cut through. She tried using her legs to break the remaining bond, but after all her work she was too weak to do so.

She reached down between her legs and felt around for

the faucet. It sounded as though it had fallen inside the tub, not out of it. She made contact and flinched as something sharp cut her finger.

"Ouch!" She raised her finger to her mouth and sucked on it. The taste of blood quickly dissipated. The cut was clearly not severe.

Then it dawned on her. Sharp! God had provided another tool. Well, same tool, different edge. In breaking it away from the wall and plumbing, a sharp edge had formed.

She gingerly fingered the sides of the faucet and determined where that edge was located. With two quick swipes, her legs were free.

She now stood and stepped out of the tub. Using both hands, she found the light switch and turned on the overhead light. She looked at the ties binding her wrist and saw that in no one place had she made real progress. The plastic looked as if it had been little more than a well-used teething ring. She winced when she saw that her wrists did, too. With light and a sharp edge to aid her, she made short work of the zip-tie.

She stepped from the bathroom. Yes, she was still in her room. She rushed to her bedside and picked up the hotel phone. No dial tone. She glanced behind the nightstand to see the cord ripped from the wall. Although she had locked her purse in the room safe when she went to exercise the evening before, she'd had her phone. She looked about and found it on the floor by the room's heating unit . . . in two pieces. Closer inspection revealed the phone's back had been removed and its battery taken, but it otherwise looked intact.

She started searching for the battery. If she could find it, then she'd take it and head for the front desk. She could reassemble the phone in the elevator and then call Richard.

As she looked around and under the furniture, she heard someone at the door. Her first thought—the woman, Charity, had come back.

Charity fumbled the keycard in her hand as she tried to enter the Gibbs woman's room. With her Taser in hand, she planned to stun the woman where she lay in the tub, fill the tub, and let her drown. She had nothing to lose by murdering the woman and one final sense of satisfaction to gain.

She opened the door and ran toward the bathroom. The door was open. The tub was empty.

"Aaahhhhhhhh!"

She heard the banshee cry come from behind her. She turned, aimed, and fired in that split second. Both barbs hit the pillow that Gibbs had raised in front of her at that moment. The woman tossed the pillow aside and was on her before she could blink.

The woman was a head taller than her and athletic, an Amazon compared to Charity. Yet, Charity used that to her advantage. She adeptly dodged the woman and used Gibbs' own momentum to throw her against the wall.

Yet, instead of bounding back toward her in a second emotional charge, the woman took up a fighter's stance. Charity thought the fight had just become interesting. She fended off Gibbs' first kick, but the woman recovered and struck out with a left jab, catching Charity on the right temple. Charity swung and missed but caught a right cross on the jaw. The woman's reach was an advantage she'd have to compensate for.

The woman looked surprised as Charity jumped onto the bed and then lunged for her. They tumbled to the floor. The woman had no height or reach advantage there. Charity landed a solid kick to the woman's abdomen.

"Uummpph."

She expected to knock out her opponent's breath and gain a window of opportunity for another attack, but the woman rolled away from her next kick. Gibbs moved to a kneeling position but seemed to struggle to get up. Charity was on her feet right then and ran toward her. Instead of putting up her hands in defense, the woman collapsed onto her back. But in doing so, she used her feet to catch Charity as she moved in. This time it was Charity's momentum being used against her. The woman lifted Charity off her feet and thrust her into the air, over the Gibbs woman, and onto her back, breaking a wooden chair next to the small table.

Charity lay there, stunned. She needed to get up or the woman would be on top of her in a flash. She struggled to upright herself and stand. If she could manage to get to her bag, which she'd dropped by the door, she could retrieve her stun gun.

Gibbs was back on her feet and moving toward her. She seemed more cautious. Charity fished out the stun gun and stood facing the woman. They circled each other once and the woman stepped toward the pillow on the floor. Charity lunged at her with the gun and the woman stepped back. She couldn't let Gibbs get anything she could use as a shield.

Yet, in that moment of overconfidence, her awareness of her enemy flagged. Gibbs kicked out with her left foot and caught her hand. The stun gun went flying across the room. Within that split second, the woman lunged and pushed

Charity to the floor. Shocked by the force of the blow, Charity found herself pinned to the floor, the woman's knees holding her upper arms down, Gibbs' right hand poised to deliver a knock-out blow.

The door burst open. Richard Nichols stood there, flanked by security guards, facing Amy.

Richard saw that Amy's door was ajar. He'd been right. Charity Lovelace had done something to Amy. Amy was her insurance plan. Were they still in the room, or had she already abducted Amy?

With two security guards behind him and the authorities on their way up from the lobby, he burst into the room. Amy had the woman pinned to the floor and appeared ready to punch her lights out. To the side of the room he saw a stun gun and not far from it, a Taser®, its wires leading to barbs in a pillow.

Smart thinking, Amy, he thought.

"Amy, you're . . . Hey, we got her. The FBI and police will be here in a moment."

Charity Lovelace jumped up as soon as Amy released her. She charged for the stun gun, but Richard stepped in to block her. She stopped and Richard kicked the gun toward the nearest guard. He then placed himself between Lovelace and Amy. She'd have to go through him now.

"I'm not letting you take me. Jail or no jail, they will ensure that I have a slow, painful death. Shoot me. Make it quick."

Richard knew what she was implying. *They* were The Assembly.

The older of the two guards looked at her, "Ma'am,

we're not armed. The police will be here in a minute, but they're not going to shoot you either." He took a step toward her. The younger guard blocked the door.

Fists up and rage filling her face, she raced at the younger guard who reflexively stepped aside. But she didn't veer toward him to attack. Instead, she sped out the door. She took two steps across the walkway and dove over the railing into the free air of the atrium. A moment later, Richard heard a loud crash followed by louder screams.

Forty-seven

As Lynch led his caravan through the gate to exit the cargo area at Lambert, he saw his first news truck arrive. He knew they'd get wind of something happening there. He wondered how creative they'd be to get good video, though, since they would not be allowed inside the perimeter.

True to his word and with 15 minutes notice, Seamus and his friends had closed the streets between Lambert and the Southworth's home. The caravan arrived there in five minutes. Ferguson PD had secured the block around the Southworth home and people were standing on their porches and behind the police cars, craning their necks to catch a glimpse of whatever was causing such a stir.

The caravan stopped in the middle of the street, right in front of the house. Lynch drove the lead vehicle, while he had Zach in the rear and Mack in front of Zach, so Zach could keep his eyes on him. The limousine pulled out of the driveway and pulled into position right after Lynch and Tony, within the middle of the caravan.

With the procession lined up and ready, the doors to the vehicles flew open and the Blues and Royals regiment filed out onto the street. In short order, they lined up and marched up the front walkway to line the steps and front walk. In unison, they put their hands to their swords and the front door opened. Out came Prince Alexander followed by the Prince of Wales and his family. As they stepped onto the porch, each soldier drew his sword in salute as the royals came to him. At the base of the steps, the remaining soldiers drew their swords as one unit.

With a simple command, half of the soldiers turned to face the path to the cars. The royals stepped in behind them and the remaining half closed ranks behind them. In lockstep, they marched to the street, protecting their charges until they were safely inside the limo.

Lynch saw Mary following the proceeding with her cell phone, no doubt recording the whole thing. He wondered how many times he'd be forced to watch it over the next five years, or longer.

With everyone loaded into their assigned vehicles, Sir David emerged from the limousine and rejoined Lynch in the lead car. As police cars, with lights flashing, provided an escort, Sir David leaned toward Lynch and said, "I just got off the phone with my deputy in London. We've caught the bugger responsible for bombing the RAF drone. And, after a little water *therapy*, he's implicated one of my people here."

The police escort peeled away from the caravan as they entered the air cargo parking area, allowing Lynch and his vehicles clear passage through the gate. Lynch saw a mob of news people lining the fence. Apparently, the earliest arrivals had claimed locations for their trucks so that their cameras could video the event from above the fence.

As they approached the plane, Lynch saw that additional men had arrived.

Sir David pointed. "The rest of my team is here. The family, along with the Blues and Royals, will depart shortly in this plane, while my men and I finish up here and take the other plane home later today."

"What will happen to the traitor, Sir David?"

"Well, we are about to find out."

The vehicles parked about a hundred feet away and the soldiers emptied onto the tarmac, where they quickly lined up. The two mounted officers met the limo at the gate and were quickly joined by their men, who surrounded the vehicle. Together, they led it to a spot near the cargo ramp in a show of pomp never before seen in St. Louis. One of the officers barked a short command and the soldiers formed a human barricade for the Royal Family. The family emerged from the limo, Prince Alexander first, and in unison, the regiment pulled their swords in salute, as they had done at the Southworth's home.

The soldiers led Prince Alexander and his brother's family aboard via the same ramp, but Prince Arthur stopped outside the limo. He said something to the closest officer, who then rode toward Lynch.

"Sir," he said to Lynch. "His Royal Highness wishes for you to join him for a moment before he boards."

Lynch felt honored and walked alongside the officer to meet with Arthur. As he did so, he saw Sir David talking with two of his men. Lynch noticed a smile cross Arthur's face as he approached. Arthur extended his hand to Lynch and they shook hands.

"Lynch, for a while I never expected to see home again, but you and your man, Mack, took our minds off the trouble while guarding our lives as well. I owe you a debt of gratitude that I'm not sure I know how to repay."

At the mention of Mack's name, he looked about for him but didn't spot him with the others. In fact, Zack wasn't visible either.

"Your Royal Highness, it has been my pleasure to serve you and to get to know you and your lovely family. I hope—"

A commotion beyond the ranks of the soldiers interrupted him and caught their attention. One of the Royal Protection team members was forcing his way through the ranks. His arm was in a sling. Nigel Barrington, per Sir David's description. He had eluded the two officers Sir David had sent to arrest him.

Someone yelled, "Gun!"

In a flash, other members of the Royal Protection team jumped into action and piled onto Barrington. The man had no opportunity to shoot.

With all eyes on Barrington, Lynch felt uneasy. His "gut" sent warnings to his brain to be alert. His gut never failed him.

Out of the corner of his eye, he saw new movement. Someone else was pushing through the ranks, using Barrington as a distraction. A shot rang out. Instinct kicked in and Lynch stepped in front of the prince. And yet, another body flew in front of his. The bullet intended for Prince Arthur caught this third person. The soldiers quickly subdued the second shooter. As they dragged the man to his feet, Lynch was shocked to see that it was Zach Darst. Confused, Lynch looked down to see who had taken the bullet for both him and Arthur.

"Ow! That smarts!" The man's hands were all over his chest inspecting it and then he lifted up his shirt to reveal body armor and the bullet lodged within. "Man, I'm glad that worked. I hope I never have to do that again."

Mack. Ghost Rider had lived up to his name and materialized out of nowhere.

Forty-eight

Karolus sat at the desk in his study and prepared for the next day, a day destined to be full of more rhetoric about peace in Syria. In his mind, the question popped up, "What Syria?" Little remained of the country with the ongoing war between Assad and ISIS, Russia and various NATO countries bombing both sides of the conflict, and the majority of its populace having fled to Europe. Added to that mix, Hezbollah had begun to concentrate its forces along the northern border of Israel, along with claims to the Golan Heights and the oil fields discovered beneath those mountains.

And of course, the never-ending debate over global climate change waged on. The President's pedantic insistence that climate change exceeded ISIS jihad as the greatest threat to mankind had come across as silly. But then, the man surrounded himself with members of the Muslim Brotherhood, so such a position was only natural.

"Sir?"

Karolus turned to see Francois in the doorway.

"Yes, Francois?"

"You have a visitor in the living room. Mr. Mabry again, sir."

Karolus felt a twist in his gut, the same discomfort he had experienced the last time the man had stopped by. He would really need to talk with him about calling ahead.

Mabry stood at the windows near the door to the

balcony, looking out over the bright, city nightscape of New York.

"Truly dazzling, but I still prefer Katonah," said Mabry as Karolus entered the room.

"So, again, Martin, you chose to surprise me. Haven't you a cell phone? They're marvelous devices and make it so easy to call ahead."

Mabry turned to face Karolus. He did not look amused. He also made no move to sit down, unlike before.

"So sorry. It's not a mistake I'll make with you again."

Was that a tone of sarcasm that Karolus heard? Or was it something more ominous?

"To what do I owe your visit this time, Martin?"

"Last time, I came as a friend. This time, not so much. A majority of the executive council has given you a vote of no-confidence, Karolus."

Now, something more than a twisting discomfort filled Karolus.

"Why? The mission is still in process. It will simply require more time. We *will* succeed in claiming the Throne of Promise as directed. Perhaps it's time we meet and I can present to them my plan in its entirety. I can show them how it meshes with our larger plan. The Chinese economy is set to collapse and allow us to usher in our global currency. War plans are being made as we speak to invade Israel and claim their newly discovered oil fields. We have ISIS cells and race protesters positioned throughout this country, ready on command to foment unrest and allow us to trigger Martial Law. It's all coming together. Just as the Mahdi has directed."

Mabry shook his head. "I'm afraid it's too late for a meeting. The bloodbath in Missouri, which failed to kill its intended targets I might add, has drawn too much worldwide attention. It was one thing to stage an explosion in England, or even a car accident or two, but this was an obvious assassination attempt, not an alleged mass shooting incident which seem to be occurring with more frequency in this country." He walked up to Karolus and faced him.

"And then, you made this personal with your foolish desire to get rid of Bradley Graham and that security man of his. You put pride ahead of the organization."

For the first time in his life, Karolus felt fear—raw, knee-buckling fear.

"But . . . but I was groomed to be Secretary General . . . to lead the world into a new era of peace by putting into motion our plan in the Middle East and then elsewhere . . . to make the United Nations the global governing body it was always intended to become."

"Again, pride, Karolus. Do you not recognize who it is we *really* serve? You are a 33-degree Mason, are you not? And yet, you do not acknowledge the true architect of the universe? Call him Osiris, if you wish. Or Lucifer. Or Allah. He has had many names. *He* is the one who predestined a man greater than you to sit as leader of the world, as the Mahdi. You were to be little more than his cheerleader, a mouthpiece for him. But your intense sense of self-importance, your pride, has taken you out of that running. We will move another world leader into that position when he leaves his current position nine months from now." Mabry looked toward the front entrance and nodded. Francois and two other men appeared. They walked up to Karolus and the two men grabbed him by the arms. Francois, in turn, unlocked the door to the balcony and opened it.

"Francois? What . . ."

The aide stood there, mute but for a moment. "Charity Lovelace was a friend. She jumped to her death out of fear of you."

Mabry placed his hand on the aide's shoulder. "Francois has always been loyal to the council and an excellent source of information. He will be rewarded well. Charity, too, was a valuable asset."

Many have said that at the time of one's death, your whole life flashes before your eyes. For Karolus, that story became one of tragedy, death, and betrayal. He began to struggle, but the two men were far stronger and lifted him off the floor. He no longer had any leverage with which to fight. They carried him with ease onto the balcony and Karolus now saw how his "retirement" was to play out. Charity had simply led the way. He glanced back toward his beloved residence and saw Mabry standing in the door. He began to fight with every ounce of his strength.

"By the way, Karolus, should we meet again, I won't be calling ahead." He nodded at the two men.

As Karolus felt himself fly up and over the railing, he saw Mabry make a call on his cell phone and heard, "Karling is taken care of . . ." before all he heard was rushing air around him. His life story ended as he passed the 22nd floor.

Forty-nine

Lynch had yet to rejoin the campaign but the urgency of doing so had abated. After two days of debriefings, interview requests, and countless emails and phone calls, Lynch and the Southworths came together at their home for a midday meal. Nothing fancy. Mary asked Lynch if he wanted to help them with the leftovers from her two days of cooking for the Royal Family. How could Lynch refuse?

"Drink?" asked Mike.

"It's not yet five. Well, maybe in England. Do you still have some of that Scotch or did Arthur empty the bottle?"

His host laughed. "He came close. Not that I blame him. If I was the target of assassins, you'd probably find me imbibing a bit more than usual . . .no, make that a lot more." He handed Lynch a short glass with two fingers of Scotch. "Here. I have to get the new bottle."

While Mike searched out a new bottle of the expensive liquor, the doorbell rang. Lynch went to the door expecting to shoo away some reporter. Instead, there stood a man dressed in a tailed morning coat, vest, striped pants, white gloves, and a top hat. He looked like a character from *Downton Abbey*, not that Lynch would ever admit to having watched the show.

"Good day, sir. Are you Michael Southworth?"

The man's London English accent made him sound like a character from the show as well.

"Uh, no, sir, I'm not. I can get him for you. One

moment."

Mike walked up just as Lynch turned to find him.

"What's up, Lynch?

The eyes of the man at the door brightened.

"Are you Mr. Lynch Cully then?"

"I am, and this is Michael Southworth." It seemed strange to call his friend by his formal name. 'Mike' was so much more fitting.

The man seemed relieved. "Finally, sir. I have been trying to locate you as well. Perhaps you also know where I might find Desmond Macklemore Gilman."

Lynch smiled. That seemed even more inappropriate for the man than 'Michael' was for his friend. He doubted he could ever get away with calling Mack by his first name any more than anyone could get away with calling Lynch by his. Besides, he owed Mack. Big time.

That story had been intriguing in itself. Mack had been working for a private security company under contract to the CIA when they got wind of a plot to infiltrate the Graham campaign and kill Bradley Graham should his popularity continue to rise. The operative was alleged to be a veteran, possibly a SEAL. When the CIA told them the Graham campaign was not their concern, Mack left the company on his own and came to the campaign to stop that plot. Interestingly, the story about Ghost Rider and Zombie 10 in Afghanistan was true, according to Mack, but SEAL Team 3 had been involved, not DEVGRU. As for his change in appearance, an IED and multiple reconstructive surgeries were responsible for that. Lynch now had medical records to corroborate that story.

Yes, Lynch owed Mack. For doubting him, mistrusting him, and for taking the bullet "claimed" by Lynch when he stepped in front of the prince.

"Yes, I know how to reach Mr. Gilman," said Lynch.

"*Very* good, sir. You will save me much time, and that time is short." The man extended an envelope to Lynch, as well as one to Mike.

"What's this?"

"Invitations, sir. From His Royal Highness, Prince Arthur. Now, how might I find Desmond Gilman?"

Lynch reached out. "I can get it to him this evening. He's out of town at the moment."

"Oh, thank you, sir." He extended a third envelope toward Lynch. "Everything is explained in the invitation. Good day, gentlemen." He bowed, turned, and walked off the porch.

Lynch followed him part of the way and saw a car with diplomatic plates waiting for the man. As he returned to the house, he saw Mike standing in the foyer with his mouth open in disbelief.

"Mary is going to faint." He held up a beautifully engraved invitation bearing the royal crest of the House of Windsor. "We've been invited to Arthur's coronation. But more than that, he's sending a private jet to pick us up and bring us home. And . . . we're allowed to invite a guest each."

Lynch read the same thing on his invitation, but Mike hadn't read far enough. "Mike, keep reading."

The flight from St. Louis to Heathrow was like a holiday party. Lynch had quickly discovered that Brad Graham and his wife had also been extended personal invitations due to his willingness to stay behind in harm's way at the museum while tasking his personal security team to protect the

Royal Family. Lynch's invitation also requested that he extend the invitation to any and all family members, who would be invited to a special event following the coronation. The invitation did not hint as to what that event would be.

"Wow, this is the way to travel," said Richard. "Dr. Cully, can I pour you another glass of wine?"

Lynch's father held up his empty glass. "Please."

Seamus O'Connor sipped on a Guinness. "This is how I should travel when I visit family in Ireland." The others laughed.

Amy, Mary, and Lynch's mother huddled together discussing something. Lynch couldn't make out what they were saying. He made his way along the seats to where they were.

"Mother, are you causing trouble again?" He grinned.

"Not at all, dear. We're speculating on just what this special event will be."

"I think we're going to get a private tour of Buckingham Palace, or maybe Windsor Castle," said Amy.

Mary shook her head. "I hear the Queen has recovered enough to receive guests. She might even attend the coronation of her grandson. I think we might get introduced to her."

Lynch laughed. "Well, I have absolutely no idea, so keep guessing. We'll find out in two days."

Two days later, after fittings for formal attire and lessons on protocol, the morning of the grand celebration dawned. Crowds already lined the streets leading from Buckingham Palace to Westminster Abbey. Street vendors hawked souvenirs of the event. All of London, indeed, the country, seemed ebullient. Even the weather cooperated with a nearly sunny day that was ten degrees warmer than the seasonal average.

Limousines arrived to pick up the special guests from the U.S. Lynch started to climb in after his parents, but the chauffeur stopped him.

"Please, sir. You, Mr. Gilman, and the Southworths will share a separate vehicle."

Lynch stepped back, surprised and unsure of what to expect. He watched as the others departed from the hotel. A moment later, another limo arrived for them.

"Where're we going?" asked Mack. "I saw the others head that way."

"Me, too." Lynch took in the scenery as they traveled slowly away from Westminster Abbey. Soon, Buckingham Palace came into view and Mary gasped as they turned into the gate and were saluted by the guards.

Upon exiting the limo, a member of the Blues and Royals came up to them and saluted. Lynch recognized him from their trip to St. Louis.

"Welcome to London. I hope you have found everything suitable."

Mary began to say something, but her husband stopped her.

"That would be an understatement," replied Lynch. "We have been overwhelmed by your generosity and graciousness."

"It is the least we could do. Please follow me."

He led them to an open, horse-drawn carriage and ushered them aboard. "You will be part of the procession, following the family. Upon arriving at Westminster, you will be ushered inside to sit with the family. And afterward, you are to return to the carriage which will return you to the palace here. You will receive further instructions upon returning."

"I don't understand. What—"

The soldier broke protocol and smiled. He then winked. "You will, sir. Please take this all in and enjoy this day. You will never experience another like it."

That's for sure, thought Lynch. As he sat back in the carriage, he saw Mary pinch herself.

"This *is* a dream, right? I feel like a princess, too."

The man had been correct. The procession to Westminster seemed surreal. Lynch wondered what the people thought, seeing this carriage of Yanks following the extended Royal Family. And yet, they cheered even louder as their carriage passed by. Lynch couldn't help but smile and wave, even though Mary's smile was wide enough to fill the cab.

After being escorted to their seats in the fourth row, Mike's eyes widened yet again. He nudged Lynch with his elbow.

"There it is. I never thought I'd see it in person."

"What?"

"I don't want to seem rude and point. The coronation chair. There." He nodded toward an ancient chair up front. "King Edward's Chair, and look, under the seat . . . it's the Stone of Destiny, Jacob's Pillar. I wish I could take pictures."

The ceremony with its pomp and glitter had been more

than Lynch could take in. He wished he could have videoed the entire event, but that wasn't to be. The ride back to Buckingham Palace was as incredible as the ride from it. Lynch couldn't see anything ever surpassing the experience of this day, except perhaps his future wedding.

Upon arrival, the four were escorted into an anteroom within the palace. A short while later, the rest of their party joined them.

Amy rushed up to Mary. "OMG, Mary. You got to ride in the procession and sit with the dignitaries. I can't believe it."

"I know. I'm still pinching myself."

They talked among themselves, nibbled on finger sandwiches, and drank tea and coffee for roughly half an hour. Speculation about what was to happen next filled most of the conversation.

The door opened and a valet entered. "His Majesty the King wishes to see you now. Before we go to the throne room, Mr. Cully and Mr. Gilman, might I talk with you for a moment?" He led them to the side of the room. "When we enter the throne room, your group will approach the King. It is appropriate for the men to bow and the women to curtsy. Please let your friends know that. Should the King call you forward individually, you should again bow. If he asks you to kneel, you may kneel on one knee or both, but you should probably agree on which way so you both do the same."

Lynch and Mack looked at each other. Lynch had no idea where this was leading.

"One knee?" asked Mack.

"Works for me."

A moment later, the valet ushered them into the throne

room. The old-world beauty of the chamber amazed Lynch—the embossed, red velvet walls; the ornate ceiling and carvings on the tall walls just below the ceiling. Two winged figures held garland over a proscenium arch under which sat the thrones. And on those thrones sat Arthur and Helen, now King Arthur and Queen Helen. Seeing them in their royal garb up close was another surreal experience.

As a group they approached the thrones and stopped as directed by the valet. Together, the men bowed and the women curtsied. That felt strange to Lynch, who firmly believed in the American ideal of rugged individualism. But this was Arthur, and according to Mike, the man now held the throne of David. If God had placed him there, how could Lynch argue?

Arthur stood and stepped forward on the platform. "I realize this is probably strange for a bunch of Yanks who have never dealt with a monarchy, but I would like to thank you all for participating in this day with me. Lynch, would you please introduce me to your parents and friends?"

Lynch went around the group and made those introductions, although protocol kept them from approaching the King or shaking hands. When they were done, Arthur said, "Carson Cully and Desmond Gilman, will you please approach the throne." He gave the men an impish grin as if he knew what he'd done by calling out their given names.

Lynch and Mack looked at each other and Mack raised one brow. Together they walked forward and stopped just below the platform.

"Gentlemen, my words alone cannot begin to repay you both for what you did for me and for my family." Helen stood and came to her husband's side. "You not only took us into your protection, you did so at some significant threat to your own lives. And, you safeguarded us while plans could be made to bring us home, to make this day possible. You have served the Crown in a way not expected of someone to whom the idea of a monarchy is an abstract, even foreign, concept. I'd like now to reward you for your service to the Crown and to my country. Again, this might seem foreign to you but please kneel."

A valet appeared next to the King and presented him with two badges. The King took the first and Lynch saw that it appeared to be a Maltese Cross of white enamel edged in silver with silver rays between the points of the cross. It was attached to a ribbon of blue with a central white stripe. Outward from the central stripe, the ribbon was edged with red, white, and red stripes. He kept his gaze forward as Arthur placed this badge around Mack's neck and fastened the clasp at the back. A moment later, he did the same with Lynch.

"As my very first royal decree as King, I appoint you both as Knights Commander of the Royal Victorian Order, for your service to the Royal Family. Please stand, *Sir Lynch* and *Sir Mack*." Lynch smiled as he saw the mirth in Arthur's eyes at using their nicknames.

From his group of friends, he heard Seamus O'Connor say, "*Sir* Lynch? A knighthood? How in the world are we ever going to be able to work with the guy again?"

Afterword

I know. You're probably thinking, how in the world did you come up with this idea? David's throne evolved into the British throne? Really? Isn't this stretching things . . . a lot?

Actually, that was my first reaction to being presented with this idea. Yet, God *did* promise David that his throne would be perpetuated throughout eternity. So, what *did* happen to that promise?

Ready for a brief Bible/history study? And this will be brief, mostly the highlights, because there is much, much more to the story.

When Jerusalem fell to the Babylonians, King Zedekiah and his sons were taken captive to Babylon just as the prophet Jeremiah had foretold. The sons were murdered and Zedekiah had his eyes put out. Yet, Jeremiah stayed behind under the charge of the remnant's captain of the guard. Responsibility was given to Jeremiah for two things—Jacob's Pillar (the coronation stone) and the king's daughters, who might have also been Jeremiah's granddaughters. These are known through Scripture and early historians. The captain of the guard forced Jeremiah and the daughters to flee to Egypt, despite God's warning that all who did would die if they stayed in Egypt. Historical accounts tell us that they stayed at a Milesian fortress (Tahpanhes, or "Fort of the Jew's Daughters") in northern Egypt and then fled with the Milesians to

Greece. Although the Milesians flourished in Greece (the Trojans?), a number of them soon followed the maritime route of another group to Spain. That group? The Israeli tribe of Dan, which had established coastal communities in and populated what are now Spain, France, Ireland, and Scandinavia. Irish lore talks of *Ollamh Fodhla* (Holy Seer) and his servant, *Bruch*, on an Iberian <u>Dan</u>aan ship being shipwrecked at Carrickfergus along with a royal princess and the *Lia Fail* (Stone Wonderful). That princess was Tamar Tephi (Scota and Tea Tephi are also names used), a daughter of Zedekiah, who married *Eochaidh*, or Heremon, the King of Ireland.

So, how could a daughter fulfill this destiny? God had already settled that issue through Moses, when He declared that the daughters of Zelophehad could inherit their father's land in the absence of a male heir (Numbers 27:7). Since Zedekiah had no male heirs, his daughters could continue the royal line.

How, then, did the lineage flow to the British throne? In Ezekiel 21:27, the prophet foretold of the monarchy being overturned three times and would not be overturned again "until He comes Whose right it is to reign in judgment . . ." The first overturning occurred when Jeremiah took the stone from Jerusalem to Ireland, where the monarchy stayed for over a thousand years. In 503 AD, Fergus took his reign, along with the stone, to Scotland where it became known as the Stone of Scone—the second overturning. In 1296 AD, Edward I, while battling the Scots, took the stone to England. Subsequent wars resulted in the unification of Wales, Scotland, and England, with the monarchy residing in England—the third overturning. Interestingly, the stone became incorporated into King Edward's Chair, the coronation chair that has been used with every English coronation including Queen Elizabeth II and which will be used again should Prince William gain the throne before the return of Christ.

There are two other aspects of the British Monarchy that are of interest with respect to the Throne of David. In Genesis 48-49, Jacob blessed Judah with the scepter, to become the ruling, kingly line to which Christ was born. Yet, Jacob gave Ephraim, a son of Joseph, the birthright, the right of the first born and its position of preeminence. Over the course of history, these two became two separate nations—the House of Judah and the House of Israel/Ephraim. Judah, with Jerusalem as its capital, ultimately became the Jewish nation we have today.

But, what of Ephraim? The House of Israel, based in Samaria, was seen as evil in the sight of God. After it was exiled to Assyria, the Bible makes no mention of it ever returning to the Promised Land. In fact, Assyrian rulers populated Samaria with foreigners, with whom the Jews were continually at odds. Today, we call these the Lost Tribes of Israel, but as recently as two centuries ago, they weren't so "lost." Although many historians of today will argue this, prominent historians of the 18th and 19th centuries believed, and wrote, that much of the House of Israel escaped the Assyrians and moved into what is now Europe. They blended into or became the Scythians, the Gauls, the Anglo-Saxons, the Scandinavians and others as we know them today. The royal crests of these nations reflect this Israeli heritage.

The other interesting aspect of this history goes

back to Genesis 38 with the birth of Judah's illegitimate twins—Zerah ("scarlet") and Perez ("breach"). At birth, Zerah presented first and the midwife tied a scarlet thread on his wrist to indicate his being royal seed. Yet, he retracted back into the womb and Perez was then born first. Perez had disrupted, or breached, the natural order of the firstborn. I mentioned the overturning of the throne above. One verse earlier in Ezekiel 21: 26, God states that the crown of the king is to be removed and that the low is to be exalted, while the high will be brought low.

So, getting back to the English Monarchy, how does this play out? Let's look at the breach between Zerah and Perez first. Through Perez we get the line of David and, ultimately, Christ. Yet, the lineage of the five sons of Zerah is believed to be interwoven into royal lines of Europe.

Also, in Ezekiel 37:16-22, God directs Ezekiel to take two sticks. On one he is to write "For Judah" and on the other, "For Joseph," the stick of Ephraim. In verse 19, Ezekiel was to take both sticks in one hand to symbolize becoming one once again. In verse 21, God states He will gather the children of Israel from among the nations to which they had gone, return them to the Promised Land, and join them with Judah to become one nation in the land with one King (capital K, i.e., Christ).

In following the genealogies of the kings and queens of Europe, you can see the lineages of these kings flowing to a defining point in history. Through various marriages interweaving between European royal families, we come to the Danish Princess Alexandra who married King Edward VII of Britain and produced a son who became King George V. George V married Mary of Teck, a product of French and German royalty, and from them came Edward VIII and

George VI. Edward abdicated the throne to marry a commoner, Wallis Simpson, and George ascended to the throne, followed by his daughter, Elizabeth II in 1953. When (or if) Prince William ascends to the throne to follow his grandmother, he will be the continuation of this prophecy as God also continues to gather His people to become one nation.

With the births of Edward VIII and George VI, we finally see the breach between Zerah and Perez sealed, and the lower (Zerah) being elevated to the throne. In addition, for the first time in centuries, the House of Judah and House of Ephraim became united in one throne, with the lineage of David carried through Ireland and Scotland to England, and the lineage of Ephraim carried through the royal lines of Europe.

Still awake?

Okay. I know I've presented this in a very factual way, while there is zero definitive proof. After all, we don't have ancient documented genealogies to confirm anything I've said. Some historians will scoff at what I've presented here. Yet, there is more in the Bible, as well as from early historians, to suggest what I'm saying has validity. As I said, I've presented the "highlights." But that leads us back to the first question, what happened to David's throne in light of God's promise? If you have a better answer, I'd love to hear it.

If you're interested in researching this further, I can recommend the following books:

"Judah's Scepter and Joseph's Birthright," by J. H. Allen, 1902

"History of the Anglo-Saxons," by Mr. Sharon Turner, 1805

"Where is the United States in Bible Prophecy," by Michael D. Hodge, 2010

There are also genealogy charts and other materials available through Artisan Publishers of Muskogee, OK (www.artisanpublishers.com).

Sneak Preview:
A Kidnapped Nation

One

The moonless but starry night provided perfect cover as the dark SUV pulled up to the single metal bar that served as a gate to the facility. Streetlights were non-existent in this "neck of the woods." Only the straying light from a passing vehicle's headlamps had a chance of revealing the two men who emerged from the late model Ford Expedition, whose driver had used night vision goggles for the last mile.

"Got it," said the younger of the two as he snapped the padlock with a pair of bolt cutters.

Together they swung open the gate. Then the older used his cell phone to broadcast a message to the group waiting for his word. He waved the driver through the gate and met him by the driver's window.

"Go on up to the main building. You know what to look for, right?"

"Yessir. We'll get 'er done."

"Good. Check it out and then start setting up."

The SUV, lights still extinguished, crept along the narrow, paved road and disappeared around a bend, hidden by tall pines. The man returned to a spot near the entrance where he could see the road as it stretched out both north and south. He turned to the younger.

"Go ahead and close the gate. Stay close by. We need to move folks in as quickly as they get here. We have three hours before dawn."

Over the next two hours a ragtag caravan, of sorts, arrived at staggered times. Each arrival was noted by a preset signal with the headlights. Only two cars passed by that did not belong.

The assortment of pickup trucks, SUVs, and older sedans would not have appeared out of place for this remote location. Even the generator in the bed of one pickup and the small fuel tanker were typical for the traffic expected along that rural highway. What would seem strange to the locals was the wide collection of states represented by the license plates on those vehicles. Besides the locals from Oregon, Nevada, New Mexico, Utah, Colorado, Arizona, Idaho, Montana, and Wyoming were well represented, too. Even one vehicle from each of the Dakotas arrived.

The western states were under siege. These people, men and women, intended to get word of that siege out to the rest of the country . . . before it was too late.

As each vehicle moved into the area around the main building, a team of men removed those license plates. Only the plates of the Expedition and a Chevy Tahoe were left in place.

"Got 'em all?" asked the older man, as the last of the vehicles lost its obvious means of identifying the owner. "We expect they'll be using drones to watch us within two days. Don't want to make it easy for them to ID any of us."

"We have them, except for yours and Adam's."

Their leader nodded. "That works. They'll know who I am soon enough."

They would indeed. The Feds who would soon descend upon this place already knew the name Simon Slattery. They didn't yet know he'd left his ranch in Nevada to lead this protest over land seizures by the federal government, and to support two local ranchers whom the Bureau of Land Management had targeted and were now in jail on what Slattery saw as the latest in trumped up charges against private landowners.

He walked over to a small group of men talking around the camp lantern one of them had set on his lowered tailgate. He glanced from face to face and saw serious commitment. But then, he knew *that* about each of them. They'd already driven hundreds of miles to participate in what Slattery hoped would remain a peaceful protest. Should the Feds turn it otherwise, he also knew each man was willing to become a martyr for the cause.

Yet, he knew that saying you'd die for the cause was easy to say and not so easy to accept if you felt the burn of lead in your chest. He prayed that none of them would take on that level of engagement.

"Hanson, no rush, but take Brandy and secure the southern access road. Use that beat up Fairlane we nearly had to tow here to block the road and then take up a suitable observation location. You'll have company sometime tomorrow I'm sure. The Feds will make sure they have eyes on that road."

He turned to two of the others. "Buddy, you guys take that hay trailer and block the main road in. We need something we can move in and out of position easily, and that should work. And find two people to man the fire tower. Make sure they have binoculars. They need to be in place by the time the sun rises." He paused and looked around. The lone security light over the main building illuminated the area well. Most of the people who had joined him that night took advantage of it to perform their initial tasks.

"Any of you guys see the electrician from Montana? Forget his name."

"Busby."

"Yeah. Him."

"Helped him position the generator near the meter box. I think he joined Comer and Thompson. Looking to see if there's an active alarm system before someone accesses the building."

Slattery nodded. He loved that these guys knew the plan and took the initiative. They made it that much easier for him.

"Good. We should be ready come morning." He smiled. "BLM staff is in for one hell of a surprise."

To most western landowners, their biggest enemy wasn't some foreign-born terrorist allowed into the country by the politically-correct crowd in Washington. Their enemy had become Washington itself. Ranches that had been in their families for generations had become targets for the government, which used the Bureau of Land Management to push those families off their land under the guise of protecting the environment. The real goal wasn't hard to see. The government elites wanted full control of the resources under those lands to pass on to their cronies in Big Business. The Edmond Ranch was the latest target . .

. after the U.S. Geological Survey discovered oil, natural gas, and uranium in the valley.

A quick note from Braxton . . .

I hope you enjoyed *A Zealot's Destiny* and thank you for purchasing it. Please consider writing a review at Amazon, Barnes & Nobel, iTunes, Goodreads, or elsewhere. Reviews are crucial to Indie authors. It doesn't have to be lengthy. Just a couple of sentences will do.

Also, if you'd like to stay informed about my new books, book signings, and more, please sign up for my newsletter. You can do that at my website: **www.braxtondegarmo.com**. As my thank-you for signing up, I'll give you my eBook, *And Then One Day*—a prequel to the MedAir Series. If you've wondered how Lynch and Amy met, and what led to their breakup, this is the book for you.

And did you know you can purchase signed copies of my paperbacks at my website? With shipping included in the price, ordering them directly from me is typically cheaper than ordering them online.

About the Author

Braxton can't lay claim to wanting to be a writer all his life, although his mother and seventh grade English teacher were convinced he had what it would take. A bachelor's degree in Bio-Medical Engineering led to medical school and a residency in Emergency Medicine. He served for a decade in the U.S. Army Medical Corps with tours such as the Chief, Emergency Medical Services at Fort Campbell, KY, and as a research Flight Surgeon at Fort Rucker, AL. Who had time to write?

By the 1990s, as a civilian, his professional and family life had settled down, somewhat, and his mother once again took up her mantra, "Write a book. You're a good writer." In 1997, a Valentine's Day writing contest convinced him that maybe he could write fiction. He spent the next fifteen years learning the craft of writing.

Now, twenty-plus years after that first hesitant start, he has sixteen novels published, as well as non-fiction books and a children's book, and can't find enough time to write. As a Christian, he writes "true-life" Christian fiction (suspense and thrillers) that many call "cutting edge," as he's not afraid to take on such issues as human trafficking, racism, and more. His characters are real-life as well, with all the flaws and blemishes real people have. As such, his books are never likely to gain acceptance by the Christian Bookseller Association. But then, he never intended to tell stories just to the choir.

Books by Braxton DeGarmo:

Still Here Series:
The End Begins - 1
The Shaking - 2
The Beasts – 3
The Trumpets – 4
The Mark - 5

Non-fiction Study Guides:
Still Here! Surviving the End Times
Still Here! The Apocalypse is Now
Still Here! Countdown Revelation

MedAir Series:
Looks that Deceive – 1
Rescued and Remembered – 2
The Silenced Shooter – 3
Wrongfully Removed – 4
A Zealot's Destiny – 5
Kidnapped Nation - 6
The Khmer Connection - 7
Resurrected Trouble - 8

Seamus O'Connor Thrillers:
The Militant Genome
Ten Seconds 'Til

Other Books:
Indebted

Children's Books:
The Toucan Who Can Can-can